Peter James was educated at Charterhouse then at film school. He lived in North America for a number of years, working as a screenwriter and film producer before returning to England. His novels, including the number one bestseller *Possession*, have been translated into thirty languages and three have been filmed. All his novels reflect his deep interest in the world of the police, with whom he does in-depth research, as well as science, medicine and the paranormal. He has produced numerous films, including *The Merchant Of Venice*, starring Al Pacino, Jeremy Irons and Joseph Fiennes. He also co-created the hit Channel 4 series, *Bedsitcom*, which was nominated for a Rose d'Or. He is currently, as co-producer, developing his Roy Grace novels for television with ITV Productions. Peter James won the Krimi-Blitz 2005 Crime Writer of the Year award in Germany, and *Dead Simple* won both the 2006 Prix Polar International award and the 2007 Prix Coeur Noir award in France. *Looking Good Dead* was shortlisted for the 2007 Richard and Judy Crime Thriller of the Year award, France's SNCF and Le Grand Prix de Littérature award. *Not Dead Enough* was shortlisted for the Theakstons Old Peculier Crime Thriller of the Year award and the ITV3 Crime Thriller of the Year award. He divides his time between his homes in Notting Hill, London and near Brighton in Sussex. Visit his website at www.peterjames.com.

FAITH

Peter James

An Orion paperback

First published in Great Britain in 2000
by Orion
This paperback edition published in 2000
by Orion Books Ltd,
Orion House, 5 Upper St Martin's Lane,
London WC2H 9EA

An Hachette UK company

10

Reissued 2005

A CIP catalogue record for this book is available
from the British Library.

ISBN 978-0-7528-3711-6

Printed and bound in Great Britain by
Clays Ltd, St Ives plc

The Orion Publishing Group's policy is to use papers that
are natural, renewable and recyclable products and
made from wood grown in sustainable forests. The logging
and manufacturing processes are expected to conform to
the environmental regulations of the country of origin.

www.orionbooks.co.uk

To the memory of my mother Cornelia,
an absent best friend.

Acknowledgements

I owe a great debt to a number of people who generously gave me so much of their precious time, their knowledge and their wisdom, and added whole dimensions to this book. In particular, I would like to thank Anna-Lisa Lindeblad-Davies, police surgeon and coroner, Dr Peter Dean, hypnotherapist Dr Christopher Forester, the fiendishly creative mind of Detective Chief Inspector David Gaylor, and Mr Nicholas Parkhouse DM MCh FRCS who gave me invaluable insight into the world of the plastic surgeon.

I also had treasured help from Mr David Albert, Dr Andrew Davey FCAnaes, Dr Celina Dunn, Dr Ian Dunn, Dr Bruno Von Ehrenberg, Dr Dennis Friedman, Danny Green, Mick Harris, Amanda Hemingway, Nurse Marion Heath, Nurse Becky Holland, Dr Bruce Katz, Rob Kempson, Dr Nigel Kirkham MRCPath, Tracy Lewis, Lynn Magos, Dr Richard G Mathias, Tim Parker, Dr Rick Ross, Nurse Jacqui Scott, Dr Geraldine Smith MRCPath, Roy Shuttleworth, Mr Brent Tanner DM MCh FRCS, Dr David Veale, Elizabeth Veale and Arnie Wilson.

As ever, deep thanks to my UK agent Jon Thurley, to my crucial unofficial editor, Sue Ansell, my late mother and best ambassador, Cornelia, my copy editor, Hazel Orme, and my editors, Simon Spanton and Selina Walker. A very big thank you is reserved for Helen, for more reasons than I can list.

And finally, of course, thanks for the patience of

Bertie, ever curled beneath my desk, occasionally pausing from his slumber to fart, chew my computer cables, or shred a fallen sheet of manuscript . . .

Peter James
Sussex, England, 1999
scary@pavilion.co.uk
www.peterjames.com

Prologue

Someone told Maddy Williams that people always knew when they were going to die. Or maybe she'd read it somewhere. A newspaper? Magazine? She read a lot of women's magazines – particularly the problem pages and stories of human angst, about people like herself who had complexes about the way they looked. Noses too big, breasts too floppy, pointy ears, ratty lips.

There were faulty cars known as Friday cars, and maybe there were Friday people – people who had bits of code missing from their genes, or error messages that manifested by placing their eyes too close together, or giving them too few fingers or a hare-lip, or, like herself, a port-wine stain birthmark the shape of Texas, covering half of her face. Defects that the victims had to display for the rest of their lives, as if they were carrying a banner that said, *My genes did this to me*.

But not any more for Maddy Williams. She'd been saving since she was ten years old, when she first heard about plastic surgery in a television documentary. Ever since Danny Burton and every other classmate, and just about every stranger she'd ever encountered, had stared at her in a way that made her feel like a freak, she had been saving for this series of operations that was going to transform her life. And one of the most famous plastic surgeons in Britain was performing them.

Some months back he'd sketched on paper and shown her on the computer in his consulting room how she was going to look with her new face, and three weeks ago he had started on her. It wasn't just Texas that was going: that hooked beak of a nose was morphing into a Cameron Diaz snub, her lips would be filled out, her cheekbones reshaped. After thirty-one years of hell she was going to be transformed!

And now on the operating table, woozy from the pre-med, her thoughts rambling, she hardly dared believe it was all happening ... that it was *really happening!* Because nothing good ever did happen to her, that was the pattern of her life. Always, when she was on the edge of something going her way for once, the wheels would fall off. She'd read about this too, people who were dogged by bad luck. Maybe there was a bad-luck gene?

In truth the two operations she'd had so far weren't quite as great as she'd hoped. She was disappointed with her nose, the arches were too flared, but the surgeon was going to correct that now. Just a tiny op today, pre-med and local anaesthetic, a little bit of tweaking and hey presto!

When I come round I'm going to have a nose like Cameron Diaz.

Soon I'm going to be everything I ever wanted to be. Normal. I'm going to be an ordinary human being. Just like everyone else.

The ceiling above her was cream plaster; it looked tired, the kind of ceiling where spiders hang out and bugs crawl. *I'm a pupa curled up inside a chrysalis and I'm going to emerge as a beautiful butterfly.*

The table shook slightly beneath her, a faint rumbling sound – wheels? Like a drum roll. Now she was under bright lights. She could feel their warmth. Get a suntan! she thought.

Two figures in green surgical scrubs stood over her, their faces anonymous behind their masks and beneath hats like scrunched J-cloths. The nurse and the surgeon. His eyes locked on hers. Last time they had been sparkling with warmth and humour, but now they were

2

different: cold, devoid of any emotion. An icy wind squalled through her, and the faint apprehension of a few minutes ago now turned into mounting terror that she was not going to survive this operation.

People know when they are going to die.

But there was no need to be afraid. Hey, this surgeon was Mr Nice Guy! This was the man who'd shown her how beautiful he could make her, who'd held her hand to reassure her, who had even done his best to convince her that she looked fine as she was, that she did not need surgery, that the blotch on her face and the kink in her nose all added to her character . . .

But this surgeon was in a strange space today – or was it just in her imagination? She looked for reassurance at the nurse. Warm concerned eyes stared back. She wasn't aware of anything wrong. But . . .

People know when they are going to die.

The words were screaming inside her now. She was not going to make it through this operation, she needed to get out, now, this minute, cancel, forget about it.

Maddy attempted to speak, but as she did so the surgeon leaned over her, holding a cotton bud in his gloved hand, and began to work it around the inside of first her left nostril, then her right. She wanted to move, to shake her head, to shout, but it was as if someone had disconnected her body from her brain.

Please help me! Oh, God, one of you please help me!

Darkness was descending, swabbing up her remaining thoughts before they were fully formed, before they could turn into words. And now, as she stared back into the surgeon's eyes, she could see a smile in them, as if he had been holding something back from her and now he didn't need to hold it back.

And she knew for certain that she was going to die today.

1

Late on a wet May afternoon, Faith Ransome, walking around the downstairs rooms of her house, checking for errant bits of Lego, thought, Is this it? Is this my life? Is this all there is?

Alec, in the kitchen, called, 'Mummy, Muummeeeee! Come and watch!'

She stooped to recover a bright yellow corner piece from behind the sofa, relieved. Ross would have seen it for sure. And then . . .

She shivered, feeling a little queasy. It was cold in England after three weeks of hot, dry sun in Thailand. They'd been home four days and it felt much longer. Four centuries.

'Muummmeeeee!'

Tuning out his voice, she walked upstairs, the ritual, checking each of the stairs for marks, mud, paw prints, and the walls for any new blemish, the lights for blown bulbs. Her eyes scanned the landing carpet and she recovered another Lego brick, went into Alec's room, and put the two pieces in the box on the table. She looked around carefully, picked up a robot space-walker, crammed Alec's trainers into the cupboard and closed the door, rearranged the Star Wars bedcover and straightened the row of fluffy heads on the pillow.

Spike, Alec's hamster, as fat as its Rugrat namesake was skinny, was trundling around inside the treadmill in his cage. She scooped up a few spilled grains from the table-top and dropped them in the waste-bin.

As she finished she heard the drumroll bark of

Rasputin, their black Labrador, b-woof . . . b-woof . . . b-woof . . .

A rush of adrenaline. Then the unmistakable mashing of tyres on gravel.

Not good adrenaline this – like seaweed-laden storm waves breaking inside her. Barking steadily, Rasputin lumbered from the kitchen, through the hall, into the drawing room where, Faith knew, he had leaped on to his chair in front of the bay window so that he could see his master.

He was home early.

'Alec! Daddy's home!' She sprinted for the bedroom, peered in, checked. Bed neat inside the four-poster oak frame. Shoes, slippers, stray clothes, already put away. *En-suite* bathroom. Basin spotless. Towels hung the way Ross liked them.

Hastily she pulled off the jeans, sweatshirt and trainers that were her habitual daytime clothes. It wasn't that she felt like dressing up to greet her husband, she just wanted to avoid criticism.

In the bathroom she stared at her face in the mirror. In the cabinet was a plastic vial of pills. Her *happy* pills. It had been over a month since she had taken one and she was determined to stay off them. Determined to beat the depression that had dogged her on and off for the past six years since her son had been born – to kill it dead!

She put on some eye-shadow, fresh mascara, a dash of rouge, dabbed a little powder on her perfect snub nose (her husband's craftsmanship, not her genes) pulled on black Karen Millen slacks, a white blouse, a pale green Betty Barclay cardigan and black mules.

Then she checked her hair in the mirror. She was a natural blonde, and favoured classic styles. Right now it was parted to one side, cut just short of her shoulders at the back and slanted down across her forehead at the front.

You don't look bad, girl, not for a thirty-two-year-old mum.

Although, of course, she had Ross to thank for a lot of that.

The key was rattling in the front door.

And now she hurried down the stairs, as it opened in a flurry of leaping dog, swirling Burberry raincoat, swinging black case and distressed-looking Ross.

She took the case and the raincoat, thrust at her as if she was a hat-check girl, and proffered her cheek for a perfunctory kiss. 'Hi,' she said. 'How was your day?'

'Total hell. I lost someone. Died on me.' Anger and pain in his voice as he slammed the door behind him.

Ross, six foot four, black hair gelled back in high-gloss waves, reeking of soap, looked like some handsome gangster: starched white shirt, red and gold silk tie, tailored navy suit, trousers with creases to slice cheese, black brogues flossed to military perfection. He seemed close to tears.

At the sight of his son his face lit up.

'Daddy, Daddy!'

Alec, face brown from Thailand, was leaping through the air into his arms.

'Hey, big guy!' Ross held his son tightly to his chest, as if in this animated bundle of child he was holding every hope and dream in the world. 'Hey!' he said. 'What's been happening? How was your day?'

Faith smiled. No matter how low she felt, seeing the love between her husband and her son was the one thing that gave her strength and the resolve to make her marriage work.

She hung up his coat, set down the case, and went into the kitchen. On the television, Homer Simpson was being berated by his boss. She poured a three-finger

7

measure of Macallan into the glass, then pressed the tumbler up against the ice arm of the Maytag fridge. Four cubes clinked into it.

Ross followed her in and set Alec down. The boy's attention returned to the television.

'Who died?' Faith said, handing her husband the glass. 'A patient?'

He held up the rim to the window, checking for dirt, lipstick, and God-knew-what-else he checked the rims of glasses for before committing them to his sacred lips.

One finger of whisky went down. She reached up, loosened his tie, half-heartedly put a comforting arm around him, which was the most she could do, and the most she wanted to do, then withdrew it.

'I scored two goals today, Daddy!'

'He did!' Faith confirmed proudly.

'That's terrific!' Ross stood behind his son and wrapped his arms around him again. '*Two* goals?'

Alec nodded, torn between accepting praise and watching the show.

Then the smile faded from Ross's face. He said again, 'Two goals!' but the sparkle had gone from his eyes. He patted Alec's head, said, 'Just great!' then went down the hall to his study and sat down in his leather Parker Knoll, still, unusually, with his jacket on. He levered the chair to its furthest back-reclined, footrest-up position, and closed his eyes.

Faith watched him. He was suffering, but she could feel nothing for him. Part of her still wanted everything between them to be as it once was, although now it was more for Alec's sake, than her own.

'Died. I can't believe she did that to me.'

Quietly, 'A patient?'

'Yes, a fucking patient. Why the hell did she have to go and die on me?'

'What happened?'

8

'Allergic reaction to the anaesthetic. That's the second this year. Jesus.'

'Same anaesthetist? Tommy?'

'No, Tommy's away. I didn't use anyone. It was only a tiny correction, for God's sake – just the flare of the arches. I used a local anaesthetic – don't need an anaesthetist to do that. Could you get me a cigar?'

Faith went to the humidor in the dining room, took out a Montecristo No. 3, clipped the end the way Ross liked it, and brought it back into the room. Then she held the flame of the Dupont lighter as he drew several deep puffs, rotating the end until it was burning evenly.

He blew a long jet of smoke at the ceiling, then, eyes closed, asked, 'How was your day?'

She wanted to say, Actually, it was a shitty day, the way most of my days are, but she didn't. She said, 'It was OK. Fine.'

He nodded, silently. Then, after some moments, said, 'I love you, Faith. I couldn't live without you. You know that, don't you?'

Yes, she thought. And that's a big problem.

2

The small boy stood in the alley in the darkness that lay beyond the throw of the streetlight. Above him, on this warm September night, the glow of a weak bulb spilled through drawn curtains behind an open window.

A car was accelerating down the street, and he pressed himself flat against the wall. There was a crash of gears, then it went past. Somewhere down the street he heard the words of a new song called 'Love Me Do' playing loudly over a radio. He wrinkled his nose against the stench from the dustbins beside him.

A breeze swayed the curtains and a streak of light

played across the windowless side wall behind him. Somewhere close by a dog barked, then was silent. And in the silence he heard a woman's voice. 'Oh, yes, oh, my God, yes! Harder, fuck me harder, oh, my God, oh, yes, oh yes, oh *yes*!'

In his right hand the boy held a heavy rectangular oil can, with a round screw cap, and a thin metal handle with a sharp edge that dug painfully into his palm. The words SHELL OIL were printed on the side. The can smelt of car engines. It contained a gallon of petrol, which he had siphoned from the tank of his father's Morris.

In his pocket, he had a box of matches.

In his heart, hatred burned.

3

Ross's semen trickled between her legs. Faith lay still, listening to the stream of his urine, grey daylight through the open curtains, stark shapes of the beeches in rich green leaf framing the horizon. News drizzled from the clock radio, slightly off tune, across the far side of the bed, gloomy Kosovan war-dead news. Then a time check: 6.25 on Wednesday, 12 May.

She reached for her contact lenses, picked up the container and unscrewed the top. Twenty minutes and she would have to get Alec up, fed, to school, and then . . . ?

The queasiness she'd been feeling for the past few days seemed worse this morning, and a thought struck her.

Pregnant?

Oh, God, please no.

A year after Alec was born they'd begun trying for a second child but nothing had happened. After a year,

Ross had arranged tests, but they'd shown everything was working fine. The problem, it seemed, was with him, but he would not accept that and refused flatly to go to any specialist.

At first this had angered Faith, but increasingly she'd seen it as a blessing. She loved Alec to death but he was hard work, all the time, and her energy levels had been so low she didn't know how she could have coped with another child.

And she knew that a big part of the reason she had stayed in her marriage was that she couldn't imagine life without Alec. There was no way, in her depressed state, that Ross would have let her keep him if she had left, nor, in that state, could she have coped very well with him on her own. And there was no questioning the intensity of Ross's love for Alec. But from that love would come influence. Alec carried Ross's genes and she couldn't do anything about that. But with love and guidance she could maybe bring out in him all the good things he had inherited from Ross and try to damp down the bad.

From the bathroom, Ross called out, 'What are you wearing tonight, darling?'

Brain into gear, fast. 'I thought the dark blue – the Vivienne Westwood you bought me.'

'Slip it on for me?'

She put it on. He came out of the bathroom, stood naked, hair wet, toothbrush in mouth, staring at her. 'No. It's not right. Too frivolous for tonight.'

'My black Donna Karan – the taffeta?'

'See it.'

He went back into the bathroom then reappeared, shaving foam on his face, one strip razored clean.

She turned around for him.

'No – that's more suitable for a ball. This is just a dinner.' He marched across to her wardrobe, flicked through the hangers, pulled out a dress, tossed it on the *chaise-longue*, then another, then another.

'I have to get Alec up.'

'Just pop these on. You need to look right – it's really important tonight.'

Turning away, she mouthed a silent curse. It was always *really important*. But she put the dress on. And another. None of her reflections pleased her. Bad hair day today, it was a tangle, and the lousy wet weather of the past three weeks had bleached away most of the remains of her tan, returning her complexion to its usual early-morning just-risen-from-the-grave pallor. Her friend, Sammy Harrison, had told her a couple of years back that on a good day she looked like Meg Ryan on a bad day. And today was not a good day.

'Need to see it with shoes,' he called, watching her in the mirror, razoring away the last of the foam. 'And your bag.'

Ten to seven and he was dressed, dabbing at a fleck of blood on his chin. On the bed were laid out the dress, the shoes, the bag, the necklace, the earrings. Alec was still asleep.

'OK, fine, good. Wear your hair up.' He cupped her face in his hands, kissed her lips lightly, and was gone.

Life's a bitch, and then, thought Faith, it's not that you die, you just start, without even noticing it, to become someone you never wanted to be.

All those dreams you had at school, all those glossy lives you looked at in magazines, of people who seemed to have it all. But she had never minded that, never envied them. Her father, a gentle, uncomplaining man, had been bedridden throughout her childhood, and she'd worked since as far back as she could remember to help her mother keep the family. Weekends had been spent on the living-room floor stitching thumbs to mittens for the local glove factory where her mother worked part-time, and every morning, from the age of twelve, she'd left home at a quarter to six to do a paper round.

Faith had never been ambitious for wealth. All she had ever sought to do with her life was to be a caring person, and to try to make a difference to the world. There was no Grand Plan, it was just her simple philosophy. She had always hoped that when she had children, she could teach them to respect the world around them, try to give them a happier childhood than she'd had, and to make them decent people.

But now, at thirty-two, her life was as remote from her modest origins as it was from her dreams. She was married to a plastic surgeon who was a seriously wealthy perfectionist, and they lived in a house that was absurdly grand. She knew she *ought* to count her blessings, as her mother told her. But she and her mother would always see things differently – she hoped.

She decided to avoid the chemist in the village, and drove instead to Burgess Hill, the nearest town, where there was a large Boots.

As she waited in the queue at the car-park barrier, she stared out at the cloud-laden sky, could almost feel it pressing down on her. She tapped a fingernail against her front teeth, aware that she was shaking slightly, her nerves jangling. That indefinable dark fear that was part of her depression, along with slack energy and the occasional, very frightening sensation that she wasn't quite inside her body, never stayed away for long. She was glad she kept the Prozac capsules in the bathroom cabinet. If she had had them in her bag she would have taken one now.

There was just one car in front of her, driven by an old woman who had pulled up too far from the machine and was having to open her door to reach out and get the ticket. Faith glanced at the Range Rover's mile-ometer: 8.2. She mentally doubled it for the return home. Then doubled it again for the return trip to the station this evening, to catch the train to London for the medical dinner with Ross: 32.8 miles that would have to be accounted for – Ross checked the mileage every day.

To justify this trip to him, she stopped at Waitrose and did a major groceries shop. It was easier this way – best to find ways to sidestep the mines and booby traps Ross planted in her daily life. That way there was some kind of peace, at least in her waking consciousness if not in her troubled dreams. Dreams in which the same theme recurred endlessly.

When did my life with Ross start to change?

Had there been a point in the past twelve years at which Ross, the kind, caring, fun-loving young house-man she had loved to death had turned into the vile-tempered monster whose arrival home she dreaded? Had that side of him always been there? And, in those early, heady days, had her love for him, or the prospect of a glamorous life, blinded her to it?

Or had he masked it?

And why was it only she who could see it? Why couldn't her mother, or her friends? But she already knew the answer to that. Ross never gave them the chance – he could charm the birds out of the trees. Even though the medical world had been able to do nothing to ease her father's slow, painful and undignified descent into death over twenty wretched years, her mother had remained in awe of doctors. She adored Ross – was even perhaps a little in love with him herself.

Sometimes Faith wondered if the fault lay with her. Did she expect too much of her husband? Did her depression cause her to see only the bad and ignore the good? Because even now there were happy moments and good days with him, although in the end his temper or his criticism usually soured them. She had tried on this recent holiday in Thailand, as if it had been a last attempt at salvaging their marriage and getting back to how they had once been. She'd given it her best shot, but in the end could feel nothing for him.

There was a borderline in life. You could push people up to it, but then no further. Beyond that everything changed irrevocably. Airline pilots called it the point of no return: that critical moment when you were too short of runway to abort take-off, when you had no choice but to become airborne. That or crash. And that was where she was now. That was how far Ross had pushed her.

In those early days Faith had loved him so much she'd let him do *anything*. She had believed in him so completely that she'd endured the pain and discomfort of six operations, and he had transformed her from being plain into someone, well, less plain. And in a way it was flattering. As his reputation began its rapid ascent, she had enjoyed being taken to conventions where he had pointed out the reshaping he had done on her lips, eyes, mouth, nose, cheeks, chin and breasts. That, at least, was one of the bonuses to have come out of twelve years of marriage, the huge boost to her confidence, which was now being almost as thoroughly undermined.

Hidden in an attic bedroom they rarely used, she kept a pile of books and magazine articles about marital problems. She'd read and reread *Men Are From Mars, Women Are From Venus*, and even left it lying around the house in the hope – or, more likely, *delusion* – that Ross would pick it up and read it. Also, recently, she'd discovered an Internet chatline for abused wives. Her head was full of advice. And plans.

Life can be good again, she thought. Somehow I'm

going to find a way to make it good – for Alec and for myself.

In a sudden fit of extravagance in the supermarket, she bought a couple of frozen lobsters – Ross's favourite – for their dinner tomorrow, some spicy chicken wings, for which Alec had acquired a taste in Thailand, as well as his favourite caramel-crunch ice-cream. Then she remembered to buy a couple of tins of Ambrosia rice pudding with sultanas for her mother, who was coming to babysit tonight.

Oh, Ross, why do I still keep trying to please you? Is it just to buy a few moments of peace? Or do I delude myself that if I'm sufficiently nice to you, you'll release me from this marriage, and allow me to take my son with me?

She turned the Range Rover into the drive, past the grand stone balls topping the pillars and the smart brass sign, Little Scaynes Manor. The approach to the Elizabethan house was stunning, down the tree-and-rhododendron-lined gravel drive, up to the gabled, ivy-clad façade – her heart used to flip with excitement each time she drove in.

It was a grand place, no question, in a beautiful location, close to the foot of the soft, rolling hills of the South Downs. Ten bedrooms, drawing room, library, billiards room, a dining room that would seat thirty, a study, a huge kitchen with oak planks on the floor, and an acre of utility rooms. Yet none of the rooms – except perhaps the dining room – felt too big when it was just the two of them on their own. The house was just small enough to be homely, but large enough to impress Ross's colleagues and the occasional reporter or television crew.

There were fourteen acres of garden and grounds. Once, when it had been a true manor house, several hundred acres of farm and downland had belonged to it, but over the past couple of centuries previous owners had gradually sold off outbuildings and parcels of land. What remained was more than enough, though: fine lawns, a mature orchard filled with apple, pear, plum and cherry trees, a lake and dense woodland badly in need of coppicing. To visitors who came for an evening, or a weekend, it was idyllic.

Yet there was an atmosphere about the place that prevented Faith from feeling entirely comfortable, enhanced by the narrow, heavily leaded windows with glass that seemed black from the outside, the timbered exterior, the impossibly large and ornate chimneys – and the rumour that a woman had been bricked up inside one. She had been the mistress of the man who had built the place, and, as local village lore had it, could be heard hammering away at night, trying to get out. Faith had never heard her, although she had an open mind on ghosts, and felt bricked up in some way here herself. Sometimes, entering the house when it was empty, the large gloomy hallway, the sharp tick of the grandfather clock at the foot of the carved stairs, and the slits in the helmet visors of the armour Ross collected gave her the creeps big-time.

Today it was OK. It was Wednesday and the cleaning lady was here: Faith could hear the whine of the vacuum-cleaner up in one of the bedrooms. She was glad Mrs Fogg was in, but equally glad that she was upstairs: although the woman was an excellent cleaner, she could talk for England, mostly about how it was only a series of disasters that had led to her being forced to take this job, that she wasn't really a cleaning lady, not by a long shot.

Speedily, Faith lugged the groceries into the kitchen then, before unpacking them, removed the pregnancy-testing kit from the Boots bag and squinted at the instructions.

Above, Mrs Fogg was still Hoovering.

Faith removed a small plastic pot, a pipette, and the plastic test disc from the box, carried them into the downstairs cloakroom, and locked the door. She urinated into the pot. Then she drew some urine into the pipette and, following the instructions carefully, released five drops of urine onto the indent in the disc.

The nausea was back and her head felt warm as if she were running a slight temperature.

A red minus sign.

She was praying for a red minus sign.

She looked everywhere except at her watch. She looked at the horse prints on the wall, the old-fashioned brass taps on the brilliant white sink, the emerald wallpaper, the pile of *National Geographic*s on the shelf by the seat. She noticed a spider's web up in a corner and made a mental note to tell Mrs Fogg. Then she looked down and raised the stick.

She had to look at it twice to make sure, then checked the instructions.

Minus!

A red minus sign filled the central window of the disc. And, with her relief, the nausea was gone.

4

Oliver Cabot was distracted by several things tonight, but principally by the woman at the next table, who had caught his eye twice and looked as bored with her companions as he was with his.

He had accepted the invitation to this dinner at the Royal Society of Medicine, hosted by the pharmaceutical giant Bendix Schere, not out of love for his profession, or admiration for his host's company – an organisation that he despised. Rather, he was interested in keeping up to speed with every advance being made in medicine, and staying in the frame in a profession of which he was becoming daily more mistrustful. But right now this woman, on the far side of the round twelve-seater table behind a jagged skyline of wine bottles and water jugs, with her streaky blonde hair framing her face – a cute face, pretty rather than classically beautiful – was reminding him of someone and he couldn't think who. Then at last he got it.

Meg Ryan!

'You know, Oliver, it took us twelve years to develop Tyzolgastrine.' Johnny Ying, Vice-President, Overseas Marketing, a Chinese-American with a Brooklyn accent and spiky hair, probed his meringue basket. 'Six hundred million dollars of research. You know how many companies on earth can afford to spend that kind of dough?'

Tyzolgastrine was being hailed as a revolutionary ulcer treatment. It had recently been listed by the World Bureau of Ethical Medicine as one of the hundred most important medical advances of the twentieth century. Not many people knew that the World Bureau of Ethical Medicine was wholly funded by Bendix Schere.

'You didn't need to spend that kind of money,' Oliver remarked.

'How's that?'

With a wry smile, he said, 'You didn't discover tyzolgastrine, you ripped it off. You only started marketing it after you'd wasted four hundred million dollars trying to bury the concept of an antibiotic ulcer treatment. You don't have to bullshit *me*.'

Meg Ryan was listening to a lean, bald man who was talking enthusiastically while she nodded. Her body language told Cabot that she had not taken to this man one bit. He wondered what they were discussing. And as he did so she caught his eye again and immediately looked away.

'Normally aspirated – *normally aspirated, right?* – she'll give you two-eight-five BHP, but what I did, I took the heads to a firm in Tucson, had them polish them, skim an extra two thou ...

Faith had to look at his place-card to remind herself of his name. Dighton Carver, Vice-President, Marketing. He had been talking about car engines for the past fifteen minutes. Before that he had talked about his divorce, his new wife, his old wife, his three kids, his house, his power-boat – more cubic inches of testosterone and grunt – and his workout programme. He had not yet asked her a single question about herself. Her companion on the right had introduced himself with a strong hand-pump at the start of the meal, and had then proceeded to talk to the woman on his right throughout the five courses they'd had so far.

Her dessert lay untouched on her plate. The queasiness she'd felt this morning had returned and she'd barely eaten anything. This was one of those occasions that Ross enjoyed and Faith hated. She liked the company of individual doctors, but *en masse* they seemed to unite in an élitist way that always made her feel an outsider.

Ross, the son of a Gas Board clerk, now a celebrated plastic surgeon, was being courted and fêted by his profession. His name was there on the printed menu, on the left side of the sheet, opposite the lamb noisettes in onion marmalade, opposite the Bâtard Montrachet '93 and the Langoa Barton '86. It was featured alphabetically on the same column as the Queen's gynaecologist and a host of other distinguished medics. He was one of the guests of honour: Ross Ransome MS, FRCS (Plast).

In spite of everything, she felt proud to see his name

in print on that menu, knowing that, in her own small way, she had contributed something towards his success. At Ross's insistence she'd had elocution lessons to change her suburban London accent into a more refined one. For years she'd dutifully read her way through the lists of books Ross had prescribed for her: classics, the great poets, Shakespeare, the major philosophers, ancient and modern history. At times she had felt like Eliza Doolittle in *My Fair Lady* – or, as Ross would have preferred, Shaw's *Pygmalion* (also ticked off the list). He wanted her to be able to hold her own at any dinner table.

Many times she had wondered privately what it was about her that he had fallen in love with. He'd changed her face, her breasts, her voice, and re-educated her. And sometimes she had wondered if maybe it was just that: he had been attracted to her because she was malleable. Maybe he'd seen her as a *tabula rasa* he could shape into his perfect woman. Maybe that's what the control freak inside him needed.

He was watching her now, seated diagonally from her across the large round table, next to a man with a perfect tan and even more perfect teeth, who was talking to him intently, underlining his points with a sideways slice of his hand through the air. On his right was a woman with big, peroxided hair, who'd had one face-lift too many. Her skin gave the illusion of defying gravity altogether, rising upwards from her facial bones and muscles to give her mad, staring eyes, while her mouth was stretched into a permanent humourless smile. No chance of Ross taking anything other than a professional interest in her, Faith thought.

A pity.

Casting her eyes around the room for familiar faces, Faith saw that a man she'd noticed watching her before was looking at her again. She glanced at Ross, but he was immersed in his conversation, then looked back at the stranger. Their eyes met, and he smiled. Flattered, she looked away, feeling like an excited child, and suppressed a guilty grin. It had been a long time since she had flirted with anyone and it felt good, darkened only by the shadow of Ross and the anger he would take out on her later, if he saw.

She glanced back and the man was still looking at her. She lowered her eyes hastily this time, aware that she was blushing.

'Then what I did was I raised all the tolerances – suspension, shocks, brakes – we ripped out the whole lot and started again. Actually we used a racing matrix . . .'

Once more she tuned out her companion, then cast a furtive glance at the next but one table. Her admirer was engrossed in conversation with an Oriental man on his left, and she had a chance to study him. He was about the same age as Ross, mid- to late-forties, she guessed, and something else set him apart from everyone else, but she couldn't immediately decide what.

He sat straight-backed, tall and lean. He wore hip, wire-framed glasses and his face, beneath a tangle of grey curls, was serious and intellectual. He had a bigger, less perfect bow-tie than the neat little black satin numbers that seemed to be the uniform standard here, which gave him a rather reckless, louche air.

Who are you? she wondered. I really like the look of you.

He might be a scientist – maybe working in the research and development division of their pharmaceutical hosts.

The bang of the gavel snapped her out of her thoughts. A liveried toastmaster pronounced, 'My lords, ladies and gentlemen, please be upstanding for the loyal toast.'

As they sat down, Ross pulled a tube from his inside pocket, unscrewed the lid and shook out a large Havana. Now he watched her with a dry, humourless smile that said, 'I see you looking at him, sunshine. I see you looking at him.'

5

The house was divided into two flats. There was a metal fire-escape at the rear of the building, accessed from the glass-panelled kitchen door of the first-floor flat.

The boy climbed the fire-escape now, struggling under the weight of the gallon can of petrol, his plimsolls silent on the cast-iron treads. He was eleven, tall for his years, and strangers always guessed his age wrong; to a casual onlooker he might have passed for sixteen. He knew that no one would take any notice of a boy of sixteen out on his bicycle at eleven o'clock at night on the quiet south London streets, and no one would have seen the can, which he had transported here strapped to his chest inside his windcheater.

'Love Me Do' by that new group, the Beatles, who were on the telly all the time, was still playing, and he could hear shouts and laughter too, as if a party was going on somewhere down the road. The words of the song's refrain repeated over and over, strengthening the hatred inside him.

Two hours ago, his father had come into his room and said good night, and an hour later the boy had heard him go to bed. Half an hour after that he had left the house through his bedroom window, and shinned down a drainpipe. When he returned, he would go in via the same route.

He had been planning this for months, every detail, right down to the puncture-repair outfit, the spare bulbs for his bicycle lamps, wrapped in tissue paper in his saddlebag, and the rubber kitchen gloves, which he was putting on now. He had a sharp eye and an enormous capacity for detail, as well as being good with his hands. He had practised and practised until he had made an art of the shaping of his bedclothes to look like himself asleep. He had topped them with a wig he had bought in a joke shop, now cut and dyed to match his own hair.

He had pedalled the route dozens of times from his home to here, timing the journey, and he had rehearsed what he would say to a policeman if he got stopped, and the name and address he would give. And he had had to wait for a night when there was no moon but no rain either to minimise any footprints.

Last night, lying awake, thinking about everything that might go wrong and wreck his plans, he had been nervous. But now that he was here he was feeling fine, calm.

Calmer than he could ever remember feeling in his life.

6

At a quarter to one in the morning, in a former artist's loft close to the Portobello Road, Oliver Cabot sat at his desk, which had been fashioned from the door of a ruined Indian temple.

He stared at his iMac screen, with the numb patience of a hardened cybertraveller, as the small colour photograph of Ross Ransome downloaded inch by reluctant inch.

It was almost there. As if to help, he clicked the cursor on to the scroll bar, moved it up, then down again, but it made no difference. All he could see so far was the top half of the surgeon's head and what looked like bookshelves behind him.

He yawned. In the still of the night, the threshing of the computer's fan reminded him of the dead sound in an airliner. On his desk, trapped in the glare of his Anglepoise lamp, Jake grinned at him from a tortoise-shell picture frame.

Freckled Jake, with his brown fringe and gappy grin – two teeth missing from the front row, taken by the Tooth Fairy and never to be replaced.

Jake, frozen in time, running out of the front door of their waterfront house in Venice, Santa Monica, with its view on to the canal and the appalling stench of sewage. Jake, on his brand-new mountain bike, unaware of the horror waiting for him just five days away.

The tightness in his throat, which always came when he allowed the memories to creep in, was there now. Oliver looked back at the screen, moved the cursor, scrolled down. Now he could see the full picture of Ross Ransome and, to his disappointment, there was no one else in the frame. No Faith Ransome.

Hey, Shit-for-brains, he thought, what kind of a sad bastard are you who trawls the net at this time in the morning looking for a photograph of someone else's wife, a woman you've never even met?

An Oliver Cabot kind of a sad bastard.

7

Silence in the car. Ross driving fast. Darkness unspool-ing from the road ahead, an endless loop, sometimes with brilliant lights bursting from it, sometimes a void. Brahms playing, the violin mournful, as if a prelude to something bad ahead. The smells of Ross's cigar and leather filled the interior of this macho Aston Martin cocoon.

Her father had smoked cigars, and this smell always reminded her of him and of their little semi-detached house. She remembered when her father's arms had stopped working and she had sat by his bed while he clamped his lips doggedly around the soggy butt and looked up at her with a desperate smile to say, 'At least my mouth still works, at least I can still thank God for creating me.'

Faith's mind returned to the man, the stranger in the crush at the bar after the speeches were over. He had been alone. All she needed to do was take four steps and she'd have been in front of him. Ross hadn't even been in the room; he'd stayed at the table talking to someone. Just four steps. Instead, she'd bottled out and broken in on a conversation between Felicity Beard, the wife of a gynaecologist acquaintance of Ross – one of the few medical wives she liked – and another woman, and talked mostly about their holiday in Thailand until Ross had appeared and said he wanted to leave, an early start in the morning.

'I saw you,' he said calmly.

'Saw me what?'

Silence again. Just the violins and the night. A signpost to Brighton flashed past. Eighteen miles. She knew what. There was no point in going through the rigmarole of denial. Ross was calm but there was brooding anger inside him. Best to let it simmer and maybe by the time they were home he'd be too tired to make a big issue. Right now she didn't feel well enough for a fight.

She thought about Alec, long tucked up and asleep by now. He'd be fine, he adored his grandmother, who spoiled him. She enjoyed staying over – Ross had made a palatial space for her in the house, a whole suite of rooms. She'd be awake now, sitting in front of the sixty-inch television he'd bought for her, chain-smoking and watching movies into the small hours, just as she had throughout Faith's childhood, keeping Faith's bedridden, insomniac father company.

It seemed from what she read and people she talked to that few mothers got on with their sons-in-law. But her mother and Ross had taken to each other from the start, and Ross had always been good to her – and to her father during the last years of his life. But this created a problem: Faith found it hard to talk about her marital problems to her mother, whose standard response was that all marriages had their difficulties and that Faith should count her blessings, and accept Ross's behaviour as due to the stress of being a man in his position.

It was twenty past twelve. She thought again about the stranger at the dinner, wondered what life would be like with a different man, a different husband. How could she get out of Ross's clutches? How would Alec –? And then, suddenly, the nausea erupted inside her. 'Stop! Ross quick, pull over!'

The interior of the car seemed to close in around her. Hand rammed over her mouth, just one thought in mind as he pulled on to the hard shoulder, *Must not . . . Not in the car . . .*

They jolted to a stop. She threw the seat-belt clear, found the door-handle, pushed, stumbled out into the sharp, cold air. Then, on her knees on the tarmac, she threw up.

Moments later, Ross's hand on her forehead. 'My baby, darling, you're OK, my darling, you're fine.'

Sweating, she threw up again, Ross holding his palm firmly against her forehead, the way her mother used to when she was a child, holding her with his firm,

27

comforting hand, then wiping her mouth with his handkerchief.

Back in the car with her seat reclined, the heater turned right up, Ross said, 'Probably that seafood cocktail. Duff prawn or something. If you get seafood poisoning, you know about it within a few hours.'

She wanted to tell him he was wrong: he knew she'd been feeling like this for days, but she was scared to talk in case she threw up again. She lay back, with the darkness and the lights revolving around her and inside her, her contact lenses feeling gritty and uncomfortable, dimly aware from the motion of the car, the changing resonance of the tyres beneath them, the stops and turns they made, that they were getting closer and closer to their home.

To a glass of water.

She was sitting at the wide pine table in front of the Aga, listening to Rasputin barking, probably chasing a rabbit outside somewhere, and Ross calling him back in. The clock on the kitchen wall read ten past one.

She heard the patter of paws, then Rasputin was nuzzling his face into her lap. 'Hey, boy, sweetie-pie, how are you?' As she stroked the dog's silky hair, he looked up at her expectantly, two big, soulful eyes. Then he gave her a gentle nudge. Smiling, she said, 'You want a biscuit?' Easing him away, she took one from the store-cupboard, made him sit nicely for it and popped it into his mouth. Then, while he crunched happily, she went over to the sink and swilled her mouth with water, trying to get rid of the sour taste of vomit.

A key clattered, then moments later she heard the rattle of the safety chain as Ross locked up for the night. He came up behind her, rested his hands on her shoulders, and nuzzled her cheek. 'Alec's sound asleep. How're you feeling now?'

'A little better, thanks.'

'The pills kicking in?'

'I think so. What were they?'

'They'll calm your system down.'

It irritated her that he always resisted telling her what pills he gave her, as if she were a child.

He knelt, examined her eyes, told her to stick out her tongue, then examined it with a worried frown.

'What is it?'

'Nothing.' He smiled. 'Bed. There's something I want to show you before we go up – won't take a sec.'

Behind the smile, she again detected a faint unease. 'What did you notice with my tongue?'

After a momentary hesitation, his voice, full of confidence, said, 'Nothing to worry about.'

She picked her evening bag up from the kitchen table, and followed him down the corridor, which was lined with prints of historical military uniforms, interspersed with shields and swords hung in brackets, into his study. Whether it was the throwing up or the pills she did not know, but she was definitely feeling better now – and wide awake.

Ross walked across to his computer, touched the keyboard and the screen came to life. Then he switched on his desk light, snapped open his briefcase, took out a disk and pushed it into the slot. Once Faith had liked the manly, solid feel of this room, but now she felt uncomfortable, like a child in a headmaster's study.

It was spotlessly tidy with deep, leather-upholstered armchairs and sofa. Fine Victorian seascapes hung on the walls, there was a bust of Socrates on a plinth, and bookshelves lined with medical books and periodicals. He worked at a handsome antique walnut partner's desk, which she had bought him for his birthday shortly after they'd moved here, and which had made a big dent in the savings she'd built up during her short career in catering.

She'd given up work at Ross's insistence shortly before their marriage, twelve years ago. Although she loved her job, and the small firm she'd joined after catering college, doing mostly directors' lunches, she had been happy to concentrate on making a home for herself and Ross. Once they were settled she could do what she had always wanted: a degree in nutrition.

But Ross had rejected both the idea of her going back to college, and of her taking a part-time job. While he had made a big issue of not wanting her to exhaust herself though studying or being at work, what she now realised was that he had wanted her at home so that he would know where she was.

Instead, she had plunged into local community life. Their neighbouring hamlet of Little Scaynes consisted of little more than a few rows of Victorian cottages, originally built to house railway workers constructing the London–Brighton line, a haphazard scattering of larger, more recent houses and bungalows, and a Norman church that boasted some fine early frescoes, dry rot, a thriving colony of deathwatch beetle, and a curate whose false teeth rattled when he addressed his puny congregation.

Little Scaynes had no shop and its only pub had closed in 1874 when the main Lewes–London road had been moved three miles to the south. The nearest place for groceries was two miles on, a village store which was facing closure due to the nearby superstore. Faith had been co-opted on to the committee to save the little shop, although like everyone else – and just as guiltily – she only bought emergency items there.

Despite its paltry size Little Scaynes was a hotbed of

local politics, with an army of tweed-skirted, stout-shoed, iron-haired activists. It seemed to Faith that country people spent most of their time either trying to save things or trying to halt progress. Ever since moving to the house, ten years ago, she had been a participant in numerous such projects, partly because she wanted to contribute to the community, partly as a way of making friends, and partly because she always found it hard to say no.

Right now, in addition to the village-store campaign, she was on committees to save the church roof, the local library, an ancient copse of beeches threatened by a housing estate, a public footpath blocked for years by a stubborn farmer, and she was an active member of the local branch of the NSPCC. She was involved in attempts to stop the modernisation of a rustic barn on the edge of the hamlet, reverse the approval of a new bypass, foil the building of yet another golf course, and prevent the merger of their parish council with a neighbouring one.

However, the achievement that had given her most satisfaction in recent years was helping to raise over fifty thousand pounds to send the leukaemia-stricken daughter of a local herdsman to America for an operation – Ross had pulled strings – which had saved the five-year-old's life.

Her own face appeared on the computer screen. Moments later it was replaced by another photograph showing it in profile.

'That's how you look now,' Ross said.

She yawned, suddenly leadenly tired again, trying to remember when they had been taken. On the beach outside their hotel in Phuket three weeks ago, she recalled, looking at the background.

Ross was pointing at her nose on the screen. He was making a curve with his finger along the bridge. 'A simple operation, just a few days of discomfort, and then . . .' He clicked the keyboard and her face disappeared, then reappeared again in profile, but now with a new nose.

Even though she had been expecting something, from the throw-away remarks Ross had been making recently, it shocked her when it came, and even more so that it was now, at this hour, and when she was feeling ill. She realised it was probably for these reasons that he had chosen this moment.

'Can we talk about this in the morning, Ross? I'm too tired.'

'I've organised a room at the clinic next Monday. Your mother can take Alec—'

'No,' she said. 'I've told you, I don't want any more surgery.'

The anger that had been pent-up inside him since dinner was now coming out. 'Faith, do you know how many women would give their right arm for what you get free?'

Smiling acidly, she held out her right arm. 'Cut it off – you've cut bits off just about every other part of me.'

'Don't be ridiculous.'

'I'm not. If you don't like me the way I am, then marry someone else.'

He looked so genuinely hurt that she felt a pang of guilt, which changed rapidly to anger with herself for allowing her feelings to be manipulated like this. Ross was like a fine actor who had his audience in the palm of his hand. He had played with her mind and emotions for years, and she'd been sucked in. But not any more.

'Darling,' he said, 'every plastic surgeon in the world operates on his wife. Hell, when you come to conferences with me, you're the best credentials I can have. People look at you and they see perfection. They think,

Look at this guy's wife – he must be brilliant at his work!'

'You look on me as your professional sample? Is that all I am to you? A *sample*?'

He looked even more hurt now. 'Darling, you always told me you weren't happy with your face – you didn't like your chin, you wished you had stronger cheek-bones. That's all I ever did to you – and it made you look stunning, you know that, you told me yourself.'

'And my breasts?'

'I didn't cut anything off your breasts, I added to them.'

'Because they weren't big enough for you.'

He moved closer to her, his voice raised. 'Listen, don't ever forget that you were nothing, you were just a plain little girl. I saw your potential. I made you the beautiful woman that you are. You and me – we made each other successful. This is a two-way thing. I help you, you help me in my career, with your looks, personality, your—'

'So why didn't you leave me as I was, if you can't bear to see other men looking at me? Why didn't you let me remain an ugly duckling?'

He stared hard into her eyes, quivering, and although he had never struck her, she had a feeling that now he was going to.

'You weren't just looking at that man at dinner. He was fucking you with his eyes.'

She turned away. 'You're being ridiculous. I'm going to bed.'

Ross gripped her shoulders so hard she cried out in pain. Her handbag fell to the floor and her lipstick and compact spilled out. 'I'm talking to you.'

She knelt and scooped up her things. 'Well, I'm not talking to you any more tonight. I feel ill and I'm going to bed.'

As she reached the top of the staircase he shouted out, 'Faith, I am—'

But she barely heard him as the nausea got her again. She tried to hang on to the banister rail, but her grip slipped and she stumbled forward.

Ross caught her. She braced herself, but now his grip was gentle, and his voice tender. 'I'm sorry, I didn't mean to shout at you. You just don't know how much you mean to me. I love you to death, Faith. You are everything to me. You and Alec. I didn't have a life before you, not a real one. I didn't know what love or warmth were before I met you. I know I'm not easy sometimes, but that's probably because I care about you too much. Can you understand that?'

She stared at him dully. She'd heard this speech so many times and, yes, she knew he meant it. But it had long ceased to mean anything to her.

'You know how scared I get when you aren't well, don't you? I want you to see a doctor, see Jules tomorrow. I'll have Lucinda call him first thing.'

Lucinda was Ross's secretary, and Jules Ritterman was their family doctor, whom Ross had known since being lectured by him at medical school. Faith did not care for him, but right now she felt too weak to argue. She just wanted to lie down, to sleep.

Her head was swimming. 'I'll be OK,' she said. 'I'll be fine.'

'I want you to see Jules.'

Something in his tone caught her. Insistence.

'I'll be fine. Probably just jet-lag from Thailand still catching up with me.'

'You've been feeling sick for a week and it's not clearing up. You may have picked up a bug in Thailand and if so it needs to be knocked on the head. *Capisce?*'

She went into the bedroom, sat on the bed, removed her lenses and put them into their container, then gratefully leaned back. Ross stood over her and she tensed, warily, but he had become again the gentle, caring Ross.

'*Capisce*?' he said again.

She tried to think it through. It meant going back up to London tomorrow. But it was Ross's birthday in a few weeks and it would give her a chance to do some shopping for him.

'Ok,' she said, reluctantly.

'Besides,' he said, putting his arms around her and holding her tightly, 'we've got to get you right before we go into surgery.'

8

It was 6.05 in the morning, 13 May. Five weeks away from the longest day, yet it felt cold enough to be February. On the news it had said there had been falls of snow overnight in some northern parts of the country.

Oliver Cabot, dressed in a tracksuit, gloves and trainers, removed the padlock and chain from his dark red Saracen hybrid, opened the front door and wheeled the bicycle out of the communal hallway of the apartment building, shivering. There was a dampness in London that seemed to drive the cold deep into your bones, he thought, and corrode whatever warmth you'd ever had in your body. It had been a shock after life in southern California, and he still hadn't got used to it, and doubted, now, that he ever would.

He pulled on his crash helmet, mounted the bike, zeroed the mileometer, then pressed down on the pedals. He built up speed along the Portobello Road, quiet and empty on weekdays, and at the end swung left into Ladbroke Grove.

The air felt glacial against his face, and he pedalled hard to work up a sweat. In spite of the cold, he always liked London at this hour. There was something special about being out in a city ahead of the rest of the world. He liked seeing the street-cleaners, the paper-boys, the milkmen, and the occasional woman, bleary and dishevelled, climbing out of a cab still in her evening wear.

Today the street seemed even emptier than usual. A couple of cars passed him, then a cab rattled by, its occupant an anonymous silhouette in the rear window. A line of a poem about London, came into his head and he tried to remember the name of the poet. Thom Gunn, perhaps?

Indifferent to the indifference that conceived you ...

He kept up his fast pace. The anonymous world he was passing remained just as indifferent to him as it did every morning. But there was a change inside him today. The memory of that woman at the dinner last night. Faith Ransome. Her glances across the crowded room towards him. Those glances weren't indifferent. They were—

She's married, Oliver Cabot. Get her out of your head, man.

He pedalled along handsome terraced side-streets up towards the Bayswater Road, crossed into Hyde Park and headed for the Serpentine. He cycled around it, watching the ducks, the reflections.

In those immediate days, weeks, months after Jake's death, he had gone out running in the early morning along the canals of Venice, California, along the beach beside the ocean, running before the sun came up, measuring distance by the lifeguard towers that rose eerily out of the darkness ahead, like the watch-towers of a concentration camp.

That was how he had felt. A prisoner in his own life. A prisoner of his own thoughts. Waking every morning from the escape of sleep and dreams to the overcast reality of having to live in a world in which Jake had been ripped from his life. From *their* lives.

Now eight years on, the paralysing pain of grief had gone, but the feeling of dumb helplessness remained, and there were reminders everywhere he turned his head. That was another reason he liked this hour: he had started going out early in those immediate weeks so as not to see other children.

He pedalled past a group of workmen unloading road-mending gear from the back of a truck. The air no longer felt cold. *Faith Ransome. I like your name. Faith. Something tells me you are not happy in your life, Faith. You were flirting with me last night. There was desperation in your face. So lovely, yet so desperate.*

Dismounting, he leaned his bicycle against a tree and walked the few yards to his usual spot beside a massive laurel bush, with the reflection of the trees on the far bank rising like shadows from the flat water in front of him.

Three words went repeatedly through his mind like a silent mantra. *Man. Earth. Heaven.* He stood as still and silent as a tree, allowing Chi, the universal life energy, to flow through him. And as he entered into his state of meditation, he thought of just one person.

What are you desperate about, Faith?
Will I ever get to meet you again?

9

On the hard couch behind the screen in the Wimpole Street consulting room, a strap tight around her arm, Faith held her breath. She'd never liked injections. The needle was touching the skin now, indenting it. She watched and did not watch at the same time. Then she

37

flinched as it pierced the skin. A sharp prick that felt as if it had gone right down into the bone, followed by a duller ache. Out of the corner of her eye, she saw the hollow tube of the syringe steadily fill with crimson blood.

Two faces above her looked down in stern concentration. Dr Ritterman's nurse, a sour woman of about fifty, and Dr Ritterman himself.

'OK, Faith,' he said, walking round to the far side of the screen. 'You may get dressed now.'

A few minutes later, Jules Ritterman, seated behind a desk the size of a small country, was studying her notes. A solemn, diminutive man of sixty, his face had the texture of parched leather, criss-crossed with deep, horizontal trenches and shallower creases, which gave him the air of a sagacious tortoise. With his grey, pinstriped suit, crinkly hair and unfashionably large glasses, he could have passed for a chartered accountant or a lawyer, if it wasn't for the flamboyance of his salmon pink shirt, and a bow-tie the colour of a roadkill frog.

The room was far larger than it needed to be, and Faith, in a wing chair before the desk, glanced around at the walls, the alabaster mantelpiece, the gauze of rain across the window and the greyness of the May morning beyond. According to Ross, Jules Ritterman was the top socialite general practitioner in London. He was GP to anyone who was anyone. It was typical of her husband, in his craving to distance himself from his humble roots, to have courted this man and made him a close friend.

Perhaps Ritterman, too, had begun with nothing, Faith thought. Maybe he'd been the child of penniless Jewish refugees and had created this grand practice through his own determination, talent and strength of character. She had never warmed to him, nor to his equally cold wife, but she could understand why he appealed to Ross, and also that to have established such an A-list clientele he must be a fine doctor. She just wished she had a doctor she could talk to. But every time in the past when she had tried to discuss this with Ross, he became furious. In his eyes, Ritterman was the best; he refused to see how she could want someone inferior.

Ritterman leaned forward on his elbows. 'Well, Faith, I don't think there's anything to worry about. Probably a little hostile bacteria from your trip to Thailand. That's one of the hazards of travel, I'm afraid – encountering bugs our immune systems aren't familiar with. It'll probably clear up of its own accord. But I'm going to have some analysis done on your blood and urine, just to make sure, and I'll let Ross know if they show up anything.'

'Why can't you let *me* know?' she asked, a little sharply. It was always the same with Ritterman: she felt he treated her like a schoolgirl.

'Don't you think you're fortunate to have a husband who is able to explain medical things to you?'

'Actually I don't,' she said. 'I'd really rather *you* did.'

He gave her a placatory smile that failed to signify compliance. It infuriated her, but she said nothing. This was how it always was with Ritterman. Even when they had been trying for a child, and the test revealed she was pregnant with Alec, it was Ross whom Ritterman phoned, not her.

'It's been a while since I've seen you. Other than this, how have you been feeling?'

'My depression?'

'Yes.'

'A lot better. I haven't taken any Prozac for over a month.' She couldn't read in his expression whether he approved of this or not.

'And you are feeling more positive?'

'About life?'

'Generally.'

'I – I think – a little, yes.'

'I wouldn't worry about staying on the Prozac longer if it makes you more positive, it—'

'I'm doing OK without it,' she said.

'Right.' He nodded. 'I'll have my secretary telephone a prescription for your tummy-bug through to Ross.'

'Why can't you give it to me?'

Chiding now, he said, 'Much easier. It will save you the bother of having to queue for it.'

'I don't mind that.'

His eyes slipped to his watch and the signal could not have been clearer.

She left, feeling dissatisfied and belittled.

It was half past eleven. Outside, in the teeming rain, she took a cab to the General Trading Company in Sloane Street. Ross was a stickler for smart labels. Shirts and ties had to come from Jermyn Street, and only from Turnbull and Asser, Hilditch and Key or Lewin's, food from Fortnum & Mason, Jackson's or Harrods, anything to do with smoking from Dunhill. The General Trading Company was on his approved list for a broader band of gifts.

Faith loved the rich atmosphere of the General Trading Company. It felt like being in a private club, its small interconnecting rooms packed with treasures, and tinkling with the cut-glass accents of the staff. Silk scarves were *de rigueur* for every female customer here, draped around their necks and shoulders, like totems of rival tribes: Cornelia James versus Hermès versus Gucci.

Faith wore one herself, the Cornelia James signature proudly displayed across the front of her black Max-Mara raincoat. Before she had met Ross, she had had little interest in fashion or in designer labels, partly because she had always been short of money. Ross had turned her into a label snob, but she enjoyed it. Retail therapy, she had joked with him. When she had been at her lowest ebb with the depression, she had raised her spirits by coming to London and having a blitz in expensive designer shops. Ross never minded how much she spent – he even encouraged it. He wanted her always to be dressed in the latest and best. But she never really felt at ease in her fabulous outfits.

She knew that outwardly she blended in here, that there was no trace of her stark origins and state-school education, yet she felt an outsider. Half the people in this shop seemed to know each other, as if they'd grown up together. And that was the difference, she thought. You could tell in their faces the confidence their upper-crust breeding gave them, and that was something you could never buy, and never change with a surgeon's scalpel. You were either born into it or you weren't.

Faith tapped a glass display, pointing at a crocodile-skin wallet, and asked an almost absurdly handsome male assistant if she could look at it.

'It's a wonderful wallet,' the Adonis told her, as he unlocked the cabinet. 'Awesome.'

She turned it over in her hands, brought it to her nose and savoured the rich aroma of the leather. Then she opened it and checked out the compartments inside. 'Would you know if it takes dollar bills? My husband has always complained that English wallets are just that bit too narrow.'

'I'd better go and check up on that one,' the young man said.

But before he could move, a hand reached from behind Faith, and laid a crisp, brand-new-looking one-dollar bill on the counter. 'Here,' an American voice said, 'want to try this?'

Faith turned round, then stared, in a mixture of

amazement and disbelief, at the tall, lean man in a black greatcoat. 'Er – thanks – er – hi,' she said, awkwardly, fighting her excitement, in case she was mistaken.

He smiled. 'Hi! How did you enjoy the dinner?'

It *was* him. Her admirer from two tables away last night.

10

'The dinner was fine,' Faith said.

His smile told her he did not believe her.

She liked his face. It wasn't handsome in any conventional sense: it was long, almost equine, and his nose, which was also long – and craggy – looked like it had been plucked from a box of spares in a tool shed as an afterthought. But it was filled with warmth and sparkle, a wise, yet playful face beneath a tangle of curls that, although grey, seemed youthful. She had the strange but comfortable feeling that somehow they already knew each other well. His eyes, titanium grey and hypnotically strong, were flirting with her, yet somewhere in them, she saw sadness.

'Actually,' she confessed, 'I didn't have that great a time. In fact, it was incredibly dull.'

With an effort, she glanced away, aware she needed to stop the game. But it was good, just for a moment, to feel flattered by this man in his black polo-neck, black jeans and dramatic black coat.

To feel *wanted*.

Their eyes locked again.

Behind her, a triumphant voice said, 'Yes, look, a perfect fit!'

She turned and saw the assistant holding up the wallet with the dollar bill inside it.

'Fine, good,' she said. 'I – I'll take it.' She dug her

purse from the entrails of her handbag, handed her gold card to him, then turned back to her admirer.

'Nice wallet,' he said.

'For my husband,' she said, then instantly regretted saying that.

'Lucky man.' The eyes were flirting again.

Fumbling for the right words, she said, 'Would you – um – think that was a good present for someone to give their husband?'

'Uh-huh.' He reached past her to pick it up, and she smelt his cologne, strong and masculine, a scent she didn't recognise but which she found appealing. Turning the wallet over in his hands he said, 'This is really neat. Beautiful, I guess, so long as you don't have any conscience about crocodiles.'

She couldn't tell whether he was joking or serious. 'Do you?'

He put the wallet down. His voice, deep and laconic, rumbled around inside his throat. 'I guess they make better wallets than bathing companions.'

Faith laughed.

'You have time for coffee?' he asked.

She looked back into those flirting eyes. Danger flags were running up inside her head. And she had more presents to buy today, including, she must not forget, Godiva chocolates. It didn't matter what else she got Ross, if she did not include those chocolates in his birthday packages he would sulk. She glanced at her watch: 11.45. She could spare half an hour. Her mother was collecting Alec from school today, so it would be OK if she was late back – and, anyhow, she would tell Ross she'd been shopping for his birthday. 'Sure,' she said. 'Why not?'

He put out his hand. 'I'm Oliver.'

'Faith.' She took it. He had long fingers and a firm grip.

'Faith Ransome,' he said.

She wondered for a second how he knew. Had he just read her name on her credit card?

His eyes again fixed on hers, he said, 'Faith. A good name. The writer H. L. Mencken defined faith as "illogical belief in the occurrence of the improbable". Is that you?'

'Probably,' she said, with a grin, and signed her credit slip.

Downstairs, in the basement café, Faith considered ordering a cappuccino, then decided green-leaf tea would be more settling for her nausea. As her admirer carried the tray to a vacant corner table, Faith followed at a distance, looking nervously around for any familiar faces.

Calm down, girl! she had to tell herself. *You're not having an affair with the man, for Christ's sake, you're just having a cup of tea with him!*

But all the same, her nerves were jangling. Jangling because of her attraction to this stranger, and jangling because if Ross discovered she'd been in a café with another man, she would never hear the end of it. She settled down in her chair at the tiny round table, her back pressed to a wall of plants, which smelt pungently damp. 'What's your surname?'

'Cabot,' he said.

'Like the explorer?'

'Uh-huh. I'm a distant relative.'

'You'd have to be pretty distant,' she retorted.

'Why's that?'

'He's been dead for five hundred years.'

He grinned. *'Touché.'*

She never normally took sugar, but feeling in need of energy she tore open a packet and tipped the contents into her cup.

'The infusion of a China plant sweetened with the pith of an Indian cane,' he said, with a flourish, as if he were delivering a line of poetry.

'That sounds a lot more elegant than calling it a cuppa with one lump.'

He gave her a warm gaze, and she no longer cared if anyone saw her. She was beginning to feel deliciously liberated, as if sitting tucked away with this eccentric stranger was her own little revolution against the tyranny of Ross.

'So,' she said, 'what are you buying here?'

'I came to look at a wedding list – a work colleague's getting married.'

'Great place to have a wedding list.'

'Actually, I told him to have it here. This is my favourite store in the whole world. It feels so quintessentially English. More so than Harrods or Harvey Nichols.'

'What about Liberty's?'

'More than Liberty's. Don't you think?'

'It's always been my favourite shop too.'

They were silent for some moments. Then she said, 'Tell me, I'm curious – how did you know my name?'

'It wasn't that hard. You're married to the plastic surgeon, right?'

Cocking her head cheekily, she said, 'Anything else you'd like to tell me about myself?'

There was, but Oliver Cabot held himself in check. He was still in shock at seeing her here. This was his favourite store, that much was true, but he hadn't been here since before Christmas. And he hadn't needed to come today. He'd already bought the wedding present, a porcelain jardinière, over the phone.

This stuff works, he kept thinking. If you *really* want something, you can make it happen. *Power of the mind.*

If he had understood it eight years back then maybe, just *maybe*, Jake would still be alive . . .

This morning, on his bicycle, he had been thinking about Faith and had put her out of his mind. Suddenly she had come back in, so strongly that it was as if they'd made telepathic communication. He'd presumed it was just down to wishful thinking. But now she was here, sitting with an expectant grin, waiting for a reply to her question, in her stunning silk scarf and elegant coat. Eight years ago he would have dismissed this as coincidence. His medical training told him there was no such thing as telepathy. And yet, it had taught him what all other doctors learned: that the most powerful drug in the world was the placebo. *The power of the human mind*.

She had on little makeup, and her eyes were warm, alert, but that desperation he had seen last night was there too, in her movements, her aura. And there was something else, which he didn't like.

Without saying anything, he reached across the table, took her left hand lightly by the wrist and began to study her palm. Her wrist was firm, slender, sensuous, but he tried to block that from his mind. Tried to block the smell of her perfume, to ignore the pleasure of holding that warm, soft hand, and just *concentrate*.

As Oliver Cabot gently traced Faith's lifeline with his forefinger, a tiny erotic tickle coiled through her, startling her, as if a switch had been thrown deep inside her.

He continued to trace further creases. 'Love line, health line.' He frowned.

The feeling she had had upstairs, that they were old friends, was deepening.

'That's your life line.' He pointed to a second line that intersected it. 'It's broken just over a third of the

46

way down, which means you're going to have a change around your early thirties.' He paused. 'I guess that's where you are now, right?'

'What kind of change?'

'Could be anything. But it's a pretty major change.' Then, 'Could be a change of relationship. Divorce.'

She looked away, awkward now. 'Anything else you can tell from my palm?'

'Sure. How much else do you want to know?'

'Just the good stuff – you can edit out the rest.'

Smiling, he studied her palm again, and suddenly his expression darkened a fraction. When he looked up at her there was concern in his eyes. 'How's your health?'

She did not tell him that she was feeling queasy. 'It's fine, thanks.' With a nervous shimmy in her voice, she added, 'Why?'

'No big deal.'

'What did you see?'

His hands were attractive and he kept them in good shape. 'I don't want you to worry.'

'I wasn't worried sixty seconds ago, now I'm scared stiff.'

'Don't be. Your health-line shows . . .' He fell silent.

'Shows?'

'A possible problem. Just be aware of it. It doesn't necessarily mean a thing.'

'What kind of a problem?'

He shrugged. 'Could be anything. Just make sure you have regular check-ups.'

I just have, she nearly said. *This morning*. He must be picking up from her that she had some bug. Maybe he could see it in her eyes or her skin or something. 'Is this what you do?' she asked, incredulous. 'Are you a palmist?'

He laughed. 'I can read palms but I'm not a fortune-teller. I'm interested in all the different ways the outside of the human body can tell us what's happening on the inside.'

'So what do you do exactly? Are you a doctor?'

'Did you hear of the Cabot Centre for Complementary Medicine?'

The name sounded familiar. She had a feeling there'd been some press coverage recently. Then she remembered. 'In *The Times* about a month ago? Was that you delivering a pretty blistering attack on the medical profession?'

He stirred his espresso thoughtfully. 'No disrespect to your husband, but the average conventional Joe Doctor just about any place in the western world is a puppet on a string. A clerk, tied hand and foot, with a decade of wasted training behind him. A victim.'

'Of what?'

'A system he helped build because he thought it would make the world a better place. Instead all it did was make a few organisations rich enough to afford absurd dinners like last night.'

'But you didn't have a problem accepting their hospitality?' she ventured.

'I was there to snoop, although, actually, I am a paid-up, card-carrying doctor of medicine – I just don't practise as one.'

'Tell me about the Cabot Centre for Complementary Medicine.'

'You ought to come and see it – we're doing some real interesting work.'

'What kind?'

'I guess we're multi-disciplinary. We have a homeopathy practice, osteopathy, acupuncture, hypnotherapy, chronotherapy—'

'Chronotherapy?'

'It's a newly evolving therapy that revolves around the human body clock. We're doing a whole lot of research into circadian rhythms. There's some evidence that humans don't live a twenty-four-hour cycle. Instead we live a twenty-five-and-a-half-hour cycle, which makes us kind of unique on this planet. I have a theory it causes a lot of our health problems. Let me show you the stuff we're doing sometime – or is the wife of an eminent plastic surgeon forbidden to talk to quacks like me?'

She smiled. Ross always rejected alternative medicine and most forms of complementary medicine too. They'd argued about it in the past. Ross had been furious when Faith had tried acupuncture, on the recommendation of a friend, for a skiing injury. No, more than furious. *Incandescent* with rage.

So far as Ross was concerned modern western clinical medicine was the only medicine anyone in their right mind should ever contemplate. He deeply resented that anyone could set themselves up as an alternative medic after only a few weeks of a correspondence course, when he had spent nearly twelve years as a student and apprentice, learning everything that could be learned about every molecule in the human body.

Ross hated alternative medics even more than he hated the charlatans of plastic surgery – the doctors who set up cosmetic-surgery clinics without any qualifications in plastic surgery, yet were allowed to practice.

'Maybe your husband would like to come too?' Oliver asked. 'A lot of our treatments and therapies are for post-operative care.'

She felt a tad disappointed. Was this just a sales pitch? And she could picture Ross's face. 'I don't think so – I mean, he's incredibly busy.'

She detected his relief and was glad. The invitation to include Ross had been a courtesy, nothing more. It *was* her he was interested in.

'How about tomorrow? I can check my diary –

maybe you could come over and have some lunch afterwards?'

'I'd love to, but I live in Sussex. I don't come up to town that often.'

'Nice part of the world. OK, so next time you're in town?'

Their eyes met again. This was so good but so dangerous. She was flattered by him, yet common sense was shrieking at her to finish her tea, thank him politely and walk out of his life. Getting entangled with another man was the last thing she needed at this point. She had to sort out her life with Ross, and somehow find an exit for herself and Alec. It was possible that Ross could accept her leaving him to be on her own, but she knew for certain that hell would freeze over before he could accept her leaving for someone else.

But it felt so incredibly good being here with this man. As if a chink had opened up in the darkness, through which she could see the possibilities of a life beyond the one she had.

Oliver Cabot proffered a business card. 'Call me next time you're coming up.'

She slipped it into her handbag, intending to drop it into a waste-bin before she got home, scared of Ross finding it. 'Thanks,' she said. 'I will.'

He gave her a yearning look that said, *I want you to, but I think you won't.*

11

The boy stood at the top of the fire escape and put the Shell can down as softly as he could, making only the faintest clink.

Then, hands clammy inside the rubber gloves, he unzipped the breast pocket of his windcheater, carefully removed the brand-new key and inserted it in the lock of the kitchen door. Holding his breath now he turned it slowly. But in the still night air, the final click sounded as loud as a pistol shot.

He froze. The sound seemed to take for ever to die away, and as he stood, staring anxiously through the glass panel into the dark kitchen his calm deserted him and he began to panic. But he talked himself through it, and after a couple of minutes he was fine again.

He glanced down at the small backyard, then up at the skeletal tower block under construction immediately beyond the rear wall. No sign of anyone. This was as he had hoped. So far so good.

He turned the handle then pushed open the door. It moved noiselessly on hinges he had oiled himself a few days earlier. The stale, greasy smell of a fry-up greeted him, along with the hum of the fridge. He picked up the petrol can and went in, closing the door silently behind him, then stood still in the darkness in the cramped little room, listening.

He could hear the muffled cries and shrieks of the woman beyond a closed door. 'Oh, yes, oh, my God, yes, do that!'

He was familiar with the layout of this flat – he'd been here on two previous occasions, always when she was out at work.

On those visits it had been easy to calculate how much time he had. All he'd needed to do was stop his bike near the Co-op, and from a concealed position behind a tumbledown wall he had a clear view across the road and through the window to the checkout till where she sat throughout her shift, except for her breaks. He simply waited until she arrived for work, and he knew then that he had eight clear hours. Although the most he had ever needed was two.

That had been on the second visit. The first had been

mere curiosity. Fact-finding. Rummaging through drawers, lifting out her garments, smelling the scent of this woman he barely knew. He had lifted out black lace lingerie and had been quite confused by the strange feelings he had experienced when he had pressed the cups of a brassière to his nose.

His mission on that visit had been to discover if she kept photographs of him, to see how much he might still mean to her. There were plenty of photographs of herself in frames in the little sitting room, the bedroom and the kitchen. One, the largest of all, a framed black-and-white, had been taken in soft focus. It was a close-up of her head and neck, black ringlets tossed back. She was smiling at someone, her face full of vanity.

There were more photographs of her in drawers, and in two albums. Photographs of her alone, and with men. On boats, at a horse race, at a motor race, in restaurants, in night-clubs.

There was just one photograph in the entire flat of himself.

He found it lying face down at the bottom of a drawer in a wooden chest, amid a jumble of letters and documents. It was small, two inches across, badly creased and curled at one edge, with much of the colour faded. It was of the two of them, sitting together, side by side on a pebble beach. He was about four, wearing swimming trunks, painfully thin, knees drawn up, hair tousled, squinting into the sun. She was sitting next to him, but she could have been a thousand miles away. Dressed in a bikini, wearing dark glasses, she was pouting into the camera. This was a photograph of her and her alone. The boy beside her . . . did she even know him?

Would she even remember him today?

You can't go forgetting people. Not the people who

love you. You can't just discard them, walk away from them. You really can't.

I promise you.

12

'Come on, darling, eat it up, it's your favourite.'

Alec, at the kitchen table in a Rugrats sweatshirt, brown hair, Ross's hair, flopped down over his brow, spaghetti bolognese going cold in front of him, chopsticks stuck in the bowl – he'd been refusing to eat with anything else since Thailand – was rotating a Lego helicopter in his hands.

'You can play with that later,' Faith said, on edge. 'Granny cooked the spaghetti specially for you.' She was feeling irritable, a combination of her curse due and two drawn-out meetings. This morning she'd spent three hours on the church-roof committee, looking for ways to fund much-needed repairs, and straight after that there had been a village meeting, preparing battle-lines for the public inquiry on the proposed golf course. The bouts of nausea were persisting, despite some Zantac tablets Ross had given her, which he thought might clear it up; it was almost a week since her consultation with Jules Ritterman yet she'd heard nothing.

Ignoring her, Alec plucked a piece of yellow brick from the fuselage, puckered his lips, then pushed it into another slot.

Faith stood up so sharply her chair fell over. Rasputin, asleep on a bean-bag in front of the Aga, jumped up in surprise. She tore the helicopter out of Alec's hand. 'Eat your supper,' she snapped.

'Don't want it.'

She put the helicopter down on the black marble

work surface, seized Alec's chopsticks and smashed the spaghetti into small pieces. Ross and her mother spoiled him.

Her mother sat in silence, at the other end of the table from Alec, fag dangling from her lips, ash dangling from the fag, eyes screwed against the thin thread of smoke, brow furrowed in feigned concentration on the pages of *Hello!*, which lay open on the huge old pine table in front of her. Occasionally she cast a glance at *Neighbours* on the television, which was blaring too loudly for Faith's comfort.

Faith didn't turn the sound down. After all, her mother had looked after Alec all day – it was half-term already. But that was the problem. It didn't matter how old you were, she thought, you'd always be your mother's child, which was one of the reasons she could never bring herself to tell her mother not to smoke at the table while Alec was eating. And, in spite of their differences, she respected her mother. Margaret. A sensible, solid name, and that's how she looked now: sensibly dressed for the country, for this damp night, in her chunky cable-stitched pullover, corduroy trousers, cosy shoes.

A few months south of sixty, with short grey hair, she had a handsome face lined with sadness and with too many years of heavy smoking. She'd been through her share of suffering. Twenty years of nursing Faith's bedridden father, of watching him steadily deteriorate.

Ross had been wonderful during those last terrible years, with her father little more than a vegetable. He'd paid for twenty-four-hour nursing care, helped her mother out financially and secured for her father the finest treatment in the country, even though there was little that could be done for him. That was why in her mother's eyes Ross could do no wrong.

Faith scooped up some spaghetti, mixed it with the

meat and held it in front of Alec's mouth. He closed his lips tightly.

'Eat!' she hissed.

Cigarette bobbing from her lips, 'We had a lovely day, darling,' her mother said. 'We went to—'

'Alec! Eat this!'

'Not hungry.'

'The Bentley Wildfowl Trust,' her mother said. 'Tell Mummy what we saw, Alec.' She took the cigarette from her mouth and coughed.

Faith rounded on her. 'Have you been giving him sweets all day?'

Looking at Alec, her mother said, 'We had a cheeseburger for lunch. At McDonald's.'

'What time was that?' Faith demanded.

She caught a conspiratorial exchange of glances between her mother and Alec. God, her mother who was normally so sensible. When she was with her six-year-old grandson, her brain turned to mush.

'Mummy, what time did you have lunch?' Faith asked again.

'It was – er—'

'I've told you, I want *routine*. Routine is important for a child. Lunch at one, supper at six, that's Alec's routine. That's the damned routine I used to have as a child.'

'Ross said that—'

'To hell with Ross. He's not here all day. I'm Alec's mother, and what I say goes, all right?'

Again she saw an exchange of glances between the two of them. Like they were sharing some guilty secret. Alec smirked.

Faith stormed out of the kitchen.

She walked along the corridor and into the hall, her brain swirling, then through into the snug, with its big old sofa, armchairs, shelves of well-thumbed paper-backs and the massive sixty-inch television, which was on, its sound muted. A newscaster was mouthing words, then the cameras cut away to a woman reporter holding a mike to a man.

Faith sat on the sofa, seething with anger. Irrational anger, she knew. Routine was important to Alec, but it really didn't matter if there was the odd exception, and if her mother got pleasure out of spoiling him so what? God knows, her life was short enough of pleasures, and being able to summon her down here to babysit at a moment's notice, from her dull little flat in Croydon, was a real boon.

There was something else, too, that was causing her bad mood. Something she had been brooding about, for days – and nights, waking often in the small hours of the morning and thinking ... thinking ... thinking. Trying to get this thing out of her mind and not being able to.

Her memory of their encounter at the General Trading Company, remained fresh and stubbornly persistent. Several times she'd been tempted to lift the phone and take him up on his offer to show her around the centre, but each time wisdom – or maybe nerves – got the better of her.

Rasputin padded into the room and came across to her. She put her arms around his neck and hugged him tightly. 'Good boy,' she said. 'You never have any problem about eating, do you?'

Levering herself up from the sofa, she climbed the stairs and went into her bedroom. The dog followed her and stayed in the doorway, watching her. She sat on the bed, opened her handbag, rummaged her way through the contents, down to the bottom, and pulled out the business card, which she had concealed beneath a bunch of petrol receipts. 'Dr Oliver Cabot. The Cabot Centre for Complementary Medicine,' she read, guiltily.

She read it thoroughly, the phone number, the fax number, the e-mail and website addresses.

You're the real reason, Dr Oliver Cabot, aren't you? You're the real reason I'm so damned uptight.

13

'Brandenburg.'

'Any in particular?' the scrub nurse asked.

'Number two, in F, Jane,' Ross said, without looking up from his suturing. 'I think this is a number two in F morning, don't you?' He beamed brightly, a real *this-is-what-the-Big-Cheese-wants-and-this-is-what-the-Big-Cheese-is-having* beam.

Under the bright octopus lamp, the young woman lay on the table, her eyes open, glazed, motionless as a cadaver. Only the digital displays on the anaesthetics monitor and the constant beep, beep, beep told the six in the operating theatre that she was still alive.

Imran Patel, the registrar, watched closely, studying Ross's technique. The surgeon was coming to the end of the thread. The scrub nurse, wordless, passed a fresh one up to him. This was how Ross liked his theatre to run. The old-style way, where the scrub nurse was there to serve him, where they were *all* there to serve him, the runner nurse, the anaesthetist, the operating-department assistant, or ODA. Operating theatres needed to run like clockwork. Hierarchy. Discipline. A tight ship.

And pretty nurses.

He liked pretty nurses around him, and considered flirting a perk. He wasn't interested in anything beyond that, though.

Strains of the Brandenburg Concerto No 2 filled the

room. Ross pushed the needle through the thin flap of flesh, cropped only minutes earlier from the young woman's thigh, and then through the thick roll of scar tissue from the terrible burns that covered her upper torso. Sally Porter, twenty-seven, a pretty girl before the fire had ravaged her looks. Ross did not know much about the fire, other than that it had happened on a boat. When he was doing reconstructive surgery, he avoided finding out the cause of any tragedy because it might affect his judgement: if he found out a patient had done something really stupid, such as throwing petrol on a barbecue, or deliberately setting fire to themselves, it might anger him and cause him to do a less good job.

Sally Porter would always be an innocent victim. A long-suffering girl, on whom he had operated ten times in the past two years, and on whom he would probably have to operate at least another ten times, trying, one small step at a time, to give her back her life. He admired her guts, her stoicism in coping with the setbacks.

And she'd had her share of setbacks. On one previous operation, the new skin had become infected and died and she'd had to endure the whole operation again. Today's operation was a repeat of one he had performed six months earlier. There had been a micro-circulation problem: the skin had constricted too much, pulling her head permanently downwards. It was the endless battle every plastic surgeon fought between beauty and blood supply.

He finished the last of the sutures, stood back and nodded at the photographer, who had returned to the theatre. She stepped forward and took three pictures of his work. Then the registrar began to lay the strips of gauze in place, and the scrub nurse handed Ross the stapler.

*

Twenty minutes later Sally Porter was hoisted up while a Fatslide board was slipped under her. Then she was lifted across on to a trolley, and wheeled out to the recovery room. The runner nurse turned off the CD, and the atmosphere in the operating theatre became slack. Then she helped Ross remove his gloves, and binned them.

Ross flipped his mask down, slackened the tapes of his gown, and began writing his notes, the registrar looking over his shoulder. He was interrupted by a young nurse holding a cordless phone. 'Mr Ransome, there's a call for you.'

'Who is it?' he asked, irritated. They were on a tight schedule today, and Sally Porter's operation had taken longer than he'd anticipated. It was two thirty, he was hungry and he wasn't going to have time for lunch.

'Um . . .' The nurse covered the receiver with her hand. Her name was Francine West, she was pretty and she was looking nervous.

'I don't bite,' he said. 'Just find out who it is.'

She went out of the room and returned some moments later. 'It's Dr Ritterman. The third time he's called.'

He slipped out of his gown, handed it to a nurse, then took the phone and went into the corridor. The line was bad, he couldn't tell whether it was this handset or whether the GP was on a mobile.

'Ross,' Ritterman said, in his calm, dry voice, 'sorry to chase you like this.'

'No problem. What's up?'

There was a long pause and Ross, listening to static crackle, wondered if they'd been disconnected. Then the GP spoke again. 'You recall you asked me to see Faith last week?'

'Yuh.' Ross entered the changing room and untied the front of his pyjama trousers with one hand. 'This

59

nausea she's been having, Jules, it seems to have been going on a long time.'

'I had some tests done on her fluids,' Ritterman said, sounding hesitant, 'and I needed to have further analysis on what came back. I – Is this a good time to talk, Ross?'

Urinating, Ross said, 'Actually, no, I have to get back into the theatre.' But GP's tone had worried him. 'What is it, Jules? What do the tests show?'

'Look, Ross, I think we ought to have a chat about this. What time will you be free? I could come over and see you.'

'Can't we do this over the phone?'

'I'd prefer not to, Ross. What time will you be finished today?'

Alarmed, Ross said, 'About six, but I have to dash to the flat and change. I have a livery dinner in the City.'

'What time do you have to be there?'

'Seven thirty.'

'I could pop in about six thirty for a few minutes – I'd have to be away before seven, we're going to the ballet.'

'What's wrong with her, Jules?'

'I think it's best if we discuss this face to face, Ross. It's not good, I'm afraid.'

14

The second visit had been to get the key.

Previously the boy had squeezed in through a tiny lavatory window that seemed to be left permanently open and which was out of sight of any neighbours. But there was a six-foot drop to the floor – far too much risk of being heard if she was in. So he had removed the key that hung on a hook beside the kitchen door, taken it to an ironmonger and had a copy cut, which he'd paid for out of his meagre savings. As an extra precaution he had also bought a can of oil and lubricated every hinge in the house.

Now, enough light spilled through from the hall for him to see the squalid state of the kitchen – just like it had been before: dirty plates piled in the sink, an open tin of spaghetti rings sitting on the draining-board, two plates crusted with congealed food on the Formica-topped table, both with cigarette butts crushed out in them. On the floor beside the pedal bin lay an egg shell and a curled length of orange peel.

It was disgusting. Embarrassing.

He took this personally.

There was a sharp click and the fridge stopped humming. In the silence her voice seemed even louder. 'Oh, yes, don't stop!'

And as he listened to her cries, he thought, You didn't like the mess I made and yet you live like this?

15

The house was silent. Alec had been taken to see the wild animals at Longleat by a schoolfriend's family. Faith missed him. She worried about him constantly when he was out of her sight, fretted about him travelling in a stranger's car, hoping he had his seat-belt on properly, or getting out of the car in the safari park. She could not imagine life without Alec. She wondered where he was now as she sat in the leather swivel chair in Ross's study, in front of his computer, logged on, entered her password, and checked her e-mail.

Not much this morning – the date of the next committee meeting about the blocked footpath, a brief message from an old friend who had moved to Los Angeles, some junk mail and the daily collection of news from the abused women's network, to which she had subscribed a while back when she had been feeling particularly down.

She went on to the web, read the address on Dr Oliver Cabot's business card, then carefully typed it in.

Outside, in the teeming rain, Morris the gardener, in a cagoule with the hood raised, pushed a laden wheelbarrow past the window. Rasputin growled, padded over to the window and barked.

'Quiet, boy! It's only Morris,' she said. The gardener was nervous of dogs, and Rasputin made sure he stayed that way. 'We'll go walkies later, when it eases up.'

Suddenly, on the screen appeared the words:

> Cur'd yesterday of my disease,
> I died last night of my physician.
> Matthew Prior, 1664–1721,
> 'The Remedy Worse Than The Disease'

Faith smiled. Moments later the words faded and large letters proclaimed:

WELCOME TO THE CABOT CENTRE FOR COMPLEMENTARY MEDICINE. YOU ARE VISITOR NUMBER 111926.

Then a picture of the exterior of the Centre appeared – it looked like a tall, narrow church – with a photograph of Oliver Cabot: he was dressed all in black, eyes twinkling behind those tiny oval glasses.

She felt a tiny lump of excitement at the sight of him. Gripping the mouse she moved the cursor and clicked in the top right corner of the frame. Instantly the frame enlarged, and a few seconds later his face filled the screen.

The gardener trudged back across the window and,

absurdly, she knew, she looked away from the screen to the wall, as if studying the framed picture of Ross shaking hands with Princess Anne at a charity function.

She looked back at Oliver Cabot's image once more, and felt a deep yearning to see him again. *Crazy*, she thought. I'm like an infatuated teenager. Crazy, and yet . . .

She scrolled down and his image disappeared. A list of the services offered at the centre came up: acupuncture and Chinese medicine, aromatherapy, chronotherapy, craniosacral therapy, colonic irrigation, colourpuncture, counselling and psychotherapy, homeopathy, hypnotherapy, manual lymphatic drainage, manumassage, osteopathy, reflexology, reiki, shiatsu.

Below that it said:

All our therapists at the Cabot Centre meet the highest international standards, and all, where policies permit, are practitioners accredited by major health-insurance companies. Come and visit our oasis of tranquillity in the heart of London.

There followed a phone number, fax number, e-mail address and a link to other related sites. She read the phone number, then found herself checking it on Oliver Cabot's business card. Hesitating, she eyed Ross's dark grey Bang and Olufsen phone. A knot tightened in her throat.

He's just going to show me around the clinic, that's all, no big deal or anything.

And maybe Dr Oliver Cabot could give her something to knock this bug on the head.

Picking up the receiver, she was about to dial when she saw a car, headlights on, nosing through the front gates. A white Mercedes estate came down the drive, its occupant obscured behind the rain-lashed windscreen.

She watched it with a frown, displeased at the interruption.

Then, as the door opened, she instantly recognised the driver. Wrapped in a riding coat, and beneath a practical but ludicrous looking rain-hat, it was the world's most boring woman.

Felice D'Eath.

Shit.

Faith had been co-opted with Felice D'Eath on to a sub-committee of the NSPCC, organising this year's Hallowe'en Ball. Although it was nearly six months away, the woman had been bombarding her since before Christmas with posted memoranda, then faxed ones, and finally, horror of horrors, she had discovered the Internet and now her e-mails poured in. Every damned gift donated for the tombola was scrupulously detailed to Faith, and so far the tally was three hundred and twenty prizes.

She logged off the site and hurried to the door as a volley of raps from the knocker echoed around the hall.

In her reedy voice, Felice D'Eath said, 'Ohhhhh, Faith, I'm sooo pleased to have caught you in. I've got the car compleeetely filled up with prizes.'

Faith stared past her at the rain, which was now coming down even harder. Felice peeled off her hat, shook free her dreary brown hair, then began unbuttoning her coat. 'What a horrible afternoon,' she said, 'but it's clearing from the west – it'll stop in about half an hour. We can unload the car then. You look pale, Faith – are you all right?'

'I'm fine.'

'You really don't look it. Anyway, Let's sit down and discuss the tombola layout – I've had some thoughts about this – and we can go over the list. Last year they raised seven hundred pounds on the tombola. I think we should try to double that at least, don't you?'

'Yes,' Faith said, resignedly, closing the door behind her. 'At least.'

As they went into the kitchen, Felice said, 'An Aga. Lovely to look at, but so terribly wasteful. They keep pumping out heat when you really don't need it. There was one in our house when we bought it, but we had it taken out.'

'Really?' Faith said. 'We had one put in. Tea or coffee?'

Plonking herself in a chair, Felice unwrapped a sodden silk scarf from around her neck and laid it on the table. 'Do you have any herbal tea? Tannin is so bad for the stomach lining and I find coffee quite devastating – it kills all the minerals in one's system.'

Faith put the kettle on the Aga hotplate. 'I didn't know. I have camomile.'

'Anything else?'

'Only camomile.'

'Well, I suppose so, then, but camomile always sends me to sleep.'

Faith dropped two bags into her cup.

16

Ross, in stockinged feet, braces of his dinner-suit trousers hanging loose, ushered Jules Ritterman into the living room of his small flat close to Regent's Park, and steered him to one of the two-seater chesterfields opposite each other in front of the fireplace, separated by a low oak chest that served as a coffee table. Gas flames leaped up among the imitation logs. Chopin played on the CD.

He felt strained: Ritterman's words had been preying on him all afternoon, whittling away at his concentration. His mind had begun to wander when he was cutting through a cheek muscle, and he had nearly severed a nerve, which would have left the patient with one side of her face partially paralysed.

He wanted desperately to hear what the doctor had to tell him, but he said, 'Can I get you a drink, Jules?'

'Well, just a very small whisky, thank you, if you have time. A livery dinner, you said?'

Hurrying out to the kitchen, Ross called, 'Barber-Surgeons Hall – I'll have to leave just after seven. You're going to the ballet?'

'*Les Sylphides.*'

It was one of the few ballets Ross knew. Faith had a CD of it at home. He poured some Macallan into a crystal tumbler and shouted, 'Any water or ice?'

'A splash of water.'

Oh, God, please be all right, Faith.

As Ross padded back into the room, the doctor's eyes were roving approvingly over the fine pieces of antique furniture and the oil paintings on the walls, mostly eighteenth- and nineteenth-century naval scenes. 'It really is a most charming place this, Ross. Are you using it a lot?'

'Three or four nights a week. It's a little small, but it suits me fine. Faith hardly ever comes to town these days. You and Hilde will have to come to dinner again when I can drag her away from Alec and up here for a night.'

'That would be very nice.' Ritterman smiled. 'How's your golf these days?'

'Crap. I've got into shooting, joined a couple of syndicates.' He sat opposite the GP, leaving his glass on its coaster on the oak chest, glanced at his watch anxiously, and said, 'So?'

The doctor leaned forward, pressed his hands firmly on his thighs, as if to iron out creases in his trousers. 'Um,' he said. 'I . . .' He raised his glass and stared hard at it. 'Look, there are a few more tests I could do, just to make certain, but I'm sure in my own mind, Ross. And I've had a couple of informed opinions as well. How familiar are you with hydrophobia?'

Ritterman's tone was making Ross even more frightened. 'Hydrophobia – as in *rabies*?'

Ritterman nodded.

'Faith has *rabies*?'

Ritterman stopped him with a raised hand. 'No, but I'm afraid she has something that attacks the human neurochemistry in much the same way.'

'As severely?'

'I'm afraid so.'

'Wh-what kind of a disease? Viral? Inherited? Communicated? What's the prognosis, Jules?'

Ritterman massaged the base of his neck. 'It's viral, probably waterborne. All the known cases have contracted this disease after visiting areas in the Far East bordering the Indian Ocean and South China Sea – which, of course, includes Thailand. It's known as Lendt's disease.'

'*Lendt's* disease?'

'Named after Hans Lendt, the American immunologist who identified it. I've had a look at several case histories in the past week, and they all share similar characteristics. The first symptom is prolonged nausea – the patient usually feels this for two to three months. Increasing disorientation with delusions of persecution follow. Night terrors. Terminal features include fluctuating levels of consciousness and hallucinations. Then a gradual loss of motor-control functions.' Ritterman fell silent.

Ross tried to picture all these things happening to Faith. He lifted his glass, turned it round and set it down again without drinking. His mouth was dry. 'What's the treatment?' He asked the question, although he could already read the answer in Ritterman's face.

'There isn't one, Ross,' he said, baldly.

'Nothing?' It came from Ross's throat like a yelp of pain.

'There are clinical trials in progress but no specific treatment as yet. The disease was only identified eight years ago with a handful of cases around the world, mostly visitors to that area from Europe, the United States and Australia. But it's growing rapidly. About three thousand people have been diagnosed with it and the numbers could double in the next twelve months.'

Ross fiddled with one of the studs in his dress-shirt. 'What's causing it?'

'No one knows yet. Could be pollution causing some new viral strain to breed. Could be susceptibility resulting from our own weakening resistance – antibiotics are slowly destroying our immunity to some diseases.'

Ross nodded; he knew about this theory.

Ritterman took a sip of his drink then watched Ross levelly. 'Ross, I'm afraid the survival rate is not good.'

'*Survival?*' Ross stood up, unable to sit still any more. 'This Lendt's disease is terminal?'

'In a large number of cases.'

Ross walked over to the window and stared down at the rush-hour traffic streaming along Wellington Road. Brake-lights, indicator-lights, headlights daubed in erratic streaks across the wet tarmac. Londoners were heading home to normality. He felt as if his whole world was collapsing in on him. Faith, terminally ill. Faith, whom he loved more than he had ever thought it possible to love someone, and with whom he had never questioned that he would spend the rest of his life.

Terminally ill.

He turned to look at Ritterman, feeling sudden blind panic. 'Tell me I'm not hearing this, Jules.'

The doctor said, quietly, 'I'm sorry, Ross.'

'And you're absolutely certain of your diagnosis?'

'All the evidence points to it – and you have just come back from Thailand. I've sent the tests to three different labs as a precaution, and all their findings tally. But I'd be happy for you to get your own second opinion.'

Ross felt drained. A terrible dark dread swirled inside him. *Night terrors . . . Hallucinations . . . Gradual loss of motor control functions . . . Terminal.*

It couldn't be possible that these things were going to happen to his darling Faith.

No, God, you bastard, don't do this to her – to us. Not to her, she doesn't deserve any of this.

He felt so helpless. 'I want to understand this disease, Jules. I want to know everything that you know about it. I want you to let me have all your research sources. I want every bit of information that exists in the world on this bitch. Faith is a great girl, she's strong, a fighter.'

Ritterman nodded, without conviction.

'What did you tell her when you saw her?'

'I told her the truth,' Ritterman said. 'That I thought it was probably some bacterial infection she'd picked up – just a tummy bug.'

'So she knows nothing about the Lendt's disease diagnosis?'

'Not yet.'

Ross was silent for some moments, thinking. Then he said, 'Who's doing the trials?'

'Moliou-Orelan.'

Moliou-Orelan was a US pharmaceutical giant with an impressive record for fast-tracking drugs on to the market. 'They're a good outfit, Jules. How can we get Faith on to a trials programme?'

'I've been in touch with them already,' the GP said.

'They're being very secretive but I understand they've had positive results with their phase-two trials.'

Ross's eyes widened. 'And?'

'I don't know specifics, Ross.'

'You haven't heard anything?'

'No. But—'

'It's going to be months before they start phase three,' Ross interrupted.

'No, they're already down the road.'

'Can you get her on them?'

'I have a good contact who's working on someone in Research and Development there—'

Interrupting again, Ross said, 'I don't want her taking a placebo, I want her taking the real thing.'

Ritterman smiled wistfully. 'I think I can get her on to the trial, but I cannot guarantee what she'll be taking, you know that. No one can.'

All phase-three drug trials involved two groups of people, one who took the drug itself, the other who took a placebo. The trials were either single or double blind. In a single blind the doctor knew who was taking the drug and who the placebo. But in a double blind trial – and all phase-three trials were double blind – neither the doctors nor their patients knew which were which. Only a handful of employees at the pharmaceutical company running the trials held the keys to the codes.

'Jules, I want you to get the real thing. Do whatever you have to. There must be a way of getting the genuine thing from the phase-three trials. Surely you can swing it to get her on a named patient basis?'

'I'll do my best.'

Ross walked away from the window slowly. 'Look, do me a favour – I'd rather you didn't say anything to her, Jules, OK? About how serious this is. Let me break it to her in my own time.'

'Of course. What would you like me to say to her?'

Shakily, Ross took a Havana from the humidor on a side-table, and held it in his hand. Without answering the doctor's question, he said, 'Jules, she's not going to die. We *are* going to find a way. Right?'

There was helplessness in the GP's expression.

Ross perched on an arm of the chesterfield opposite Ritterman, tears trickling down his face. 'You've got to help me, Jules. I couldn't live without Faith. I don't even like being apart from her.'

'Of course I'll do everything I can.'

Ross pulled out a handkerchief and dabbed at his eyes. Then he said, 'You have to understand, Faith is a child, Jules. Emotionally, she has never grown up. She's very vulnerable, needs protection – that's what I give her.'

'I think she's mature and sensible, Ross. You're mistaken.'

Sniffing, Ross said, 'Maybe that's her act when she comes to you.'

Ritterman smiled. 'I don't think so, Ross.'

Ross began picking at the band on the cigar with his thumbnail. It was ten to seven, but he no longer cared about tonight's dinner. 'I know what's best for her, Jules. I don't think it would be good for her to know how serious this disease is, OK? Not now or at any time.'

'You want me to lie to her?'

'I didn't say lie, I just don't want you to tell her the truth. Jesus! If we can't do anything for her, at least we can give her the illusion of hope.'

'You're putting me in a difficult position.'

'Jules, you don't tell everyone who has terminal cancer that they're going to die, do you?'

'If they ask me outright, I tell them the truth. I may

71

try to dress it up as positively as I can, but I do tell them the truth.'

Ross stared at him. 'We have a good relationship, don't we? We trust each other implicitly. I need you to trust my judgement on Faith.'

Ritterman stared back at him. 'Faith is a very sick woman. What do you expect to achieve by keeping her in the dark?'

'What would you achieve by telling her the truth? You're going to terrify her and yet you can't offer her any realistic hope.'

'I believe that if patients know the truth, it gives them time to prepare . . .'

'For death?'

'Yes.'

'Don't you think you're being defeatist?'

'I'm being realistic.'

'What's the first rule of medicine?'

Ritterman shrugged. 'Do no harm.'

'Right. If you tell someone, particularly someone of Faith's mental fragility, that they are going to die, they will die. They put themselves into a state of panic – it becomes a self-fulfilling prophecy. She will have a far better chance of surviving if she doesn't know.'

Ritterman looked at his friend, thinking, Maybe it's you, Ross, who can't cope with the reality, not Faith. 'I don't agree with you,' he said.

This isn't real, we are not having this conversation, we can't be. Ross closed his eyes and shook his head for several seconds, as if somehow, when he opened them again, Ritterman would have vanished and none of this conversation would have taken place.

But Ritterman was still there, and his calm was beginning to anger Ross. How the hell could he stay so damned calm? Because Faith was just one of hundreds –

maybe thousands – of patients that Ritterman had. *Faith Ransome.* Just a name on a list.

Registering Ritterman's faint look of disapproval, Ross lit the cigar and sent clouds of rich, heavy smoke swirling to the ceiling. 'I'm her husband. Surely to God I'm qualified enough to be able to tell her?'

'Of course you are, but I can't lie to her if she asks me outright.'

'All you have to do is tell her she's picked up a virus and that you're giving her a course of treatment for it. End of story.'

'Well,' Ritterman said, reluctantly, 'I'll go along with it – for the moment – but I don't like it.'

Anger roiling inside him now, Ross stood, glowering, over the doctor. 'You don't like it? Me neither, Jules. And you know what I really fucking don't like? I don't like the idea that my wife has Lendt's disease. So it seems we're both stuck with things we don't like.'

17

On the television a sea of people, young women mostly, erupted into screams. It seemed to Ross, standing in front of it, that every girl in the whole world was there. And now, stepping out of the darkness of the Boeing, four adolescents, all in dark glasses, with limp hair and big grins, waved into a lightning storm of popping flash-bulbs.

The newscaster said, 'Crowds of fans almost brought London's Heathrow airport to a standstill this morning when the Beatles arrived home from their latest American tour.'

Sweeping across the room now, his father, Joe Ransome, reached down, turned a dial, and the Beatles vanished. At school everyone was talking about the

Beatles. One of Ross's friends, Thomas Norton, had brought in a copy of a magazine called *New Musical Express*, which was full of pictures of them and of the Rolling Stones. Several of his friends had posters of groups and singers up on their bedroom walls. Ross had nothing in his little bedroom in the small terraced house in Streatham in south London. He was not allowed anything. There were just two pictures in the entire house, a faded, framed print of Anne Hathaway's cottage half-way up the stairs, and another framed print, of *The Haywain*, above the electric log fire in this room.

With the screen dark now, his father, dressed in his brown suit, shirt and tie, and brown leather shoes – polished by Ross every morning – sat down in his armchair with his newspaper, the *Sporting Times*, his pen and his pewter tankard of beer, coughed, then opened a fresh pack of ten Kensitas, filter-tipped. His muscular frame seemed to dwarf the room, which was crammed to capacity with a leatherette three-piece suite, an upright piano and a side-table, both covered in darts trophies.

Ross stood beside the chair, watching the ritual, waiting to do his duty. First the Cellophane from the cigarette packet was carefully flattened, then folded, flattened once more, then folded again and again, until it was too small to fold any more and his father placed it carefully on the little table, which, when he had got home from school this afternoon, Ross had polished until it shone like a mirror, as every surface in this house shone.

Even his father's shock of thick black hair shone, Brylcreemed back against his scalp. He could smell the hair cream, and the faint, sweet reek of the Old Spice he splashed on his face each morning.

Now came the gold foil. Again, with the concentration of a man entrusted with the most important task the human race had yet devised, Joe Ransome carefully flattened it and began the folds. Then he put it carefully beside the Cellophane and began the third part of the ritual, the removal and inspection of the gift certificates.

Now as his father took out and lit, with a Swan Vesta match, the first of the ten cigarettes he would smoke this evening – always exactly ten, never fewer never more – Ross carried the foil and the Cellophane out of the room and put them in the kitchen waste-bin. Then he returned for the certificates and, without disturbing his father who was now studying racing form, took them through to the kitchen and placed them in the white jar with the cork lid. On the notepad beside them he added, with the pencil kept there for the purpose, the new total: 437.

A catalogue of gifts for which the certificates could be exchanged was kept on a pine shelf in the kitchen, just above the bread-bin where the recipe books his mother had used were kept. In the catalogue were exciting things like fishing-rods and bicycles, and boring stuff like electric Teasmaids and lawnmowers. Ross nurtured the secret hope that his father was saving up to buy him the new drop-handlebar Raleigh Blue Streak bicycle he so desperately wanted.

But somehow he did not think it was likely.

'*Boyyyyyyy!*'

Ross ran back into the living room, frightened by the tone of his father's voice.

He was pointing at the floor, his face white with anger. To his dismay, Ross saw the object, a Dinky car, lying on its side at the foot of the settee.

'Why is that there?'

Ross stared back in silence.

'*Why is it there, boy?*'

Stammering with fear, Ross said, 'I – I – don't know, Daddy.'

Holding his cigarette tightly between his forefinger and thumb, Joe Ransome brought it to his lips, inhaled deeply then, holding it like a dart, jigged it furiously at his son. 'You know that's why your mother left, don't you, boy? She couldn't stand the mess you made everywhere. She couldn't stand your untidy room, your toys always lying around everywhere. You drove your mother away, Ross. You understand that, boy?'

Ross picked up the Riley saloon, then stood, his head drooping in shame, his eyes moist, shaking with fear.

'Fetch me the cane, boy.'

'Daddy, I—'

'The cane.'

Ross reached behind the piano, pulled out the thin bamboo cane and carried it over to his father.

'Kneel, boy!'

Ross stuffed the car into the pocket of his shorts, knelt in front of him and stretched out his hands, palms up.

His father raised the cane, then brought it down, with all his considerable strength, six times on to each hand.

'Now get up to your room and do your homework, boy.'

Tears sliding down his face, hands numb and stinging, Ross replaced the cane behind the piano and left the room.

As he climbed the stairs, the pain hit him and his whole body twisted in agony. He raised his hands, lowered them, opened the fingers, clenched them against the pain, banged the knuckles together, trying to do anything, *anything* to stop this agony. They were burning as if they had been immersed in boiling water or concentrated acid. And above his whimpering, he heard his father bellowing in fury.

'You drove her away, boy. Remember that. You remember that always.'

18

The building *was* an old church, Faith realised, as she stepped out of the cab. In a residential street, shoe-horned into a gap between two Victorian terraces, it sat hunched but proud, an imposing edifice of raw red brick, gargoyles and smoked glass.

Winchmore Hill was an area of London she barely knew. On the northern edge of London, it was a smart, leafy pocket, with a well-heeled air. She recalled that a couple of years back she'd been to a dinner party somewhere in this area, hosted by a particularly vulgar music promoter who kept telling her how Ross had improved his sex life. Then the man had insisted his wife bared her breasts half-way through the meal to demonstrate to the assembled company what a great surgeon Ross was. 'He's given her tits,' the man had said. 'She din' have no tits before, flat, like a little boy she was.'

Now Faith stepped up to the massive oak door and read the brass plaque beside it: THE CABOT CENTRE FOR COMPLEMENTARY MEDICINE.

Nervous, she dug her hands deep into her pockets, hugging her long raincoat tightly around her against the cold, gusting wind. Her hair whipped her face.

Come this far, no turning back now, girl.

But she knew she *could* turn round, go back into the street, hail a taxi and head home.

And then?

She tested the door, which opened a few inches. Boldly now she pushed it wide open and stepped in, and was immediately surprised. In contrast to the stern exterior, the interior was airy, modern and visually stunning. It could have been an art gallery: split levels of pine floors, soft white walls hung with abstract paintings that reminded her of views through microscopes, plants and pieces of sculpture strategically arranged to break up empty spaces, massive white candles burning in wall sconces and on free-standing holders. New Age relaxation music played from speakers, and Faith could smell the pleasant but intense aroma of a scented oil.

There was a reception desk directly in front of her, manned by an attractive young woman with gelled ginger hair. She was wearing a navy blue polo shirt embroidered with the words 'The Cabot Centre', and glowed with such an aura of health and vitality that Faith instantly felt a wreck. Displaying teeth to die for, she gave Faith a welcoming smile.

'I've come to see Dr Cabot,' Faith said, noting a box of advertising leaflets for the centre on the desktop.

'Do you have an appointment?'

'Yes.'

The receptionist took her name, then pointed her to an encampment of high-tech-looking seats beyond a screen of potted plants, where several people were seated.

'Is there a lavatory?'

'Yes, just down to the right.'

Faith could see it. She walked down a corridor and went into a spacious room, tiled in white, with massive white candles burning. She went into a cubicle, sat down, and closed her eyes. The nausea, which had been coming and going all week, had returned with a vengeance. Dr Ritterman hadn't come back to her or, rather, to Ross with the results of the tests. Why not? Surely a week was long enough? She wondered whether to say anything to Oliver Cabot about how she was feeling. But Ross would be furious if he discovered that she was taking some kind of alternative medicine.

And Ross *would* find out: he was constantly snooping, looking through the medicine cabinet, criticising any vitamins or health supplements she bought. He even went through her handbags.

She knelt at the lavatory and threw up. Her head was swimming, and she stayed where she was, clutching the rim, close to passing out.

It was several minutes before she felt better. She flushed the lavatory, then rinsed her mouth at a basin. She checked her face carefully in the mirror, put on some lipstick and adjusted her hair. At least all the time I'm feeling grotty, Ross isn't saying anything about more surgery, she thought.

She turned her head to the right and looked closely into the mirror. The scar was almost invisible, but not quite. And there was a matching one on the opposite side of her face, just at the point where her jawbone met her ear-lobe, an inch and a half long either side. The legacy from the operation Ross had performed to heighten her cheekbones.

In the daytime, under makeup, no one could see them. It was only at night that they were more clearly visible. Ross insisted he didn't notice them and that was all that mattered. But they bothered her. They were the tell-tales that this was not her natural face.

Sometimes she wondered if Ross had deliberately made the scars more prominent than they need be, as insurance that she would be prepared to have more surgery. He told her that the next time he operated on her he would be able to make them less visible. There were scars under her breasts also, from when he had put in the implants, and he had said he could deal with those when she was older and needed a breast-lift.

79

Besides, as he had told her, 'No one other than me is ever going to see them – so what's your problem?'

Back in the waiting area, Faith perched on the edge of a sofa that was more comfortable than it looked. In front of her was a small indoor Zen garden with a fountain trickling water down an assembly of round, flat stones. She glanced at the other people here: an emaciated man in his late thirties, his clothes hanging loose, eyes sunken, an Aids sufferer, perhaps; a smart-looking man working feverishly on a Psion computer; a rotund earth-mother garbed in what looked like an Inca blanket, sitting with her eyes closed, holding a baby with an inch of green snot hanging from its nose; a young, neatly dressed, Asian woman in a pin-striped two-piece reading *Health and Fitness* magazine.

Faith glanced at the magazines strewn on a side-table. There were several alternative- and complementary-medicine newsletters, and a whole stack of Cabot Centre leaflets. Then she noticed a copy of the Hypnotherapy Research Society magazine, flagging an article by Dr Oliver Cabot on the front cover. She picked it up and turned to the article. It was titled 'Remission of Cancer through Circadian Reprogramming'. She began to read but had difficulty concentrating. A phone warbled faintly in the background.

She had taken a lot of care deciding what to wear today. Informal but not sloppy. Casual smart, but not too smart. Eventually she'd settled on a thin grey cashmere polo-neck, black sueded cotton jeans, black boots and her long camel coat. She looked good today, she thought. Good hair day. Good face day. Looking good but not feeling good. Nausea and nerves. Great.

A shadow fell, then a harried woman with two small boys, all three with streaming colds, sat down beside Faith.

'Mummy,' one of the boys said, 'I want to go to the toilet.'

'You only went half an hour ago. You'll have—'

'Mrs Ransome?' Faith turned. A woman in clothes identical to the receptionist's greeted her with a smile. In her early thirties, she had short brown hair, Latin good looks and, like the receptionist, she had a complexion so healthy it was unreal. 'Dr Cabot can see you now.'

The woman floated up a flight of stairs as if she were weightless; Faith felt the drag of gravity in every molecule in her body.

If he's surrounded by women like these, what chance do I have?

Then she chided herself, *I don't want any chance. This is purely a courtesy visit. I'm here because of my nausea – because so far my own doctor doesn't seem to have been able to diagnose anything. That's all. That's why I'm here.*

She followed the woman along a corridor, past a sign that said, 'Relaxation Therapy', and another, marked, 'Hypnotherapy'.

'Faith!'

Oliver Cabot was standing in a doorway dressed in a black jacket, grey collarless shirt, black chinos and black suede brogues. He was even better-looking than when she had last seen him, but he seemed more serious. It felt as if she was visiting Oliver Cabot, doctor, rather than Oliver Cabot, friend. Yet as she reached him, his expression changed to one of joy. And as she shook his hand and looked at that craggy, equine face beneath the tangle of grey curls, he gave a huge lopsided grin. Instantly all her anxieties melted away and she felt a surge of excitement.

'Faith!' he said again, staring directly into her eyes, making her feel that she was the most important thing in his life. 'Faith! This is so great, I can't tell you! Great that you came! Hi!'

'Hi!' she said.

'How *are* you?'

'Fine, thank you,' she said.

They were still holding hands, Faith realised, but it seemed the most natural thing in the world to be standing in the doorway, soaking up the warmth from those sparkling, crystal-clear grey eyes.

Happiness flooded through her. It was so good to be standing here with this man, so absurdly good. She felt something she had not felt for many years.

She felt free.

19

Ross finished his round in the day-surgery unit and went into the staff room to grab a cup of coffee. It was small and narrow, with chairs on either side and a kitchenette. Tommy Pearman, his regular anaesthetist, followed him. A short, squat man with a figure like a bean-bag, his baggy blue surgical pyjamas made him look even more shapeless than he already was. A widower, he lived for his work and for his diverse hobbies. He was an avid collector of Etruscan art, vintage cars, antique navigational charts, medical text-books and, bizarrely, diseases. He had accumulated over the years, through his medical-research connections, a terrifying array of bacteria and viruses, which he kept in a cold store at his baronial home in Kent. One Sunday when Ross and Faith had been having lunch there, he'd taken Ross down to the store and shown the collection to him.

Included among the hundreds of carefully labelled vials was a smallpox culture, five strains of hepatitis, viral meningitis, anthrax, bubonic plague and a Soviet virus called Marburg, developed for germ warfare, which would melt internal organs. When Ross had asked him whether he had any qualms about keeping these things – particularly smallpox which had allegedly been eradicated – Pearman had replied that he felt more comfortable knowing they were here, safely hidden away in his cellar, than at large anywhere else in the world. The anaesthetist was brilliant at his job, and Ross trusted him implicitly, in spite of the way he got into terrible flaps about things. And right now Pearman was flapping. 'I've just seen Mrs Jardine,' he said. 'She has a terrible cold, coughing up sputum. I'm not happy about her.'

Ross glanced at his list. Elizabeth Jardine was at the top for this afternoon. A full face-lift. She was fifty-seven, married to a film producer and off in mid-July to spend three months in Los Angeles. A nice woman, he had liked her when she had first come to see him. She was desperate to have the operation before going to the States.

He mentally timed the list. After Elizabeth Jardine, a seven-year-old girl with a burn scar on her chest, then another child, a nine-year-old boy with a patch of thickened skin on his scalp, preventing hair growth, a woman with a skin tumour on the back of her calf, another woman with a malignant tumour on her face, and a teenage boy with a penile deformity – erections were painful because too much skin had been removed during circumcision. It was a lot to get through. Even so, he said, 'I'm reluctant to postpone. She should have come in a month ago but she went down with 'flu – she's going to be very upset.'

Pearman shook his head. 'I really don't think it's wise.'

'How bad is she?'

'Bad. I think you should take a look at her, see for yourself.'

Normally Ross would have trusted Pearman's judgement. The only thing holding him back was his concern for Elizabeth Jardine. 'Yes, OK, I'll go and see her in a minute.'

As he poured himself a cup of coffee, he noticed a large, half-eaten carrot cake in a tinfoil box on the work-surface. The sight of it made him feel hungry. He'd been operating since seven fifty this morning and hadn't stopped for breakfast. 'Whose is that?'

'Sandra – her birthday. Thirty-seven. She doesn't look it but, of course, she thinks she does, poor thing.'

There was a tradition in the clinic that on someone's birthday they provided cake for the rest of the staff. Sandra Billington was the chief administrator. Ross cut himself a slice and picked it up. It was sticky and crumbled in his fingers.

'I hear Sandra's going out with Roger Houghton. Have you come across him? Admin, accounts, dull stick, but who knows, they might be suited?' Tommy Pearman was the clinic's matchmaker and conductor of gossip.

Ignoring the remark, as he ignored all gossip because it did not interest him, Ross crammed some carrot cake into his mouth, and said, 'Tommy, what do you know about Lendt's disease?'

The anaesthetist had a passion for the history of medicine. He'd written two books on the development of modern medicines and was currently working on a history of anaesthesia. His small stature, hunched physique and eagerness to please often reminded Ross of Ratty in *The Wind in the Willows*.

'Rings a bell. I was reading something on it recently – maybe in *Nature*. Umm, viral, I think. Inflammatory symptoms. Attacks the brain's neurochemistry. Very rare. I can do a bit of homework on it, if you like?'

'I'd be grateful. There's a lot of stuff on the web about it – I took a trawl through it late last night.'

'It's quite an exciting disease, actually,' the anaesthetist said, enthusiastically.

'Exciting?'

Detecting disapproval in the surgeon's voice, Pearman said, defensively, 'Well, yes. I think new diseases are exciting – medicine would be a dull profession without them. What's your interest?'

'Relative of – of a friend of mine has it.'

'I'll see what I can come up with.'

'I'd appreciate it.'

Pearman looked worried suddenly. 'You know, I still don't understand the Maddy Williams thing.'

Maddy Williams was the young woman patient who'd died during the small operation by Ross to correct the flare of her nostrils.

Ross pretended to be involved with the cake. 'Uh-huh?'

'Has an inquest date been set yet?'

'Yes, in about three weeks.'

'I mean, that was terrible luck.' He shrugged helplessly. 'The cardiac problem wasn't on her records, but her doctor wrote to warn you about it, and you never got his letter. I wasn't aware of it and it's not on her records. She could easily have died during one of the major operations. There's obviously a fault in our system if an important letter can go astray, don't you think?'

Ross glanced at him. The cake was good, he cut some more.

'The only thing is,' said Pearman, 'and this is absurd speculation, that someone deliberately lost the letter or wiped details of it from the computer. But I can hardly imagine anyone doing that, can you?'

Ross did not respond.

20

I thought you would be perfect. I thought you would live in a house that was all white and spotless and that light would shimmer around you when you walked. I thought you would be dressed in white furs and lie all day on a white sofa like a lady I saw in an ad on the telly.

The door to the bedroom was open just enough for him to see in. To see the woman lying on her back, her ankles scissored around the man's naked waist, as his bony white buttocks twitched up and down between her thighs. He couldn't see the man's face and he didn't care. The man wasn't important. It was the woman. He could see part of her face and that was enough.

You left me because you couldn't stand the mess I made, and yet you live like a pig and do dirty things with men.

You left me and you don't even have a picture of me anywhere on display.

Holding the can of petrol in his hand, he tiptoed away from the door and walked silently into the sitting room. The television was on, but the sound was right down. On the screen the Beatles were being interviewed. Several boys at school were wearing their hair in Beatle fringes.

Their mothers hadn't left them.

There were more dirty plates in here. An ash-tray on the floor was so full of lipsticky butts that some had fallen on to the carpet. Near them was a teacup lying on its side in a saucer. He saw a high-heeled shoe, then a nylon stocking under a side-table. Then another teacup, this one with a disintegrated cigarette butt floating in the bottom.

In the next-door room she was screaming, 'I'm coming, oh, God, I'm coming!'

Now he had only moments left. Gripping the cap of the petrol can, he gave it a sharp twist then unscrewed it and discarded it on the floor.

21

Oliver loved the way Faith looked around his office. When some people came into a room, it didn't look like they noticed anything. Faith seemed to notice *everything*. Her eyes were roaming the furniture, the walls, the pictures, the certificates.

He helped her off with her coat, and it was good feeling her firm shoulders, breathing in the perfume that rose from inside the coat. She looked even more gorgeous today than she had at their meeting a week ago. *Faith Ransome, you are incredible!*

He hung the coat in a cupboard behind his desk, placing it carefully on the hanger, still savouring the scent and the warmth that arose from it.

When he turned back, she was looking at the framed black-and-white photograph of Jake on the wall. Jake in his Bart Simpson T-shirt sitting up on the transom of their yacht, off Catalina Island, hair tousled by the breeze, grinning that big, cheeky, Jake grin.

And Faith was thinking, That's his kid. Oh, shit, he's married. Why the hell did I imagine he was single?

She caught Oliver's eye and he smiled, but she saw his deep discomfort. 'Jake,' he said.

'Your son?'

He nodded, his face wretched. Then he ushered her to a deep sofa and said, 'Get you a drink? We have almost anything.'

Wondering why mention of his son made him look so unhappy, she said, 'Yes, I'd love a . . .' She hesitated, not sure what she did want. Something to settle the queasiness. 'Tea.'

'Something herbal? Green-leaf? Ordinary English?'

'Ordinary English with milk, please.'

She sat down and looked around to see what other clues about Oliver Cabot she could pick up. She liked the feel of this room: it was airy and bright, the furniture modern, with clean lines. It barely felt like an office at all – a couple of large, green plants, horizontal Venetian blinds half closed against the view out across the street, a pristine antique phrenology skull on top of a white filing cabinet. Several framed medical certificates, one stating that he was a fellow of the Hypnotherapy Society, added an authoritative tone. There were several large unlit candles, an ioniser, a framed reflexology chart, a dramatic framed black-and-white photograph of Stonehenge, with beams of the rising sun bursting across the lodestone, another photograph of the same small boy dressed up as a vampire for trick-or-treating, and a battered, full-size Shell petrol pump, complete with nozzle.

No photograph of his wife.

She wondered why not.

Smiling again now, Oliver perched on the arm of a chair opposite her, crossed his legs and swung them up and down, like a big kid, Faith thought. 'So,' he said, 'did he love the wallet?'

She looked at him blankly. 'Wallet?' Then she realised what he was talking about. 'Oh, Ross doesn't get it for another fortnight, not until his birthday.'

'Lucky man.'

Faith smiled thinly. There would be something wrong with the wallet, inevitably: it would be too long for Ross's suit pockets, or not have enough space for his credit cards, or not be *exactly* the right shade. In twelve years of marriage to Ross she couldn't recall many presents he'd approved. But now she wanted to talk about Dr Oliver Cabot, not Ross. Looking up at the photograph of the kid in his vampire rig, she probed, 'Is that Jake too?'

That pain in his face again. 'Uh-huh.'

'How old is he?'

His legs stopped swinging. A long, dark pause, and then, 'He'd have been just coming up to sixteen right now.'

In the silence that followed she felt a tightening in her throat, as if he was transmitting his pain to her. 'I'm sorry,' she said. 'I had no—'

He patted his thigh a couple of times and stood up. 'Don't worry about it, you didn't have any reason to know. You have kids?'

'A son, Alec. He's six.'

His secretary came in with tea for Faith and a can of mineral water for Oliver.

Faith was curious to know about this son who had died, but sensed he didn't want to talk about it. When the secretary left, she tried to keep him on the subject of his life. 'What does your wife do?'

'Marcy's a writer – she works in LA, writes television sitcoms, but we ...' He grimaced, good-naturedly. 'Let's say we inhabit the same planet but that's about the limit of what we have in common, these days.' Then he added, 'We're divorced.'

'I'm sorry,' she said.

He shifted off the arm of the sofa and sat down on it properly. 'You want to know something, Faith? People are lucky if they change together. Mostly they don't.

They either stay together for the sake of their kids, or for fear of being alone, living their lives of quiet desperation, or else they move apart. Those are the brave ones.' He smiled wistfully. 'Guess that's what I tell myself.' He thought for a moment, then said, 'Tragedy can bring people closer together, but sometimes it throws them apart.' He crossed his legs, then reached forward and gripped the toes of his trainers, and stayed there, like a coiled spring. 'How about you?'

'I suppose . . . I sort of fit into the *quiet-desperation* category.'

'Too personal if I ask why you feel that?'

She would have loved to pour it all out to him, yet a part of her was thinking, Not here, not now, too soon. Way too soon.

His secretary put her head around the door. 'Sorry to interrupt, Dr Cabot, Mrs Martyns is on the line. She wants to have an urgent word with you about her visualisations.'

He raised his eyes. 'Third time this morning. I'll call her back, Tina.'

'And a reporter called Sarah Conroy phoned from the *Daily Mail*. They're doing a piece on London's alternative clinics. Said she's interviewed you before, when she was with *Focus* magazine. I told her you'd call her back – she needs to speak to you before four o'clock.'

'Sure – remind me.'

She left and Oliver tore the tab off his can. Some water bubbled out, pooling on the top. He drank a little, then dabbed his mouth with the back of his hand.

'I'm curious,' Faith said. 'Why the Shell pump?'

He turned to look at it, as if he had totally forgotten its existence. 'I saw it in a junk store. I guess its true purpose here is that it has no purpose. We get too hung up on *meaning*. I like the spontaneous, the irrational. I try to do something irrational every day. Are you irrational, Faith?'

She used to love the irrational and the zany. She'd been a total addict of *Monty Python* from the first series. But there was no room in Ross's life for the irrational. She tried to remember the last spontaneous thing she'd done, and realised, with dismay, that it had been years ago. Years since she'd unzipped Ross's trousers while he was driving down a German *autobahn*, years since she'd stolen that great big brass ash-tray from a hotel foyer late one night, right under the nose of the night porter, and crammed it into her suitcase, light years since the days of getting drunk and dialling people with silly names, like Smellie, in the middle of the night, and saying, '*Hallo, are you smelly?*' then collapsing in giggles.

God, how serious life was these days.

'I never wanted to be a grown-up,' she said.

He hunched his shoulders and gave her a big grin. 'There are times when I think life's too short to grow up. Part of me just wants to remain a kid. I get the sense you're still a kid at heart.'

'I wish,' Faith said.

'Is that what you'd wish for,' he asked, 'if you could have one wish granted? That you could be a kid again?'

'No. Older, early twenties, maybe.' Her memories told her she had been happy then, in those early heady days of courting – such a *quaint* word. She *had* been happy then, in love, and with her whole life ahead of her.

They were interrupted by the rising cadence of a phone ringing. Oliver shot a glance at his desk. Then Faith realised it was coming from her handbag. She pulled out her Nokia, embarrassed, and glanced at the dial. It was Ross at the clinic. She pushed the END button with her thumb, killing the call. Then she dropped the phone back in her bag, surprising herself at finding the courage for this small act of defiance. There'd be hell from Ross later, but right now she did not care.

Not one bit.

22

'This is where I come most days in my lunch-hour,' Oliver said.

In the distance below them, the rooftops of London stretched far away, fading into a grubby smudge beneath the threatening charcoal sky. The wind tore at her hair and ripped through her coat, a savage, glacial wind, but she scarcely noticed as she walked alongside him, down the path between the gravestones.

Oliver, in his long black coat, hair streaming, holding the small carrier-bag containing their sandwiches and two bottles of mineral water, strode at an easy pace. She glanced at the names on the tombstones. *Mary Elizabeth Mainwaring, beloved wife. 1889–1965. Harold Thomas Sugden, 1902–1974. William Percival Leadbetter, 1893–1951. At Peace in the Kingdom of the Lord.*

Then she looked up at him. 'Does death fascinate you?'

He stopped and pointed down at the headstone of William Percival Leadbetter. 'You know what fascinates me? It's the dash. That little mark between the dates. I look down at someone's grave, and I think, That dash represents a human being's entire life. You and I are living out our dashes right now. It's not important when someone was born or when they died, what matters is what they did in between with their lives. And all we have here in this graveyard are just thousands of anonymous dashes. That makes me sad.'

'You think people should have their entire biographies etched on their tombstones? Or some kind of video hologram that replays all their achievements as you pass the gravestone?'

'There has to be something better than this.' He walked on.

'Do you think about your own death?'

'I try to think about life. I try to think what I can do with my little dash to make a difference. I—' He fell silent and they walked for some moments without speaking. Then he said, 'You lose someone close and you realise how helpless we are. We can put people into space, we can map the entire human genome, we can plot the floor of the ocean with a little sonar device, and sometime soon we'll be able to make the rain fall wherever we want it to. But so many diseases still defeat us.' He tapped his head. 'We have the ability to beat any disease if we could just find the way to harness the power we have inside our heads.'

'I think that too,' she said. 'Is it true we use only a very small part of our brains, something like twenty per cent?'

'Around twenty per cent of what we know to be there. What we don't know is what else we are connected to that we could draw from.'

'Some other dimension?'

They were approaching a bench. 'This is a good place to sit,' he said. 'You're not too cold?'

Faith was freezing, but the cold air, or maybe it was Oliver's company, had blown away her nausea. 'I'm fine.'

He dug a hand into the bag and pulled out a tuna

sandwich. Handing it to her he said, 'Guess I should really be taking you to some smart eatery. But—'

'No, I'm happy we came here.' And she meant it. With every moment she spent with Oliver Cabot she grew more comfortable with him, and more intrigued by him. And felt more free.

As she began to unwrap the Cellophane from her sandwich, her phone rang again. She checked the display, in case it was Alec's school, but it was Ross again. Once more she pressed the END button and dropped the phone back into her bag.

'Where are you from in the States?' she asked.

'LA.'

'How long have you been in England?'

'Seven years, coming up to eight.' He was unwrapping his own sandwich, with long, slender fingers. Pianist's fingers, Faith thought, watching them. Everything about this man seemed attractive to her, she realised, even the way he unwrapped a sandwich.

'I came to get away from the memories of my son. California haunted me. And, you know, this is a good place to be. If you could just find a way to reconfigure the circuitry of your brain so that the weather seems tolerable.'

She laughed. 'You mean so that when there's a biting wind your brain will tell you it's a really nice wind?'

'I'm working on it.'

She picked away at the wrapping on her sandwich. 'How did your son die?'

'Leukaemia. He had a nasty virulent form of the disease. I knew there wasn't anything in conventional medicine that could help Jake, but my wife refused to go along with any alternative treatments because she thought it would be gambling with her child's life.' He gave a wry smile. 'I gave up practising conventional medicine after his death – too many vested interests at stake that don't care about the patients. Modern medicine has itself in a box and I decided to dedicate my life to trying to get it out.'

'What kind of a box?'

The quiet was suddenly broken with the clatter of a fast-approaching helicopter, and at the same moment, Faith's phone rang again. With an apologetic look at Oliver, she pulled it out of her bag. 'Just need to make sure it's not to do with my son,' she said. On the display no number was identified.

She pressed the green button to answer it.

'Where the hell are you?' Ross demanded.

The helicopter was passing right overhead.

'Can't hear you!' she yelled.

The voice became a few decibels louder. 'Faith, please tell me where you are and what you're doing.'

'I'm in town.'

'Where?'

She hesitated. 'Knightsbridge,' she said.

'What's that sound?'

'A helicopter.'

'Why didn't you tell me you were going to be in London, Faith? We could have arranged to do something this evening. *Les Sylphides* is on at Covent Garden.'

She wondered what Ross was on about: he had never before expressed the slightest interest in ballet. The noise of the helicopter was subsiding. 'Spur of the moment. I had to collect a birthday present for you.'

'You should have told me. I don't like it when you don't tell me things, Faith. You know that, don't you? I always need to know where you are because I care about you so much, darling.'

'I was planning to come up next Monday, but it looks

like I'm going to be tied up with the golf-course public-inquiry committee.'

'Fuck that. How's Alec getting home from school?'

'It's half-term this week. He's with Nico Lawson.'

'He was with other people yesterday too. You should be there for him, Faith. It's unsettling for him to keep spending time with different people.'

Seething, she glanced at Oliver, who was folding the Cellophane into a tiny ball. You damned hypocrite, Ross, she thought. In one breath you're telling me we could have had a night in town and in the next you're angry I'm not at home for Alec. I'm always at home for Alec. That's why I don't have a career. But she kept calm. 'It was his choice – he was invited and it happens to be Nico's birthday,' she said. 'I'm spending all of tomorrow with him. We might go to Thorpe Park.'

'It seems to be happening more and more, these days.'

She glanced again at Oliver, embarrassed now. 'I don't think so. How's your day?'

'Fine, Faith. Who are you with?'

'I'm on my own.'

'I hope you're telling me the truth.'

'I'll see you tomorrow. Call me at home, later?'

'I don't like the sound of your voice, Faith.'

'The reception's bad here.'

'The reception's fine. There's something about your voice, Faith. You sound different.'

'I – I don't feel that brilliant.'

There was a long silence. Again she glanced at Oliver, who was turning his sandwich in his hand, as if inspecting it.

'Tell me how you're feeling, Faith?'

'Just not brilliant.'

'In what way?'

'The same.'

'The nausea?'

'Yes. I don't understand why I haven't heard anything from Jules Ritterman. You haven't heard anything?'

A little calmer suddenly. 'From Jules? No. I'll give him a call, chase him up. I love you, Faith. I really love you, darling. You do know that, don't you?'

'Yes.'

'I'll call you later,' Ross said. 'Love you.'

'And you.'

'Tell me you love me.'

Good-humouredly she said, 'I do, you know that.'

'I want to hear you say it. Say it to me, Faith.'

One more glance at Oliver, and then, tersely, 'I love you.'

'I love you, too.'

He was gone.

She put the phone back in her bag. Oliver looked at her. 'I'm sorry. Hope I'm not causing you any hassle?'

'You're not.' She shrugged. 'My husband's very possessive.'

'Guess I can't blame him. Think I'd be pretty possessive about you if you were my wife.'

She glanced away, blushing but smiling.

'You're not feeling too good?'

'I feel – *brilliant!*'

He grinned. 'You know, I once heard a great definition of a bore. It's someone who deprives you of solitude without providing you with company. I think that defines a lot of marriages.'

'Ross is never boring,' she said, surprising herself by how defensive she sounded.

'No offence – I didn't mean to imply—'

'No, it's OK. What I mean is . . .' She wasn't sure why she'd sprung to Ross's defence. She hadn't wanted to say that at all. It was as if the shadow of Ross was all

97

around her, a dark fear from which she could never be free, no matter how far away from him she was.

Alec was part of that fear. Something churned inside her every time she allowed herself the luxury of thinking that it could ever be possible to end her marriage. Alec. The thought of what divorce might do to him. The knowledge that Ross would use him as a pawn and would fight tooth and claw over him. It was far, far worse than any fears about what Ross might try to do to her.

Oliver took a bite of his sandwich. She looked down at her own, but she had no appetite. 'What I mean is,' she said, 'Ross isn't boring, but that doesn't . . .' Her voice tailed away.

'Doesn't?' he echoed.

She smiled. 'Tell me about you. Tell me about *your* life since your divorce.'

'Well,' he looked coy, 'I've been celibate.'

'Seriously?'

'Eight years. So, before your husband gets too jealous, you can tell him that. It's true.'

'Why?' she asked. 'Do you have a reason? Or you just haven't met anyone?'

'You know about the Jing Chi?'

Faith shook her head.

'It's the name the Chinese have for sexual energy. They believe that if you control it through celibacy it transforms into a higher energy you can use at a spiritual level for healing. I wanted to try that,' he said simply, and bit into his sandwich again. 'I wanted to try to concentrate my mind and reach up into higher levels of consciousness. I did a lot of studying, and figured that was what I needed to do. So I made a decision. And I never met anyone who made me want to reverse that decision.' He looked at her again, focusing those clear grey eyes directly on her own. 'Until you.'

23

She was a mess. The seat-belt mountings in her mother's ancient, crappy little Russian car had sheared, and she'd taken out the last non-laminated glass windscreen on Planet Earth, face first, at forty miles an hour. The blades of a rotary mower, Ross opined, wouldn't have caused much less disfigurement.

Leah Phillips was a teenager. Blind in one eye, most of her nose, lips and chin were gone, and her face, gridded with scars, looked as if it had been soldered back together. She was sitting in the consultation chair in front of his desk, constantly glancing at her mother on the sofa a few feet away.

Even Ross, who had been hardened by countless harrowing sights during his career, was moved by this one, and tried hard to let only reassurance show in his face.

His office was designed to reassure. It was decorated in the same masculine style as his study at home. Rich, dark woods, leather upholstery, oil paintings of naval battle scenes, bookshelves lined with leatherbound medical tomes, a white marble bust of Hippocrates on a white Doric plinth.

'And your date of birth, Leah?' he asked.

She glanced again at her mother, who was clutching a large brown envelope and who answered for her, in a timid, nervy voice, 'Nineteen eighty-three.'

He wrote down the details with his Mont Blanc. 'Can you tell me how you came to see me?'

Again Leah left her mother to respond. 'Our doctor gave us a list of names, you see. My husband looked you up on the Internet, and he thought you seemed the most suitable for what Leah needs.' She was wringing her hands and smiling a desperate, for-God's-sake-help-us smile.

He shot a glance at the Psion Revo lying on his desk. Ten past three. Surreptitiously, he tapped up the organiser's diary. This was the last of his afternoon consultation patients and he was due back in theatre at four. It was an effort to concentrate when his mind was on Faith. Where the hell was she today?

In town.

No, you're not in town. You're lying to me, you bitch. Where are you really, Faith? You might as well tell me because you know I'm going to find out anyway, don't you?

He studied his notes to get his bearings. 'Yes, OK, the Internet.' He wrote that down, then looked up again. One of the skills he had acquired over the years was the ability to look at any patient, no matter how badly disfigured they might be, without giving away any emotion in his face. He crossed his arms and leaned forward over his desk towards the girl. 'So, tell me, Leah, what can I do for you?'

Her mother nodded for her to speak. 'I want to look how I used to look.'

'Leah was doing modelling work,' her mother said, 'with a top agency. She did a fashion spread for *17* magazine in the June issue. Everyone says she had – I mean, *has* – the talent to get right to the top.'

All their eyes met for an instant, like the flash of a spark.

She stood up and passed him the envelope she had been clutching. 'These – these are of her.'

Ross opened the envelope and shook out several professionally taken photographs of a strikingly beautiful young brunette. Even with all his experience, it was hard to believe this was the same girl, and he felt a swirl of anger at whoever in the A and E department after the crash had done this botch-up on her. It looked more like she had been treated by someone apprenticing in sheet metal work than by a doctor.

Putting the photographs down, he looked at the mother and then at the girl. As gently as he could, he said, 'I think I can improve you, Leah, but it's going to take a long time and several operations. I can't promise what the results will be, and it's very important you both understand that.'

'How much improvement will you be able to make, Doctor?' her mother said.

Not enough, he thought. He could give her some kind of life, but he couldn't give her her modelling career back.

He told her the truth, all the while thinking, Faith, you bitch, you don't realise how lucky you are. I made you beautiful. *I could just as easily make you look like this.*

When they left, the girl was sobbing. The knowledge that she would have to endure probably ten operations over the next couple of years was tough for a youngster of her age. But it was important she and her mother both knew the score: you had to have determination to go through what Leah was facing, and he didn't want them coming back angry and disappointed with the final result.

Ross closed the door, then asked his secretary to hold any calls for a few minutes. He turned towards his computer, entered a command, followed by a password, and moments later was connected to his computer at home in Sussex. Soon he had in front of him on the screen a complete log of every phone call made and received by Faith at home in the past seven days. At a single click of his mouse he could listen to a recording of any of them.

OK, my sweet little bitch queen, let's see who you've been speaking to recently.

24

'I have to get going,' Faith said, feeling a flash of guilt that, for these past few hours with Oliver Cabot, she hadn't given Alec a thought. It was as if she had been taken back fourteen years, to her late teens, to a time when her whole life had been ahead of her.

As she sipped the last of the cappuccino, her body thawing now, the door opened. She looked up warily, returning to the real world. A guy and a girl in their twenties. Strangers. She relaxed again.

There was a cheery fug in the café, which reminded her of her student days. Formica table-tops, the haze of cigarette smoke, the smell of meat sauce, the chatter of people at tables crammed close together, and news-papers swinging on their wooden poles each time the door opened.

It was five past three. It would take her a good forty minutes to get to Victoria, half an hour on the Gatwick Express and a further twenty-five minutes' drive from there. She wouldn't be home much before five thirty, she calculated. Just in time to have supper with Alec.

Across the table, Oliver, his unruly hair even more tangled by the wind, asked, 'Did you do anything about having a medical check-up?'

She remembered him studying her palm in the café at the General Trading Company. 'Actually, I did.'

'I'm glad. All OK?'

She hesitated. 'I'm waiting to hear – the doctor took some blood tests and stuff.'

'I hope you didn't mind my—'

'No.' In the warmth, with the cigarette smoke, her

nausea was returning, but she did not want to tell him this. 'It was a good thing. I – hadn't had a check-up for a while.'

'And you're fine?'

She didn't want to tell him about her depression because she didn't want to appear flawed. 'In rude health, I think the expression is.' She could see doubt in his eyes – or maybe that was in her imagination?

'Good. I'm glad.' There was a long silence, and then he said, 'You know something, Faith, it's really been good seeing you.'

'Thank you. I've enjoyed myself too.'

'Can I see you again?'

Her attraction to him was scaring her yet boosting her. It felt so good being with him. She knew she ought to say no, but instead she heard herself say, 'I'd like to – yes.'

'Can you get away tomorrow?'

'It's half-term and I'm taking my son and two friends of his out for the day.'

'Sometime next week?'

Hesitantly she said, 'Perhaps we'd better talk on the phone when I see how my diary is. I have several committee meetings, and it's Ross's birthday on Wednesday.'

Bad thoughts swirled through her. Thoughts about Ross finding out, throwing her out, forbidding her ever to see Alec again.

Oliver raised his palms to her with a genial grin. 'Look, whenever. Cut yourself some slack when you have the chance, and if you feel like seeing me, I'm here. I'm not going anywhere.' He prodded around inside his empty coffee-cup with his spoon, and scraped some remnants of froth from the sides. 'I just want you to know that I really do want to see you again. OK?'

As she stepped outside, the wind slashed her hair

against her face, and then, suddenly, it seemed to have found its way inside her and was swirling in her belly. She was so cold she almost cried out, and then the nausea rose. The whole street seemed to come loose, as if it had been torn from its mountings, and she saw the pavement tilt, coming straight at her face.

She was dimly aware of Oliver's arm catching her, strong, firm, saw his blurred face. Heard his disembodied voice.

'Faith? Jesus. Faith?'

He helped her back to her feet and she stood, unsteadily, supported now by his arm around her waist. She breathed deeply, felt the air cooling her burning face, stared at him, could see the lines of deep concern etched like charcoal around his eyes.

'Want to go back inside?' he asked.

'No, I'm OK – just the – the air—'

'Let's go back in, sit down for a few minutes.'

'No, I'm OK, I have to get back. Can you call me a taxi? I'll be fine, really.'

'I'm not putting you in a taxi. I'll drive you.'

'Thanks, no, I'm OK, really.'

She felt a little better – until suddenly there was a blinding pain behind her eyes, as if she'd been stabbed through the head. Another bout of the nausea hit her, and she clutched him, bile clawing up inside her throat, everything around her a blur again. Her legs buckled.

The seat in Oliver's dark blue Jeep was soft, like an armchair, giving her the sensation that she was on a boat, swaying, rocking. She listened to the solid rattle of the diesel, the whir of the fan, felt the warm stream of air, heard the faint strains of Mozart on the sound system, which was turned right down but not off. She was concentrating hard on one thing.

Don't throw up. Don't throw up. Don't throw up.

He changed gear, pulling away from lights. 'What did your doctor say to you, Faith?'

A ringing sound. Her mobile. Inside her handbag. *What had the doctor said? Nothing.* The phone was still ringing. She found the zip, pulled it, dug in the bag, pulled out the phone, looked at the display.

It was Ross again.

She switched it off, dropped it back in her bag. Speaking was an effort. 'Just . . . something I picked up . . . in Thailand . . . They have different bacteria . . . I'm – OK.'

'The hell you are.'

He was braking again, stopping at a light in a corridor between two juggernauts. She could hear the hammering of their engines, could feel them shaking – shaking her whole world. Oliver felt so strong, so good to be with. A deep, terrible fear seeped through her, a darkness like a black lake of ink spreading through blotting paper, a fear of what was wrong with her, a fear of Ross's anger, and this Jeep, this sanctuary, was going to deliver her to Victoria, to her train home.

Her train to hell.

25

The petrol tumbled unevenly from the can. Panicking, Ross had to tilt it back then forward to get the best results. *Come on, please, please, please.* The smell was intense, and his eyes stung from the vapour. He poured some over the sofa, *come on, come on,* the carpet, the dining table. Then, making a continuous trail, he backed out of the door into the hall and continued the trail all the way to the kitchen door.

The man was making all the noise in the bedroom

now. Ross could hear the springs creaking, the man grunting louder and louder.

Still pouring he hurried back to the bedroom door. Then, angling it carefully so that the petrol would pour in through the open chink, he laid the can down on its side.

There was a dull, booming sound from the can as the petrol continued to pour out in uneven spurts and flowed away, through the crack, into the bedroom. But the sound was drowned by the noises the man was making.

'Yes!' the man screamed. 'Yes, yes, yes!'

Ross retreated through the kitchen to the door. He waited as long as he dared, then tried to pull the matches out of his pocket.

This was the one bit he hadn't rehearsed. His rubber gloves stuck in the lining of his trousers.

Don't do this to me.

Panicking badly now, the stench of petrol all around him, he ripped off the glove, dug his hand into his pocket and pulled out the box. As he opened it several spilled on the floor. When he knelt to pick them up, all the rest emptied on the floor also.

He heard a shout of surprise. 'Hey? Jesus – what the hell—'

A door crashed open. Footsteps.

No time to look up, no time to do anything except seize one matchstick, strike it, toss it.

WWHHHUMMMPPPPPHHHHHH.

The speed at which the line of flame travelled across the floor took him by surprise. He looked up in time to see, for one fleeting second, a naked man standing in the hall, and in the next instant, with a truly terrible cry of pain and fear, the man was engulfed in a brilliant yellow and green fireball.

The crying was even worse now, terrible, desperate,

agonised howls. And suddenly there was another voice, a woman screeching, hysterical with fear.

Ross allowed himself one moment to savour the cries and screams as if they were music. Then he snatched up his rubber glove, slammed the door shut behind him, turned the key, pulled it from the lock and, clutching it in his teeth while he pulled on the glove, sprinted down the fire-escape.

He clambered over the back wall, dropped on to the cement foundations of the construction site, and immediately scrambled down a ramp into what would eventually be the underground car-park. There was enough of an orange glow from the streetlighting outside for him to see reasonably well in here.

His bike was waiting, tucked carefully behind a cement-mixer where he had left it. He jumped on it, keeping the lights off for the moment, and pedalled furiously across to the far side, up the ramp and out into the busy main road.

When he considered himself a safe distance away, he stopped and switched on his front and rear lamps. Then he pedalled on at a relaxed pace, just part of the night and of interest to no one.

It was a full five minutes before he heard the first fire engine bells.

26

'Mr Ransome, I simply fail to understand how you cannot see it,' Lady Geraldine Reynes-Rayleigh said. 'Absolutely everyone else can. Absolutely *everyone*.'

Each syllable was articulated with slow, tortuous precision, underpinned with disdain, as if she were criticising a servant who had only the most rudimentary grasp of the English language, and as if the act of speaking to him was something she considered utterly beneath her.

She had the kind of body a lot of women would kill for – especially at her age: tall, willowy, with a terrific bust, whose shape and preservation she owed to her previous plastic surgeon, equally terrific legs, which she owed to her genes, and sensational long blonde tresses, which, her tell-tale black eyebrows told the world, she owed to the skills of her hairdresser.

Internally, her biological clock had just ticked up fifty-two, but the press gave her age as forty-seven. Externally, her previous surgeon had nipped, tucked and liposuctioned away a good twelve of those years. Not many thirty-five-year-olds managed to look this good, Ross thought. Shame surgery couldn't do anything about her personality.

Poised on the armchair in his office, she was power-dressed in the way that only the very rich can. There was something about truly expensive clothes that set them and their wearers apart from lesser mortals, and Lady Geraldine Reynes-Rayleigh was a whole planet away from lesser mortals. He had long tried to get Faith to have this kind of air about her, but it didn't seem to matter how much money he spent, the exact formula had always eluded him.

'I came to you, Mr Ransome, because everyone I spoke to said you were the number-one surgeon in this country,' she continued.

The true reason she had changed surgeons, Ross knew but did not reveal to her, was that her previous surgeon, a brilliant man called Nicholas Parkhouse, had found her so impossible that he had refused to operate on her again. Ross had usually been able to cope with troublesome patients, but he was bitterly regretting having taken this one on.

It was the Reynes-Rayleigh name that had seduced him. She had fast-tracked herself from page-three bimbo to A-list socialite through three marriages, each to a richer, better-connected man than the last. Her current conquest, a shrewd, flamboyant baronet, had been ranked in the top one hundred richest men in the *Sunday Times*, and the pair were scarcely out of the society columns throughout every season, from polo with the Prince of Wales, to Wimbledon with Tom Cruise and Nicole Kidman, to Glyndebourne with the King and Queen of Norway. She had wanted the face-lift prior to a *Hello!* photo session at their revamped Palladian stately pile, but she was not happy with the results. It was inevitable, he realised now to his chagrin. She was not a woman it would ever be possible to please.

Perhaps some of the sniping about her that Faith had pointed out to him in the Dempster diary column in the *Daily Mail* was true. Two or three times he had seen pieces alluding to her reluctance to pay bills, despite her wealth.

'The two sides of my face are simply not even – you absolutely *must* be able to see this.'

'Lady Reynes-Rayleigh, if you study the *Mona Lisa* you'll see that her face is asymmetrical, too.'

Plumed horses, parading through the folds of couture silk that encased her neck, rose gently up and down as she spoke. 'She's an old boot, if you want my opinion. I don't find the comparison flattering. You've also made a complete mess of my nose. It's now totally straight and I distinctly told you I wanted the bump *reduced*. There's no way I'm going to pay you for this mess, so perhaps you would like to tell me precisely what you intend to do about it?'

It took a supreme effort of self-will to restrain himself

from being rude to her. The woman was being unreasonable: he had done a superb job – there was simply no comparison with how she had looked previously to now. But he knew that if he did nothing, or was rude to her, she could do him a lot of damage.

Putting on the charm he said, 'Tell me, how does your husband feel about how you look?'

'I don't think that has anything to do with the issue, Mr Ransome. It's how I feel.'

Biting his tongue, 'Of course.'

'So what do you intend to do about it?'

Raising his hands in the air, he said, 'Are you prepared to face another operation?'

'I'm not a coward, you know. Do I look like a coward? With my *asymmetrical face*?'

'Of course not.'

'A second operation is going to be most inconvenient, you understand that, don't you?'

'And there are risks with every operation, Lady Reynes-Rayleigh – I do need to point that out.'

Acidly, she retorted, 'I've just said I'm not a coward, but I do have an extremely full diary. And I will expect you to compensate me for any extra expenses I incur, naturally.'

Calmly, he said, 'Can you give me some indication of what you expect these to be?'

With a smile that could corrode steel she replied, 'My solicitors are preparing a list for you.'

27

The service-station canopy seemed to be acting like a wind tunnel. Faith, head bowed against the stinging pellets of rain, stood beside the Range Rover. The pump seemed slow today as she watched the litres tick up on the dial, the rain coming at her from every direction, rattling against the worn wax coating of her Barbour, gluing her jeans to her legs and drenching her hair.

Alec, strapped into the back seat, waved at her and made a silly face. She made a face back. He leaned over, squishing his nose up against the window, then let his tongue loll like an imbecile. She laughed. You're such a wonderful child, she thought. You're funny and smart and kind and innocent. I want to get you away from Ross before he makes you arrogant, rude and cruel like himself.

For the past twenty-four hours, since almost collapsing with Oliver Cabot yesterday, she had been feeling a lot better, physically and mentally. She'd got her appetite back last night, had been hungry this morning and again at lunchtime, wolfing down a vile hamburger and soggy chips at the amusement park with Alec and his two friends, whom she had just dropped off at home. It was the first time since coming back from Thailand that she'd really felt like eating. She was hungry again now, craving something sweet.

Maybe Dr Ritterman was right, after all, and this bug *was* clearing up of its own accord.

The nozzle clicked. Fuel roared up inside the neck of the fuel tank and, moments later, gushed out and ran down the side of the car. She hung up the nozzle, closed the petrol cap, then ran into the warmth and shelter of the service-station shop.

There was a queue for the cashier. Before joining it, she stepped over to the magazine racks and allowed herself the luxury of a few moments' browsing. Magazines were one of her weaknesses, and she loved cookery and interior-design pages in particular. She finally selected the new issues of *Good Housekeeping*,

Country Homes and *Hello!*, then picked up a bag of Maltesers for herself, a tube of Smarties for Alec, and joined the queue, just ahead of a harried-looking man in a suit.

Her least favourite attendant was on duty today: a slight, cocky youth, of no more than twenty, with greasy blond hair backcombed into a quiff, an ear-stud, designer bum-fluff, and a sly grin.

He seemed to be taking an age with the people in front of her, and she was miles away when her turn came.

'Pump?'

She stared at him blankly, momentarily forgetting where she was.

'Pump?' he repeated, more loudly than was necessary.

Now she got it. *You know which pump, you little twerp, you know my car. I've been filling it up here twice a week for God knows how long. All you have to do is look out of the window.* This was his little game, she knew, flexing the only power he had.

Glancing out of the window, and taking her time, making him wait, paying him back (sad, but it felt good), she said, 'Number four.' She put the magazines and sweets on the counter, then glanced up at a poster for the national lottery. It had been a while since she'd bought any tickets – Ross disapproved.

'Sixty-eight pounds seventeen.'

She handed him her Mastercard, and looked back at the poster, tempted. She'd won ten pounds a few times, and was often lucky at raffles. But she didn't want to buy any tickets here, from this creep: they'd be jinxed.

And the creep was having difficulties. He was swiping her card for a second time now. Then he studied the display on the machine and suddenly thrust the card back at her. 'Not valid.'

She stared into his sly little eyes. 'Not valid? What do you mean?'

'Your card's not valid.'

Angrily snatching it out of his hand, she said, 'Don't be ridiculous.' Conscious of the queue of people behind her, she checked the expiry date. The card had over five months to run. Handing it back to him she said, haughtily, 'The card's valid. I think you have a problem with your computer.'

Without a word, he took back the card, picked up a phone and dialled. She felt a tug on her coat and looked down. Alec was standing there, clutching a *Beano*. 'Can I have this, Mummy?'

'I told you to stay in the car, darling.'

He screwed up his face, imploringly. 'Yes, I know, but can I have this? I haven't got this one. Please?'

'Not valid,' the attendant said again, loudly enough for everyone to hear. 'Must be past your credit limit.'

Could it be? She racked her brains. Impossible. There was a ten-thousand-pound limit on the card and she'd spent only a few hundred pounds on it so far this month. 'No way.' Faith put it down angrily, then rummaged around in her purse and pulled out her platinum American Express card, which she rarely used, and handed that to the attendant, feeling some of her dignity restored.

He took it without grace and swiped it. Then he swiped it again, all his body language showing this was merely a formality, a courtesy, before handing it back to her. 'Not valid either.'

Feeling her cheeks reddening, Faith said, 'There's something wrong with your machine.'

Behind her an irritable male voice said, 'Look, I'm in a hurry.'

Ignoring Faith, the attendant punched a couple of keys on his terminal, then took the man's credit card.

Moments later the slip printed out. With a triumphant smirk at Faith, he handed the man his card and slip for signature. Then he turned back to Faith. 'Machine's working fine.'

Now she was feeling riled and anxious. What the hell was going on? There had to be some kind of computer error, and she was going to create hell with the card companies when she got home, force each of them to write letters of apology – and, she decided, she would make them write to this cocky little bastard also. But now there was a bigger problem on her mind. Did she have enough cash on her?

'How much did you say I owe you?'

The grin was almost unbearable now. 'Sixty-eight pounds seventeen. Plus for the *Beano*, that's—'

'Don't forget my comic, Mummy, you've got to pay for that too!' Alec said.

'Have to see if I've got enough money on me, darling.' She looked in her purse, pulled out all the notes she had and counted them. Sixty pounds exactly. She emptied all the coins on to the counter.

Another irritable voice behind her said, 'Excuse me, could you serve the rest of us then deal with this woman?'

Wishing she could disappear into the floor, Faith moved to one side. Five pounds twenty-four pence. She was still short.

A little hand placed three coins on the counter. Alec's hand. 'I've got sixty pence, Mummy, you can borrow that.'

She smiled. 'Thank you, darling, I'm going to need it.' She turned to the attendant. 'I've got some money in the car – just going to get it.'

To her relief she found seven pound coins in the small purse she kept for parking meters. She went back inside, paid the attendant, then strapped Alec into his seat. He was immediately absorbed in his comic.

She started the engine, drove clear of the pumps, then stopped and dialled the number on the back of her gold card. When the customer services assistant answered, Faith said, 'Can you help me? My card has just been refused at a petrol station.'

The woman asked for the card number, then ran the usual security check of Faith's address, date of birth, mother's maiden name. Then she asked Faith to hold.

After about thirty seconds the woman came back on the line. 'I'm sorry, that card has been cancelled by the principal card-holder.'

'By the principal holder?' Faith said, astonished.

'That's correct.'

Faith thanked her and hung up. Then she rang the number on the back of the other two cards in turn.

Ross had cancelled them too.

Furious now, she dialled Ross's Harley Street consulting-room number. His secretary answered, haughtily distant as usual. The woman irritated Faith beyond belief. *Lucinda Smart*. An arid, horsy divorcée in her late forties, with a sister who had been an assistant private secretary to Princess Margaret, Lucinda always treated her with frosty aloofness.

'Could you put me through to Ross, Lucinda?' Faith asked. 'It's urgent.'

'Mr Ransome can't be disturbed, Mrs Ransome. He has a patient with him.'

'I need to speak to him the moment he's free.'

'I will convey your message to him, Mrs Ransome.'

'You'd better do more than that. Will you kindly tell him we're not going to have any food tonight if he doesn't call?'

He didn't call.

28

Once, but it seemed a long time ago now, the sound of those tyres on the gravel would have been like music to Faith. *Ross arriving home.* Once, she would have thrown herself at him as he came in at the front door, hugging and kissing him. And one summer evening, shortly after they had moved here and before Alec had come along, they had lain down on the hall floor and made love – without even shutting the door.

She could hear Rasputin barking wildly, racing down the hall to greet his master, and she could hear Alec, in his pyjamas, trailing after him. 'Daddy's home! Daddy's home!'

Looking through the gap in their bedroom curtains Faith could see the Aston Martin glinting in the security lights that had clicked on. She stepped back. She was still in her jeans and chunky polo-neck, but she didn't care. Tonight he could go hang.

She went out of the bedroom, leaving all the lights on, knowing that would irk him too. There was a toy police car on its side on the landing floor and, further on, some Lego left over from a garage Alec had been trying to assemble. She left them where they were. Downstairs, above the commotion of the dog, she heard the front door opening, then Ross's voice, greeting first the dog, then Alec.

'Daddy, can I show you what I painted at school?'

Then Ross's voice again, bellowing. 'Rasputin! Quiet boy. *Quiet!*'

'Can I, Daddy? Can I show you?'

And for the first time in their married life, Faith decided she wasn't going downstairs. She walked on down the landing and into one of the spare bedrooms at the far end.

She switched on the light, closed the door behind her and sat down in a deep armchair. The room faced out on to the rear, over the terraced lawns, the pool, the tennis court, the orchard and the paddock beyond, but on this stormy night, beneath the threatening grey of the raging sky, she noticed only the spats of rain trickling down the windows.

She shivered. The room felt cold and unused. The décor was cold, too, tasteful but impersonal, swagged curtains matching the floral bedspread, mahogany furniture, a pile of old *Country Life*s and *Vogue*s on the bedside tables. Pictures they hadn't particularly wanted in any of the other rooms hung here to fill wall spaces: a mediocre hunting scene, a couple of rather drab architectural drawings of the Pump House in Bath, and an equally dull watercolour of the Sussex Downs they'd bought when high on champagne and music at Glyndebourne.

The silence of this room felt good. Fury burned inside her and she had to let this cool. She could never win a confrontation with him, and when they'd had rows in the past it was always Alec who suffered the most becoming frightened and confused.

She closed her eyes and thought of Oliver Cabot. She tried hard to remember his face but it was elusive: one moment she could see it clearly, the next she only had a faint impression of it. Warmth was what she thought of most. Warmth and sadness, that deep, tender sadness when he talked about his son.

There was a pang inside her, a yearning of the kind she thought was left way behind in her past and that she would never experience again. The yearning she'd had in her late teens for a boy called Charles Stourton. He'd looked like Alec Baldwin and he'd adored her. He was charming, impeccably mannered, brilliant company, an amazing lover, and everyone who met him liked him.

He had a terrific job working for Sotheby's, had just been offered a two-year posting in New York, and wanted her to come with him. Then, just when she thought things could not get better with him, he had dumped her.

One brief phone call. He had met someone else.

For months afterwards she had been inconsolable. And that was when she had crashed her bike and met Ross. He'd put four stitches into her forehead, and she'd been terrified she would be scarred for life, yet within weeks of the stitches coming out, there had been no mark at all. And by then she was dating him.

He had seemed so strong, so attentive, no hint then of the control-freak he had turned into – or maybe she had been blind to it then, in her infatuation for the tall, charming, incredibly handsome, ambitious young doctor.

'What the fuck are you doing in here?'

She turned her head and saw him standing in the doorway, his face blazing with anger. She stayed put as he strode towards her.

'I said, what the fuck are you doing in here?' He stopped right in front of her, towering over her, shaking with rage, and she gripped the arms of the chair, too angry to be frightened of him, so angry that if he struck her she was going to hit him back.

'I live here,' she said, calmly. 'This is my home. This is one of the rooms in my home, and I'm sitting in it. Do you have a problem with that?'

He stared back at her as if uncertain how to handle this. 'Is this the room you like to fuck him in?'

'What on earth are you talking about?'

'Where were you yesterday, Faith?'

'I told you, I was in London.'

'You fuck him in London?'

'Fuck who? I was shopping – for your birthday. As I told you.'

'In Knightsbridge?'

'Yes. In Harrods, Harvey Nicks, then I went to the General Trading Company.'

He gave her a long, doubting look. 'I've been to Knightsbridge, Faith. I was a houseman at St George's Hospital – the building on Hyde Park Corner that's now the Lanesborough Hotel. I know Knightsbridge well.'

He turned away from her, walked over to a chest of drawers, picked up a wicker basket of pot-pourri that sat on top and sniffed the contents. 'These need replacing, they've lost their scent. You're not running this house very well. Thinking about your lover all the time, are you? I don't want *my* son to be ignored by his mother because she's off with her lover, Faith. Do you understand that? *Do you?*'

'I don't have a lover, Ross.'

He set down the basket, took out a petal and crumbled it in his fingers. 'Helicopters don't fly over Knightsbridge, Faith. They're not allowed to.' He picked up another petal and crumbled that one too.

'Helicopters?'

'When I rang you on the mobile, and you answered, I heard a helicopter. You weren't in Knightsbridge, Faith. Where were you?'

'Is that why you cancelled my credit cards? Because you heard a helicopter?'

'Don't ever think that because you have a mobile I don't know where you are. I checked with Vodaphone. They have cells all over the country, did you know that? I connected to you through their cell in Winchmore Hill in north London. Who were you with, Faith? Dr Oliver Cabot? Is that what you call being a *good mother*?'

She stared back at him, floored. How the hell did he know that?

Suddenly he scooped up a whole fistful of the pot-pourri and walked over to her, his face livid. This wasn't her husband, Ross, this was some demon. The demon said, 'You've lost your scent, too, you fucking whore.'

Then he flung them at her so hard they stung her face, strode out of the room and slammed the door behind him.

29

Faith sat, listening to Ross's footsteps receding down the landing.

Bastard.

She brushed some leaves and petals off her chest and lap, wondering how to respond to his accusations.

And then she thought, Hell, Faith, you are thirty-two years old, you don't have to account to anyone for what you do or where you go, not even to your husband.

But it was easier to think it than say it to his face. There was something about Ross that *scared* her.

Scared of my husband?

Lots of women were. There were stories all the time in the press, of women who had married monsters – and sometimes of men who had married monsters.

She was frightened that sometime Ross was going to go too far during their lovemaking and kill her. Increasingly, in the past few years, he had seemed to get aroused by roughing her up. He was terrifyingly strong, and sometimes when he was fooling around with Alec, swinging him around or wrestling him on the ground, she was certain that he did not realise his own strength.

She stood up, more debris dropping away from her jeans on to the floor, walked across the room and checked her face in a mirror. There was a trickle of blood on her left cheek from a razor-thin cut.

She dabbed the wound with her handkerchief, then dug out a leaf that had lodged in her hair and put it in the waste-paper basket. The floor around the armchair was littered with leaves, petals and strips of dried orange peel. It could stay there. Ross's problem.

How the hell do I explain the helicopter?

She didn't need to. He'd known where she was.

They have cells all over the country, did you know that? I connected to you through their cell in Winchmore Hill in north London. Who were you with, Faith? Dr Oliver Cabot?

The cut hadn't begun to clot yet, blood still trickled and she dabbed it again. *How the hell had he known she was with Oliver Cabot?*

Then it came back to her. Ross in the car after the dinner at the Royal Society of Medicine. The quiet but chilling way he had said it.

I saw you.

Had he put two and two together? The phone company telling him she was speaking from Winchmore Hill, and finding out – or knowing – that Oliver Cabot worked in Winchmore Hill? Was he having her followed? She had learned never to rule out anything with Ross. But asking her if she had been with Oliver Cabot had to have been a guess. All she had to do was deny it, and come up with some other good reason for being there.

Or tell Ross to go to hell.

And that was what she decided now, anger emboldening her. *Go to hell, you bastard.* She stormed across the room and opened the door. *You think you can pull a stunt like cancelling my credit cards and making me look a fool? Well, maybe in a parallel universe there is a Faith Ransome who'll accept that, meekly, without saying a word, but not in this one.*

You're on the wrong planet, Ross.

Alec howled, suddenly, as if he had had a terrible accident.

Faith sprinted down the landing, her stomach clenched. The child was screaming now, with pain and fear. She could see him lying on the flagstones curled up in a bundle, holding his head in his hands.

As she reached the bottom of the stairs he looked up at her, clutching his head, his face contorted. Kneeling down, putting her arms around him, she said, 'Darling, what's happened?'

He just continued the terrible bawling.

'Darling? Please tell me – did you fall down the stairs?'

'D-D-D-D-Daddy hit me.'

And she could see now, the mark below his left eye, the traumatised skin, the bruising.

Her worst nightmare. Ross harming Alec. Ross had often told her how his own father had treated him. And Faith knew from what she had read that those people who were abused by their parents often went on to abuse their own children.

Choking back her fury she checked Alec's head carefully to make sure nothing felt broken, then scooped him up in her arms and carried him through to the kitchen. She sat him down in a chair, then ran over to the freezer, jerked open a tray and pulled out a pack of frozen peas. She wrapped them in a kitchen towel, and pressed the bundle to his face.

He turned away, rejecting it, but she persisted, and slowly he calmed down.

'Why did Daddy hit you, darling?'

'I – I – I –' He began sobbing uncontrollably.

On the kitchen television, Bart Simpson was standing in front of a policeman, getting a severe dressing-down.

'It's bedtime, Mummy'll take you up.'

Near hysterics now. 'No-no-no-no-*nooooooo*.'

She carried him upstairs, screaming and protesting. Talking to him tenderly, trying to soothe him, she ran his bath, undressed him and got him into the water. He stopped crying.

'Tell me what Daddy did, darling.'

He sat in the bath in silence as she soaped him, then rinsed him and dried him.

'Tell me, darling.'

But it was as if a switch had been thrown inside him. She carried him to bed and tucked him up. He lay there, sullen and uncommunicative. Faith found that spooky: she could see Ross so clearly reflected in Alec now, that same sullenness and silence when he was angry or hurt.

She tried reading to him from his favourite book, *Charlie and the Chocolate Factory*, but he turned away with his thumb in his mouth. Finally, exasperated now, she put the book down, kissed him goodnight and turned out the light.

Instantly he began screaming.

She turned on the light again. 'What's the matter, darling? Do you want me to leave the light on?'

He stared at her in silence, with wide, fearful eyes, the left side of his face swollen and puffy.

'Light on?' she repeated. 'Talk to me, darling. Say something, please.'

Suddenly he was whispering something to her.

'I can't hear you, darling.' She stepped closer.

'Please don't let Daddy come in here and hit me again.'

'He won't,' she said. 'I promise.'

She switched off the light, closed the door and stood outside. When she was sure he had settled, she went downstairs to look for Ross.

He was in his study, seated in front of his computer, suit-jacket on the back of his chair, cigar burning in the ash-tray. Tears were rolling down his cheeks.

She went in, closed the door behind her, then stood with her arms folded, a volcanic fury erupting inside her. 'You bastard,' she said. 'How dare you?'

There was no response.

Raising her voice, she shouted, '*You hit my child, you bullying bastard.*'

Still no response.

'I'm giving you ten seconds to tell me why you hit him, or I'm going to call the police,' she said. 'And I'm going to divorce you.'

Without replying, and without turning his head from the screen, he tapped the keyboard. A second later, she heard her voice, crystal clear.

'Hi, Oliver? It's Faith Ransome.'

And then, equally clearly, she heard Oliver Cabot's voice.

'Faith! Hey, this is a surprise, great to hear you! How you doing?'

Ross turned towards her as she heard herself again.

'Fine, thanks. How are you?'

'Doing great. All the better for hearing from you!'

'I – I was wondering – is that offer to show me around your clinic still on?'

'And lunch? I said it was conditional on you letting me buy you lunch.'

Trying to look anywhere but at Ross now, she heard herself laugh warmly, and say, 'Lunch would be great!'

30

It was the silence that got to her. Those moments after Ross switched off the playback and leaned on his desk on his elbow, eyes heavy and red from crying, looking desperately, desperately hurt.

A previous version of herself, the Faith Ransome of a year back, would have reacted differently. She would probably, lamely, have given him a detailed explanation. But right at this moment she wasn't frightened of him. She was as close as she had ever come to attacking him with her bare hands.

'You're taping my calls?'

'With good reason.'

'What the hell gives you the right to think you can do that? Is that why you hit our child, you coward? You hit our child because it was easier than hitting me?'

He stood up violently, sending his chair rolling back across the room on its castors. 'I don't have any problem about hitting you, you bitch.'

'Why did you hit Alec? *How dare you hit him?*'

'You're not fucking doing your job as a mother.'

'Don't swear at me.'

'You're letting him leave his fucking toys all over the place, while you're out fucking your lovers.' He took a menacing stride towards her. 'Someone's going to discipline that child, Faith, and if you haven't time to do it because you're too busy servicing your men friends, fine.' He stabbed his chest with his finger. 'I'm going to do it, and I'll do it my way, in the language he understands. You're too soft with him, he needs some discipline.'

'Discipline? After the things you've said to me about your father?'

Out of the corner of her eye she could see him clenching his fists and braced herself, certain that she was going to be struck.

'Is he a good fuck, this *Doctor* Cabot, Faith? Has he got a big dick? Tell me about his dick. Eight-inch? Ten-inch? Cut or uncut? What do you like him to do with it?' His face was contorted in a sneer. 'Where do you like him to put it, Faith?'

Raising her voice, but keeping calm, she said, 'For God's sake, Ross, he's a *doctor*. I went to see him because he's a *doctor*. In case you've forgotten, I've been feeling like death for the past fortnight. I went to your friend, Jules Ritterman, Dr Essence of Bedside Manner, OK? I went to see him over a week ago, and he patronised me, as he always does, and he's done absolutely nothing since then. I went to see Dr Cabot because I was *desperate*, Ross.'

'What were you desperate for? A fuck?'

'I went to see him because he's a doctor.'

'He's not a doctor, he's a quack. A New Age creep.'

'Actually, he's a doctor of medicine.'

'He's a fucking snake-oil salesman.'

'He's a doctor of medicine who happens to look beyond the horizons of the narrow little boxes most doctors keep themselves in. OK? I may be married to you but you don't own me, and if I want to see a doctor of my choice, I'm going to do that, and if you don't like it, then divorce me.'

Backing off a fraction, he said, in a cracking voice that sounded more hurt than angry, 'Why didn't you discuss it with me?'

'Because you wouldn't have agreed.'

He stared at the Bitch Queen From Hell through a mist of tears. You made me mad. You made me hit the son I adore more than anything in the world, and now you are daring to answer me back.

You made me mad, bitch. You made me so mad I lost my temper with him. See what you are doing to me? Do you see? *Do you see?*

He wanted to hit her, wanted to smash her so damned hard right in the middle of her smug face, punch those lips, stove those teeth in, see how *Dr* Oliver

Cabot would feel having a split-open lip and buckled teeth clamped around his eight-inch dick.

This answering-back was so out of character. Was this coming from *Dr* Oliver Cabot? Was this man poisoning her against him? Faith had never answered him back before. And she wouldn't be answering him back now if she knew the truth about what was wrong with her.

Tommy Pearman had come back to him with a ton of information about Lendt's disease. Twenty per cent of people diagnosed with it were still alive a year after diagnosis. Eighty people died, twenty lived. That eighty were going to die anyway. Negative people. You only died if you wanted to die, you died if you were told you were going to die. Faith was not going to die because no one was going to tell her. She wasn't going to know, therefore she was going to be fine.

Taking a step towards her and changing his tone he said, 'I love you, Faith. I love you more than anything in the world. You know that, don't you?' He put his arms on her shoulders and it hurt him to see her flinch. 'Christ, don't you realise how much I love you? I want to love you, not harm you. I want to make you better and I'm going to make you better. Can't you see that's what I want to do?'

'See what?'

Cold as ice.

He tried to pull her closer to him, to hug her, but she resisted, kept a space like a block of wood wedged between them.

'Do you think I'd have sent you to Jules Ritterman if I didn't believe he's the best doctor in this country?'

'I don't like him and I don't intend seeing him again.'

The way she was staring at him, that look of defiance, as if she believed she was scoring some kind of triumph over him. A triumph like the first spores of cancer in a biopsy. It had to be excised now.

He slapped her cheek so hard she staggered sideways, cracked her head on the corner of a bookcase, flailed with her hands, then went down, sprawling on the carpet, and lay still.

Motionless. Blood dribbling from her lip, staring at him with one glassy, motionless eye, like a fish.

It seemed as if some valve inside him had been wrenched open and his blood was draining out.

'Oh, Christ,' he said, kneeling down. 'Faith. Oh, sweet Jesus. Oh, Christ.'

31

The smell of that first cigarette of the evening always tantalised Ross. He watched his father, in his armchair, in his sharply polished shoes, jacket and carefully knotted tie, *Sporting Life* open on his lap, holding that tiny cigarette in his massive fingers and drawing deeply. The end glowed and, like some fiery caterpillar, ate away a quarter-inch of paper and tobacco, leaving behind a neat cast of ash.

A storm of blue smoke blew around him as he exhaled, then quieted into wispy strands and curls as it drifted out across the room. Ross, reading the *Eagle*, breathed it in. He loved that sweet smell.

His father made a mark on a page with a ballpoint pen and said, 'Three thirty at Chepstow. River Beat. Does River Beat sound like the name of a horse that's going to win a race tomorrow, boy?'

Ross had long learned that the only way to survive his father's unpredictable temper was to steer a middling course, and to try to come up with an open-ended answer to any question. When he had been asked to give opinions previously, if he had been wrong and the horse lost, it would be deducted from his pocket money. But no bonuses had ever been added for the times he had been right.

'How long is the race, Daddy?'

'Two miles.'

'Jumps or flat?'

Joe Ransome gave his son a withering look. 'This is summer, boy. The flat season.'

'How long is a beat on a river?' Ross asked.

Irritably his father said, 'How do I know? Depends on the bloody river. Or else it depends on how big the estate is, or the syndicate, or whatever. How long is a piece of string? Eh?'

'Depends how many strands go into making it.'

'Don't get smart with me, boy.'

Ross returned to his comic. His father drank some beer from his pewter tankard, wiped his mouth with the back of his hand, then gripping the smouldering stub of the cigarette between his lips, concentrated again on the paper.

Suddenly he said, 'It's of no consequence, but your mother's had an accident. They don't know if she'll live.'

She was still alive? Ross glanced up, but his father was looking at the paper again. For three days he had been waiting for news. He'd looked in newspapers in a shop near his school but had seen nothing. There was a local paper, but that was only weekly and it was still another two days before it came out.

For three days he had been afraid every time a car had driven down the street that it was a policeman coming for him.

She was still alive, and he had wanted her dead. It was a terrible anticlimax to learn that she was still alive, that he had failed.

They don't know if she will live. Maybe she won't. 'What happened?'

Unhurriedly, his father removed the cigarette from his mouth and crushed it out in the ash-tray. 'I said it was of no interest.' He turned the page of his paper and began scouring another race field. After some moments he said, 'Fire.'

It took a supreme effort of will for Ross to turn back to Dan Dare and read. He knew from previous experience that his mother was a no-go area with his father. Whenever he had tried to find out about her, his father had gone berserk. After several minutes had passed, Ross looked up. 'What happened to Mummy?'

Joe Ransome lit another cigarette, stuck it in his mouth and squinted at the paper through the smoke. 'God punished her for leaving you.' Then, quietly but even more bitterly, he added, 'And for being a whore.'

'What's a whore?'

His father made another mark on his form. 'A woman who does things with men.'

Ross thought of the naked man in the hall engulfed in flames, and the terrible screams. The man whose naked buttocks had been hammering up and down between his mother's thighs. He hoped this man who had done things with his mother had remained in agony until he had died.

As his father turned the page, he said, 'What kind of fire, Daddy?'

'You're asking too many questions. Do you want to fetch the cane?'

'No, Daddy.'

'Then sod off up to your room.'

The following day, two police officers came to the house. They stayed, talking to his father in the living room, for over an hour. Ross crept up to the door and tried to hear what they were saying, but the voices were too muffled.

32

'Tell me what it feels like when you eat.'

Kylie Spalding was just about as nice a person as any member of the human species he'd yet met, Oliver Cabot reckoned. She was nineteen, with long brown hair and a pre-Raphaelite face that, despite her painfully emaciated body, was simply gorgeous.

She was lying on the wood-framed couch in his office in a roll-neck sweater, jeans and socks, eyes shut, bony hands by her sides. When he'd first met her, just three weeks ago, suffering cardiac arrhythmia and showing early stages of renal failure, she had been close to dying. Now she was close to living again.

'Eat?' Her voice was slurred and slow.

Sitting beside her, he said, in the calm, steady voice he used in hypnotherapy, 'You like bananas, don't you, Kylie?'

A long pause and then, 'Uh.'

Kylie had bulimia, which had been preceded by anorexia nervosa. Her body was depleted in essential minerals, and her teeth were pitted and discoloured by gastric acid. Her parents had brought her here in desperation, and already, after just two sessions, there was improvement – slight, but significant.

'I want you to imagine you're eating a banana, OK? Just hold this banana in your hands and take a real hard look at it. This is some banana, right?' No reaction, and that was fine, she was thinking about it, absorbing it. 'It's in great condition this banana, just how it should be for eating. There's some green streaking on the skin, in the bright yellow. I want you – just go very slowly – I want you to peel off the skin and take a look inside, take a look at the flesh ... It's firm, hard but sweet, you've never seen a banana this good before. Now I want you to put it in your mouth, Kylie, and take a bite.'

She mimed taking a bite.

Her throat constricted then expanded.

'Terrific! Now tell me, how does it feel as you start to eat it?'

She sat bolt upright, her eyes wide, and began to retch into her cupped hands.

He didn't move.

She stared at him, terror in her eyes. After some moments she pulled out her handkerchief and wiped her mouth.

'I – I'm sorry.'

He handed her a glass of water and, his voice unruffled, said, 'Drink a little.'

She drank, gratefully, then he took the glass.

'I'm really sorry.'

'You don't have to be sorry, Kylie. I want you to close your eyes and try again now. I want you to think about the banana. You like bananas, right?'

She nodded, then closed her eyes.

'Now you have a new banana ...' and Oliver continued as before, soothing and relaxing, but his mind drifted away from his patient.

Faith Ransome, you are the most adorable woman I've ever met. My God I could fall in love with you, but you are married. I know you are not happy, but I can't start messing with your marriage. I can try to help you with your health, but I have to stop these thoughts I'm having about you. Somehow I have to put a stop to them.

And it's so damned hard.

'This is great, Kylie, I'm really proud of you. I'm

going to wake you in a few moments and you are going to go home, and when you get home the first thing you are going to do is eat a banana. You understand that?'

'Uh.'

He looked up at the photograph of Jake, and thought about how he and Marcy had felt as they'd watched him slowly slip away from them, and he stared at Kylie Spalding and thought about her parents sitting downstairs in the waiting area right now, thought about the helpless desperation in their faces when they'd first come to him, and thought, Kylie Spalding, there is no way in hell I'm letting you do that to yourself or to your parents. There's no way in hell anyone's going to lose you.

And then he tried not to think it, but the thought just bullied its way into his head anyway. And there's no way, Faith Ransome, that I'm going to lose you, either.

33

He was on his knees, crying, touching her face with his hands. 'Darling? I love you. Darling? Are you OK?'

Ross pressed his face against Faith's, breathed in the smell of her hair, whispered, 'Darling, I love you, oh, my God, I love you.'

Then he reached down, held her slender wrist, feeling for a pulse. The solitary blink told him, yes, she was OK, she went down hard but she was OK, on the floor, not moving, but OK.

This thing she did, this not-moving business, playing possum. Animals played possum to deceive predators, but Faith was doing it to panic him, to make him think he'd hurt her more than he really had. She was doing it to make him think she was dead. Her sad little way of trying to get back at him.

Well, you're not dead, you bitch. When I want you dead, *then* you'll be dead.

He kissed her forehead and she moaned softly.

Cradling her face in his hands now, he whispered, 'I love you, darling. Faith, I love you so much.'

Droplets of blood stained the beige carpet – there was a whole damned pool of blood – and a contact lens lying beside it. 'Hey!' he said. 'Hey, Faith, careful.' He lifted her face a little, dabbed at her lip with his handkerchief, stemming the blood, then saw the gash on the left side of her head, where she must have struck the bookshelf. It was one hell of a gash, he could see raw white bone exposed inside it. Jesus. It needed stitches.

You hit the bookcase, you stupid bitch. Karmic revenge. You fuck Dr Oliver Cabot, then the bookshelf pays you back. Bad karma.

Have to get you off the carpet, you're making a stain.

He dropped the contact lens into his shirt pocket, lifted her on to her feet, then half carried, half dragged her out into the hallway, edging past Rasputin, then took her into the kitchen and propped her in a chair. She was limp, but conscious, not saying anything. That was her style: she often did this after she'd angered him, just stayed motionless, tracking him with her eyes.

You think it bothers me when you do this silence bit, don't you, bitch? Well, I'll let you in on a secret, shall I? It doesn't bother me at all.

He cleaned the wound, then froze it with a local anaesthetic and, with painstaking care, began to suture it. 'You're lucky it's me doing this, darling – this is the kind of gash that could leave you with a nasty scar if it's sewn by some Johnny-come-lately houseman in A and E.'

Carefully he pricked the skin, pressed the needle through. 'Three weeks and there won't be a mark.' He tried to look her in the eye, but each time her pupils

134

swung away, looking anywhere but at him. 'You're probably not appreciating it now,' he said, 'but you will.'

When he had finished, he covered the gash with a strip of flesh-coloured Elastoplast. 'There, all set.'

Still she refused to meet his eye.

Ross put his medical box away in his study, then came back into the kitchen to get water and a cloth to clean up the bloodstains from his carpet. His eye fell on a bone in front of the Aga. 'Rasputin been eating a bone in here?'

She ignored him.

He raised his voice. 'Faith, has the dog been eating a bone in here? In my kitchen?'

Her head was beating some rhythm totally out of synch with the rest of her body. A deep bass thump that sent shock-waves through the core of her skull.

'Faith, I'm talking to you.'

The nausea was back now with a fury. She put her hands on the edges of her chair, gripping with her fingers, scared she was going to overbalance and fall off it.

Ross's voice softened. The anger was replaced with reproach. 'Darling – Faith, darling, you do realise you've put blood on my carpet? I'm going to clean it up for you – would you like me to?'

Her eyes were still averted.

'Faith, I know you can hear me. I'm going to say this to you once,' he said, 'and then I'm not going to say it again. *I'm deeply hurt.* All the years that you've had credit cards, you've never ever *once* thanked me for them. You know that? Not *once*. But the moment I stop them all hell breaks loose. You're like a spoiled child sometimes.'

He went out of the room, ran up the stairs and

opened Alec's bedroom door. He could hear his son sobbing.

Even though the curtains were drawn it was still light in the room. Alec was facing away from him, thumb in mouth. Ross knelt by the bed, put his hand on Alec's shoulder and, to his horror, his son flinched.

'Hey, big guy!' he said softly. 'You didn't tell me if you scored any goals today. Did you?'

Alec continued to sob.

Ross leaned over and kissed his cheek. 'I love you. You've got to learn to be a little tidier, that's all, OK?' Ross bit his lip. This was him and his father all over again. He didn't want it to be that way, did not want Alec to go through the kind of hell he'd been through as a child, had promised himself that he would never let that happen. And yet . . .

A child had to have discipline. A child had to realise there were rules that society lived by, that he couldn't just leave toys strewn all over the place, and that if he did leave a toy car at the foot of the stairs, someone was going to stand on it and take a fall, maybe the kind of fall that could break a bone or even kill them. Alec needed to learn that, and some lessons were painful.

You couldn't make an omelette without breaking eggs.

He stared at his son, then nuzzled his face against Alec's, his tears mixing with his son's, feeling the warmth of his little body. God, you mean so much to me. You'll never, ever have any idea how much. You're my life, Alec, do you know that? You are, you and your mum. You are everything I have in the world, and everything I want.

He kissed Alec once more. 'Goodnight, big guy, I love you.' He left the room with a heavy heart. Tonight he had done his duty, however painful it had been.

A child had to have discipline.

*

Faith stayed put in the chair. When Ross was in these moods he was like a stranger, as if some other person were inside him. In the past she had kept quiet, thinking it would calm him if she didn't answer back, but that didn't work. Now she was standing up to him and that didn't work either.

'I don't smell anything cooking.'

She looked at Ross, who was standing in the kitchen doorway, shirt-sleeves rolled up, sponge and bucket in his hands.

'Food?' he said. 'Dinner? I don't smell any dinner cooking. Why is that, Faith? Can you explain that to me?'

She closed her eyes, and in the giddying darkness behind her eyelids she searched for some place to crawl into. She had planned to tell him there was no dinner because he had cancelled her credit cards and she had not been able to buy food. Her head was hurting so much, and with the disorienting spinning it was all she could do to remain upright and conscious. And then all her emotions burst through the fragile dam that restrained them, and she started sobbing uncontrollably.

Moments later she felt Ross's arms around her, cradling her like a baby, and her mind went back to all those nights, years ago when they had been so much in love, when they had been two spoons in bed together, her naked body held safe and firm by those same arms.

He was nuzzling her now, warm cigar breath on her cheeks. She turned her face sharply away.

'I love you, Faith. You don't know how much I love you.'

Suddenly, through her sobbing, she said, 'You hit Alec and you hit me. What are you? I don't know you any more. I used to be so proud of you, Ross, you taught me so much about everything. You taught me about people, about life, about how to look at things. You taught me how to enjoy good food, you taught me to love wine, how to listen to music. I used to look up to you and think I was the luckiest woman in the world to be married to you.'

She tried to pull free of him, but he held her tightly, gripped her face, forcing her to look at him.

'I'm the luckiest man in the world to be married to you, darling. I love you more than anything on this earth.'

'I hate you,' she said, struggling against him.

'You're the most beautiful thing that ever happened to me, Faith, my darling. I couldn't live without you.'

'I hate you.'

'You taught me the meaning of love, my darling.'

'You've taught me how to hate.'

'I just love you so much.'

She broke free of him, stood up and walked across the kitchen. 'I hate you more than I ever knew it could be possible to hate someone.'

34

'Are you sure you want to know? I ask all my clients this question before I proceed. Are you *absolutely* sure you want to know?'

It was half past eleven on Monday morning. Ross, seated behind his desk in his Harley Street consulting room, said, 'That's why you're here.'

Ross had never met a private investigator before, and Hugh Caven, seated in the armchair normally occupied by his patients, did not fit his mental model at all. A thin, soulful-looking man in his late thirties, dressed in a tired grey suit, Bugs Bunny tie and clapped-out trainers, he sported a number-one close-shave haircut and a gold earring in his left lobe.

It was possible that when he was younger he had been quite striking in a lean, mean, Terence Stamp way, but now his misshapen face, with its broken nose, slack skin and sallow complexion, seemed to be paying him back for years of late nights and substance abuse. He had more the appearance of a has-been rock star than a detective. A man who had suddenly found himself deposited in his own shadow.

Although he did not care for the man's appearance, he was perfect for the job, Ross thought. A chameleon. Sit him on a sofa and he would disappear into the pattern of the upholstery. Yet he had achieved notoriety: Ross had seen his name in the papers only recently. Hired by a suspicious wife, his investigations had caused the resignation of a cabinet minister whom he had photographed frolicking with his bisexual lover. Hugh Caven had been highly recommended by one of the divorce-law partners at Ross's solicitors.

He spoke with an Irish accent, his voice soft but insistent. 'I always say this, Mr Ransome, because some people like the *idea* of finding out but then they have the problem of facing the *reality*. The Bible tells us that the truth shall set us free, but that's not my experience. The truth can shackle you for the rest of your life. I think it's only fair to warn clients of the pain they might face if their suspicions prove true.'

Ross stiffened. 'Look, if I wanted a shrink, I'd have phoned a shrink. I want my wife followed, I don't want a fucking sermon.'

Hugh Caven stood up. 'Then I'm afraid I'm not your man. Been nice talking to you, Mr Ransome.' He ducked down and picked up a nylon laptop bag from the floor.

Ross stood up also, clumsily, in surprise. 'Hey, what do you mean?'

Caven turned to face him and now, for the first time, Ross could see the true toughness of the man.

'Clients hire me, Mr Ransome, because they have a problem. I've seen it all, believe me, I'm talking about *everything*. You want some sleazy gumshoe with a long lens, take a look in the *Yellow Pages*. What you're asking someone to do is to turn your life upside down, your wife's life and, if she does have a lover, her lover's life as well.'

His eyes opened wide and looked even more soulful. '*Three* lives, Mr Ransome. We all have to rub along on this planet together, that's my philosophy. I like everybody to be cool. If you don't want to be cool, I don't need to work for you. It's a fine morning, I'll take the day off, go fishing down the Thames estuary on my boat. I'll be happier and you might be happier too.'

'Look, wait a second – I'm a little confused—'

'I don't think a man of your intelligence needs to be confused, Mr Ransome.' He put the bag back down on the floor. 'It was Charles Darwin who wrote that the highest possible stage in moral culture is when we recognise that we ought to control our thoughts. You're a smart man, you're a pretty good example of survival by natural selection. I'd like you to listen to me, or I'm through that door and on to my boat.' He opened out his hands, palms outwards. 'You tell me.'

Do I want this cocky little shit working for me? Ross wondered.

But if not it would mean finding another agency, starting again. Losing valuable time. He took a deep breath and said, 'I'm listening.'

The private investigator nodded. 'Good, then we're cool. How about we sit down again?'

He pulled his computer out of the bag, settled it on

his thighs and opened the lid. 'I want you to think about the implications very carefully all the time I'm working for you, Mr Ransome. Any time you want out, you call the mobile number I'm going to give you.' He gave Ross a searching look, then busied himself with his computer.

'You seem to have a problem with your conscience,' Ross said.

'I like to sleep at night.'

'I'd like to be able to sleep at night too,' Ross said. 'I'd like to sleep at night without wondering who my bitch wife has been screwing during the day.'

Caven peered at his screen. 'Address that you'd like me to use in communications with you, please.'

Ross gave him the address of his consulting room. 'What's your success rate in cases like this?'

Caven was still typing the address. 'If your wife is having an affair, Mr Ransome, I will find that out for you.'

'How long will it take you?'

Caven raised his hands in the air. 'I can't answer that without more information. Depends how careful she is. Could be a week if I'm lucky, could be a couple of months or more if she's being clever. And it depends how far you want me to go – and how much you're prepared to pay. Do you want just one person, or a full round-the-clock surveillance, nine men, three shifts of three? Are you happy to pay for phone taps? Audio bugging? Stake-outs? Video surveillance? Satellite tracking? There's a whole package of options I can offer you, depending on your budget and your urgency.'

'When can you start?'

'As soon as I have details of both parties, and your retainer, Mr Ransome, I can move as quickly as you want. I can start having the lady watched from this afternoon, if you like.'

'I want photographs,' Ross said. 'Clear photographs

of her and her lover doing whatever it is they do to each other. Blow-ups. You can do that?'

'You're the client, Mr Ransome, you can have as many photographs as you want.'

'It's not quantity, understand? *Quality*. I'm making myself clear?'

'Very clear. Quality. Not a problem. We stand for quality. We're very cool about quality.'

Ross reached down and pulled his cheque-book out of a drawer. 'Money isn't an issue, Mr Caven. I want the best you've got.'

35

At ten to twelve Faith pulled on her coat, stepped off the train at Victoria station and began to walk down the platform, with butterflies in her stomach.

She'd spent an age deciding what to wear and had changed clothes in front of the mirror three times. Finally she had settled on a navy trouser suit, scarlet body, and ankle boots she'd paid an extravagant sum for. But she was glad she'd bought them: they made her feel good every time she wore them. Especially now.

Zipped into an inside pocket in her handbag, and safely switched off, was her old mobile phone. In her hand she carried the tiny brand new Nokia, with its new number, which she had bought earlier this morning with cash from her personal savings account.

When she reached the end of the platform she used her new phone to call Oliver Cabot's mobile number.

'Oliver? I'm here!'

A booming Tannoy announcement almost drowned his reply. She could just hear, 'Make a left – I'm parked outside the Grosvenor Hotel.'

Excitement coursed through her and she had to make a conscious effort to stop herself breaking into a run.

She barged into a large Middle Eastern man lugging a suitcase on wheels and apologised. Then she collided with a backpacker. 'Sorry,' she said, and carried on, threading through the crowds who seemed to be pouring into the station and leaving it at the same time.

Then she was outside in chilly spring air, the smell of petrol fumes, the thunder of buses, the rattle of a taxi, angry blasts of a horn. She hurried past the window of a foreign-exchange stall, a news-vendor, ducked around a gaggle of Japanese students who were blocking the pavement, heard the ting of a bicycle bell and the blare of another horn. Then she saw the navy blue Jeep ahead, flasher winking.

Oliver!

He was standing there, anxiously scanning the crowds, a blur of silver hair, huge smile, black polo-neck, outstretched arms. He seemed even better-looking than the image she had carried in her mind during the past three long days.

'Faith!'

'Hi! I'm sorry, the train was late!' She felt his outstretched arms close around her and they kissed, left cheek then right cheek. Gently, he pushed her back to arm's length, his smile changing to a frown.

'Your face – what happened?'

She'd been rehearsing this, but her delivery came out sounding clumsy. 'Oh – I just, um, tripped on one of my son's toy cars, caught my head on the corner of a wardrobe. It's nothing.'

'Is it hurting?'

'No – it hurt like hell last night after the anaesthetic—' She stopped. She'd already said more than she intended.

'Anaesthetic? You had stitches?'

143

'Just a few.'

'Where? In hospital?'

'No, er, Ross – happened to be around.' Her feigned innocence sounded just that. 'Couldn't really have a better person to do it!'

'No,' he agreed, with a laugh that ran out of steam half-way up his throat.

A traffic warden was approaching. Oliver ushered Faith into the car and started the engine. It felt warm as toast in the Jeep, and as they pulled out into the traffic, she felt snug, safe.

Free.

He turned his head. 'Do you like Thai food?'

She hesitated. Thailand, where she'd recently been with Ross. And from where she had returned with the bug. The choice seemed a lousy omen, but she wasn't going to let it bother her. 'Love it.'

'There's a great little place I go to. One of London's best-kept secrets.'

'My lips are sealed.'

The wipers flicked away a few spots of rain. Classic FM was playing on the radio, Elgar, a rousing, uplifting piece, the kind of music men held in their hearts as they marched towards battle; the kind of music that could make you feel invincible. And she felt joyously, recklessly invincible. Sitting high up in the Jeep someone they knew might easily spot her, and she knew she ought to be worried, but she wasn't. She felt higher than any happy pill could have made her.

Oliver turned right, past the coach station, heading into Belgravia. There was an easy silence between them. She watched the traffic through the windscreen, detached from it by the cocoon of the car and the music.

This felt so good. So damned dangerously good.

Then the dark shadow of Ross's attacks on Alec and her on Thursday evening was stalking her again. She'd had nightmares for the past four nights. There was no question that, however much she tried to play it down in her mind, Ross's behaviour was getting worse. He had never hit Alec or her before.

He'd been full of remorse the next day. On Saturday afternoon after playing golf he'd brought home a massive bunch of flowers for her, and an electric car for Alec, which he could actually sit in and drive. He'd taken her out to dinner on Saturday night. On Sunday he'd made her breakfast in bed, something he'd done maybe twice before in their entire married life. Then he'd taken Alec on a bike ride. After Sunday lunch the three of them had gone out for a long walk, something they used to love doing together but hadn't done for a long time.

But none of it had meant anything to her. She had done her best to get through the weekend without another confrontation, scared that now Ross had finally crossed the Rubicon of violence he might now hit Alec or her again at any time.

'Your husband hit you, didn't he?'

Oliver startled her. Had he been reading her thoughts?

She considered the question carefully, unsure whether she wanted him to know, deeply humiliated. Slowly, she turned towards him and nodded.

36

The newsagent's was busy, filled with kids on their way home from school, buying sweets and cigarettes. No one took any notice of the tall schoolboy standing by the newspapers, browsing the latest edition of the *Streatham Advertiser*, which had come in today.

Ross found what he was looking for on page five. He couldn't have missed it. He had expected to find a couple of lines, but this was almost half a page, with the headline: MAN DIES IN ARSON BLAZE, and a photograph of his mother with the caption, ROSAMUND RANSOME. CRITICAL.

Glancing round to ensure that no one noticed, he scanned the article, then read it through again carefully.

An arsonist was almost certainly responsible for a blaze on Monday night that claimed one life and left another person critical.

Streatham taxi driver Reginald Malcolm Tyler, 24, was rushed to King's College Hospital following a blaze at a first-floor flat in Lackham Road on Monday night, but was pronounced dead on arrival. The flat's tenant, Mrs Rosamund Ransome, 36, a cashier at the Co-op, was transferred to the burns unit at East Grinstead Hospital with 60 per cent burns to her body and face.

Police have refused to confirm reports that a can of petrol was recovered from the blaze scene. DCI David Gaylor of Streatham Police said, 'I am treating this blaze as suspicious and we have opened a murder inquiry on the dead man. We would welcome calls to our incident room from members of the public who saw anything suspicious in the vicinity of Lackham Road on Monday night.'

The police have no leads at present, but DCI Gaylor confirmed they are anxious to interview acquaintances of Mrs Ransome. A neighbour, whose name and address is withheld, said that divorcee Mrs Ransome had a number of men callers.

There was no mention that she had a son. That both relieved and angered him.

The following morning Ross emptied his savings from a small metal box into his jacket pocket. Then, instead of attending school, he took a bus to Clapham Junction railway station, and bought a return ticket to East Grinstead. He only just had enough money.

The events of the past week had depleted his cash reserves. But they had been well worth it.

37

'Do you eat shrimp?'

'Shrimp?'

'They do a terrific shrimp starter.'

'You mean *prawn*?'

'Uh-huh.' Then, mocking, he put on an exaggerated English accent: 'I say, old girl, they do an absolutely ripping line in jolly old *prawns* here, don't you know? Top-hole and all that. Spiffing.'

Faith laughed, and the happiness in her face seemed to Oliver to fill the whole restaurant with light and warmth. He stared at her across the fresh linen, the tall, gleaming glasses and the single-stem vase with a purple orchid. It felt so good to see her pretty face all lit up with laugh lines, those gorgeous, alert blue eyes, the blonde sheen of her hair, her elegant clothes. He wanted to reach out and touch her, to hold her in his arms, hug her tight.

Protect her from her bastard husband.

But she was protecting herself right now, sitting very upright, arms folded, a classic defensive position. He needed to get her out of guarding mode before they could move on. So he began to mirror her, so subtly she would never notice. First, he studied the rhythm of her breathing, and matched it, breath for breath. Within a couple of minutes they were synchronised. Then holding eye-contact, he folded his own arms. Moments later she took a drink of her mineral water, and he did the same, rapport building, setting down the glass exactly when she did.

Leaning forward a little, Faith said, 'So many words in the States are different from ones we use here.'

Oliver leaned forward too, poker-faced, and said, 'You know, I find absolutely the same thing over here.'

After a moment's hesitation she laughed, and Oliver laughed too, not because he was mirroring her now but because her laughter was so damned infectious.

Their waiter came. Oliver encouraged Faith to select the prawns in coconut sauce starter, ordered the same, then changed his order to prawns with spiced mango.

'Have you had the – er, the *shrimp* in coconut?' she asked.

'Uh-huh,' Oliver responded, with deliberately downgraded enthusiasm. 'I think the mango's a little more interesting.'

'I'll have it, too,' she said.

Oliver ordered lemongrass chicken, with a spicy nut salad to follow, and to his secret delight, Faith ordered the same.

When the waiter walked away, Oliver lifted his glass and drank some more water. Faith followed suit. When he set down his glass, he leaned back a little in his chair; seconds later, Faith did too.

Now she was unconsciously mirroring him, which meant he had control and she would be compliant. It was a technique he used on his patients to encourage them to believe that they were making the decisions themselves on courses of treatment. If they believed that the treatment was going to work from the outset, its chances of success were greatly enhanced. Right now he needed Faith to believe in him, to open up to him.

Tapping his forehead above his left eye, he said, 'Tell me more about this.'

Raising her finger and touching the plaster, she looked embarrassed. 'I—' She was interrupted by the waiter presenting a bottle of Sancerre to Oliver for inspection.

He nodded the man away, and she continued, 'I – it – it wasn't deliberate. He didn't mean to—'

'Why are you defending him, Faith?'

'No, it's not that I'm defending him, it just needs to be in context.'

The waiter poured some wine for Oliver to taste, and he saw, to his disappointment Faith folding her arms again.

When the waiter left, Oliver folded his own arms, held the position, then reached out and picked up his glass again. He held it towards her. 'Cheers.'

She raised her glass and chinked it against his. 'Cheers.'

He drank and set his glass down, and now she was mirroring him again. He prompted her: 'You were saying about your husband?'

'He has a lot of good points.'

'You wouldn't have married him if he didn't.'

'Do you believe people can change?'

'Heraclitus said that you can't step into the same river twice.'

'Because we move on?' she suggested.

'I think dumb people don't change, because they're not affected by anything that happens to them, but intelligent people change constantly.'

She nodded. 'And can you change from being a kind, caring person into a monster? A psychopath?'

Oliver shook his head. 'We call them sociopaths. You

are born one, you don't become one. But the smart ones know how to play the game. When you first meet them they are outwardly kind and caring, until they've gotten what they want. Then they don't need their masks any more and their true character emerges.'

He stared at her, and could see the fear in her eyes, the fear that seemed to be ingrained in her. She was too lovely, too decent a person to have to live in fear. Fear was a hideous, corrosive thing.

Your husband's a sociopath, Faith. You may not be ready to admit that yet, but any man who can hit a woman like that is a monster. And you're in danger because he's going to get worse. And one day he might just hit you so hard you won't get up again. And he'll tell the world he cannot imagine what has happened to you. That you just vanished into thin air. He'll appear on television and do a wonderful job of weeping and parading your little son, who's desperate for his mummy to return. And in twenty years' time they'll find what's left of you under a cement patio.

He shuddered, aware that his thoughts were running wild, but this was what he felt.

Faith was giving him a strange look and the colour was draining from her face. She placed both her hands on the table, steadying herself, as if fighting for control. Control of what? Was she having another bout of what she'd had last time?

Alarmed, he said, 'You OK?'

Even whiter now she nodded but did not speak.

The waiter brought over two tiny appetisers on elegant saucers.

'Faith?'

She was shivering, staring wide-eyed at him. Then she got up and ran to the back of the restaurant, through to the washrooms.

When she returned, she was even paler than when she had left the table. 'I'm sorry,' she said.

Her skin looked clammy, like someone having a heart-attack.

'The bug?' he said.

'Yes. It sometimes – comes on so suddenly.'

'You want to lie down?'

'I'll be OK, really.'

'You need air?'

She looked back at him with such an expression of defeat in her face that he felt a chill deep inside him. Was she more sick than she was letting on? *I've only just met you. Don't let me lose you before I've even got to know you.* He said, 'What's really wrong with you, Faith? I don't think you're telling me the whole story.'

She was gripping her glass as if desperate for something to hold on to. In a frightened voice, that was barely even a whisper, she said, 'I don't know, no one will tell me.'

'You're married to a doctor and he won't tell you anything?'

'No.'

'You're going to come back to London tomorrow, Faith, to the clinic, and I'm going to take a good look at you, run some tests of my own, find out what's really going on. OK.' It wasn't a question.

Faith nodded, and the fear in her eyes was replaced with a film of gratitude as watery as January sunlight.

38

At eight thirty the following morning, Ross stood in a corner of the Harley Street operating theatre, face mask dangling below his chin, writing up his notes after the first operation of the day. He'd slept badly last night and the operation had not gone well.

It was the kind of work he enjoyed least. A repair: a skin graft he'd performed a month earlier on the neck of a man badly burned in a chemical plant accident had become infected and failed. Now he'd had to crop a fresh flap of skin from the man's thigh and try again. The failure of the first graft had not been his fault, but he didn't see it that way. In his mind, all failures were his fault.

His failing marriage to Faith was his fault: he gave her too much freedom, too much time alone, too much money. And, in some way he didn't fully understand, he felt her illness was his fault and it was down to him to cure her. All these problems could be dealt with: they had to be taken in hand, the bad bits excised, like the necrotic flesh he'd just excised and replaced. There were always solutions. And now, out of the corner of his eye, he saw his anaesthetist, Tommy Pearman, balding, perspiring, misshapen, sidling up to him.

'Came second in my class on Sunday, did I tell you?'

'Didn't know you went to Sunday school, Tommy,' Ross said.

'Ha bloody ha! In my Bentley.'

'Ah, yes, your Bentley.' Ross had a clear picture in his head of the anaesthetist in his green 1930s Bentley. Once Pearman had turned up for Sunday lunch in it, wearing a leather helmet and goggles, as if he was auditioning for the part of Toad.

'At the hill climb. I told you about that?'

Ross tuned him out while he wrote down an important detail.

Like a child wanting attention, Pearman continued, 'It was at Prescott Hill – home of the Bugatti Owners Club – an open meeting, for all kinds of vintage sports and racing cars.'

'Why didn't you come first, Tommy? You should

always try to come first.'

'I just went for a bit of fun,' the anaesthetist said, defensively.

'Coming *first* is fun,' Ross said, finishing his notes and handing them to the scrub nurse to write up on the computer. 'You shouldn't ever be pleased to come second, Tommy.'

Then he was interrupted by a houseman. 'Mr Ransome, the photographer wants to know if it's for the next operation you need her.'

Ross used photographs for his papers and he put up some of his best operations on his website. 'Mrs Reynauld?' he said. 'She's next – we're going to do quite interesting work on the jawbone. Yes, I do want photographs.' Then he put an arm around the anaesthetist. 'I need a quick word, Tommy,' he said, and propelled him towards the door.

Out in the corridor, Ross said, 'I have to do a talk in Prague in September for the World Confederation of Plastic Surgeons.' Then he dropped his voice as a nurse walked past. 'I'm talking about micro-circulation, and I want to spice it up a little. You're into all the future-technology stuff, as well as your old cars, right?'

The anaesthetist nodded dubiously.

'I want to get nanotechnology into my talk. Do you know anything about it?'

'Miniature robots.'

'That's it. Dig something up for me, will you?'

'I've got more for you on Lendt's disease, all the data on the drug cocktail Moliou-Orelan are using, the phase-two trials results.'

'And?'

'Just over thirty-five per cent survival rate beyond one year of people taking it.'

Ross clutched him excitedly. 'Thirty-five per cent?'

Pearman rolled his eyes affirmatively.

'That's ace news, Tommy!'

'I wouldn't call it that. Sixty-five per cent of people with the disease die within twelve months – eighty per cent if they're not on the drug – and it's not a pleasant way to go. I don't think a thirty-five per cent cure rate is that impressive.'

'It's brilliant, Tommy! There wasn't anything and now there's thirty-five per cent. Thank you.' He left the anaesthetist in the corridor and hurried into his office, closed the door, then rang Jules Ritterman.

'Ross! I was just going to call you!' Ritterman said.

'I just heard some information about the Moliou-Orelan phase-two trials.'

'That's what I was going to call you about. It's not brilliant, but there's some progress.'

'You have to get her on those phase-three trials, Jules, right now. You've just got to pull any strings you can.'

'I'm working on it. But it is only thirty-five per cent,' he cautioned, 'against twenty-five per cent for the placebo. That's only a ten per cent difference. And, as I told you, we'll have no way of knowing whether Faith will be given the drug itself or a placebo, which cuts the odds in half again.'

Ross barely heard the caveat. 'Faith is fit, she's a strong woman, and she has the right mental attitude. Those are the things that count. It's going to work, Jules, I know it.'

39

Report One. Tuesday 17 May. Surveillance Operative HC.

0915 – **Activity.** The subject left Little Scaynes Manor unaccompanied, in dark green Range Rover registration S212 CWV. Subject proceeded to Gatwick

Airport, car park 3, purchased ticket from Gatwick Express ticket office, boarded the 10.00 Gatwick Express train to London Victoria, and sat on her own in the standard section.

At 10.03 subject made brief call from mobile phone to person (presumed from subsequent actions to be Dr Oliver Linden Cabot – home and office addresses at end of report). The following is the transcript of the recording made of the subject's end of the call by directional microphone (DM):

'Hi, how are you? I'm on my way – caught the ten o'clock, should be in Victoria by ten thirty. Can't – sorry, can't –' (connection terminated by train entering tunnel).

At 10.05 subject redialled (presumed to be same number). Transcript continues: 'Sorry about that, we went into a tunnel. This (indecipherable word) is a bad – (15 seconds indecipherable – passing oncoming train) – same place as Friday? Me too . . . 'Bye.'

10.07. Subject's rail ticket examined by inspector. No exchange of words.

10.10. Subject acquired coffee from trolley. Passed rest of journey reading Daily Mail newspaper. No communications or interaction with any other person.

10.32 – Activity. Arrival in Victoria. Subject left train, exited west from west concourse on to Buckingham Palace Road and met with male, mid-forties, American accent, six foot tall, thin build, wavy greying hair, (later tentatively identified from digital images taken compared against his website photographs as Dr Oliver Cabot – final identity to be confirmed. Photograph 1.1 appendixed). Oliver Cabot was waiting in a navy Jeep Cherokee, registration P321 MDF (registered owner, the Cabot Centre for Complementary Medicine). Transcript from directional microphone (DM):

Dr OC: *Faith, hi, great, you made it. Great to see you.*

FR: *And to see you too. You didn't have to come and collect me again.*

Dr OC: *I wanted to. OK?*

FR: (reply inaudible from passing traffic)

Subject and Cabot enter Jeep Cherokee. Cabot in driving seat. Audio signal lost.

10.37 – **Activity.** Jeep Cherokee departed from Buckingham Palace Road. Surveillance maintained by taxi. Jeep Cherokee headed into North London. Journey time 43 minutes. Parked outside the Cabot Centre for Complementary medicines, Chapel Hill, Winchmore Hill, London, NW13 3BD.

11.25 – **Activity.** Subject and Cabot exited Jeep and entered Cabot Centre for Complementary Medicine. Observer unable to get close enough for audio.

11.28 Magnetic tracking transponder secured on underside of Dr OC's Jeep Cherokee.

11.31 Positive voice ID by window scanner microphone on subject and Cabot. Transcription from scanner on first-floor window:

Dr OC: *Glass of water you said? Sparkling?*

FR: *Still.*

Dr OC: *Coming up. OK, let me slip your coat off. Now, I want to start by taking a complete medical history from you. Let's begin with a few basics –* (Voice lost).

40

Oliver sidled across to the wall and peered out furtively through the slats of the blinds. Suddenly he raised a finger to his lips, and walked towards the door, signalling urgently with his eyes.

Faith, puzzled by his behaviour, stood up from the chair in front of his desk, followed him through to his secretary's office and out into the corridor.

He closed the door quietly, then said, 'Is your husband having you followed, Faith?'

Oh, Christ.

She felt a sudden heave of panic inside her as she flashed back to Ross confronting her on Friday night with the recordings of her phone conversations. The possibility *had* occurred to her. 'Why do you ask?'

'A cab trailed us from Victoria – I'm pretty sure it was the same one all the way. I took a detour but the driver followed. Now there's a man in the street, lurking behind my car – he's talking on a mobile phone, keeps looking directly up at my office, angling the antennae towards my window, like he's trying to pick up our conversation.'

A few moments ago she had been feeling safe, here with Oliver. Now she could sense the darkness of Ross closing around her. 'Anything's possible with him,' she said.

Oliver glanced at the plaster above her eyebrow. 'I don't know much about surveillance except what I've read and seen in movies,' he said, 'but I do know there are devices that can pick up sound waves bounced off glass. We'll go to another room where we aren't going to take that risk.'

'What does he look like?'

'He's—'

They were interrupted by a good-looking man in his mid-thirties, in a grey roll-neck sweater and blue blazer. 'Oliver, when you're free I need a few minutes with you – I want to show you the insulin graph.'

'Can it wait till this afternoon?' Oliver asked.

A moment's hesitation, then, 'Sure.'

Introducing them, Oliver said, 'Dr Forester – Faith Ransome. Dr Forester is in charge of hypnotherapy.'

'Nice to meet you,' Faith said, shaking his hand.

'Good to meet you too.'

'Chris,' Oliver said, 'is there anyone in your office right now?'

'No, I have a patient in –' he glanced at his watch '– ten minutes.'

'Can we borrow it?'

Looking surprised, he said, 'Yes – yes, of course.'

Signalling Faith to be silent again, Oliver walked in, then made his way stealthily to the window, edging past a therapy couch to keep out of view of the road below. Then he stopped and pointed towards his Jeep.

Faith followed his finger, but all she could see at first were parked cars. An elderly woman shuffled into view, progressing laboriously along the pavement with two grocery bags. A white van with ladders on the roof flashed past. Then she saw him. A slip of a man with shorn hair, wearing a leather jacket, jeans and trainers, was leaning against a wall, shooting furtive glances up at the clinic. He was holding a mobile phone with a wire trailing to his ear and his lips were moving.

She moved away from the window, and joined Oliver in the corridor. After he had closed the door, he said, 'You haven't seen him before?'

'I don't think so.'

A young woman was clumping on crutches down the corridor towards them.

'Susan, how you doin'?' Oliver greeted her.

She stopped, short of breath. 'OK, I think. The acupuncture's really helping – I just had another session. But I don't like it. It hurts.'

'No gain without pain. Right?' He followed it with the kind of smile that could charm birds out of trees.

'Give me a call when you come for your next appointment – I'd like to take a look at your leg myself and see how it is doing. You seem so much better than when I saw you last. I really mean that.'

Faith followed him up a flight of stairs and along another corridor. 'Do you know all the patients here?'

'I try to see everyone for the first consultation, then decide what treatment would work best. In conventional medicine, most of the time there is just one treatment and you deviate at your peril, risking the wrath of your profession, the insurance companies, malpractice suits, you name it. In the medicine we practice here, every case has different needs. That young woman has a very rare form of rheumatoid-arthritis. Her mother brought her to see me two years ago – she was in a wheelchair and unable to hold a pen. Now she just has problems with one foot. She drives here herself. We've given her her life back.'

'Amazing.'

He stopped outside another door. 'We don't do anything *amazing* here. We only do what the pharmaceutical industry ought to allow conventional medics to do, but doesn't. You have to understand where much of the pharmaceutical industry is coming from. There's no money in curing people with a one-off knockout drug – the development costs are too high. The big bucks are in disease management. The industry likes chronic conditions that don't actually kill you, but keep you in a state of permanent ill heath, on medication and drug-dependent all your life. That's how it can recoup the hundreds of millions of pounds that drugs cost to develop.'

He raised his eyes. 'Our sole interest is to see patients *cured*. That's the reason the pharmaceutical industry does everything in its power to trash what we do. It gets upset when we cure people using techniques that are not patentable, or natural remedies that are freely available.'

She gave him a quizzical smile. 'So why do the big bosses invite you to their dinners?'

'I think they just like to know their enemies.' He knocked, then went in. The windowless room was dark while he groped for a light switch, then twin fluorescents on the ceiling flickered into life. One buzzed loudly.

It was a small consulting room with an array of high-tech equipment and an examination couch. There was a strong smell that Faith always associated with modern offices and hire cars, the anodyne smell of brand-new, synthetic upholstery. It reminded her, suddenly, of the Toyota they'd been driving in Thailand.

They'd been home barely a month but it seemed far longer than that. Now, her recollections of their holiday were more like a television travelogue she had watched, than anything she had experienced. The travelogue showed a tall man with a blonde wife and a small son. The man played with his son and, when he wasn't doing this, he was sitting at the bar, chatting to anyone who happened to be around, the very model of charm itself.

The blonde wife seemed to be struggling a bit. She had been badly sunburned on her shoulders and chest, and had spent several days in the shade reading, alternating between thrillers and one serious book about the psychology of human relationships.

They had taken several trips around the island in a rented Jeep, visiting the monkey forest and a spectacular waterfall. They had gone with their little boy to an aquarium where he had been fascinated by a giant squid and had made bold faces at a hammerhead shark.

They seemed like any other family on holiday, having a good time. It was easy, Faith thought, to give the world the illusion you were happy. All you had to do was to walk along holding hands, and everyone figured you were fine, you were in love, you were having a nice life. Few people knew what went on behind your locked doors. Few people knew that she prayed every night at dinner that Ross would drink too much and fall asleep the moment they went to bed instead of wanting to make love to her.

Oliver tapped the keyboard in front of a computer and the screen woke up. She saw her name appear at the top of a large, blank form.

'OK, let me get a few basics down. I need your date of birth.'

She was feeling queasy again. The nausea she had woken up with and which had stayed with her on the train had gone when she had seen Oliver at Victoria. This queasiness was of a different kind – not the sort born of illness, but the sort born of fear. Fear of the man in the leather jacket down in the street.

She gave him her date of birth.

'Your GP – this Dr Ritterman – gave you a thorough check-up when you went to see him?'

'Well, it seemed pretty thorough.'

'And you're generally in good shape, other than this thing?'

She shrugged. 'I try to keep in reasonable condition – I walk the dog three or four miles every day, swim quite a lot in summer, go to a local gym twice a week and do aerobics – well, before I went away. But Jules Ritterman . . .' she fell silent.

'What about him?' He gestured for her to sit.

'He's never been communicative, and over this thing, nothing at all. I don't know if this is because there's nothing wrong or because there's something seriously wrong that he's keeping from me.'

'Why would he do that?'

She looked up at the thrumming light. 'Because I'm

just Ross's wife – this genetically challenged X-chromosome thing somewhere down the bottom of their mental food chain.' She bit her lip. 'Sorry, I don't mean to rant. It always hacks me off, being patronised.'

'It ought to. That shit is all part of the voodoo of conventional medicine. Like the way doctors always used to write things in Latin so you couldn't read their prescriptions.'

Oliver pulled up a chair close to her, and was silent for some moments, studying her. It was a comfortable feeling. She could smell the subtle, masculine scent of his cologne, could feel the energy coming off him; despite his intellect, there was a quality about him that was pure animal, something muscular and powerful, a lion, or maybe a leopard. He was wearing a quietly fashionable black jacket, black roll-neck jumper, black trousers, Chelsea boots. The colour emphasised the fine bone structure of his face, the alertness of those titanium grey eyes behind his glasses, the silver streaks in his unkempt curls.

And she could see something she had sensed before: the inner toughness of a man who has absolute confidence in what he is doing, and is comfortable in his skin.

Something stirred deep within her: the need for this man that increased with every moment she spent with him.

And she had to stop this, needed to remember why she was here: he might be able to make her better. That was all. She had to be able to say that to Ross, and to look him in the eye while she said it, because there was going to be a mighty confrontation when the private detective reported back.

'Oliver, can I ask you something? I want you to promise you'll be honest with me. You will tell me straight if you find anything wrong with me, however bad it might be?'

'Let's work on the assumption that we're not going to find anything of the magnitude you're worrying about. OK?'

'Now *you're* patronising me!'

He laughed. 'You're right. I apologise. I want you to understand that if we *do* find something bad, whatever that thing is, it's in big trouble, because it's going to have to deal with *me*.' He tapped his chest hard.

She grimaced. 'OK.'

'Whatever we find, we're going to deal with it. I promise you that.'

She believed him.

41

They were kissing. Their faces pressed hard together. Faith and Oliver Cabot. *Dr* Oliver Cabot.

The man had the gall to call himself *Dr*?

Joke.

Tight close-up, taken with a zoom lens, fast film, short depth of field, the small areas of background visible in the frame were just a blur.

Cheek to cheek.

His wife and *Dr* Oliver Cabot. *Intimacy in the fucking street, for God's sake!*

Ross rested the photograph against the wood-rimmed steering wheel of his Aston Martin and turned, simmering, to the private detective in the passenger seat beside him. The man was exuding a stale, unpleasant odour of musty fabric and last night's tobacco.

They were in the west car park of the Queen Victoria Hospital, in East Grinstead, in a courtyard bounded by tired red-brick buildings and a solitary prefab.

Ross always found it hard to believe that this unprepossessing place was where modern plastic surgery had begun. In 1939, this group of buildings that looked like workshops had been turned into a burns unit for fighter pilots and become world famous. They still looked like a collection of workshops today, and maybe that was a good thing, he thought sometimes. Good to remind surgeons that they were craftsmen, nothing more; they might carry the title Mr today as a snob thing to set them above mere doctors, but not so long ago they were mere barbers who did amputations as well as haircuts and shaves. However, he wasn't thinking that today. He was thinking that he wanted to kill the man who was kissing his wife.

'It's a joke,' Ross said. 'This man's a bloody quack. You tell me how this bastard has the gall to call himself a doctor.'

From the computer bag on his lap, Hugh Caven removed a sheet of paper and handed it to Ross. In a non-judgemental tone, he said, 'This is Dr Cabot's curriculum vitae.'

Ross glanced down the sheet.

1976 Grad. Princeton Medical School. Magna cum laude.
1979 Doctorate, Hons, Immunology. Pasteur Institute.
1980–82 Junior Registrar, Oncology, Mount Sinai Hospital, Beverly Hills.
1982–88 Jnr Consult. Oncologist at St John's Hospital, Santa Monica.
1988–90 Doctorate in psychology. California Masters in clinical psychology then specialist training in hypnosis.
1993 Established Cabot Centre for Complementary Medicine, London.

Passing it back dismissively to the detective, Ross said, 'The man's a traitor to his profession.' He focused his attention on Caven's report. 'My wife and this charlatan were together for two hours inside this building, during which you have no idea what they were up to. Then he drove her back to Victoria Station. They could have been screwing for two hours.'

'With respect, Mr Ransome, I don't think so. I believe it was a *bona fide* medical examination. There was nothing improper in their body language when they emerged from the building, nor when they parted at Victoria Station. Nothing at all, in my experience, to suggest anything other than a professional relationship.'

Ross looked at him. '*Professional* relationship? You can go to all the alternative doctors in the world, Mr Caven. You can swallow all the useless homeopathic pills you want, you can have people stick acupuncture needles in you until you look like a hedgehog, you can listen to them telling you how they can cure this or that by pressing their thumbs into the balls of your feet, you can believe whatever you want. I don't have any time for that crap and I won't have truck with the con-artists who peddle it.' He shook his head. 'Do you really want to put your faith in the kind of primitive stuff witch doctors were doling out two thousand years ago? I'll tell you something, Mr Caven. One hundred years ago, if you got acute appendicitis it was almost always terminal – there was nothing anyone could do for you. Now it's little more than a minor inconvenience. The Second World War was the first time in the history of the human race that more soldiers died in hospital from their *wounds*, than from the infections they had picked up while they were being nursed. And do you know why?'

The detective shook his head.

'Penicillin. In the Western world, life expectancy has doubled in the past hundred years for one reason only: the progress of the *science* of medicine. People who turn their noses up at modern medicine make me sick. And I'm not having any Johnny-come-lately quack messing with my wife's health. Do you understand what I'm saying?'

'Very clearly, Mr Ransome.'

Ross stared at the car clock. 'My wife and Dr Oliver Cabot are either currently fucking each other or about to start fucking each other. And I want the photographs. Another gift that our modern world has gained through science.'

42

The boy walked from the station. It was a hot July morning and he stopped on the way to buy himself a Lyons Maid orange ice-lolly. He was licking it as he entered the gates of the hospital, a tall, gangly boy in shorts, Aertex shirt and school blazer with a badge sewn on the breast pocket, carrying a small bunch of flowers. He was looking forward to seeing his mother, the woman who had abandoned him seven years ago because she couldn't put up with him being untidy.

A kind-faced receptionist told him the name of the ward his mother was in. She was a little hesitant, but she looked at the flowers, smiled sadly at him and told him where he could find the ward sister.

There was consternation when he identified himself at the nursing station. A short, rather severe woman with a badge on her lapel, 'Marion Humphreys. Staff Nurse' and a watch on a chain glanced at a younger nurse, then back at Ross. 'You are Mrs Ransome's son?'

Ross nodded. He wore the doleful expression he had been practising in front of the bathroom mirror.

Marion Humphreys took him into a small room with vinyl-covered chairs, sat him down and closed the door behind her.

'Ross?' she said. 'That's your name?'

'Yes.'

'Your mummy's not at all well. She's terribly burned and she's on a lot of medication. I think you might find it upsetting to see her.'

He dropped the ice-lolly stick into a wastepaper basket. 'Is she going to die?'

The woman looked awkward. 'We're doing everything we can to save her, but when you have very bad burns like hers, the lungs get damaged and so do a lot of important organs. We do a lot of our breathing through our skin, and she has very little skin that isn't damaged.'

'Do you think she will die?'

'I don't know, Ross.'

'Will she be badly scarred if she survives?'

The nurse frowned at the question. 'She's in the best place for burns. We have the finest plastic surgeons in the world here. If anyone can make her better, the doctors in this hospital can.'

'You're nice,' Ross said. 'I like you.'

'And you're a nice boy to care so much for your mummy. Have you taken the morning off school?'

'My teacher said I should come.'

'Where's your daddy?'

'He and Mummy don't get on very well.'

'I see.'

'Can we go to her now?'

'Just for a few minutes.'

She took his hand and held it all the way down the corridor and as she opened the door into a small room.

As he went in he noticed a strong smell of chemicals, and an even stronger, sweet smell of cooled grilled meat. He stared down, past a bank of monitoring machines and through a forest of drip lines, at a blackened, hairless head, covered in a glutinous, translucent jelly, protruding from a body almost entirely swathed in white gauze.

For a moment he thought her head was turned away from him towards the far wall because all he could see was a mass of dark blisters, which had to be the back of her scalp, surely.

Then he realised it was her face.

Pads were taped over her eyes. Her lips, through which a breathing tube was inserted, were bubbles the colour of parchment. The only sound for a moment was the steady clunk-puff . . . clunk-puff . . . clunk-puff . . . of the ventilator.

The nurse said, 'Mrs Ransome, your son is here. Ross. He's brought you some flowers.'

There was a strange sound, a rattling moan somewhere deep in her throat, and tiny beads of spittle appeared at one corner of her mouth.

'Beautiful flowers, Mrs Ransome!' The nurse cast a glance at Ross and lowered her voice. 'All her airways have been burned. I don't think she can smell them, I'm afraid. But she understands you're here.'

'She looks very tidy,' he said.

43

OUR NEWS! *At the end of September we moved into a beautiful old house on the river right in the middle of Shrewsbury, only five minutes' walk from the cinema (for Simon) and from Marks and*

*Spencer (for Bridget) and a good pub only two
doors away. We have settled in happily despite the
worst floods for fifty years, which arrived three
weeks after our move – waist deep in water in the
basement, all character-forming stuff!*

Rain was falling steadily outside. At the kitchen table,
Faith sipped camomile tea to try to settle her stomach as
she read the morning post. She was feeling lousy this
morning, her head ached, and her eyes felt raw, as if
there was grit inside her contact lenses. Upstairs, in their
bedroom directly above, she could hear Mrs Fogg
Hoovering. The machine clunked against the skirting-
board and Rasputin, lying on his bean-bag in front of
the Aga, lifted his head and growled at the ceiling. He
was in a grumpy mood because she'd only taken him for
a short walk.

'I know you don't mind the rain, but I do today,' she
said to him. 'Sometimes, just very occasionally, we do
what I want, not what you want.'

The dog looked at her hopefully, eyes bright, pink
tongue out, panting. Then he stood up, trotted out into
the hall and returned moments later with his lead in his
mouth.

Faith laughed weakly. 'No, I'm sorry, boy, I'm not
going out now.'

Ignoring the plaintive bark that followed, she
returned to the chatty circular letter, envious of her
friend's happiness. She and Bridget Nightingale had
been close friends at school, but now, living two
hundred miles apart, they communicated only rarely.
Bridget had gone into nursing, and also married a
doctor, a neurologist, but that was where their similar-
ities ended. Bridget and Simon were happy, they had a
great marriage, lived a normal life. They'd had their

share of ups and downs and tragedies, but they adored each other.

The tone of the letter deepened Faith's sense of failure. Above her the Hoovering stopped and she listened to the rain thudding against the windows. Then the phone rang.

She answered it quickly, her heart lifting, in the hope that it might be Oliver – even though she'd told him only to use her new mobile number. But it was the Aga service engineer, calling to arrange a visit. She stood up and walked across the kitchen to her diary.

Then she sat down again, turned to the next letter and slit open the large, thick envelope. It was information on a nutritionist course at the Open University she had requested, together with an application form. She was glad it had arrived today and not tomorrow, when Ross would have seen it. It would have been something else for him to get angry about – he didn't approve of her doing anything that smacked of independence. He barely even tolerated her charity work.

Next there was another circular letter, this time from the husband of her closest friend, Sammy Harrison, whom she was having lunch with today. John had entered a charity bike ride in Uganda in aid of Children In Need and a sponsorship form was enclosed. She set it to one side to ask Ross how much they should give.

Then, changing her mind, she picked it up again. Sod it, she thought, glancing down the column, looking at the rest of the donations and picking up her pen. *I'm* going to decide.

She rubbed her eyes, then dabbed them with her handkerchief. The clock on the wall said twenty to ten. Friday today. Ross would be home tonight, and Alec was going to stay the weekend on the Isle of Wight with a schoolfriend. She had mixed feelings about that. She was glad that he was going to be distanced from the bad atmosphere between herself and Ross, but she missed Alec when he was away. And it meant she was going to be stuck with Ross on his own. It was a long weekend. Bank Holiday. Three whole days.

She opened the local paper and turned to the back of the property pages, looking at the classifieds for rental properties. The two-bedroom flats started at around eighty pounds a week, and she knew that even in grotty areas of London, they would be far higher than that. She was going to need around ten thousand pounds a year just for rent and food for herself and Alec, and she needed to run a car on top of that, plus all the other costs of living.

Hopefully she could get work in catering, but it would be a struggle on their own. A struggle, yes, but better than this existence.

If Ross would let her go.

And if he wouldn't let her go freely she would run away with Alec. Ross could argue for custody on the grounds of her depression, but now that he had hit both her and Alec no court would allow that.

She could hear Mrs Fogg, in a spare room now. She went up to her room, took out her contact lenses and put them into the solution in their container. When she put them back in, her eyes felt just as raw. It was probably from tiredness because she was barely sleeping, worrying about Ross and about what was wrong with her.

It was now three days since Oliver had examined her, and he'd told her it would take time to get the results from the blood tests. She thought about him constantly. Nothing had happened between them, yet she missed him. Badly, dangerously.

She picked up the cordless phone and, walking

downstairs, dialled Dr Ritterman's number. His secretary answered, her usual cold, defensive voice.

'It's Faith Ransome speaking, I'd like a word with Dr Ritterman, please.'

'You rang yesterday.' The woman made it sound like an accusation.

'I did, and he still hasn't rung me back. I came to see him over a fortnight ago and now I want the results of my tests.'

'Dr Ritterman is very busy. He will be in touch when he has some news.'

'That's not good enough,' Faith said. 'I expect my doctor to return my calls. I'd like to speak to him now, please.'

'I'm afraid he's with a patient and cannot be disturbed. I'll tell him you phoned.'

'Look, I'd—'

But the woman had hung up.

Faith stared furiously at the receiver, on the verge of redialling, when Rasputin raced out into the hall, barking. Moments later the front doorbell rang.

Faith's heart sank. Felice D'Eath stood in the porch in a bright yellow sou'-wester, looking as if she'd just climbed out of a lifeboat. She was clutching an ornate bottle of extra virgin olive oil in one hand, a basket of pot-pourri in the other, and had a large pink teddy bear crammed under her arm. The tailgate of her Mercedes estate was open, piled high with another load of tombola prizes for the NSPCC ball.

'Beastly weather. You were expecting me, weren't you? Ten o'clock, you said?'

Faith had forgotten. As she helped unload the contents of the car, and lugged everything into the upstairs room where they were storing and labelling the prizes, Felice reminded her twice, and then a third time for good measure, that it was less than six months to the ball, and Faith silently wondered where she and Alec would be in six months' time.

She knelt amid a sea of prizes, most of them tat, being the dutiful committee woman, labelling each in turn under the command of Felice, who was reading out the entire list of all five hundred gifts and their donors.

'Christ, I pity anyone who wins this,' Faith said, holding up a prancing china horse with a clock growing out of what appeared to be a tumour in the side of its stomach. 'Who on earth donated it?'

'I did.'

Faith felt her face burning with embarrassment.

'My first husband gave it to me – I've never been able to stand it.'

Smiling with relief, Faith said, 'I didn't know you were married before.'

'I got rid of him ten years ago. Best thing I ever did.'

'Tell me more, Felice,' she said eagerly. Suddenly the woman was interesting.

With her wet-weather kit removed, in a jumper and baggy black trousers, the other woman looked small and vulnerable. But her expression was tough and proud. 'Jonathan was a bully, and one day I decided life was too short and I wasn't going to put up with him any more. I packed, collected the children from school and left home with them while he was away at work.'

'And?'

'He came after me, made my life hell for a couple of years, poisoned the children against me, beat up my boyfriend. But,' she shrugged, 'in the end it was worth it. Sometimes in life you have to stand up for yourself. You're lucky if you have a good marriage. You and Ross seem happy together.'

Faith smiled thinly. 'I suppose I should be grateful for small mercies. At least he never bought me one of these.'

44

Ross came through the front door with a huge smile. He barely acknowledged Rasputin's greeting, just scooped Faith into his arms and held her tightly. 'Faith,' he said. 'My darling. My *darling*.'

Faith wondered if he had been drinking, but there was no smell of liquor on him, just the faintest antiseptic redolence of operating theatres.

'God I missed you,' he murmured. 'I love you so much, Faith. I want to stop staying up in London, we shouldn't be apart so much. I miss you terribly. Do you miss me?'

A hesitation in her voice too faint for him to notice. 'Of course I do.'

Rasputin, upgrading his efforts at getting attention from his master, launched a volley of deafening barks.

'Of course? Only *of course*? Don't you miss me terribly, wildly, every second of the day?'

Uncertain where this was leading, she said, 'You know I do.'

He kissed her again. 'Do I? How do I? You don't ring me to tell me how much you're missing me. You used to – do you remember? – when we were first married?'

Tiptoeing through a minefield, knowing his mood could swing at any moment, she eased his coat off his shoulders, and said, 'You don't like me calling you at work – you always sound so annoyed when I do, these days.' Then she walked to the cloakroom and hung up the coat. When she came out, Ross was sifting through his post on the hall table.

Casually he said, 'I fixed that problem with your credit cards. They should all be OK now.'

'They are.'

'You booked the tickets?'

'Yes.'

'*Life Is Beautiful*?'

'You said you wanted to see it.'

They had missed it on previous occasions when it had shown. Now it was on for tonight only at an art-house cinema in Brighton.

'Where's Alec?' he said casually.

'Gone to the Isle of Wight for the weekend with the Caiborns.'

His face fell. 'That was this weekend?'

'Yes.'

'I'm not going to see him? At all?'

'He'll be back early next week.'

'I don't remember agreeing this.'

'We discussed it,' she said.

'I'd never have agreed to it. I don't see enough of him as it is – I mean, I don't mind if he goes out for a day or something, but a whole *long* weekend? I miss him – don't you understand that? I *really* miss him.'

'I miss him too.'

He slipped his arms around her waist and nuzzled her neck. 'At least I have you to myself for the whole weekend. You know something? I fancy you even more now than I did twelve years ago – that's got to be a good sign, hasn't it?'

She felt only revulsion for him, wanted to push him away, but she squeezed him back. She could feel his hardness pressing against her, and could see the signal in his eyes. 'We have to leave in a minute,' she said. 'The film starts at eight.'

'I need a quick drink.'

'I'll get it for you,' she said, relieved to have an excuse to ease herself away from him. 'Are you going to change?'

'Yes.'

But instead of going upstairs he followed her into the

kitchen, and leaned against a pine dresser, loosening his tie and unbuttoning his collar. 'We don't have to see the film, if you don't want to.'

'I do want to, very much.'

'We could have dinner somewhere instead.'

'I've paid for the tickets. We agreed we'd eat afterwards.' Faith took a crystal tumbler from the display cabinet, held it against the spigot on the fridge and pressed hard. Several ice cubes were ejected into the glass.

Then she walked across to the cabinet where she kept the whisky bottle in permanent readiness. Ross was now peering intently at the framed photographs ranged along the pine shelves between the willow-pattern china. He picked up one that sat between the gravy-boat and the teapot. It was of the two of them skiing in Zermatt, with the majestic peak of the Matterhorn towering behind them. 'I can remember this photograph being taken,' he said. 'It was our second wedding anniversary. It was freezing up there and you tried taking your bobble hat off but the wind hurt your ears. Do you remember?'

She poured three fingers of whisky. 'Yes.'

He picked up another photograph. 'Mount Vesuvius! I put the camera on a rock with the timer and you said all we'd get was a photo of our feet. Remember?' There was a look of childlike joy on his face.

Handing him his glass, she said, 'I remember we climbed all the way up, and when we got to the top we saw there was a chairlift on the other side.'

He picked up a photograph of Alec sitting on a lawn, hugging Rasputin, and studied it. 'I love you, Faith,' he said, then took a sip of his drink. 'You don't have any idea how much I love you.'

The show of affection was puzzling her. It was unusual for him to be this loving without having been angry first, and she was not sure how to respond. She said nothing.

'How much do you think?' he insisted.

'I don't know. Tell me.'

He drained half the whisky in one gulp, replaced the photograph on the shelf and leaned back against the work-surface. 'To the end of the universe and back – that much.'

He was scaring her. His mouth was smiling, but there was darkness in his eyes.

'Just this universe?' she teased.

Suddenly, as if a switch had been pulled inside him, he seemed barely to hear her. He rotated his tumbler thoughtfully. 'Oh, by the way,' there was a forced casualness in his voice, 'I spoke to Jules Ritterman today. He apologised for not being in touch – some hiccup in the lab. They got some of your samples mixed with someone else's and it took them a while to unravel it.'

'I rang him, too. His secretary hung up on me. I want a new doctor, Ross.'

He continued to stare at his glass. 'No, he's a good man.'

'Ross, I'm not having my doctor's secretary hang up on me.'

'I'll talk to him about her.'

'No, Ross, I'm sorry, it's not about him talking to her. I'm going to find myself a doctor I'm comfortable with.'

'So, anyway,' he continued, as if he hadn't heard her, 'there's nothing to worry about. You do have a bug – one of those tourist things, the locals aren't affected by it, but our western immune systems are susceptible. It's the same thing if these people come over here – they get bugs that we don't because our bodies are used to them.'

'How do I get rid of it?'

He dug his right hand into his jacket pocket and pulled out a small cylindrical container, which he handed to her. On the exterior was printed in green letters on a white ground, 'Moliou-Orelan (UK) plc. NOT FOR SALE. PHS. 2', then several rows of numbers and letters.

Smiling encouragingly he said, 'Brand new antibiotic – Jules managed to wangle some for me. Guaranteed to nuke any tummy-bug. You take two three times a day with food.'

There was an eagerness in Ross's voice that felt wrong to Faith.

'Isn't it better to take some established antibiotic? I'm not sure I like the idea of taking something new – what about side effects?'

'The ones I gave you last week are an established antibiotic and they've had no effect,' Ross replied. 'Moliou are a great company, good people, lot of integrity, I have total confidence in them. The problem with existing antibiotics is that we've all taken so many of them, they're losing their efficacy and bugs are getting more resistant to them. These are what you need, trust me.'

She unscrewed the lid, pulled out the cotton wadding, then tipped two tiny grey capsules into her palm. Each had a row of numbers printed in bright blue, too small to read.

'Take them with you,' Ross urged. 'Swallow them in the restaurant before we eat. We're going for a Chinese after the film, right?'

'Or a curry, if you prefer.'

'No, you prefer Chinese. We'll go to the China Garden, have their special starter assortment, yes?'

'Great.'

'And after that some crispy duck with pancakes. You love crispy duck, don't you?'

'I didn't think you cared for it.'

'No, I love it!'

He was acting very strangely, she thought. Was he worrying about his behaviour last Friday when he'd struck her? Contrite about it? Or scared? There was nothing he could have picked up from any phone bugging this week – she had been careful to say nothing at all over the phones at home, and her new mobile was now switched off and safely hidden in the cellar. At any moment she was expecting him to start quizzing her about her visit to Oliver Cabot's clinic.

But he said nothing about it, not a word. He was meek as a lamb.

All weekend.

45

Three days was the longest Faith had ever been apart from Alec, and by Tuesday morning, she was missing him dreadfully. They'd spoken every day: Alec was having the time of his life, gabbling breathlessly about multi-coloured sands at Alum Bay, and seeing needles that weren't really needles at all but rocks called The Needles.

From their bedroom window, she watched Ross's car disappear down the drive, her emotions in turmoil. In the hall, Rasputin was barking furiously, the way he always did when his master left the house.

'Quiet!' she yelled.

In the bathroom the radio chattered, but she wasn't listening, her mind was elsewhere. Tightening the belt of her dressing-gown, she went downstairs, her slippers slapping across the flagstones of the cold hall, and into the warmth of the kitchen.

Her breakfast place was laid on the table, the two capsules on the side plate so she wouldn't forget them, not that they'd made much of a difference so far. The bouts of nausea had continued to come and go over the weekend, and she was having a minor one now.

She went down the brick steps to the cellar, switched on the lights and walked past the racks of wines to the far end where the chest freezer sat. Reaching into the space between it and the wall, she retrieved her mobile phone and carried it upstairs.

Rasputin padded into the room, snuffled around, then picked a rubber bone off his bean-bag and began worrying it. Faith yawned. The clock said 5.50.

She switched on the phone. There were three new messages.

Only one person knew the number.

'Faith, it's Oliver, seven thirty Friday evening, sorry I didn't get back to you sooner – I had to wait on some of the tests. Give me a call as soon as you can. I'll be on my home number or my cellphone all weekend.'

'Hi, Faith, Oliver again. Saturday morning. I'm going to be tied up with patients until noon. I'll be on my cellphone the rest of the day.'

There was anxiety in his voice, which worried her, and which seemed to increase with each message. In the final one there was distinct urgency.

'Faith, it's Oliver, Sunday, eleven. I really need to talk to you about the tests as soon as possible. Appreciate it may not be easy for you to call. If for any reason you get through to my voice-mail, leave a message where I can call you back.'

Faith waited until eight before she tried his home number. There was no answer. She tried him on his mobile and left a message for him.

At nine, Oliver rang her back. At ten, she was on a train to London.

46

At ten, the Boeing 737 touched down at Malaga airport in Spain. Ross, carrying his leather briefcase, squinted against the brightness as he stepped out into the humid, kerosene-drenched sunlight.

He followed the other passengers down the gangway and into the bus. Ten minutes later, still carrying only his briefcase, he walked out through the customs area into the din of the arrivals hall, and scanned the sea of jostling placards. KUONI. THOMAS COOK. M. A. BANOUN. DR PETER DEAN. AVIS. DAVID ROYSTON. Then he saw the rather shabby rectangle of cardboard. SNR ROSS RANSOME.

The man looked like a pimp and spoke no English. He insisted on taking Ross's briefcase, then led him outside to a spotless white Mercedes with a chauffeur behind the wheel.

The pimp opened the rear door for Ross, handed him back his briefcase, then climbed into the front passenger seat. The leather interior of the car reeked of cigar smoke and the temperature felt below zero.

In broken English the driver greeted him. 'You have good flight, Señor Ransome?'

Pulling on his seatbelt Ross said, 'Thank you, it was fine.' He opened his briefcase, removed his mobile phone and the copy of the *British Journal of Plastic Surgery*, which he hadn't finished reading on the plane, then his sunglasses which he slid into the top pocket of his jacket. Addressing both men he said, 'How is *il capitano*?'

The driver, easing the car away from the kerb, turned his head with a broad smile, parading an erratic mouthful of gold. 'Señor Milward? Señor Milward very well.'

'Good.'

Ross dialled his secretary. She had no idea he was in Spain and he did not enlighten her. She knew only that he was taking this Tuesday off as part of the long weekend. He did not want anyone knowing he was here.

As they left the airport behind and wound up the fast road into the hills above, Ross barely glanced at the views across the dry, scrubby landscape down towards the Mediterranean as he concentrated on going through his appointments for the following three days with Lucinda. On Thursday, she told him, he had the corrective operation on Lady Geraldine Reynes-Rayleigh. And, she added, she had opened a letter this morning from the woman's solicitor putting him on notice that their client was dissatisfied with his work, was inconvenienced by having to have further surgery and would be seeking compensation.

When he finished the call, he pulled out his Mac PowerBook, made several notes on it, then concentrated on his reading, trying to put aside his anger towards Lady Geraldine Reynes-Raleigh.

An hour later, when he next glanced out, they were crawling in heavy traffic past a parade of smart shops. He looked at a Bang and Olufsen display in a window. A few minutes later, they pulled up on the quayside of the Puerto Banus yacht basin.

Ross felt a tightening of anxiety in his chest. The chauffeur turned, gave him another glinty smile and said, 'Just a short walk, Señor Ransome. Two hundred metres.'

47

The taxi made a right turn off Notting Hill Gate. Faith looked out of the rear window to see if any other vehicle followed them. Nothing did. Then, after a short distance, the taxi made a left into Ladbroke Avenue. Again she peered through the rear window. When she turned back she saw the cabby's eyes watching her in his mirror.

She glanced at her Rolex: it was twenty-five past eleven. To save her the trek across London to his clinic, Oliver had suggested they meet at his home – he had a patient at the clinic at nine thirty whom he had to see himself, and he would drive across after that.

She swallowed nervously, scared by the urgency in Oliver's voice.

Faith, I have the results back from your tests. I need to see you.

What the hell did they show?

The taxi slowed, then halted outside number thirty-seven. Faith climbed out, paid the driver and tipped him, then stood on the pavement as he drove off, looking warily around her. It was a fine morning, and the sky was cloudless. She was wearing a blue blazer, jeans and boots, and already wished she had on lighter trousers and shoes.

Suddenly she shivered. There had been something about the tone of his voice. Something not good at all.

Ladbroke Avenue was a grand residential street, wide and quiet and lined both sides with plane trees in full leaf. Behind them rose imposing terraced houses, with columned porticoes and tall sash windows. The multiple entryphone panels showed that, like most London homes of this size, they had now been carved up into flats or bedsits. The quality of the cars parked along the street showed that they were still occupied by money: Mercedes, BMWs, Audis, Porsches and assorted off-roaders. No sign of Oliver's jeep. Maybe he had a space at the rear. A Jaguar rolled past, then a people-carrier, then a flatbed truck loaded with scaffolding, followed by two crash-helmeted riders on mopeds with clip-boards on the handlebars – apprentice cabbies doing the Knowledge.

She checked both directions for any sign of the man in the leather jacket she had seen outside the clinic last week, or for anyone else who might be watching her. Then she walked up the steps to the columned porch, glanced around once more, scanned the list of names and found Oliver's.

Moments later a voice crackled over the intercom. His American accent sounded more pronounced than usual. 'Hallo?'

'It's Faith,' she said.

'Come right up – top floor, no elevator, I'm afraid.' There was a buzz then a sharp click, and she pushed the door. Nothing happened. The buzzing continued and she pushed again until it yielded and she stumbled into a narrow, gloomy hall, with bare floorboards and tired paint.

She walked past a row of mail-boxes, a mountain bike propped against the wall, and a large box with a DHL delivery note taped to it, then began climbing the stairs, her boots clumping loudly on the bare treads.

When she reached the third floor, she heard a door open above her.

A chirpy English voice said, 'I've checked all the sensors. The one in the bedroom was definitely on the blink and I've replaced it – no charge for that, it's still under warranty.'

Then Oliver's voice. 'Thanks, appreciate it.'

She heard footsteps, then a man in his mid-thirties,

wearing a blue tunic with Languard Alarms sewn on the breast pocket, and carrying a tool-box, crossed her on the stairs.

She was breathless, which surprised her. Before Thailand she'd considered herself reasonably fit. And in Thailand, she'd swum fifty lengths of the pool every day.

Why am I breathless? A month of no exercise? That all it takes?

'Faith?'

She stared back at him, puzzled. It was Oliver Cabot, and yet it wasn't Oliver Cabot at all. He was wearing a green sweatshirt over a t-shirt, baggy blue jeans and trainers. The same build, the same features, the same hair colour, and almost the same voice. But this man looked a good five years older, and there were subtle changes in his features. He wasn't so good-looking, he—

Stretching out a hand, he shook hers with a firm grip. 'I'm Harvey, Oliver's brother.'

Surprised, she said, 'Oh, hi. I'm sorry, I didn't know Oliver had a brother.'

He grinned. 'I guess if I had a brother like me, I wouldn't go around bragging about it either.'

She laughed as he ushered her in and closed the door. 'He just called, the traffic was bad, he'll be right here. Can I fix you something to drink?'

She barely heard him. She was staring around in awe. 'Some tea, please. This is incredible!'

'It's kind of a neat place,' he said.

It was vast. Like something out of a lifestyle television commercial. A loft apartment that seemed to stretch far away into the distance, finishing in a fine metal staircase that rose gracefully up to a crescent-shaped mezzanine sitting area. The ceiling was a good thirty feet high, girdered with raw oak beams. Picture windows looked out across miles of rooftops. A polished wood floor covered with Persian rugs ran the length of the apartment, and the place was richly but sparely furnished with stunning Oriental pieces. There was a fine Chinese screen, a black lacquer dining table and chairs, an ornate fireplace set amid rows of bookshelves, several tall jardinières, and some massive sculptures of what looked like Indonesian gods. Tapestries, mirrors and abstract paintings hung on the walls, and every hard edge was softened by a flourishing plant. Exotic fish swam slowly in a handsome tank.

Faith was entranced by the atmosphere. 'So much space and light! You both live here?'

He sounded almost apologetic. 'I'm just on a visit right now – I live in the States, North Carolina. Ever been there?'

'Not to North Carolina. I've been to New York, Washington and Florida.'

'It's beautiful. I'm an hour's drive from the Blue Ridge mountains. Great place to live. Different pace from London, but London's a great city, don't you think?'

They went into a starkly modern kitchen. He filled the kettle. In the same laconic voice as Oliver he said, 'Guess you're pretty brave, letting an American make you tea.'

Smiling she asked, 'Are you over on holiday?'

'Work and holiday mixed.' He ducked down and produced a tin of biscuits. 'Cookies?'

'I'm fine, thanks. What work do you do?'

'Research. Quantum physics. I'm over to give a paper at a seminar in Switzerland next week, and I'm grabbing a few days' vacation in London either side, hanging out with my kid brother.'

It was strange watching him move, and listening to him speak, because there was so much of Oliver in him.

Little gestures, expressions, the way his eyes widened as he talked, the way his hands moved, even the articulation of his lean frame. And then, behind her, she heard Oliver.

'Hey, I'm sorry, the traffic!'

She turned, and he was standing in the kitchen doorway.

'Faith, good to see you.'

And it was good to see him, too. He was looking smart, wearing a jacket and tie, chocolate brown chinos and brown suede loafers. It was the first time she'd seen him in a tie and she liked the serious, authoritative air it gave him.

As he smiled, she could see the shadow of worry in his eyes. They kissed, each cheek in turn, Oliver holding her tenderly but firmly. But she sensed a distance and her fear deepened.

'My bro taking good care of you?'

'He's making me very welcome.'

Harvey raised a hand in the air. 'I'm outta here – going to check out your Royal Academy and the Tate and the Wallace Collection. Oh, the alarm guy came, said he found the problem and fixed it. One of the sensors was toast.'

'Good,' Oliver replied. 'Thanks.'

'No problem.' Then, putting on the same jokey Oxford accent Faith had heard Oliver use, his brother said, 'And old bean, who's to know – might even get invited to join your jolly old Queen for a spot of tiffin.'

Faith laughed.

'Nice meeting you, Faith. See you again.' He pumped her hand, then turned back to Oliver. 'What time is the theatre tonight?'

'Seven forty-five,' Oliver said.

'Great!' And he was gone.

For a moment Faith and Oliver stood still, smiling at each other.

'Nice guy,' she said.

'He is,' Oliver replied, with feeling. 'Got a terrific wife and three great kids – they're in school right now which is why she isn't with him.' He looked at her for a moment. 'How have you been feeling since I saw you?'

'Up and down. The attacks come and go.'

'Any change in their frequency?'

She nodded. 'They're getting more frequent – and stronger.'

The kettle rumbled, steam belched from its spout, then it clicked off. 'Tea?'

'Thanks.'

He unscrewed the lid of a glass jar. 'Clear or with milk?'

'With milk.'

He pulled out two tea-bags. 'I have triple glazing here – I don't like noise. I checked with a scientist friend who knows about radio signals, and just in case our friend from last week is lurking around, he won't be able to hear us through it.'

'I wasn't followed,' she said.

He looked at her again, and she could see that the worry in his eyes was more pronounced. Suddenly she felt uncomfortable, and walked back into the vast living area, in need of its calming space.

She went across to a row of bookshelves and looked at some of the tomes. *Organic Psychiatry* William Alwyn Lishman. *Risk and Probability*, Dr David Veale. *The Social Transformation of American Medicine*, Dr Zara Cholimsky. *Health and the Human Circadian Cycle*, Dr Oliver Cabot.

She pulled it out, turned it over and looked at the photograph on the jacket. A small square black-and-white of Oliver looking serious. It wasn't a good photograph, she decided. It captured none of the essence of the man, none of the passion for life he exuded. She opened the book and glanced at the table of contents, but she was too nervous to read. Her eyes skittered over the words.

Oliver came out of the kitchen carrying the two mugs, and they sat in deep sofas, looking out across the west London skyline. Oliver hunched forward, watched Faith intently. She cradled her hot mug in trembling hands and, trying to ease the tension, said, 'So, tell me, how many hours have I left to live?'

A thin smile, then he looked deadly serious again. 'Plenty, Faith. But the news from your tests isn't good and we have to deal with that.'

Some of the light seemed to drain from the room, as if it had suddenly clouded over outside. 'Wh-what did they show, the tests?'

'Did Dr Ritterman tell you *anything*?'

'No. After I rang again on Friday and gave his secretary a rocket, he phoned Ross, told him I have some bug, a tourist thing, and he's given me some antibiotics.'

'You have them with you?'

She opened her handbag and passed the Moliou-Orelan container to him. He read the exterior wording. 'Dr Ritterman provided these?'

'Yes – via Ross.'

He shook out one pill into his palm. 'What are your instructions?'

'I have to take two three times a day.'

'Faith, what did Ross tell you these were?'

Disturbed by his tone, she said, 'A new antibiotic.' Hot tea slopped over the edge of her mug and on to her hand, and she put the mug down on a mat. 'Do you know about them?'

'I know Moliou-Orelan, sure, but this is a new drug

that's not on the market yet – it doesn't even have a brand name, only a code. Did he say anything to you about taking part in a clinical trial?'

'No.'

Oliver examined the pill for a few moments. 'Have you ever heard Ross mention something called Lendt's disease?'

'I don't think so, no. What is it?'

'You have it, Faith. I wish to God you didn't, but you do.'

She searched his face for comfort, and for the first time felt none. Outside, somewhere beyond the tranquillity of this room, a siren howled. And deep in her heart, a siren howled also and she shuddered with the vibrations. 'What is Lendt's disease, Oliver? I want to know everything. Please tell me the truth. Tell me everything you know.'

Slowly, and in as positive a light as he could frame it, he told her.

48

The pimp opened Ross's door, relieved him of his briefcase, and pointed a warning finger at a bollard that was hazardously close to the Mercedes. He stepped out of the air-conditioning on to the quayside of Puerto Banus, into bleaching sunlight and a salty breeze tarred with the smells of rope and marine paint. Ross had been here once before about fifteen years back, on a men's golfing weekend and hadn't cared for the place then. It used to have a reputation for housing British villains – taking advantage of Spain's lax extradition laws – as well as a few ageing dregs from the Third Reich eking out the last of their looted gains. It seemed smarter now.

A gull circled above the boulder breakwater of the

harbour mole, soared for a few moments, then began to tack lazily westward.

Putting on his sunglasses, he looked around. The whole port reeked of money. Flash boats lined the pontoons. Young blondes lined their sundecks. Paunchy middle-aged men dressed in shorts and yachting caps strutted around their bridges, holding beer cans and cellphones.

The riff-raff were kept at bay by security guards, permitted only to watch from the seamless row of bustling bars, cafés and restaurants lining the waterfront. A two-million-pound Sunseeker motor yacht was capturing the attention at this moment. Holidaymakers watched her nosing out towards the harbour mouth, listening to the bellow of her engines as enraptured as if they were listening to an orchestra.

It was the morning exodus. Cast-off time. A chain-gang of Filipinos were loading cool boxes on to a gin-palace. A wooden Riva reversed erratically from a pontoon, engine revving too hard, the skipper making a pig's ear of it, sweating profusely and shouting instructions at his blonde companion who was waving a boat-hook like a demented lion-tamer at other boats in her attempts to fend them off.

Ross followed his escort past a security guard, and along a pontoon where the largest yachts of all were berthed. It was quiet here; just the clattering of slack halyards, the flapping of ensigns and the faint beat of music coming from the interior of one floating villa.

The pimp stopped at the gangway of a boat that seemed more like a liner than a yacht. The name *Soozie-B-too* was emblazoned in gold copperplate capitals on her rounded stern, and beneath, in slightly smaller lettering, was the name of the flag of convenience under which she was registered, *Panama*. Ross, who knew a fair bit about boats, priced this extravaganza well north of fifteen million pounds.

Two flunkeys in dark suits and designer sunglasses materialised from the aft saloon, and eyed Ross as he followed the pimp up the red carpeted gangway, past a small red and white sign showing a pair of stiletto heels crossed out, and on to the teak decking.

Ross pocketed his sunglasses as he entered the saloon, which was dimly lit and vulgarly plush: white leather furniture, deep white carpet, gilded mirrors and a curved bar covered in animal hide in one corner. There was a strong smell of cigar smoke, and Ross, his eyes adjusting quickly to the gloom, could make out its source, the instantly recognisable, short, stocky figure of Ronnie Milward.

He was lounging on a sofa near the bar, wearing a dark polo shirt buttoned to the top, white trousers, crisp plimsolls, and sunglasses the size of patio doors. A smouldering stogie was clamped between his lips and he was in deep concentration, playing an electronic game on the glass table in front of him. A tall tumbler containing ice and the remnants of a pink drink sat next to the ash-tray.

Ronnie Milward was in his late sixties, but with his sleek, tanned face, which reminded people of the late shipping tycoon Aristotle Onassis, and his hair dyed black, with only flecks of silver showing stylishly at the temples, he passed easily for a man in his mid-fifties.

Without looking up as Ross approached, Ronnie Milward said, in his coarse east London accent, 'You ever play bridge, Ross? I'm trying to learn. Everybody's playing it these days. You want friends, you gotter play bridge.' A thin curl of smoke rose from the cigar as he pressed one key, then another. 'Good for the brain cells. That's what I need now, new brain cells. You gimme everything else, Ross, but you din't give me what I really need, you see. Fresh grey stuff. Maybe a fresh dick, too.'

'I can give you one of those.'

Milward pressed another key. 'Fuck it, you broke me rhythm.'

Ross studied the man's face with interest. Five years, almost exactly. It was wearing well. Milward switched off the machine, stood to his full height of four feet, eleven inches and seized Ross's hand with a grip of steel that belied his size. Then he swung his arms around Ross's midriff and gave him a huge bear-hug. 'Hey, hey, hey! Good to see you, Ross, boy!'

Hugging him back, Ross said, 'Good to see you too, Captain.'

Milward gazed at him. 'Yeah, you look all right. Done some surgery on yourself, have you?'

'Just clean living.'

'Bollocks to that.'

They sat down. Even though they were berthed in harbour, Ross could feel a slight sensation of motion.

'So, how are you, Captain?'

'I'm drinking a Sea Breeze. You like one?'

Ross frowned.

'Vodka and cranberry. Healthy, you know. Cranberries. Good for the cholesterol.'

Milward shouted, and a leggy red-headed woman in her mid-thirties, wearing a chiffon shirt-waister and too many baubles, appeared through a door.

'Mandy, this is Ross Ransome, most famous plastic surgeon in England.'

Ross stood up. She gave him a vacuous smile and a limp, moist handshake. 'Nice to meet you.'

'When your tits start drooping, this is the man's going to do 'em.'

'Really?' she said.

'He could make 'em bigger. I'd like 'em a bit bigger.'

'Great,' she said, with a giggle, as if she had just won a minor prize in a game show.

'Get us two Sea Breezes, darlin', and some cashews.'

As she walked away, Ross looked hard at the parts of Ronnie Milward's face that weren't obscured by his ridiculous sunglasses. 'You're wearing well.'

'I'm clapping out on the inside,' he said. 'Diabetes. Prostate. Blood pressure. Cholesterol. The joys of ageing.'

At least you're ageing in style, Ross thought. At least you're ageing on a fifteen-million-pound yacht, free to spend your ill-gotten loot, free to come and go as you please, instead of being locked up in a prison cell and butt-fucked twice a day, which is probably the kind of old age you deserve.

Ronnie Milward was not his real name, nor was the Aristotle Onassis face the one he had been born with. Ross had changed it for him in a clinic in Switzerland more discreet than any bank. Two hundred and fifty thousand pounds had changed hands, out of sight of the British tax man. But seeing this boat now, Ross regretted not having charged him even more.

Holding the flame of his gold Dupont to the smouldering tip of the cigar and puffing hard, Milward said, 'You got to be away by three for your flight?'

'Yes.'

'I been back a couple of times in the past year.'

'That's taking a risk.'

'Me own mother din't recognise me.' He grinned. 'You gimme skin grafts on me fingers. No dabs are going to give me away. Shame you can't gimme new DNA as well.'

Mandy brought them their drinks and was about to sit down with them when Milward brushed her away. 'Fuck off and leave us in peace. Mr Ransome din't come all this way to talk about your tits.'

As she sauntered off, he turned to Ross with a quizzical smile. 'So, you want to see me, but you din't want to talk over the phone.' He stirred his drink with the plastic swizzle stick, then grabbed a handful of nuts. 'What's on your mind?'

'You told me five years ago that you owed me a favour, Captain. I've come to call it in.'

Laying his cigar in the ash-tray Milward said, 'I done owe no favours Ross. You did a job, I paid you. We're all square.' He chucked the nuts into his mouth and washed them down with a swig of his drink.

Without being able to see the man's eyes, Ross found it hard to tell whether he was joking or not.

'Don't come to me talking about favours, Ross. You want something, I'll see what I can do, that's how I work, everything's business with Ronnie Milward. I don't do no favours, I do business. You want to do business, tell me what you want.'

'I want to know if you can arrange something, or put me in touch with someone who can.'

From his briefcase, Ross removed a brown envelope. He shook two photographs out of the envelope and handed them to him.

Milward glanced at the first photograph, a face-on close-up of a man. The second was a longer shot, showing the same man in profile. A tall man in his mid-forties, with a lean face and a tangle of silver curls.

He laid them down on the table and looked back at Ross. 'Am I meant to know him or what? Looks to me like that French singer geezer, wozzisname?'

'No, you don't know him. He's American, lives in London. His name is Oliver Cabot. *Dr* Oliver Cabot. He's screwing my wife.'

'You want someone to teach him a lesson? Give him a good hiding?'

Ross's mouth felt dry suddenly. Picking up his glass,

he drank some of the icy vodka. Then leaning forward and staring hard into those dark, impenetrable glasses, he lowered his voice and said, 'I want him dead.'

49

'A year?' Faith said. 'A *year*?'

'For eighty per cent of people diagnosed.'

It was taking time to sink in. And Faith didn't want it to sink in, she wanted to keep talking, as if somehow if she talked for long enough they might arrive at some new way of looking at this *thing*, this Lendt's disease, this savage pack of micro-organisms that invaded human bodies and killed two out of every three of their victims.

Oliver was showing her a picture of one now on his iMac screen. A blow-up of a photograph taken through an electron microscope. It was hard to make out at first exactly what she was meant to be looking at in the uneven, swirling mass of green and red hues. Then Oliver pointed to a white area, the shape of a kidney bean.

'That?'

'Uh-huh.'

'How – how big is it?'

''Bout a hundred of them could sit on a pinhead.'

She stood up, feeling as if she had been abandoned by the entire world. Her eyes were moist but she wasn't about to cry: she was too shocked for that, too numb, too bewildered. Thoughts were unravelling around her.

Eighty per cent.

Four out of five dead within twelve months.

She stared out of the window. A hundred or so yards away was a pretty roof garden, lush with leaves and hanging plants, many in bloom. May had ended; this might be the last spring she would see. Her last summer. The last Christmas. She was never going to see Alec grow up.

I'm only going to be here for one more birthday for Alec.

Did Ross know? Was that why he'd been so sweet to her this weekend? Was he lying to her about the capsules – lying about what they really were?

Oliver stared at the iMac screen. There wasn't any easy way to break bad news, and to break it to Faith, of all people, was a really tough call.

He wished there was room for doubt, but the results of the tests were coldly unambiguous, and that Faith was being given a Moliou-Orelan clinical-trials drug was all the confirmation he need. They were the only company so far developing a drug to treat Lendt's disease.

And neither her GP nor her bastard husband had told her the truth – or even part of it.

Sixty-five per cent of people with this disease died within a year. There was no proof that the other thirty five per cent, those on the Moliou-Orelan drugs trial who were still alive at the end of a year, were cured. All that was known so far was that the drug seemed to offer some hope.

But he suspected – although he could not prove – from his own research in the past that Moliou-Orelan manipulated drugs trials. They were scrupulously careful not to be caught out, but their ethics were dubious. He wasn't prepared to trust any results published by that firm, and even less so in a life-threatening disease – life-threatening to the one woman he had met in the past decade with whom he could fall in love.

Oliver also knew that the reality was that twenty per cent of people would survive almost any disease for a longer period than the rest, simply because of their genetic makeup or immune system, or sheer willpower. It wasn't about drugs. It was about luck and determination, and Faith was going to need both of these.

He watched her standing silently, staring out of the window, face ashen, trying to understand what it must feel like to a person to be given a death sentence. They'd never told Jake – he'd been too young for such news, and besides, neither he nor Marcy had ever wanted to acknowledge to themselves that Jake was going to die. It was as if by denying it to themselves they could somehow save him.

Was Faith's husband doing the same thing?

The thought occurred to him that he was meddling in someone else's life here, telling Faith something that her husband had deliberately not told her, maybe with the best intentions.

But then he thought about the sticking plaster above her right eye. He did not know what Ross Ransome's intentions had been; all he knew was that a man who hit a woman was not a man he would ever trust.

I'm going to make you better, Faith. Whatever it takes, you and I, we're going to beat this thing. I've lost one battle in my life and I determined then I'd never lose another.

She was walking back towards him, looking utterly lost. He held out his arms and she sank into them, her arms wrapping tightly around him, as if he were a piece of driftwood in a raging ocean. 'I'm scared,' she said. 'I'd like to be brave but I'm not. I'm sorry.'

'You are brave – and there's nothing you need to be sorry about, OK?'

In a whisper she said, 'Is there any chance you could have made a mistake?'

'After I got the first results back, I had two more labs do the tests. Their results were identical. And the fact that you're on a Moliou-Orelan trials programme suggests that your own doctor has come to the same result.'

'Why didn't he tell me? Why did Ross lie to me?'

'I can't tell you. I guess maybe he was trying to be kind, not wanting you to know the truth.'

He felt Faith's body jig, then heard a tiny, half-hearted laugh. She looked up at him and he stared into those bright blue eyes, open so wide, so filled with fear and at the same time with trust.

Then she said, 'Make love to me.'

50

The white Renault van had 'REILLY & SONS BUILDERS. EST. 1951', in small letters on the side, and two ladders on the roof. It was parked fifty yards down the street from Oliver Cabot's apartment, facing away from the front entrance, which provided a clear view through the rear windows of anyone entering or leaving the place.

Seated in the back of the van, in an old armchair bought from a junk shop, Hugh Caven listened to a Schubert concert on Classic FM, and read his way through a collection of poems written by his late fellow countryman, William Butler Yeats.

Mounted above his head was a bank of television monitors. The kettle, plugged into the van's electrics, was taking its time to boil, and a busted spring from the chair was digging into his backside.

The van smelt as if a wet dog had slept in it. Barry Gatt, who'd done the night shift in here, was badly overweight and had a few hygiene problems. Then again, it was hard to expect someone to spend twelve hours in the back of a van and to come out smelling like they'd just spent a night at the Savoy.

His cellphone rang. 'Yup?' he answered.

'I've fixed the booster on the roof. You should have a picture now,' the voice the other end said. 'Five channels.'

'What about Sky?'

'Very witty, I like that.'

Caven reluctantly put down the book, reduced the volume of the concert, stood up and pressed a button on the control panel. All eight monitors flickered into life, and simultaneously a row of red lights began to wink.

Three monitor screens remained blank, but images appeared on the other five. All were of the interior of a large, elegant apartment: one showed the reception area beside the front door, another, part of what looked like the main living area, a third, the kitchen, the fourth an empty bedroom. But all Caven's attention was on the fifth. He saw two people he recognised instantly: Faith Ransome and Dr Oliver Cabot. They were standing next to a massive sofa, holding each other tight. The volume was too low and he turned it up in time to hear Faith Ransome's voice. 'Make love to me.'

Caven stayed rooted to his spot in front of the screen. He had been afraid that this was going to happen. He'd selected the photographs that he had given to his client Ross Ransome carefully, and he had given him a less than accurate account of his observations of the behaviour of his wife and Dr Oliver Cabot.

He watched Dr Cabot ease himself away from her. 'Faith – I don't think that's a good idea. Not right now.'

Good man. Be strong! Caven urged, silently. *Be really strong!*

'I'm dangerously close to falling in love with you, Faith. I can't get you out of my mind when we're apart. There's something very special that . . .' Cabot raised his shoulders in a shrug '. . . I guess, that you have that I . . .' His voice tailed off.

'That you what?' Faith prompted.

'Crave, I guess.' He smiled. 'I have this craving to see you all the time we're apart.'

'That's how I feel about you too,' she said.

He took her in his arms again. 'What I'm going to do is make you better, OK? I want to be your doctor. I can't be your doctor if I'm your lover – I need to keep an emotional distance for my healing to work. First I'm going to make you better and then—' He fell silent, just watching her.

'And then?'

'Then we'll see how you feel, about your life, about your husband, about your marriage.'

'And if you don't make me better?'

'We're going to. You and me together, as a team. You'd better believe it.'

Smiling she said, 'It doesn't sound as if I have much option.'

'You don't have *any* option.'

Their faces were close now, nose to nose, lip to lip. Oliver Cabot cupped her cheeks in his hands. Then he said, 'I wasn't telling you the truth just now, when I said I was dangerously close to falling in love with you, Faith. I am in love with you. I wish I wasn't, but I am.'

Caven's finger went to the stop button on the video machinery. Normally, in his experience, people committing infidelities deserved all they had coming to them. But this woman was different: she was a decent person, and he was moved by her. He didn't want Ross Ransome, whom he disliked intensely, to see this.

Jesus, woman, how in hell did you marry a shite like him?

He could stop the tape now, rewind it, erase it, tell Ross Ransome to take a hike – or tell him anything. Tell him, as he had before, that there really was nothing between the two of them.

An honourable person would do that.

Hugh Caven had a kid son called Sean and his wife was four months pregnant with their second child. He wanted his children to look up to him. He wanted them to grow up believing he was a better person than he really was. Eight years ago he'd screwed up, big-time, in his first business, importing cheap burglar-alarm equipment from Taiwan. A wholesaler who owed him a lot of money had pleaded for more time to pay, and for Caven to keep supplying him. Caven had felt sorry for the man, who faced bankruptcy if he called in the debt. The man's kids would be taken out of private school, he would lose his house, everything.

A year later the man finally did go bust, leaving Caven with an unsecured debt of one hundred and twenty thousand pounds, which threatened to take Caven's company down.

In an effort to prevent this happening, Caven attempted an insurance fraud, by setting fire to his warehouse. But he was tripped up by an eyewitness who saw him leaving, and by the forensic evidence, and spent two years in jail, during which he lost not only his business but his home as well. He lost everything except his wife.

Three years of hell followed his release, when he scraped a living first as a car-park attendant, then, falsifying his past, secured a job working nights as a security guard, before landing a more lucrative one fitting bugging equipment for a private detective agency, which gave him the inspiration to set up on his own. Now he had his life back. He had his boat, his comfortable house, and his business was going well.

His wife, Sandy, told him after he had gone bankrupt that his two big problems were that he was too soft and too picky about people. She told him what he already knew but did not want to accept, that in business, you had to be a shite at times. She had told him he needed to harden up and learn to swallow his pride, and he had promised he would.

Suddenly, the words of a Bob Dylan song began to play inside his head. It was the one about how many roads you had to walk down before you could be called a man.

Now, mouthing a wistful apology to the two players on the screen, he remembered his priorities.

51

'Should I stop taking the Moliou-Orelan capsules?'

Oliver Cabot said, 'I want you to think back to when your husband first gave these to you on—'

'Friday evening.'

'OK. When he first gave them to you on Friday evening, did you believe they were going to work?'

'Not really, no.'

'Why not?'

'I don't know, just a feeling. I suppose I've gone beyond trusting Ross. And there was – this may sound silly – but there was something almost shifty about the way he produced them. I felt something wasn't right.'

'A lot of doctors are convinced that a drug will only work if the patient believes it's going to work.'

'And even if I believe this, there's only a thirty-five per cent chance?'

'Seventeen and a half per cent. Fifty per cent of these capsules are placebos – that cuts the odds in half.'

'Could you get one analysed? Couldn't a lab tell if they're just chalk or sugar?'

'We don't even know what the long-term prognosis is for the thirty-five per cent. I doubt that people will actually be cured – the pharmaceutical industry is in the business of disease management, not of curing diseases.

They want people taking their medicine permanently – that's the way they design their drugs. Yes, I can get one tested for you. But the thing I really want to do is make you better. Whether the odds are three to one or six to one, they are still bad odds. We're not gambling a few bucks on a roulette wheel, this is gambling with your life. And I don't want to lose you, Faith.'

In a small, scared voice, she said, 'I don't want to lose you either.'

Ross, in his office, stared at his television screen, his right hand clenched tight, his nails digging into his palm. You bastard, he mouthed. You're talking about gambling with my wife's life – what fucking odds are you offering her? Moliou-Orelan are worth a million of you creeps. They can save one in three people and they can prove it. Where's your proof? What fucking Svengali influence are you exerting over her? If you were a proper doctor, practising proper medicine, I'd have enough on this tape to get you struck off for professional misconduct.

His phone rang. He ignored it. It rang again, then a third time, urgently. He jabbed the pause button on the video control, grabbed the phone and snapped, 'I told you I don't want to be disturbed, Lucinda.'

'It's ten to four,' his secretary said.

'I know how to tell the fucking time. My father gave me a watch when I was seven.'

'You have three patients waiting – Mr Sirwan has been here over an hour – and you've got the BBC coming at five.'

'The BBC?'

'You agreed to do an interview for *Panorama* on breast implants.'

'When is Lady Reynes-Raleigh booked in?'

'Three o'clock tomorrow.'

'Do I have any gaps in the morning.'

'No, none.'

'Find me an hour.'

'I can't. You've got a completely full—'

He dropped the receiver back on the cradle and pressed the play button.

On the screen, Oliver Cabot said, 'Sit down, Faith, and we'll talk through what I'm going to do.'

Ross, his insides balled up tight like his fist, watched Faith sit down on a sofa. Oliver Cabot lit a low, fat candle on the coffee table, then sat opposite her. Faith now had her back to the camera, and the weird fish-eye distortion of the lens gave Ross the top and rear of her head, and a frontal view of Cabot's face.

'Conventional medicine tends to target the disease itself. What I try to do is understand an individual's immune system and find ways to boost that. I use hypnosis and other trance states, combined sometimes with pharmaceuticals as well, and natural remedies. It's been well established over thousands of years that the mind can affect the body, that we all have the power within us to affect our own healing. There's a professor of immunology in the US who said very recently that the immune system is the mind. That's what I believe and that's what I want to work on with you. How do you feel about that?'

'That makes sense,' Faith said.

'I'd like to start by sending you to a lab I use, who will do a series of tests on your blood, which will help me understand clearly your immune system. Every human immune system is unique, and I need to establish which areas of yours we need to work on.'

'I have some savings. How much will they cost?'

'About a thousand pounds.'

You fucking con-man, Ross thought. *Jesus.*

'How quickly can they do them?'

'I'll phone them now – maybe you could go over there right away? They're five minutes by cab.'

'Please,' she said.

Ross's phone rang again, then a second time. He hit the pause button. 'What is it, Lucinda?'

'Mr Seiler is on the phone from the Credit Shiel bank in Zurich – he says he needs to speak to you urgently. And Mr Sirwan has another appointment – he can only wait another five minutes.'

'Put Seiler on.'

A moment later, Ross heard the familiar broken English of the Swiss bank manager.

'Good afternoon, Mr Ransome. We received your fax and I just would like, please, your verbal confirmation. We are to transfer today the sterling equivalent of twenty-five thousand pounds in euros to the account of the Benina Corporation SA in Puerto Banus? This is correct?'

'Correct.'

'Thank you, Mr Ransome.'

Ross hung up and stared in grim satisfaction at the frozen, flickering image of Oliver Cabot on the screen. Ronnie Milward's down-payment was on its way.

Half now, half on completion.

He switched off the television and told his secretary to send in Mr Sirwan.

52

Faith removed one wooden chip too many from the precarious tower.

'Tim*berrrrrrrrr*!' Alec shouted.

She watched helplessly as, once again, all fifty-four pieces crashed down on to the kitchen table; several rolled off the edge, rat-tat-tatting on to the oak floorboards, one coming to rest inches from the nose of the sleeping Rasputin, who didn't stir.

Alec, giggling, leaned back in his chair, pointing a finger at his mother. 'You did it! Yooouu! Silly Mummy!'

Smiling back, fighting to stop herself crying, Faith knelt, ducking beneath the table to recover the pieces from the floor – and her composure. She knew why she kept losing: you needed a steady hand to play this game and she was shaking too much.

The only time she had stopped shaking was last night when she'd got back from London after the tests, and had asked Sammy Harrison to come over for a drink. When Faith told her about the diagnosis and about Oliver, Sammy talked enthusiastically about a cousin who'd been diagnosed with breast cancer eight years ago and had gone to an alternative doctor, and was now clear of the disease.

After Alec had gone to bed they'd demolished a bottle of Chablis and for an hour, maybe even more, the buzz of the alcohol had sent her confidence soaring into orbit. Then, after Sammy had gone home, the burned-out remnants of that confidence crashed back to earth.

At three in the morning she had lain in their massive four-poster bed, wide awake, in the claustrophobic grip of fear, fighting a terrible longing to phone her mother and tell her. The thought even crossed her mind that her mother already knew, that Ross had given her the news and said, 'Don't tell Faith, she won't be able to cope.' And, of course, her mother would go along with Ross. She always did.

Instead, Faith had gone down to Ross's study, and looked up Lendt's disease on the web. There were forty sites. Among them she found a help group for Lendt's disease sufferers. It contained detailed information about the Moliou-Orelan trials, but she learned nothing new.

Another site went into the identification of the disease by the virologist, Dr Mogens Lendt, and contained pictures that looked much like the ones Oliver had shown her on his laptop. But the site was more concerned with the career of Lendt and the papers he had published. On another site there was a list of viral diseases that had been identified in the past decade, with the common link, pollution, blamed as a prime culprit.

The culprit didn't concern her. She looked for only one thing as she worked her way through the sites. A *cure*. Progress towards a cure. Hope for the victims.

She had found none.

'Can we do it once more, Mummy?'

It was the fifth time they'd played the game already, and she was tiring of it. It was seven o'clock. She didn't know what she wanted to do. *Tomorrow's World* was on television at seven thirty. It always fascinated her. She used to watch it with her father and she often wondered if he had secretly hoped that one day on the show he would see a cure for his disease. After that there was a cookery programme on Sky, and, at nine, her favourite, *ER*.

But she wasn't sure she could concentrate on television tonight.

Oliver Cabot is going to make me better.

I have to believe that.

And if he doesn't?

She looked at Alec. *What would happen to you? You'd be in Ross's hands.*

'Can we, Mummy? Once more?'

'Bed!' she said.

'Ohhhh. Please, Mummy?' That look on his face

208

always got to her. Relenting, she said, 'Once more, and then bed – OK?'

'Yeeeaaahhhhhhhh!'

Alec began to scoop the pieces back into the box, setting up the next game. While he was absorbed, she shielded her eyes with her hands, and tried, silently, to pray. Last night she had tried to say the Lord's Prayer and got the words muddled three times. For years during her childhood, she had prayed every night for her father, and every day he got a little worse. Some time, long before he had died, she had told God she was very disappointed in him, and if he ever wanted her to pray again, he'd better give her a sign by doing something good for her father.

But last night, during her lowest ebb, she had begun to pray again.

Rasputin ran out into the hall, barking excitedly. For a moment she thought Alec had startled him, but the barking persisted. 'What is it, boy?' she called.

The sound of a key turning in the lock, the door opening, a man's voice. 'Hey, boy! Rasputin! Hey, hey, hey!'

Ross?

She'd been trying to get hold of him all day, but what the hell was he doing at home? It was Wednesday. He was meant to be staying in London until Friday.

He came through the kitchen door to a squeal of excitement from Alec, who launched himself at him. '*Daddy*! Daddeeee!'

Ross scooped him up, held him in the air, and the sight angered Faith. Ten days ago Ross had struck him savagely, now he was hugging him, and Alec seemed to have forgotten all about it.

'Hey, big guy! I didn't see you all weekend! Missed you. You've grown! Haven't seen you for nine days and you've grown an inch! You're not a big guy any more, you're a huge guy!' He set the child back down on the ground. His face darkened. 'Shouldn't you be in bed? It's after seven.' He shot an accusatory glance at Faith, who remained seated at the table.

'I wasn't expecting you.' Instantly she regretted the words.

'I see. This is what happens during the week when I'm not here. You let all discipline go out of the window.'

'Why didn't you return any of my calls, Ross?'

'It's after seven. Why's he still up?'

Faith glanced at Alec. She hated more than anything else for him to see them arguing, but she was determined to hold her ground. Calmly but firmly she said, 'We're going to have one more game and then bedtime. You start, Alec.'

'He's going to bed, *now*!' Ross, a storm brewing in his face, looked around, searching for something to be angry about, and didn't have to search far. 'Why are there dirty dishes on the sideboard? Are they from lunch, Faith? Do you live like a slut when you're not expecting me home? You let my son go to bed when he pleases and leave a mess everywhere?'

Ignoring Ross, she said to Alec, 'We're playing one more game. You go first, darling.' Then continuing in the same calm grown-up-talking-to-a-child voice she glanced at Ross and said, 'Why don't you relax in your study and I'll bring you a whisky?'

She began to set up the pieces of the game, and could see Ross out of the corner of her eye, wavering. 'I left three messages for you with Lucinda,' she said. 'One yesterday and two today. I also left two messages for Jules Ritterman. I'd very much like to know why you haven't told me the truth about what is wrong with me.' She glanced at Alec, who seemed to be concentrating on the game.

Even so, he said, 'What *is* wrong with you, Mummy?'

She looked up at Ross. 'Would you like to tell him?'

'I have to send a couple of urgent e-mails.' Ross, the storm gathering in his face, turned and walked out.

Forty minutes later, Faith switched off Alec's light and closed his door. Then she went downstairs, into Ross's study, and closed that door behind her also. Ross, sitting at his computer, continued to stare at the screen as he tapped a command.

'Why didn't you tell me I'm dying?' she said. 'Why did you tell me a load of rubbish about antibiotics and lie to me about the capsules you gave me?'

He picked up a container on his desk and held it up for her to see. There was no anger in his voice now, just hurt. 'You're not taking them, Faith. These were in your handbag and I have just counted them. You didn't take the ones you should have taken at lunch and dinner yesterday, or any today.'

'What gives you any right to go looking in my handbag?'

'What do you think gives you the right not to take these pills?'

'I have every right in the damned world not to take them.'

'You're wrong. You're my wife and Alec's mother and you have a duty to both of us – especially to him. You have an obligation to remain alive, Faith. You can't bring a child into the world then just dump him.'

'Why did you lie to me?'

He stood up abruptly, hands at his side, fists clenched. 'You bitch. In twelve years I've never been unfaithful to you, you *whore*. Never.'

He took a stride towards her and she stepped back, certain she was going to be struck.

But instead his face crumpled into tears. 'I love you,

Faith. I can't bear the thought of losing you, I can't bear the thought that you might be going to die. I just wanted to do the best thing for you, that's why I didn't tell you. Can you understand that?'

He put his arms round her, pressing his wet face against her cheek. 'I want you to take those pills because they're the best chance you have. I don't want you being conned—' He checked himself. She mustn't know about Hugh Caven, he mustn't give the game away. 'I don't want you being *confident* you can just beat this by doing nothing.' Then he checked himself again. 'How do you know? Did Jules Ritterman tell you?'

She felt him clinging harder to her, and in spite of all her anger and hatred towards him, she felt pity for him. He was such a damaged man: so badly damaged from childhood that he could barely talk about it. Damaged by his ambitions, damaged by his own wiring circuitry that failed to control his emotions and temper.

His mother had died when he was young, and his bullying father from a heart attack when Ross was in his early twenties.

'I went and got a second opinion,' she said, gently.

Nuzzling even closer to her, he said, 'Faith, oh, my darling, Faith. We may have had some ups and downs lately, but I do love you. We're going to beat this damned thing. I've got everyone I know who can help with something like this on the case. I'm getting you the best medical help in the world.'

'How come you're home?' she asked.

'I blew out an interview with the BBC because I wanted to be with you. I'm here for you. I'll do anything in the world for you, my darling.'

Anything, she thought, *except the one thing I really want.*

53

At ten past eleven the following morning, Ross passed a cluster of parked motorcycles and entered the front door of a modern, rather uninspired-looking office building in a mews just off Wigmore Street. The small sign on the door said, WIGMORE LABORATORY.

Three motorcycle couriers were hanging around, crowding the confined reception area. Ross eased past them to the desk and greeted the receptionist cheerily. The woman, in her late twenties, plain but chirpy, sat behind two small towers of Jiffy-bags bantering with a biker. Ross always wondered how the hell nothing ever got lost in here. He'd been dealing with this lab for over a decade and they were always blisteringly efficient.

She turned to Ross. 'Good morning, it's Mr Ransome, isn't it? I'm still waiting for my free makeover.'

'You don't need one, you look great,' Ross replied

'Flattery will get you everywhere! Who've you come to see?'

'Dr Gilliatt.'

'I'll tell her you're here. Could you just sign in, please?'

'Of course.'

Another courier entered, holding a large package. Ross looked down at the visitors' sheet, took out his pen, then while she was distracted with signing the courier's docket he pocketed the pen without writing anything. The less of a trail he left the better.

A phone warbled. Before answering it, the receptionist leaned across and said, 'Please go up, Mr Ransome, third floor.'

Ross took the stairs and came out on a small landing. The door in front of him was labelled PATH/3. He went through and was warmly greeted by the lab's senior pathologist. Susan Gilliatt was a handsome woman in her mid-forties, attractive even in her white lab coat and with her blonde hair pinned back tightly. More than once Ross had felt that her looks were wasted on the bacteria, viruses and other assortments of low life forms with which she chose to spend her working days.

He followed her into the windowless, L-shaped laboratory, past a continuous white work-top cluttered with equipment: flow-hoods, incubators, gel solutions and PWR machines for DNA analysis, powered microscopes, computer terminals, vials, jars, test-tubes, sinks, boxes of sterile wipes, protective gloves, eye shields, warning signs, DANGER – BIOHAZARD!, health and safety instructions, and the sour reek of chemicals that would let you know, the world over, with your eyes shut, that you were in a pathology lab.

About ten people were at work in this room, all in white coats, a young team mostly, in their twenties and thirties. Some looked up as they passed, giving brief nods. They stopped behind a young, ponytailed man in his late twenties who was in deep concentration, releasing a single drop from a pipette into one of a whole row of Petri dishes, with a gloved hand.

'Niall is working on this problem now. He's been here around the clock for the past ten days.'

The young man turned his head for a fleeting instant. Ross saw bloodshot eyes behind tiny wire-framed glasses, a Joe Stalin beard and a face racked with exhaustion. 'Any progress?' he asked Susan Gilliatt.

'We've identified the strain – each one of those contains it.' She nodded at about two dozen plated Petri dishes sitting near the lab technician. Each dish contained a blood culture infected with a particularly virulent strain of septicaemia that had been found in a post-operative patient in the Harley-Devonshire Hospital, who had subsequently died.

'And it doesn't respond to any antidotes?'

'No yet,' she said grimly. 'Let's just hope it's an isolated case.'

'Any thoughts on how it might be transmitted?' he asked.

She shook her head. 'Until we understand it better, no. The woman who died had been out in India only a week before she came in here. That's the most likely source of infection.'

Ross knew that the woman, who had come in for removal of fibroids, had been admitted in otherwise seemingly good health. Two days after the operation, performed by one of the country's foremost gynaecologists, she had developed the septicaemia, and four days later she was dead. Naturally there was serious concern by the hospital that she hadn't contracted the infection there, and every effort was being made to understand the strain of the bacterium.

Niall sealed the dish he had been working on, got up from his chair and walked away up the laboratory. As he did so, Dr Gilliatt's pager began beeping.

She excused herself, then hurried to a wall phone a few yards away.

Ross watched the technician, still striding away. He glanced up at the walls and ceiling for any hint of a closed-circuit camera, but could see nothing. Susan Gilliatt was on the phone.

He seized one of the Petri dishes, checked that the lid was secure and jammed it into his trouser pocket.

Trying to maintain his composure he looked around carefully. No one was in view, apart from Susan Gilliatt with her back to him. He reached out, and moved a few of the dishes closer to each other.

When the technician returned, he noted nothing amiss.

54

There were two floors of operating theatres at the Harley-Devonshire Hospital. On the third was a suite of smaller theatres for minor operations, and on the fourth, larger ones. Originally, the majority of the work carried out in the hospital had been cosmetic and reconstructive surgery, but the insurance company that owned it had invested in setting up the most modern ITU in London, directly below on the second floor, and there was now a lucrative general surgery practice, fuelled predominantly by the long-established wealthy Middle Eastern clientele, together with an increasing stream of new Russian money.

Like all the theatres on the fourth floor, 4-2 had pale blue tiled walls, speckled terrazzo-tiled floors and a well-recessed scrub area. As befitted the prices charged for surgery here, everything in the theatre was state-of-the-art. The high-spec fittings included an internal sterilisation system up to NASA standards. The only way for a bug to get in here was by hitching a ride on a human.

And right now a whole cluster of hostile creatures, too small to see with the naked eye, slipped into this theatre inside a sealed plastic dish concealed deep in the right-hand pocket of Ross Ransome's surgical pyjamas.

It was twenty past two. Between twelve and two, Ross had performed five small operations under local anaesthetic in the small room annexed to his office that served both as an examining room and an operating theatre. At three o'clock he would be operating in theatre 4-2.

The theatre was empty. He had maybe ten minutes if he was lucky, but did not plan to use anything like that amount of time. In his white clogs he crossed over to the scrub recess, where he was out of sight of anyone peering in through the small glass portholes in the theatre doors.

Although he'd rehearsed this carefully, now that he was doing it he felt vulnerable and exposed. He grabbed a pair of surgical gloves from the dispenser and pulled them on. Then he removed the Petri dish, careful to hold it level, took a deep breath and unscrewed the lid, which he laid carefully in the basin.

Still holding his breath, he pushed the gloved fingers of his right hand into the culture in the dish, then knelt and wiped the fluid in the place he had already selected, to the right of a rivet underneath the sink.

Standing up, he checked once more over his shoulder, then replaced the lid of the Petri dish securely and dropped it into the incinerator bin. He washed his gloved hands twice in sterilising gel, peeled off the gloves and dropped them, too, into the incinerator bin.

Then he left the theatre and sauntered casually along to the small rest lounge, where he fixed himself a cup of coffee.

At two minutes past three, Lady Geraldine Reynes-Rayleigh, hooked up to drip lines, a breathing tube down her throat, was trolleyed into the theatre and lifted on to the steel operating table. While Tommy Pearman and his assistant monitored her carefully, the team began prepping her.

Ross stood at the sink, making a big deal of washing his hands and forearms, diligently using the brush to scrub his nails. He wanted them to remember him doing it. Then, for good measure, he said, 'Foul, this new gel. Stinks of cheap perfume. Can't we have something that smells better? For God's sake, this is an operating theatre, not a tart's boudoir!'

Jane Odin, his scrub nurse, said, 'It's ordered centrally.'

'And someone's probably getting a nice kickback.' Ross held out his hands for her to glove him up. 'That's the problem, isn't it? Everyone's on a bloody kickback.'

'Wouldn't mind if I was,' she said.

'I think for this operation we'll have Beethoven's Fifth, Jane.'

She grinned at his choice. 'I'll check to see if we have it.'

'I brought it in myself,' Ross said. He nodded at his patient, brightly lit beneath the octopus lamp. 'Damned if I'm going to let that bitch listen to anything peaceful. If she wants to drag us through the mill, she can suffer with it.'

'Not a nice lady, by all accounts,' his scrub nurse said, pulling the second glove tight.

Everyone in the room was concentrating on the patient. Ross secured his mask, then slipped unobserved back into the scrub recess, knelt and rubbed his left hand beneath the sink, where, half an hour earlier, he had smeared the septicaemia culture.

Moments later he walked casually over to the operating table. All that was visible of Lady Reynes-Raleigh, beneath the folds of green wrapping, was her nose.

He looked down at her with anger. *Bitch, beneath those wraps you look your age now, lying on your back, with every muscle in your body slack from the anaesthetics and gravity doing its worst to you. I'd love to take your photograph and send it to the gossip columns. What do you think they'd make of the great society beauty now? I'll tell you something, you wouldn't have screwed your way to the top of the heap looking like that.*

Since complaining about his surgery on her nose, Lady Reynes-Raleigh had decided she was displeased with his work on her cheekbones too. She was desperate to look like someone she saw in her mind and in her dreams – someone she could never ever be. Because, in truth, Ross knew that what she really wanted to look like was herself aged twenty-two.

You're fifty-two, bitch, and counting. I've cut and sewn you back to forty-two and that's as good as you're ever going to get. If you were a decent human being, I'd give you a pep talk, tell you to count your blessings, enjoy what you have and stop craving the impossible.

But you aren't.

The specialist registrar began discussing a car he was thinking of buying with Tommy Pearman. Jane Odin found the CD and put it on. As the rousing strains of Beethoven's Fifth burst out of the speakers, Ross stood still, keeping his left hand low, palm inwards, close against his gown but careful not to touch it and leave any tell-tale marks.

Raising his right arm, he began to conduct an imaginary orchestra, and said, loudly, 'Everyone knows, of course, that Beethoven's Fifth stands for victory. The opening corresponds to V in Morse code.'

Looking around at the sea of blank eyes above the surgical masks he said, 'Don't tell me I'm operating with Philistines today! This is very apposite music because today we shall have victory over Lady Geraldine Reynes-Raleigh's nose and cheeks!'

He leaned forward and made a play of studying the patient's nose for some moments. Then he announced, 'I'm going to begin with the rhinoplasty. We'll do this closed – I think it will work better.'

There was always a decision to be made on whether

to open up the nose or to work, blind, inside it. Today working blind was perfect for his needs.

'Nasal speculum,' he said.

He inserted the blade of the speculum into the left nostril and squeezed the handle, forcing the nostril wide open. Then leaving it *in situ*, he said, 'Osteatome.'

The scrub nurse proffered the chisel. He took it in his right hand and made a play of seeming dissatisfied with it, peering at the blade for a moment, then pinched it tightly between the fingers of his left hand, careful not to cut through the rubber.

'Do you want a different one?' the scrub nurse asked.

'No, it's fine.'

Feeling his way carefully with the dirty chisel, he pushed up until he could feel that the point was against the cribriform plate, which separated the cavity of the nose from the cranium, and was riddled with tiny perforations through which the olfactory nerves passed.

No one in the theatre could have any idea what he was doing. He pressed harder, forcing the point of the chisel into one of the tiny cavities, then discreetly exerted more pressure still, until he could feel the bone give and the tip of the chisel penetrate the cranium itself.

Then he withdrew it, and could see, to his satisfaction, there was a tiny amount of blood on the tip. The bleeding in the nose would mask the leakage of the CSF fluid from the tear.

More than enough to show he'd hit the target.

Beneath his mask, his lips moved, as he mouthed the great music to himself, feeling the adrenaline rush surging through his veins.

Then he began on the reshaping of her nose. He did a great job, he was inspired, he was on a roll. His eyes beamed at his staff.

She was going to look *sensational*!

55

'The thing is, that beech glade is mentioned in all the guidebooks.'

'They'll still be able to see it – we're only talking about moving the footpath fifty yards.'

'But what you have to consider is that some of the trees are over two hundred and fifty years old.'

There was a pause. Then Donald Fogarty, a retired borough surveyor and, in Faith's opinion, one of the few members of this committee to talk any sense, said, 'Yes, we're aware of that – but it's the footpath we are talking about moving, not the trees. What point are you making?'

It was the fourth meeting of the Little Scaynes Footpath Action Committee. Faith sat at the oak refectory table in Ruth Harman's converted barn, half listening, contributing little beyond her presence.

Another voice butted in. 'Gary Taylor is generously offering to donate ten acres of woodland on his farm to the community, in exchange for planning consent to move the footpath fifty yards further to the west of his property just for the two-hundred-yard stretch that passes his house. I don't see how the age of the beech trees comes into this.'

'The point is, the footpath was there long before the farm.'

I don't need this, Faith thought. I really don't. I don't want to spend what might be my last year arguing about footpaths. Or bypasses. Or saving church roofs.

She stirred her coffee.

'What are your feelings, Faith?' another voice said.

'Gary Taylor's a decent man,' she said. 'I don't see why he should have to put up with endless hordes of nerds in gaudy cagoules traipsing past his front door.

The point of a footpath, historically, was to enable people to get from one place to another – any view they happened to have was incidental. What Gary is proposing doesn't stop anyone from using the path for the purposes for which it was intended. Tell the ramblers to take a hike elsewhere.'

That made her feel a little better. She glanced with satisfaction at the startled expressions all around her, then stirred her coffee once more.

After the meeting was over, Faith drove a short distance then pulled on to a garage forecourt, stopping well short of the pumps, and switched on her mobile phone. It was nearly one o'clock. They were having a dinner party on Saturday night. Ten people were coming, four of them medics including her least favourite, Jules Ritterman, as well as the Chief Constable of Sussex, and a High Court judge, to add some gravitas. She had all the shopping to do, and at three thirty she had to collect Alec and four of his friends.

Three sharp beeps told her she had a new message. It was from Oliver.

'Faith, hi, wondering how you are. I should have the test results all back by tomorrow afternoon latest. I could see you Monday, or over the weekend if you could make it, but I guess you'd have problems getting away. Call me at the office, I've told them to put you straight through.'

She played the message a second time, just to hear his voice again.

Then she played it a third time, and saved it when it had finished, wanting to know it was there, comforted that she could dial her voice-mail and hear him any time she wanted.

I'm behaving like a besotted teenager.

Her desire for the American was intense, constant,

dominating her every thought. *Oliver Cabot*. Her secret.

Was she deluding herself about him? Was Ross right? Was he just a conman?

Never.

She had lain awake most of the night thinking, fantasising about a life with him, a different kind of a life from the one she had, far away from narrow village concerns, in a wider dimension, where they discussed things in ways that she and Ross never discussed anything. She thought back over the conversations she had already had in the short time she had spent with Oliver, on life, religion, philosophy, art, literature, travel.

She was certain that somehow – and she did not know how, but *somehow* – Oliver Cabot was going to make her better, not the pills in the container in her handbag.

It was one o'clock. She should take two now. Oliver hadn't told her not to take them, but neither had he encouraged her to take them. She pulled out from the bottom of her handbag a slip of paper he had given her to read. He had told her that it had been written in 1887, and that she should read it three times a day, with the pills, or instead of them. She obediently read it now. He said that few doctors understood it, and fewer still ever took note of it.

The wise physician, when making a prognosis, does not confine himself or herself to the virulence of the particular micro-organism involved or the nature of an abnormal growth; the wise physician makes a careful estimate of the patient's will to live and the ability to put to work all the resources of spirit that can be translated into beneficial biochemical changes.

From her handbag, she removed the Moliou-Orelan container, and tipped out two pills. Then, holding them in the palm of her hand, she climbed out of the car and dropped them into the litter-bin.

That felt good.

56

They slipped the Fatslide board beneath Lady Reynes-Raleigh three hours and eighteen minutes after the operation had begun, and heaved her on to the trolley. Her cheeks, nose, jaw and forehead had been changed in accordance with her instructions, and were now covered with rows of neat stitches. One of the talents for which Ross was highly admired was the quality of his sewing. Few surgeons could come close.

Even so, discoloured by internal bruising and trauma, she looked like a pastiche of one of Andy Warhol's 'violent period' paintings.

Less than five minutes after being taken into the recovery room, she began to regain consciousness. Another five minutes, and the breathing tube was removed from her throat. Tommy Pearman remained with her a short while longer, checking her pulse and blood oxygen levels until he was confident that she was out of danger, then joined Ross in the changing room.

As Ross removed his pyjama top and pulled on his shirt, Pearman said, 'I must give you some stuff I printed out for you – from the Net on Lendt's.'

'What else have you found?'

'Well, not much. Merck announced they've had some encouraging results with tests they are doing on rats, but I wouldn't get too excited – they're at least two years off starting any human trials.'

'Any more on the Moliou trials?'

'No.' Pearman slapped his belly, as if the mere act of doing this might reduce its girth. 'I really must do something about this.'

'You should take up running marathons.'

'My legs are too short.'

'Maybe they should have special marathons for fat midgets like you.'

Pearman pulled on his shirt, then began knotting his tie. 'There *is* something else about the Moliou-Orelan trials,' he said. 'Could be significant. This disease seems to be increasing at quite a rate and they're hoping to fast-track the drug through the FDA.'

'That means they're confident with it,' Ross said.

'It still only has a thirty-five per cent success rate.'

Pearman dragged on his trousers.

Ross put one foot on the bench and tied the laces of his black oxfords. 'Tell me something, you use ketamine a lot, don't you?'

'I've used it in certain circumstances for years – it's effective for burns patients, particularly when you have a lot of painful changes of dressings. Why?'

'It's related to LSD, isn't it?'

'Closely.'

'Do you use it in combination with other drugs?'

'No. It's a single-agent anaesthetic and non-sedative. I normally give it intravenously where it has a short half-life – about ten minutes.'

'How does a patient feel under it?'

Puzzled by his interest, Pearman said, 'They'll often hallucinate, feel delirious and scared. One of the bad things is that although it has a short half-life its effect can go on repeating for up to forty-eight hours or even longer. Paramedics use it sometimes for people trapped in accidents – it numbs pain and constricts arteries, reducing blood loss. But it also causes horrific hallucinations and some patients get the sense they're having an out-of-body experience.'

'What does it do biochemically?'

Pearman adjusted his meagre strands of greying hair in the mirror. 'It selectively excites brain activity close to mood centres. Heightens blood-flow to the brain, sending sparks of electricity to everything around it. Blood pressure rises, but it maintains muscle tone, stabilises breathing. Patients will sometimes whimper and have signs of nystagmus.'

'Can it be taken orally?'

'Well, yes, but I wouldn't administer it orally. It has a much longer half-life taken that way.'

'How long?'

'At least an hour and a half, sometimes more.'

'Does it have any taste?'

Pearman gave him a strange look. 'I don't think so, no.'

'Any acidity?'

'It's neutral. You can look it up in the pharmaceutical books – or I can scan the details in and e-mail them to you if you like?'

'I'd appreciate that,' Ross said. 'Thanks.'

Ross hung around in the changing room, checking his messages on his mobile phone while Pearman left. Then from a window in an empty office, he looked down at the street until he saw the anaesthetist's elderly Bristol emerge from the underground car park and pull out into Devonshire Place.

Immediately Ross walked along to the anaesthetics room, which, slackly, was always left unlocked, and went in. He found what he was looking for in the third cabinet he tried: a whole shelf stacked with 10cc vials of ketamine.

He palmed one and slipped it into his jacket pocket.

57

Spider sat in his regular booth at the back of Trader Vic's in Park Lane, drinking his Hawaiian Sundowner and smoking his Marlboro Light. He liked this place, with its plush leather banquettes, its exotic flavour and its smart clientele. It had tone, sophistication. And it was always dark in here, whether day or night. He liked that the most.

Although he thought of this booth as his own, he was careful not to come here too often. He didn't want staff starting to recognise him in places he went to. Doing that was like leaving tracks.

He sat quietly and unobtrusively, blending in fine, just one of the dozens of international businessmen with their laptops and palmtops and mobile phones who used this place the way they might use any transit watering-hole. That was the reason he favoured this booth, tucked away, darker than anywhere else in here. A discreet place to conduct his own business.

Spider had learned early in life that if he wanted respect, he had to work harder than most to earn it. If you had a badly repaired hare-lip and were only five feet four, with a weedy frame, you took a lot of shit from bigger boys at school.

Fighting hard and mean kept some of the bullies at bay, but that didn't earn you any friends. You had to develop other assets. You had to find something for people to admire in you. Spider found something.

He discovered long before his teens that he had a talent for climbing, and no fear of heights. He could climb just about anything. It impressed people. It even impressed some girls, who were repelled by his lip but curious about it too. He started with simple targets, like cranes, the Buckingham Palace wall, the lions in

Trafalgar Square, the Albert Memorial, Marble Arch, and graduated slowly to bigger challenges. Anything that provided a crack or a ledge for a hand or a foot he could scale. He found he could win good money in bets by climbing any building, and often with nothing more than his bare hands and rubber-soled shoes. That was how he came to be called Spider.

By the time he was fifteen he had conquered Alexandra Palace, Battersea power station, the Centre Point Skyscraper and St Paul's Cathedral.

When he was a little older, he found a better way to earn respect: he graduated from climbing things to doing things. Taking on jobs that other people shied away from. There was a lot of money to be earned in handling these tasks. And there were friends to be made. Lasting friends, who paid well.

Spider was in a good mood. Trader Vic's always did that to him. He felt a somebody here, lounging back against the plush leather, drinking his exotic drink, smoking his cigarette, which he had tapped, first, on his silver case the way his boyhood hero Sean Connery had in *Dr No*. He was cool, eyeing his surroundings through tinted glasses, his lip camouflaged by a thin moustache he had cultivated over many years, and which he had originally modelled on Charles Bronson's.

He ordered the same again.

While he waited he took out his phone, flipped it open and checked his e-mail. Nothing new, but that didn't matter. There was one sitting in a secure file that was going to keep him occupied for a while, and in funds for longer than that.

It was from his good friend, Ronnie Milward.

Uncle Ronnie.

Ronnie lived on a boat in Spain mostly. Legal problems prevented him returning to England. He was one of the few people who had ever been decent to

Spider as a kid. He was never sure why – whether it was because the old rogue had felt guilty for letting his dad take the fall in the armed robbery that jailed him for twenty years, or because he'd had a thing with his mum while his dad was locked away. Either way it was history now and both Spider's parents were dead. But Uncle Ronnie had always taken care of him and in return he took care of his uncle's business interests in England.

Mostly he collected bad debts for him, and ensured that the cash from Ronnie's drug-dealings ended up in the right accounts abroad. But occasionally he handled other matters, also. Once he had shot a man outside a pub for him. One bullet through the head. Clean. Another time he had shot a man in the groin for shagging one of Ronnie's girls.

He had plenty of trustworthy sources for guns. Clean guns, always imports, never previously used in the UK. Tonight he was waiting for a man he had done business with several times before. The man would be carrying a Heckler and Koch P9, a 9mm double-action pistol, stolen five years ago from the boot of a German police car, and ten rounds of ammunition.

Spider would pay the man two thousand pounds, four times the going rate for a handgun of this quality in London. But for the blue-chip provenance of the weapon it was cheap even at twice that price. He would use it just once, and then it would be discarded five miles out to sea in the Channel. Spider was thirty-nine, and had survived twenty years in his business. Not one weapon he had used had ever been found by the police.

He opened the e-mail from Ronnie Milward once more and looked down at the tiny but crystal sharp picture on the handset of his telephone communicator. It showed a man with a lean, craggy face and a tangle of grey curls. This man had an intellectual air about him, different from the sleaze-ball types Uncle Ronnie normally asked him to deal with. But no matter. And no questions asked. The usual routine and the usual price.

First he needed the gun, then a suitable time and a place. There was some urgency – uncle Ronnie wanted the job done quickly, and that was good. Spider had his eye on a car, a rare Subaru Impreza in green with gold trim, double overhead cams, a sixteen-valve boxer engine that had been fitted with a rally-spec supercharger. It was an animal. He was five grand light of the asking price, and Uncle Ronnie's fee of ten grand would solve that problem neatly – even after deduction of expenses – and cover the insurance. And give him some over.

He looked down again at the picture on the screen. *You're making me a very happy bunny, Dr Oliver Cabot.*

58

'What did she throw in the bin?'

Hugh Caven, seated on a sofa by the fireplace in Ross's London flat, said, 'Bin?'

'The rubbish-bin on the garage forecourt. It says here in your report that at one o'clock today she sat in her Range Rover on the garage forecourt listening to her mobile phone. Then she got out of the car and threw something in the rubbish-bin.'

The detective handed him a sealed white envelope. 'My operative found only three items in it. Several sheets of oily paper, and these.'

Ross, with an unlit Montecristo in his mouth, tore open the envelope. Inside were two capsules he recognised instantly.

'The bitch is throwing her pills away – that bastard is

persuading her to dump them. Jesus. Can you believe it? My wife is dying, these pills are the only chance she has and he's talking her out of taking them.' Choking with emotion, close to tears, Ross said, 'He's a murderer, Mr Caven.'

The detective sat in silence.

Ross looked down at the report again. 'I don't recognise that number. What the fuck number is he using?' He clicked his gold Dupont and held the flame to the end of his cigar and puffed several times, blowing out the rich blue smoke.

'It's a mobile phone.'

'It's not her phone,' Ross said. He pressed the play button and they both listened again.

'Faith, hi, wondering how you are. I should have the test results all back by tomorrow afternoon latest. I could see you Monday, or over the weekend if you could make it, but I guess you'd have problems getting away. Call me at the office, I've told them to put you straight through.'

'Where's he phoning from?'

'His office,' Caven said.

'No reply?'

'We have his office phone tapped, his mobile tapped and his flat covered by cameras. We haven't picked up any reply.'

'The bitch has got smart on me. She's using a phone I don't know about. I haven't picked up one conversation between her and this quack in ten days.'

'As I've said to you, Mr Ransome, I think you might find you're overreacting to this situation.'

'Overreacting? Is that how *you*'d feel if some charlatan was trying to kill your wife?'

Caven pulled out a pack of cigarettes, and shook one out.

'Put those away,' Ross said, glaring fiercely and taking a deep pull on his Montecristo.

Caven looked at him in surprise. 'But you're smoking.'

'I don't want that cheap cigarette polluting the smell of my Havana.'

Caven hesitated. His loathing of this man deepened each time they met. But he did a quick calculation. He was employing three men on round-the-clock surveillance at Dr Oliver Cabot's flat, plus a further rota of three men on surveillance outside the Ransomes' country house, following Mrs Ransome wherever she went. Additionally he had rented time on a satellite, which picked up and relayed back to him all calls from Cabot's office and mobile phones. Ross Ransome was aware of the costs and happy to pay. He was making more profit from this case than ever before.

He pushed the cigarette back into the packet. 'Thank you for saving me from myself,' he said.

The irony was lost on the surgeon.

59

In bed, Faith closed her book, *Wild Swans*. After reading of how women had been treated in China, she was fortunate at least to have been born and brought up in this country, if nothing else. Her head was pounding. It was twenty past eleven.

She squeezed two paracetamols from their foil wrapping and swallowed them with a glass of water. Then she took out her contact lenses, put them in the solution in their containers and replaced the lids.

Ross, naked, carried his suit jacket across the room and disappeared into the walk-in wardrobe. Moments later he emerged, strode across the room and placed his trousers in the wooden press. She knew exactly what he would do next. He would pick up his tie, examine it in the light for any marks, then carry that into the wardrobe and carefully hang it in its colour-coded slot on the rack. Then he would emerge again, check his shoes, carry them into the wardrobe, and put them in their places on the shoe shelves. After that, he would fold his underpants and place them on the *chaise-longue*. Next to them he would lay each of his socks, neatly smoothed out. And finally, he would fold his handkerchief and place that beside the socks. In the morning he would pick them all up and drop them into the laundry basket. She had never understood why he didn't just drop them straight into the basket.

His penis wasn't erect, but looked as if he was starting to get aroused.

Please let me sleep. I don't want you inside me, I don't want you coming remotely near me.

She turned off her bedside light, leaned back against the pillow and closed her eyes.

'You OK?' he said.

'I have a bad headache.'

'You took some pills?'

'Paracetamol.'

'How are you doing with the Moliou-Orelan capsules? You still have plenty left?'

'Yes, plenty.'

'How many days' supply left?'

'About a week.'

'I've got more coming. And you've been taking them three times a day, every day?'

'Ross, I have a headache.'

Downstairs in the kitchen Rasputin began barking. Probably a rabbit, she thought, or a fox.

'How's the nausea? Are the pills helping it?'

'No, not so far.'

Rasputin barked again then fell silent.

'You are taking them, aren't you, darling?'

'Of course I'm bloody taking them.'

She felt the bed sag slightly. Then his hand on her stomach, sliding down, his fingers working through her pubic hair. She squirmed away. 'Ross, I really don't feel well.'

'You had a headache on Wednesday.'

'I'm ill, OK? I'm sorry.'

His fingers persisted, working their way inside her.

'Please, Ross.'

'We haven't made love since last Saturday.'

She didn't reply.

To her relief, Ross removed his fingers. He leaned over and kissed her cheek. 'Goodnight, darling.'

Ross picked up the *British Journal of Plastic Surgery* from his bedside table, opened it and began to read. But he wasn't concentrating, he was listening to Faith's breathing, which was steadily deepening.

Then he turned and watched her eyelids. Waiting for the fluttering that signalled she was moving into REM sleep. He waited patiently, turning the pages of the magazine, glancing at her, listening.

Patience.

At ten past twelve he said, softly, 'Faith?'

She didn't respond.

Again, 'Darling?'

Still no response.

Good.

He turned out the light and lay still, eyes wide open, waiting for them to adjust to the darkness. Out beyond the closed curtains the night sky was clear, and it was almost a full moon. Within five minutes he could see all the shapes in the room clearly. Outside he heard a terrible high-pitched screeching sound. Rasputin barked a couple of times, half-heartedly. Faith did not stir. The screeching again, briefly, then silence. A fox had taken a rabbit.

Slowly, carefully, he slid out of bed and stood, motionless. In a whisper, he said, 'Faith?'

No response.

He walked round to her side of the bed, then stood still. She was breathing heavily, mouth open.

He closed his fingers around the glass jar containing her contact lenses, lifted it and backed away from the bed to the bathroom. Then he closed the door and locked it.

In darkness he walked over to the twin washbasins, and pulled the toggle for the shaving light above his basin. He opened the hinged mirror of his cabinet, took out a box of Calvin Klein Obsession For Men *eau de toilette*, and opened the lid.

Inside was the vial of ketamine he had put there earlier, with a small hypodermic syringe. He broke the seal on the ketamine, unwrapped it and dropped the seal into the lavatory bowl. Then he pierced the top of the vial with the needle, pushed it down into the fluid, and drew up a minuscule amount.

He had no idea how much was needed, or what effect the lens solution would have on the anaesthetic. This was going to be trial and error. He would start with just the smallest drop and see how that went.

He removed the top lid, marked 'L', from the jar containing the contact lenses, squirted in the ketamine, then screwed the lid back on. Then he did the same with the bottom lid, marked 'R'. Working quickly now, he put the vial and the syringe back in the Calvin Klein box and replaced it in the cupboard. Then he snapped off the light and, as quietly as he could, replaced the lenses on Faith's bedside table.

Silently, he returned to the bathroom, switched on the light once more and flushed the lavatory.

Faith slept on, undisturbed.

60

Nice neighbourhood. Plenty of flash wheels parked around here, no one about and the street-lighting wasn't that good. Nice one. Spider made a mental note that this would be a good place to trawl on his next shopping spree.

Uncle Ronnie had a lucrative business supplying luxury cars to export customers, mostly in the Middle East, and increasingly in Russia and in the growing Balkan market. Serbia was particularly good for fully loaded Grand Cherokees. Ronnie sent the shopping list to Spider, who picked up most of the cars himself, to avoid involving other people and to earn the maximum from each deal.

Spider had plenty of reasons to be grateful for Eurotunnel: it had really helped this business. Late at night, he could steal a Range Rover, a top-of-the-range Jag or even an Aston or a Ferrari to order, and have it in a lock-up fifty miles south of Calais with a brand new registration document and set of numbers long before the owner had woken up to find it missing.

Ronnie's lists came with detailed specifications on colour, trim, mileage, extras, and sometimes it took a while to find the right vehicle. Spider invested a lot of time in finding new hunting grounds and tonight he reckoned he'd lucked into one. He didn't know why he hadn't thought of this area before.

But tonight, cruising this quiet backwater of Notting Hill Gate in an unobtrusive rented Ford Mondeo, it wasn't motors that were on his mind. It was invasion of privacy. There were a lot of pressure groups about this, and Spider was right there with them, in spirit at least.

There was too much fucking invasion of privacy, these days. Surveillance cameras were a big hazard. Every city had them now, perched high up in places where you didn't notice them, silently recording everyone beneath them on tape – and they could zoom in close. Two hundred yards away they could tell what wristwatch you were wearing.

You couldn't be too careful.

There might be cameras watching him now, the registration number of this Ford being checked against a computer file on stolen vehicles, then filed away on a digital memory, ready for instant retrieval at the tap of a few computer keys. If the police wanted to, they could log the progress of this car through the whole city.

But it wouldn't help them much. He had rented it in a false name, with a false licence. That was the beauty of any system. Once you understood it, you could outwit it. No one was going to look at this vehicle twice tonight. Not even a computer.

Ignoring the no-smoking sticker on the dash board, Spider lit a Marlboro, sucked the smoke in deep, blew it out. A man was walking two large black dogs on a leash. *Shit factories*. Spider didn't like dogs, except greyhounds: they were just about acceptable if they won for you. For a time, as a kid, he'd said that a dog had bitten him in the mouth. Sometimes when he was younger, as an act of bravado in front of the lads, he'd go up to a dog, kick it and say, 'That's for you and all your fucking friends for ruining my mouth.'

But now he had his moustache and he wasn't angry about his mouth any more. He rarely thought about it. Some girls even found it sexy. Sevroula was turned on by it.

Gotcha!

Parked just four doors past number thirty-seven.

Impossible to tell the colour, but the licence plate on

the Jeep Cherokee told him all he needed to know. Dr Oliver Cabot was at home tonight.

Sweet dreams, Doctor, he thought, driving past, leaning forward and turning up the volume on Heart Radio as Jamiroquai came on.

At the end of the street there were railed gardens. He made a right turn in front of them, then another right turn, and now he was driving along the terrace that backed on to Dr Oliver Cabot's. It was another similar terrace, the same height houses, the same architecture. Probably some kind of alley running behind, separating them. He would check that out later, not now.

Now it was good just to get the feel of the place. Tomorrow he would return on his mountain bike, wearing a crash hat, dark glasses and smog mask and he would take a closer look for any surveillance cameras. More than likely there were none here, it was too much of a backwater, but he wasn't leaving that to chance.

He took another drag on the cigarette and turned up the music even more, feeling happy. This afternoon the dealer had accepted his deposit cheque of five hundred pounds on the Subaru Impreza, and in a few days he would be driving around in it. Uncle Ronnie always paid on the nail, and he was depending on this. Regardless of the deposit, the dealer refused to hold it beyond Monday.

And tonight he was going to get laid. Sevroula was a Turkish girl who had danced for him a month ago at his table at Stringfellow's. They had slept together every night for a fortnight, then her husband had come home on leave from his oil platform in the North Sea. He had flown back up there this morning.

Sevroula had told Spider he was the best kisser in the world.

In just a couple of hours he would pick her up from the staff entrance of the night-club. Maybe they'd stop and have a drink somewhere. Then he'd take her back to his flat, turn down the lights, tweak up the volume on the sound system, do some lines of Uncle Ronnie's finest coke. Then they'd get animal with each other.

He lit another Marlboro and took a second cruise past Cabot's front door. Darkness. Seclusion. Fire-escapes. Only four storeys high.

Chicken shit.

61

A narrow strip of sunlight strobed on Faith's face through a tiny chink in the curtains. She woke smiling, her body flooded with warmth. They'd been shopping in the Portobello Road, having a good time, Ross and herself, laughing at a grotesque antique demon on a stall that was several hundred years old and made of plastic. They'd broken out into helpless laughter. They were hugging each other, barely able to stand up they were laughing so much. Life was so good between them, she could feel this incredible love they had for each other, that nothing, *nothing* could ever diminish.

Then, reality closed over her, like the cold waters of the deep. And the long, slimy tendrils of reality wound tight around her ankles, pulling her further down still into a darkness blacker than any night.

Five days ago the future had stretched ahead of her, limitless, like those first few days in childhood after school broke up for the summer, when the holidays stretched further ahead than the mind could think. Then suddenly they were coming to an end, and she would find herself ticking away those final days before the new term began and the nights started drawing in. She had that end-of-summer-holiday feeling now, only worse.

She lay wondering if she would ever see another

summer, wondering if she should make a list of all the things she wanted to do while she was still well enough to do them.

She shivered. What were those things? She wanted to see Alec grow up, get married, have kids, to be a grandmother—

She wanted to go to Peru, India, Australia, to see the terracotta army in China. To Jerusalem. To—

Tears rolled down her cheeks into the pillow. I can't think like this. Can't admit it, have to be positive. Oliver is going to cure me. He's going to get rid of this thing. I feel fine today, I really do.

Outside, life went on. People came and went from this planet. There were creatures around long before man, tiny organisms, microscopic single-cell amoebae, bacteria, plankton, ants, beetles. And she had read they would be around long after the human race had died out. Some breeds of cockroach could live happily in post-nuclear fallout. They weren't aware of humans, didn't need them and wouldn't miss them when they were gone. We wouldn't even be history, she thought.

And these kidney-bean shaped creatures inside her that she had seen through Oliver's microscope, these quantum-sized living organisms that were spreading through her gut and her nervous system, that were using her as a living carcass in their food chain, these Lendt creatures, they and their progeny would be around long after she had gone. After everyone had gone.

She listened to the birds chirruping outside, and something suddenly felt unreal about them. Nothing in her life felt totally real any more.

Inside the house there was another sound. Grating voices, constant peaks and troughs of sound-effects and music. Television cartoons always sounded to her as if she was hearing them through a badly tuned radio with the volume too high. She could hear one now, faintly, a fuzz of sound that made it through all six walls separating their bedroom from Alec's.

Which meant that Alec was awake.

It was Saturday. She could see from the brightness of the sun on the curtains that it was a fine summer morning. The clock by her bed said seven fifteen. Ross was stirring and she did a quick calculation. He was playing golf at nine, which meant he had to leave here by half past eight. Which meant he would need to be downstairs, having breakfast, by eight fifteen at the latest. He would need to shower and shave so he would have to be out of bed by eight.

Which left a forty-five-minute window.

Downstairs there was a flurry of barking from Rasputin. Probably the papers arriving – it was too early for the postman. After a minute or so he quietened.

Now Ross was moving. She breathed in and out steadily, the way someone in deep sleep would breathe, eyes shut tight.

Please don't touch me. Don't start groping me, I don't want to have to make love to you.

He grunted, then rolled over, and she heard the clinking sound of the steel strap of his Rolex, and knew, from years of sleeping beside him, that he was now looking at his watch and that in a few moments he would take a sip of water from the glass beside him. And she knew what would be in his mind.

'Faith?' Just a whisper at first, then louder, more insistent. 'Faith? Are you awake, darling?'

She lay still, facing away from him, tight and foetal. His fingers began tracing a line down her back, between her shoulder-blades.

Leave me alone.

'Darling? Faith?'

Now silence. She could hear his breathing above her

own. The bed moved, feet padded across the carpeted floor. She heard him in the bathroom, first the hard stream of urine, then the sound of a tap running and the brushing of teeth, the click of the door, and the soles of his Bally slippers slapping along the landing and down the stairs. Excited barks from Rasputin in the kitchen, then louder barking as Ross opened the door for him and he rushed outside.

And she knew that, in a few minutes, Ross would be coming back upstairs, carrying a cup of tea with a freshly picked flower lying in the saucer, and there would be no staying asleep then and no way out of his advances.

She tried to go back to sleep but that was impossible. Instead, she started running through a list of everything to be sorted out for tonight. Twelve for dinner. Mixed Italian hors d'oeuvres starter of Parma ham, melon, tomato, avocado, olives, mozzarella with Ciabatta from the little Italian delicatessen in Brighton. She could tick those items off. Then salmon *en croûte* – using filo pastry – with asparagus grilled with Parmesan. New potatoes. Tick. Peas. Tick. Then she went through her checklist for the pudding ingredients. Then the fruit salad. Tick.

She worried that she didn't have enough cheese, or Bath Olivers. Ross only allowed her to serve Bath Olivers with cheese, nothing else.

He was coming into the bedroom now. She heard the clink of a cup rattling in a saucer, the click of the door closing, the swish of his silk dressing-gown. The cup being placed close on her table, inches from her face. The scent of a rose. The rustle of newspapers.

A tiny pulse tugged inside her throat and she tensed even more, waiting for the mattress to sag, the bedclothes to move. To her surprise, they didn't.

She heard running water in the bathroom. The radio came on and the shower door clicked shut.

She opened her eyes, and saw a yellow rose lying in the saucer. Maybe it was finally getting through to Ross that he needed to be gentler with her because she was ill.

But that worried her even more.

She sat up in bed.

A curl of steam rose from her tea. The *Daily Mail*, with several bite marks from Rasputin and a small amount torn from the bottom of the front page, lay neatly folded on the duvet beside her. The headlines, a little blurred, talked of peace in Bosnia and of the forthcoming wedding between Prince Edward and Sophie Rhys-Jones.

She reached across, picked up the jar containing her contact lenses, took out each lens and inserted it.

Much better. Instantly the room and the newsprint were pin-sharp. She blinked a few times. The first few moments with the lenses were often uncomfortable, and today they felt worse than usual, making her eyes water – probably because she had been crying, she realised.

Big speculation in the paper about what Sophie was going to wear for the wedding, and a comment about the vows she was going to take. She would promise to obey her husband but said she was determined not to walk in his shadow. Faith admired her courage. She had learned that to be under a husband's shadow ultimately corroded your spirit.

Then, as she read the next line, all the words slipped off the page and she found herself looking at plain white newsprint.

It did not even occur to her this was weird. She merely looked around her on the white duvet, which was now a dazzling white, almost too bright to look at, to try to find where the little black words had all gone. But she couldn't see them.

They're going to mark the duvet.

She picked up the newspaper and all the rest of the words slid off the pages like raindrops from a polished surface, and fell in a shower around her.

'Ross,' she said, 'there's something very strange—'

The walls of the room rippled like curtains in a breeze. She watched them, intrigued. 'Ross!' she called out. 'Ross, come and have a look at—'

Something crawled through her hair. With a shudder, she ran her hands through it, but it was still there. Not just one creature, but several. They were crawling down her back now, too. She swung her legs out of the bed in panic, struck the bedside table. The cup, saucer, yellow rose all fell to the floor in slow motion. The rose began to melt as if it was dissolving in acid.

'Ross—'

And now, as she stepped on the carpet, the floor tilted away from her and she fell forward, plunging down into an empty lift shaft, screaming. 'Rossssss . . . Rosssssssss!'

Suddenly she was floating on the ceiling, looking down at the floor. She could see a woman spreadeagled, naked, blonde hair pooled around her head, a brown stain near her feet with a tiny yellow flower melting away at the centre of it. It was herself, she realised.

She was looking down from the ceiling at her own body on the floor.

I'm dead.

'Ross!' she screamed. 'Ross, help me, I'm dead, I'm dead.'

He was in the shower and couldn't hear, she realised, her panic worsening. *'Ross! Help me!'*

I'm dead.

There were strands of carpet in front of her face, she was breathing in the smells of fabric and dust. Faintly, through the wall, she could hear the thrumming of the power shower. Then she was looking down again, from the ceiling. Whimpering, she said, 'Ross, please help me.'

Never going to see Alec again. Get Oliver someone, please get Oliver, he'll know how to bring me back—

A change of sound. The shower switched off, then the click of the door, and then with strange fascination she watched Ross coming out of the bathroom, striding in slow motion, dripping wet, towel around his midriff. Watched him kneel beside her, cradling her head in his hands.

Help me, Ross. My heart has stopped.

'Ross – please help me.'

If Ross can revive me I will go back down into my body and if he doesn't I'm going to drift away, further away.

The ceiling was pressing down on her back. She was feeling shut in, claustrophobic. Ross's lips were moving. Reading them, she could see he was calling her name, looking frantic.

But she couldn't hear him.

62

Ross, holding her wrist, felt anxiously for her pulse. It was strong, steady, a little fast but that was fine.

Relieved, he looked at his watch: 7.48. Making a mental log of the time, he worked his arms underneath her, lifted her up and laid her on the bed. He moved the pillows away to ensure that her head was tilted well back, keeping her airways open, and checked inside her mouth for anything that might choke her.

Her eyes were open but unfocused, pupils dilated. He cursed.

Given her too damned much.

In a voice that was slow and slurred she said, 'Ro-oss – I can see you.'

'Good.'

'I . . . I . . .' Her voice tailed off.

He sat on the bed, watching her.

'I'm up here,' she said. 'I'm up here, I can see – I—'

'What can you see?'

Her eyes rolled, as if they had become detached from their muscles; the pupils disappeared and he was staring at the whites. She was losing consciousness.

Holding her pulse again he said, 'Faith?'

A small, frightened voice now. 'What's happening, Ross?'

He kissed her forehead. 'You're going to be fine, my darling. You're just having a little turn from your illness.'

'Don't leave me.'

'I won't.'

'You – you have to play – golf this morning.'

'It doesn't matter, they can play without me.'

'I'm spoiling your morning.'

'I'm with you. That's all that matters to me.'

'We—' she said.

'We what, darling?'

'Need—'

'What do we need?'

She was silent.

Ross checked her pulse again. Her eyes were darting in all directions. Then they rolled upwards again and the pupils disappeared. Her eyes closed.

'Faith?' He pinched the flesh on her forearm, but there was no reaction. He checked her pulse; it was fine.

Twenty minutes passed. He sat, holding her wrist, monitoring her pulse all the time, not daring to leave her.

'Cheese,' she said, her eyes springing open. 'We need cheese.'

'Are you hungry?'

In a deadpan voice she said, 'You're so funny, Ross. You're so funny, you make me laugh and you make me just keep on laughing.'

Then she turned her head and stared hard at him. Stared with eyes that were focused yet sightless. He looked away, and as he did so she said, 'You're going to kill me, aren't you, Ross?'

'Why do you say that?'

'Oscar Wilde said every man kills the thing he loves.'

'Oscar Wilde was a turd burglar. I don't think a man who sodomised small boys is qualified to talk about love.'

'But you will kill me,' she said. 'You'd prefer to kill me than lose me.'

'I'm not going to kill you or lose you. I'm going to make you better, darling, we're going to beat this thing inside you.'

There was a long silence. Ross looked at his watch again. Another fifteen minutes elapsed. Then Faith said, 'I want to be back in my body, Ross, I don't like it up here. I'm so scared. Please don't let them take my body until I'm back inside it. You won't, will you?'

'Of course I won't.'

'You have to tell me what cheese to get.'

'What do you mean?'

'For tonight.'

She kept having lucid flashes, he noticed, and this was good. It was another hour and a half before the signs were clear that the drug was beginning to wear off.

It was almost noon before Faith was stable enough to go down to the kitchen to start preparing dinner for that evening. Even then, Ross was nervous of leaving her alone, and he didn't think she was yet in a safe state to drive. He took her to the supermarket himself. Standing by the cheese counter, waiting their turn, with the numbered ticket in her hand, Faith turned to him and said, shakily, 'Can you explain what happened to me this morning, Ross?'

'It's the disease advancing because you're not taking the pills,' he said. 'You must start taking them again.'

As soon as they got home Ross made her take two capsules. Then he left her in the kitchen and went upstairs. Jules Ritterman and his wife were coming to dinner tonight. And Dr Michael Tennent, a psychiatrist who had his own radio show. And another psychiatrist, David DeWitt. The perfect audience. Not to mention the Chief Constable of Sussex and a High Court judge.

He locked the bathroom door, opened the cabinet and took out the Calvin Klein box. He would have a drink with Faith before the guests arrived, as they always did, to put themselves in a party mood.

By his reckoning, just a quarter of the dose he gave her this morning should suffice.

63

The first symptom is prolonged nausea – the patient usually feels this for between two and three months. Increasing disorientation with delusions of persecution and night terrors follow. Terminal features include fluctuating levels of consciousness and hallucinations. Then a gradual loss of motor-control functions.

Ross had gone to the golf course to play a quick nine holes, then he was collecting Alec from a birthday party.

It was half past three, and he wouldn't be back for at least another hour.

Faith, glad to have the house to herself, had snatched a break from her preparations in the kitchen to sit down at Ross's computer and look up the symptoms of her disease on the Net again.

'Terminal features . . .' she read again, with deep discomfort.

She'd had the first symptom, prolonged nausea – or at least recurring nausea. Not necessarily the second symptom, though. She'd been having bad dreams but not actual night terrors. But this morning she had definitely had a psychotic hallucination. And the sensation of being out of her body was still scaring her now. Was that what death was like?

A fly batted against the window. She opened the window to let it out and savoured the smell of freshly cut grass. Then she logged off and sat for some while in Ross's leather chair, reflecting gloomily on what was happening to her. She was deteriorating. The disease was progressing. Destroying her.

What chance do I really have?

She took her mobile phone from its hiding place in the bottom of her handbag, pulled on her Barbour, and walked out through the french windows. Rasputin barged past her, ran across the wide flagstoned terrace, then waited.

She strolled, hands deep in her jeans pockets, along the immaculate lawn, down to the lake. The sun was shining, but there was a sharp wind blowing. It was meant to be summer, but no one had told the weather that. Too cold to have drinks out on the terrace tonight, as Ross had planned.

The lake was long and narrow, bordered by trees. In the middle was a small island where a pair of mallards nested. Three of their brood of eight had survived the foxes and the crows and were now almost as big as their parents.

Faith sat on a wooden bench and watched the whole family paddle towards her, then scramble out of the water, unfazed by Rasputin who treated them with the disdain he thought ducks deserved.

'Sorry, ducks,' she said. 'Nothing for you.'

They continued to squawk, jostling each other, like a bunch of elderly women at a bric-à-brac stall. Then, still protesting noisily, they returned to the water. She watched them paddling away, and the start of a poem she loved came into her head.

Happy the hare at morning, for he cannot read the
    hunter's waking thoughts.
Lucky the leaf, unable to predict the fall.

Lucky any creature, she thought, that wasn't aware it was living under a death sentence.

Fighting tears, she dialled the number, and moments later, Oliver Cabot answered. 'Faith! Hey! Where are you?'

'At home. Ross has gone out for a while so I thought I'd ring. I – I wanted to hear your voice.'

'It's good to hear yours. You sound down.'

'I had a bad experience this morning . . .' She glanced behind her, just in case Ross was back unexpectedly.

Oliver listened in silence. When she had finished he said, 'We need to start your treatment as soon as possible. I have an invitation to see a play tonight at Chichester, but I could blow it out. Would later on this afternoon work for you?'

'I – I can't. We're having a dinner party.'

'It's more important to get you right, Faith.'

'I know.'

'I'll come and tell him as your goddamned doctor that there's no way you're giving a dinner party in your condition.'

She smiled as she pictured the confrontation between Ross and Oliver. Two men so far apart in their thinking, they might be from different planets. 'I'll be OK, I'll get through it somehow.'

'What about tomorrow?'

'No, I can't do tomorrow. Monday's clear. Your message said Monday was good for you.'

'Monday's fine. Come to the apartment as early as you like.'

She did a quick calculation. One of the other mothers was doing the school run next week. She had to get Alec ready, that was all. 'I could be there by ten. What do I do if I have another of these turns?'

'Call me and I'll help you through it – and if you need me I'll drop anything I'm doing and come down.' He was quiet for a moment. Then he said, 'Faith, I will get you better, you're going to get through this. Try to be strong. I'm going to send you healing thoughts that will make you strong until I see you. I love you.'

The words brought a lump into her throat and she could barely respond. 'I love you, too,' she said. 'I wish I was with you now.' She stroked Rasputin's head, and the dog, sensing her distress, nuzzled against her legs.

'I can cancel the theatre.'

'No, go.' Tears were running down her cheeks. 'I'll be OK.'

'Call me tomorrow if you get a chance.'

'I'll try – it's going to be difficult.'

'What are you doing?'

'Ross wants us to go out for the day with Alec. He's

suddenly got into the three of us doing family things together. Probably so that he won't feel so guilty after I'm dead.'

'Faith, you're not going to die. Have you registered that?'

'OK,' she said.

'You'll call me if you need me. Promise?'

She was walking back towards the house, still deep in thought, when she remembered the pastry case in the oven. It had been there for over an hour.

'Shit, shit, shit.'

She broke into a run, but she knew she was far too late. She had been making it for a glazed strawberry and almond tart, a dessert that was always popular.

When she got there, she was greeted by a smouldering mess. Even Rasputin, normally game to Hoover up any culinary disaster, gave it a suspicious blink from a safe distance.

She didn't care that Ross had told her not to drive for the rest of the day. She got into the Range Rover and drove to Tesco. On the patisserie counter there were two ready-made strawberry tarts that would do the job fine. She could bash them about a little and no one would know that they weren't home-made. She put them both in her basket.

Then, just as she reached the checkout, she turned, walked back to the patisserie counter and put them back. Dammit, she still had time to make the thing herself.

Walking back to her car empty-handed, she tried to convince herself that it wasn't because she was scared of Ross's anger if he found out she had served a shop-bought dessert: her own pride refused to allow her to serve one.

The truth lay somewhere between the two.

64

Winter meant short days, long nights. Long darkness. Spider preferred winter to summer. He preferred cold to heat, rain to sun, but most of all darkness to light.

Darkness gave him the best cover for his work – better still when it was raining. And he knew he always looked best in the dark, or at least, in the shadows. Out of direct light he fancied he looked quite handsome.

But today, on this hot June Saturday afternoon with the sun beating straight down on him, he was having a good time. Dressed in a cotton T-shirt and Lycra shorts, crash helmet, smog mask and dark glasses, he pedalled effortlessly up Ladbroke Grove. The bike was a dream: a brand new Fisher suspension model with Ritchey Pro-Lite flat handlebars, carbon-fibre seatstay, aluminium chainstay and Shimano gears. It had cost fifteen hundred pounds, retail, but he'd paid just eighty, to a kid he knew who fenced for a bunch of junkies.

A shame, really, to be ditching it later tonight.

He changed down a gear to cope with the incline, although that was just being super-lazy, but, hey, there was no rush, and besides he was going too fast, he had a job to do, this wasn't some recreational ride.

Slow right down!

He had travelled nine miles, mostly uphill – people didn't appreciate how hilly London was until they tried to get around on a bike, but he was barely perspiring. He worked out for two hours every day in the gym, doing weights mostly, and building stamina. Over the years he had toned his once puny body into the physique of a flyweight boxer.

While he pedalled, his eyes peeled information from his surroundings. Surveillance cameras were still a relatively new phenomenon and the law hadn't yet got subtle about concealing them. They were bolted on to any high wall that provided a good vantage-point, usually at intersections to give a choice of directions, and mostly, because of budget, automatically wiped the tapes after thirty hours if no incidents were reported.

He made a right turn into Ladbroke Avenue. No cameras so far. He hadn't expected any around here, not in this quiet, posh backwater.

The navy blue Jeep Cherokee was parked in the same place as last night, just a short distance along from number thirty-seven. Slightly fewer cars parked than yesterday – some away for the weekend, Spider presumed. He braked to a halt, and looked up at the windows of Dr Oliver Cabot's flat. Then he pedalled on down the road, turned right at the end, then right again into the alley that ran along the rear of the entire terrace, pedalling slowly now, counting as he went. He dismounted when he was directly beneath the flat, looked up and around.

Not happy about this alley, he decided. Too many windows from the buildings behind overlooking it. Any number of people would be able to see him if he tried to get up this way, either on the fire-escape or just scaling the building.

On a Saturday night, plenty of people would be coming and going until late. No one would pay any attention to a man entering by a front door, no matter how late. That's what he would do. Sevroula finished work at two in the morning. And he would have finished his by then, in plenty of time to collect her, as he had promised, from Stringfellow's.

Last night with her had been brilliant. And tonight, with a big weight off his mind, would be even better. He'd only known her a month, but already he was certain he wanted to marry her. The last time he had felt this way about a woman had been six years ago. And it had taken these six years to get over her rejection. But now, he was on a roll.

Behind his smog mask he was beaming.

65

At five to eight, Ross put Bach's Brandenburg concerto on the CD. He always played Bach when guests were arriving: Baroque music, he had told Faith long ago, stimulated the brain, put people in an upbeat mood.

He was dressed in his crimson brocaded smoking jacket, open-neck shirt, cravat, black trousers and Gucci loafers. Once, Faith had thought he looked striking in that jacket, but now he just looked to her like an arrogant poseur. She was wearing the simple short black dress from Nicole Farhi that he had put out for her. Plus her pearls and her black satin Manolo Blahnik high heels.

The waitress they had booked had let them down at the last minute, and Faith had had to cajole Mrs Fogg into helping out tonight. She was now standing in the kitchen moaning that she was missing out on her bingo evening. Faith left her to it and joined Ross in the drawing room.

Rasputin lay in the hall, waiting for the first ring on the doorbell.

'Here,' Ross said, holding out a glass, 'drink this. It'll perk you up.'

She took the ice-cold champagne flute, sat down on a side chair, so as not to dent the cushions of the freshly plumped sofas, and sipped. Ross came over and clinked glasses with her. 'Cheers, darling. You look beautiful.'

'You look very nice, too,' she replied.

'Christ, woman, lighten up. Hope you're not going to greet our guests looking this miserable.'

'I'm sorry, Ross, I don't feel well.'

'We've got some serious players coming. You're fucking well going to have to feel well.' He paced the room. 'Get that down your throat and you'll feel better.'

She took another tiny sip. The nausea was back, and with it the attack of butterflies she always had before the start of a dinner party. Only they were worse tonight than ever. Large, dark death's head moths flapped their wings in her belly, filling her with deep foreboding. She wished she could phone Oliver, just to hear his voice.

Ross peered out of the bow window. 'Fucking rabbits.'

She watched two grazing on the lawn. The sky had clouded over and a fierce wind was blowing. Petals tumbled from a rose-bush. Rasputin began to bark. A Jaguar was coming in through the gates, two minutes early. Faith glared. Why the hell does anyone arrive early? Don't they know it's polite to arrive ten minutes late?

'Jules and Hilde,' Ross said.

Faith drained half her glass, put it down on a side-table and went to open the front door.

'Faith, how very nice to see you.'

Brown eyes greeted her with a warm smile. Beside them, sullen green eyes, as if their owner had come under duress. The brown pair belonged to Jules Ritterman, who was standing in the porch in a dark suit. The green ones were beneath the dated blonde fringe of his Nordic wife, Hilde, a foot taller, who was standing grim-faced, dressed in a turquoise awning, holding the smallest box of chocolates Faith had ever seen.

It took Faith a moment to sort out the eyes. She looked at one pair, then back at the other. They were there, in front of her, and then, suddenly, Faith wasn't sure that they were there at all. She felt a blast of heat as if she was standing in front of an open furnace, and then a sudden, sharp, intense chill as if a bolus of cold water had been injected beneath her skin.

Her brain locked. She couldn't remember their names. 'Hallo – hi – great – good journey? Ross is here – he's expecting you – I mean – we – we both –'

Oh, Christ, another car was coming down the drive now. A white car. She had read somewhere that people who bought white cars were indecisive.

The brown eyes were looking at her strangely. The green ones too. She wasn't sure what she was supposed to do next. Invite them in. Yes. She took a step back, but now Ross was standing beside her. He shook Jules Ritterman's hand, kissed the Nordic iceberg and Faith found herself holding the minuscule pink box of Godiva chocolates.

'My favourites,' she said.

No smile.

'Can I take your coat?'

'Actually I don't wear one tonight,' Hilde said.

Faith looked at the awning. Christ, why the hell had she thought the woman was wearing a coat? 'No,' Faith said. 'Of course. Jules, can I take yours?'

That damned patronising smile, then, 'I'm not wearing one either, Faith.'

The eyes again. What the hell was it with their eyes? Looking at her. Pity? Was there pity in them?

I'm not cracking up. Please, God, don't let me crack up.

Both pairs of eyes slid past her. She looked over her shoulder and there, by some miracle, stood the scowling Mrs Fogg in a presentable white blouse and black skirt, holding a tray of champagne flutes.

Tyres crunched on the gravel. The white car. A modest-looking car. A modest-looking man and a modest-looking woman got out. They had matching grey hair, and almost matching haircuts. On the man it looked all right, in a dull, schoolmasterly way. On the woman it looked silly. They strode towards the front door with the ardent expressions of fell-walkers approaching a challenging stile.

'This is His Honour Ralph Blakeham,' Ross said.

The judge, Faith realised.

'And my wife, Molly,' he said.

Molly handed Faith a jar of home-made quince jelly. Faith just had time to read the label before the jar slipped through her fingers and shattered on the porch tiles with the force of a mortar bomb.

While Mrs Fogg cleared up the mess, and Faith clung to Rasputin's collar to prevent him cutting his paws to shreds on ten thousand shards of glass, the rest of the guests crowded in at once.

In the kitchen, Faith sat on a chair, picking slivers of quince-coated glass off her shoes. Mrs Fogg, emptying the dustpan into the waste-bin, said, 'I really find this beneath my dignity, Mrs Ransome.'

The cleaning woman's face blurred.

'I don't have to do this job, you know. Not with my education.'

Faith was up on the ceiling looking down; she could see herself, sitting at the table, holding one shoe in her hand.

Mrs Fogg said, 'With my education I should be—'

'Help me,' Faith said. 'Please help me, I'm having another—'

From the ceiling, she saw Ross storm in through the door. 'What the fuck are you both doing in here? Nobody's got any fucking drinks.'

Faith stared down at him. Then, suddenly, she was staring up at him. He was seizing her arms, lifting her to her feet.

'Come on, woman, pull yourself together, you're the bloody hostess. Where the hell are the drinks?'

'In the hall,' Mrs Fogg said.

Ross jammed Faith's shoe back on her foot, then gripped her hand and towed her along. She followed in small, tripping steps, trying to stay upright. The walls of the hall came in towards her, then stretched away into the distance, for miles. The suit of armour swayed like a bush in a breeze.

Then she was in a sea of faces, a babble of voices. Eyes everywhere, a maze of eyes. Lips, somewhere beneath them, mouthed greetings.

'Michael Tennent,' Ross said. 'And his wife, Amanda. This is Faith.'

Looking down at them from the drawing-room ceiling, with Bach chiming around her, she heard them say they were delighted to meet her, and she knew she needed to reply, had to be polite, witty, charming, as a hostess should be, but she couldn't find the words because she was dying.

She was slipping from her body into death, right here in front of all these people, and no one realised. She blurted the only words she could. 'Please help me, I'm dying.'

She turned away from their startled faces. Only to see more startled faces. Stepping back, she collided with a slim, boyish-looking man with prematurely white hair. The Chief Constable. 'I'm sorry,' she said to him, and then to the woman standing beside him, his wife, she presumed, 'I'm sorry, I'm dying, nobody understands, please help me, please, I need everybody's help to stay in my body. Please help me, please don't let me go away.'

She backed away and now she was staring at another man, a tall, balding man in a corduroy suit, with distorted eyes; she had met him before but couldn't name him now. A shrink, she remembered, but that was all. He would understand.

Seizing his arm in terror, she whispered, 'None of them realise I'm dying. The spirits are trying to drag me out of my body, please hold on to me. Ross doesn't believe me. Please protect me.'

Now Ross was beside her, arm around her, so loving, so caring. 'Darling, it's all right, I'm with you. You're just having another of your attacks. I'll take you upstairs – you can lie down for a little while. I'll give you something to help you relax.'

'Paranoid,' a man's voice said.

'Psychotic,' said another.

'It's one of the symptoms, I'm afraid,' she heard Jules Ritterman say.

'I'll fetch it from the car,' said another voice.

Her body was some way in front of her, or maybe it was behind her. She turned her head in blind panic. 'My body,' she said. 'Where's my body?'

A prick in her arm, like an insect sting.

In moments she was back in her body. She was lying on her bed. Anxious faces looking down at her: Ross, Jules Ritterman, Michael Tennent. She smiled up at them in relief.

Then her eyes closed. She tumbled through the bed into a warm, blue ocean of sleep.

66

There was almost a full moon tonight, giving more light than he wanted, but the biggest concern on Spider's mind as he dismounted was that the machine might get stolen. All bikes in London were vulnerable and this state-of-the-art Fischer would be prize booty. The irony that it was already stolen passed him by.

The fact that *homo sapiens* has survived for four hundred thousand years owes much to the majority of humans being equipped with consciences that are tuned to the same frequency. But a minority are plugged in to a different value system. Spider could do things that other people couldn't and they didn't affect him in the slightest.

Spider the tormented child used to find solace in tormenting insects and animals. No cockroach ever judged him because he had a hare-lip. No frog ever laughed at him, no dog sneered. Spider repaid these creatures by torturing them to death. Slow deaths for beetles and spiders, being roasted alive on top of the oven. Sudden, violent deaths for frogs: he strapped them to fireworks that either blew them to smithereens, spun them round and round while incinerating them, or else carried them several hundred feet up in the air, leaving them to plunge back to the ground attached to burnt-out rocket sticks. And invisible deaths for dogs; razor blades cut up inside chunks of chicken, he discovered, were effective.

If asked to explain why he did these things, he could not have provided an answer, but it would have been obvious to any psychiatrist that he was a classic psychopath. It was only in the movies, *Silence of the Lambs* in particular, that Spider had seen a psychiatrist.

Now, dressed in a lightweight tracksuit with a nylon rucksack strapped to his back, and thin cycling gloves, Spider pedalled along the quiet darkness of Ladbroke Avenue, a geeky guy in a smog mask and crash helmet who looked like he was returning home from a geeky Saturday night out.

The street was deserted. He was relieved that the Jeep Cherokee was still there, parked in the same place as it had been this afternoon, beneath a street-light. In the sodium glow he could see that the car had accumulated a patina of dust – it didn't look as if it had been anywhere since yesterday. Slowing, he looked up at Dr Cabot's windows. Dark. Good.

At the end of the street he made a left turn, then swung the bike into an opening between two buildings, past a row of lock-up garages and into an empty, falling-down bike shed where he was invisible to anyone above.

He dismounted and heaved the rucksack off his shoulders. The Heckler and Koch P9 was a heavy brute, and the silencer made it heavier still. He also carried a photocopy of the floor layout of Dr Oliver Cabot's flat, obtained from the Planning Office, a photograph of Cabot downloaded from the Internet, a torch, a set of lock picks, a bolt-cutter, a glass-cutter and a strong suction cup for taking out window segments, an SP 300C Big Kahuna stun gun with a belt clip and two nine-volt nickel cadmium batteries, a leather combat belt, a Swiss Army knife and an empty matchbox.

He used the knife to take souvenirs from his victims. He was slowly building his own private Black Museum in a drawer in his dressing-table. Matchboxes with coded labels, containing snippets of hair, a finger nail, a tiny strip of skin, a little piece of shirt fabric. Nothing elaborate. Nothing that would give the police a signature to enable them to link his killings to one person. Just stuff.

Ripping open the Velcro stays of the rucksack, he began his preparations. First he strapped on the belt, then he inserted the batteries into the Big Kahuna, which looked like a large handgrip and felt like lead, switched it on and fired a test charge. A bolt of blue electricity arced out and crackled into the corrugated iron wall. Fine. He secured the clip to the belt, switched off the stun gun and locked it on to the clip. Then, double-checking that the safety catch was on, he jammed the loaded Heckler and Koch into his right-hand trouser pocket, which he had deepened and strengthened, and the silencer into the left-hand pocket.

Next, he clipped on to the belt the torch, the Swiss Army penknife, then the bunch of lock picks. Finally, he pushed the matchbox into a pocket in his jacket, closed the rucksack, slipped it back over his shoulders and checked his watch. Five past midnight. All set.

He pedalled back into Ladbroke Avenue. Not a soul in sight and only a few lights on here and there. The beat of music came from somewhere down the street, a persistent rap. He rode past the Jeep, an Audi, a van, an elderly Porsche. Then he dismounted again, wheeled the bike up to the front door of number thirty-seven, and chained it carefully to the railings.

The most dangerous part was now, these few steps on foot. As he climbed up to the front door, he freed the lock picks from his belt. When he was twelve Uncle Ronnie had taught him how locks worked. Like anything in life, once you understood the principles, you were nine-tenths of the way there. The rest was technique.

It wasn't much of a lock on the front door, a crappy household five-pin job, a decade old; one hard shove and it would probably have yielded, but he didn't want to draw attention to himself. He quickly sorted through the tungsten picks. Two half-diamonds, a half-round and a full-round, a full-diamond, a rake and a snake. He selected the snake, inserted the tip into the keyway and navigating the wards, pushed it firmly through the plug, feeling for the first pin. Almost immediately, he felt the snake brush against it.

Found you, you little bastard.

Gently applying pressure, he levered the pin clear of the sheer line. Then he located the second pin, and lifted that one easily. Anyone watching him would think he was just a tenant having a problem with his key, but nerves were making his hand shake and he missed the third, had to pull back for it before connecting. The fourth and fifth pins rose easily. Now he pushed the pick in the full length of the tang to the handle and gave it a twist, increasing the torque progressively. A solitary bead of sweat darted down the side of his forehead. He could still hear the fucking rap beat.

The lock clicked. The door swung forward with a rustle of paper as it dragged a bunch of flyers from a pizza-delivery house along beneath it. Red spangles glinted at him from the reflector of a bicycle propped against a wall just past a row of mail-boxes. A strip of light shone beneath a door to his left and he heard the faint sound of voices and music – someone watching a movie on television. The smell of curry filtered through his mask.

He closed the door behind him. A weak glow from the street-lighting pressed against the fanlight above the door, but not brightly enough to see by. Switching on the torch, he crossed the floor and climbed the staircase. On the first landing, a tread creaked. He slowed his pace, checking each tread carefully now, not wanting any neighbours later to be able to tell police at what time they had heard someone entering or leaving this place.

The door to Dr Cabot's flat was secured by a sturdy mortise deadlock. A pig to pick.

It took him four minutes of deep concentration before the cylinder turned and he could push the door ajar. Gently, an inch at a time, listening, feeling, sweating like a hog, hoping there wasn't a safety-chain as well. The darkness of the place poured out at him like liquid freed from a bottle.

Six inches. One foot.

No chain.

No pinpricks of red light, which would indicate an alarm system. Just a faint glow some distance away, and above it, big shadows moving on the wall. He froze, then relaxed. A fucking illuminated fish tank.

He took a step forward and a figure took a step out of the darkness straight at him. Choking down a cry of fear he jumped back, his hand diving to the stun gun. Then he stopped.

Dim-fucking-wit.

It was his reflection in a full-length mirror.

Bad omen. All his life he had hated mirrors, loathed seeing his reflection, hated being reminded that he was a freak and always would be.

He closed the door, and stood listening for any sounds. There was enough ambient light from the moon, the street-lamps and the fish tank for him to see the huge open-plan room, and work out the geography of the flat from the plans he had memorised.

He screwed the silencer on to the Heckler and Koch, then jammed the pistol down the front of his jacket. Then he unclipped the stun gun, put his finger on the trigger and, holding the torch switched off under his left arm, went to the door that showed on the plans as a corridor to the bedrooms.

It was. The first door, on the right, which by his reckoning should be the master bedroom, was ajar. The curtains were open and there was enough light from outside to show that the bed, lazily made, was empty.

Fuck.

Suddenly, the light in the corridor brightened. It took Spider a second to work out why. Lights had been switched on in the living area. He heard the click of a door, the clink of keys. Footsteps across the oak floorboards, coming this way.

Police?

Had he tripped a silent alarm? His eyes sprang to the

window, looking for an escape route. Christ, he was being sloppy tonight! He had broken his own golden rule when breaking into any place: first locate an exit route.

It was an old-fashioned sash window and he could see there were brass locks, preventing it lifting more than a few inches. *Shit*.

He stood behind the bedroom door. Footsteps coming towards him. Someone was whistling 'Raindrops Keep Falling On My Head'.

A cop wouldn't be whistling. And he'd be carrying a radio, which would make sounds.

Spider put the flashlight on the floor, gripped the stun gun, and with his right hand pulled the Heckler and Koch out of its makeshift holster and clicked off the safety catch. Holding his fingers on the triggers of both weapons, he peered down the corridor into the living area. He had a clear but narrow field of view.

A man ambled through it in a bomber jacket, chinos, loafers, carrying a booklet. He was a good six feet tall, with a mane of curly grey hair.

Exactly as in the photograph.

Spider seized his opportunity. He came out quickly from the corridor, threw a quick glance around the room to make sure no one else had come in with him, walked up behind his victim and called, 'Dr Cabot?'

The man turned, startled, but before he had time to register anything, Spider jabbed the muzzle of the Big Kahuna against his arm and squeezed the trigger, dumping three hundred volts into the muscle.

Dr Cabot seemed instantly to shrink in stature and go slack, as if all his bones had been removed from inside his skin. The booklet, a theatre programme, dropped from his fingers. He took a step back, his eyes rolling around as if they had become disconnected, then a step sideways, caught a plinth on which a sculpted bronze head stood, then went down backwards on to the floor with a grunt, and stayed there.

Spider knelt beside him. A dribble of blood rolled from the corner of the doctor's mouth – probably bitten his tongue, Spider thought absently, as he studied that equine face, comparing it against the photograph he had memorised.

No question that this was his man.

The effect of a stun gun was short-lived. It wiped the stored blood sugar from all the body's muscles and short-circuited the neuro-muscular system. Within a minute, if he gave him the chance, Dr Cabot would start to feel OK.

Spider dragged him across the floor, raised his shoulders and propped his head against the squab of a leather sofa – he didn't want to risk the bullet going through the floor into the flat below.

Lucidity was returning to his victim. Those grey eyes were focusing now. Dr Cabot spoke in a slurred voice. 'Heysh – whash—'

Spider pressed the muzzle of the Heckler and Koch against the man's forehead, two inches above his nose, savouring the faint realisation that he could see dawning in the man's grey eyes, and gave the trigger a firm squeeze all the way to the back of the guard.

The silencer was good: the gun made just a dull phut, kicking up sharply in his hands, and there was an even duller spattering sound as fragments of the back of the doctor's skull struck the sofa. The man jerked slightly and his eyes stopped moving. A neat round hole blackened by powder burns in the centre of his forehead oozed fluid.

Spider, breathing the acrid tang of cordite and the sweeter smell of singed flesh, checked to see if he could find the bullet, but there was too much mess. It might have disintegrated on entry inside the doctor's head, or plugged itself deep into the sofa. It wasn't essential.

Using the scissors on his penknife, he cut one lock of the man's hair and put it in the matchbox. Then he retrieved his torch from the bedroom and left the flat, closing the door quietly behind him. Adrenaline was pumping and he was on a high that no amount of coke could compare with. Another minute and he would be pedalling away. Ten minutes and he would be in his car. In an hour he would be collecting Sevroula.

And then . . .

On silent footfalls he made his way back down the stairs, remembering the creaky tread on the first floor. He floated over it. He had never been so silent in his life, and never felt so good about life.

A dull buzz.

Then another, sharper, closer.

Then another further away. Another. Another. Above him, then below him. Above him again. Either side of him. Doorbells.

Shit.

As he started to make his way across the hall, he heard a loud crash. Then another. Blam . . . blam . . . blam . . .

In front of him, on the front door, wood splintered.

The door of the ground-floor flat opened and a man came out, naked, with a towel around his waist. 'What the hell?' the man shouted. 'Hey!'

At that moment the lock and the door jamb gave way, and the front door crashed open. A bald, tattooed hulk in a T-shirt and jeans barged into the hall.

The light came on.

'*You!*'

The bald hulk was pointing at Spider. 'You bastard, you fucking murderer.'

The Big Kahuna was clipped back on his belt and

switched off. Spider took a step back and tried to get the Heckler and Koch out of the front of his jacket, but it snagged on the fabric. The hulk was coming at him. A hand ripped away his mask, he smelt warm breath that reeked of fried onions, then something slammed into his stomach. He crashed against a wall and fell down hard on to the fucking bicycle.

Scrabbling back like a cornered rat, hand inside his jacket, tearing at the Heckler and Koch, he kicked out with his feet and heard a howl of pain as the bicycle crashed into the hulk's knees. The hulk fell on his face, entangled in the machine.

Spider had the gun out now, pointed at the hulk who was climbing up on to his feet, and jerked the trigger back. A neat round hole appeared on the hulk's cheek.

For an instant time stopped, as if he had pressed the pause button on a video. He saw the hulk looking at him with an almost chiding expression, as if he were scolding a naughty child. He saw the naked man with the towel around him, hand over his mouth, eyes staring in shock, half-way back into his doorway.

He pulled the trigger again and half the hulk's neck disappeared. His head lolled, all the facial muscles gone slack. For an instant, there was nothing but loose ends of frayed skin and sinews, then blood began to spurt, unevenly, as if coming from a hose with a partial blockage, and the hulk rolled over to one side like a sack that had been released down a chute.

There was a stench of excrement, mixed with cordite and curry. Spider scrambled to his feet.

The naked man screamed, 'Please don't! Please don't shoot me!' and retreated into his flat, slamming the door.

Spider realised his mask had gone.
The man had seen his face.
Spider stared out at the street. *Jesus, what a fuck up.*

He heard the scraping of furniture. Threw himself against the door of the flat, then kicked the lock hard. From inside he heard a voice crying out, 'Please don't, I won't tell, I didn't see you!'

Spider fired twice at the lock, blowing a hole the size of a fist in the door. Then he charged the door with his shoulder. It budged a fraction and inside he heard a scream.

Then outside a siren.

His eyes sprang back to the open hall door.

Go.

He took one more look at the door then, reluctantly, he went. Raced down the steps to his bike. The key to the padlock was at the bottom of his fucking rucksack.

Siren getting closer.

He got the key out. A voice crackled on the speaker-phone. 'Hallo? Who is that? Hallo?'

Siren even closer now.

He dropped the fucking key.

Tried to pick it up but the gloves made it too hard. He needed the bike, goddammit, he needed that fucking bike.

One more attempt to pick up the key. Now he could see a glint of blue light skidding across the metal and glass of parked cars at the end of the street. *Abandon the fucking bike.*

He ran, oblivious now of the route he had planned for his bike, the Big Kahuna swinging from his waist, the torch under his arm, the Heckler and Koch in his hand. He jammed it down inside his T-shirt, the silencer so hot it burnt his skin, but he didn't notice. He just ran, following his nose, heading towards the silence, the smell of greenery, the huge oasis of darkness that was a park.

And his only thought right now was, *This is a fuck-up. This is a real fuck-up. Oh, Jesus, what a fuck-up.*

67

The ring of the phone came into her dream like a hollow metal scoop, trying to tease her out from her snug warm shell of sleep. The second ring came at her louder, the third louder still, shrill and stark. She tried to cling to the dream, cling to her sleep, to this other world she was in, a much better place, but it was fast slipping away leaving her high and dry, stranded on a beach.

Wind howled. She opened her eyes, saw the curtains billowing, straining like torn sails against their rails, saw bitumen black clouds beyond, heard the hooks clattering on the rail. There was an even blacker cloud inside her. Cold, hostile air blew on her face. The phone rang a fourth time and now the bed was moving, Ross rolling, reaching for the receiver. Then his voice.

'Uh?'

She lay still, grateful that the ringing had stopped. Her head was pulsing and she was feeling too nauseous to move. For a brief moment she thought, *Monday. Going to see Oliver.*

Then she realised, despondently, no, not got through Sunday yet, got to get through Sunday first.

'Whozat? Who d'you say? Oh, right, sorry, you woke me, bit of a late night . . . Yes.'

The clock on the radio on her bedside table said eight ten. A volley of rain spattered down. Goosebumps pricked her flesh; something else, something dark, pricked her mind. A gap, a void, a big empty space, a sequence of events that seemed wrong.

Ross was sitting up on the edge of the bed now, cordless held tight to his stubbled cheek, hair sticking up like a scruffy kid. He sounded worried. 'When did this happen? I mean, when did it – they – start?'

Something had been ripped away from inside her,

some big piece of memory. Last night they'd been having a dinner party and now she was here in bed and it was morning. Sunday morning?

'Oh, God,' he said. 'Do you want me to come up? I can be there in an hour and a half if you need me.'

She felt giddy, closed her eyes, which made it even worse. Her brain felt as if it was tumbling around inside her skull.

'Cross-contamination,' Ross said. 'That's what it sounds like. Why didn't anyone realise yesterday? I see. Are you on duty all day?'

She had been greeting guests and now she was in bed and it was Sunday morning. The guests were gone. She couldn't remember speaking to anyone. Or serving drinks. Or food.

Ross smelt of stale cigar smoke. 'I don't like the sound of it at all. No. Will you keep me posted? What tests are you running?' He was out of bed now, walking across the bedroom with the cordless and closing the window. 'OK . . . So you're not sure . . . same symptoms . . . The lab's not open today, right? So you can't get anything confirmed until tomorrow. No, don't worry, I'm glad you called, this is important. You realise the implications for the clinic, don't you, if there is cross-contamination?'

I dropped a glass jar of quince jelly on the porch and now I'm in bed.

'Is anyone else affected? You'd better damned well check on everyone – God knows, could be in the air-conditioning, the water, the food, anything.'

Faith heard the click of the receiver going back on the cradle.

Ross said, 'Jesus, it would have to be one of my patients, wouldn't it?'

Then the click of the television coming on, and the sound of Ross padding through to the bathroom and the door shutting. Then a newscaster's voice. 'It seems from eyewitness reports that Dr Cabot's assailant may have shot the second man, Barry Gatt, because he tried to apprehend him.'

For an instant, Faith thought she either imagined or misheard the name. The newscaster continued, 'The doctor, who was identified by his secretary this morning, came to England from America eight years ago following the death of his son from leukaemia. A maverick, who frequently made news headlines because of his controversial views on medicine and the pharmaceutical industry, Dr Cabot founded the Cabot Centre for Complementary Medicine in North London in 1990.'

She sat bolt upright in bed. There, on the television screen, was the terraced Notting Hill Gate building where Oliver lived. The front porch and steps were tented and police tapes cordoned off the pavement. She could see several police cars and unmarked vans; a man in a white protective suit was emerging from the rear of one.

No.

A sluice opened somewhere in her belly. This had to be part of the dream. Her blood was draining and ice-cold water was rising inside her.

Please no. Not Oliver. Please.

Now she could see a face she recognised, a gentle, good-looking man in his early thirties, she had seen him before. Where? On the screen beneath him appeared the caption *Dr Christopher Forester. Hypnotherapist.* He was looking distraught, and now she remembered him. He had talked to Oliver in the corridor of the clinic. They had borrowed his office to – to look out of the window at the man who was following her.

'Oliver was a wonderful man,' Dr Forester said, in a voice that was barely composed. 'I can't imagine why anyone would want to do this. He dedicated his whole life to helping people, to trying to make this world a better place.'

Faith was numb. Over and over just one thought repeated itself inside her head. *Please don't let anything have happened to Oliver.*

The newscaster was back on the screen. 'The assailant was dressed in cycling clothes, with a crash helmet and a rucksack. The police are interested in talking to anyone who might have seen someone of this description in the vicinity of Ladbroke Avenue between half past eleven and half past midnight last night.'

A policeman now appeared on the screen, and although she was listening intently, she found it hard to concentrate on his words, which seemed to drift around the room, around her head. It was a particularly savage crime, he was saying, and it was too early to suggest any motive. They had a good description of the suspect's face and would be issuing an Identikit of him shortly.

On the screen now the scene changed. The familiar gates of Stormont Palace in Belfast. Then newscaster said, 'Prime Minister Tony Blair arrives at Stormont later this morning for the start of a new initiative with the leader of Ulster Unionists David Trimble at keeping the Good Friday agreement alive.'

Had she missed something?

Whimpering, her nausea forgotten, she scrambled out of bed, grabbed the remote control and punched up Teletext, then the command for the news headlines. She hadn't even noticed she was still wearing her black dress from last night.

TWO DEAD IN NOTTING HILL SHOOTING. Page 105.

Ross came out of the bathroom, naked. He put an arm round her. 'You're awake, darling. How are you feeling?'

She punched the numbers without replying.

'I may have to go to London,' he said. 'Fucking patient I operated on last week has developed septicaemia. The worst possible patient it could have happened to . . .' He hesitated. 'What are you looking at?'

On the screen the story came up.

Police investigating double-shooting in a house in Notting Hill in which prominent London doctor Oliver Cabot and another man were killed. The shootings took place shortly after midnight.

'Jesus,' Ross said.

Faith fell into his arms. 'No,' she said. 'It can't be him. Who would kill him, Ross? Why? He can't be dead.'

Ross sat her down on the bed and cradled her head in his arms. She was sobbing hysterically. 'Why would anyone kill him?' she said.

The phone rang again. Ross answered. Through her sobs she heard him say, 'Tommy? You heard? Lady Reynes-Raleigh – I just can't believe this, what are they fucking playing at? How the hell could it have happened? I could be there by half ten. OK, I'll see you then.'

'I don't want to die, Ross,' she sobbed.

'You're not going to die, my darling angel.'

'He can't be dead, Ross. Who would kill him? Who?'

He held her tightly, kissed her sodden cheek. 'Listen, my darling, I have to go to London. The clinic administrator's called a crisis meeting. We have a big problem. I'll be back as soon as I can.'

'Don't go, please don't leave me.'

'I have to, angel.'

She flung her arms around his neck, holding on to him in terror. 'Please stay.'

'I'll get you something to calm you down.'

He released her. She sat limply, the words of the Teletext a blur on the screen, someone talking in an Irish accent about decommissioning weapons.

Ross came back holding a glass of water. He put one pill in her mouth and she sipped and swallowed, then another.

'Let's get you back into bed. I'll make Alec his breakfast.'

'Please stay with me, Ross.'

'I'll ask Mrs Appleby to come over and look after Alec.' Mrs Appleby was a widow who lived in a cottage down the lane, and was always happy to babysit.

She felt him lifting her, then she was lying on her back. On the television the man with the Irish voice was still talking.

Downstairs she heard Rasputin barking.

After a while there was silence.

68

'Mummy?'

Faith opened her eyes from deep sleep with a start, to see Alec standing over her. He was wearing a black sweatshirt with whorls of luminous green on it, and clutching a plastic Sumo wrestler with one of its hands missing. 'When are we going to Legoland, Mummy?'

The curtains were open, and rain was lashing the window so hard it looked like frosted glass. All kinds of bad stuff was stirring inside her head.

'Legoland?'

'You said we were going to Legoland today. You promised.'

She glanced at the clock: 12.25.

This took a moment to register. It couldn't be – she'd slept the whole morning.

'You did promise, Mummy.'

Now it was all returning to her. *Oh, God.*

Oliver.

Dead.

She stared up at Alec, helpless, drifting. She needed time alone for a few minutes, time to think.

Alec was close to tears now. 'You *promised*, Mummy.'

She stared at him bleakly, shivering. 'Have you had breakfast yet, darling?'

'*Hours* ago. Daddy made it for me. He burnt the toast and my egg was all hard. And Rasputin's been sick in the hall.'

'Great.'

'Mrs Appleby cleared it up.'

'Did Daddy say when he would be back?'

'He said you're not very well. Are you going to get better?'

She took his free hand, squeezed his wrist. 'Of course I am. I'm going to get better because I love you.'

He sat down, pensively, on the bed. 'Are you going to get better in time to go to Legoland today?'

Despite herself, she smiled. And she realised just how desperately she loved her son. She had to keep going for him. Whatever else, she wanted to make sure this vulnerable child of hers had a normal upbringing. Wanted somehow to make him happy. Maybe her mother could bring him up after she was gone.

'What time exactly do you think you will be better?' Alec enquired.

She smiled again. She loved the way he expressed himself sometimes.

'In *exactly* fifteen minutes.'

'I'm hungry, and Mrs Appleby says she has to go home now.'

'I'll make you something, OK?'

'What?'

'A surprise.'

'OK.' His face much brighter now, he jumped down from the bed and scampered out of the room.

Faith went across to the television, switched it on, pulled up the Teletext news. It was on the list of headlines.

TWO DEAD IN NOTTING HILL SHOOTING.

She called up the page number for details but little had been added to what she had read earlier. The phone rang and she answered. It was Ross to say he was going to be stuck at the Harley-Devonshire Hospital for a while yet. If he could get away in time, he'd try to meet them at Legoland. He said not a word about Oliver.

You're pleased, aren't you, you bloody bastard? she thought, as she hung up. She looked at the screen again, and a crazy thought went through her head. Was this Ross playing one of his sick games? Sending a false news story into the television just to torment her?

For a few moments she clung to this slim, forlorn thread. Then she remembered on television earlier, the scene outside Oliver's flat, the tenting, the tapes, the police, and she sat down on the bed, head in her hands, tears guttering down her face, trying to take on board that Oliver was dead and that she was never going to see him again.

Somehow she showered, dressed, paid Mrs Appleby who was reluctant to accept any money, and got Alec, clutching his GameBoy, belted into the back seat of the Range Rover. She started the engine, put on the wipers, opened the map on her lap and worked out a route to Legoland.

'I need to go wee wee,' he said. 'I need to go wee wee now.'

She shoved the gear shift into Drive and floored the accelerator. Gravel rattled beneath them. 'You'll have to bloody well wait.'

'You didn't make me any lunch, and I'm really, really, *really* hungry.'

'I haven't had breakfast, so we're both hungry.' She peered down the bonnet, easing the car out of the drive into the narrow lane.

Behind her she heard a sharp, twangy beep-beep . . . beep . . . blarrrrrpp . . . and, in the mirror saw Alec's face scrunched up in concentration, playing the Pokémon game they'd bought in Thailand.

'You said it was going to be a surprise, Mummy. You promised it was going to be a good surprise.'

She pulled out at the end of the lane into the main road. There was a film of grease on the windscreen and she could barely see the road ahead. Swallowing a lump in her throat she said, 'I'm afraid the surprise is that you're going to have to wait for your lunch. I've had a bad surprise too this morning, so we're both having a lousy Sunday.'

'Why isn't Daddy coming with us.'

'Because he's had a bad surprise as well. Now, play with your game.'

After they had been driving for almost an hour, she saw the signs for a Happy Eater, pulled into the car-park and they went inside. The place was packed and the smell of chips turned her stomach. A waitress came over with their menus. Alec took his and studied hard. He chose a double burger with a ring of pineapple and French fries, which Faith knew would be too much for him, but she ordered it anyway, and a coffee for herself.

Although she hadn't eaten since lunch yesterday she had no appetite.

Alec continued to play his Pokémon game. To their right, there was a young couple, leaning forward, holding hands. In love. On the left was a man reading the *Sunday Express*. Nothing about the shooting, probably happened too late for the morning papers, she thought.

Her mind was filled with the image of Oliver's face. She tried to think of him in the flat. Someone coming in with a gun. A burglar? Had Oliver gone for him and been shot for his trouble? What cheap piece of human trash killed you, Oliver? Some junkie desperate for his next fix, come for any money he could find, not giving a damn that he killed one of the best human beings in the world to get it?

'Why are you crying, mummy?'

She looked into the little boy's round, concerned eyes and cracked. She got up, asked the waitress to keep an eye on Alec, made her way to the washroom, locked herself into a cubicle, sat down and wept into her hands.

It was several minutes before she felt composed enough to make her way back to the table. When she got there, Alec's meal had arrived. He sat behind it, with a ketchup bottle in his hand, and most of its contents on the table, his face, his shirt and his hands. 'The top came off, Mummy. It wasn't my fault.'

As she cleaned him up, he said, 'Are you crying because Daddy isn't with us?'

She gave him a thin smile. 'I'm OK, just a bit sad today.'

'You said you were going to ring Daddy because he might meet us there.'

'I'll phone him now.'

Then she realised she'd forgotten to bring her normal

mobile with her. What the hell? It didn't matter now. She dug into her handbag, pulled out her private phone and switched it on. Before she had a chance to dial, the message indicator beeped. She jammed the phone to her ear and listened.

'Faith, hi, this is Oliver. Call me as soon as you can on my mobile.'

She listened, fighting back her emotions. The message must be from yesterday, when he was still alive. She played it again. He sounded subdued. Had he known something was wrong, that someone was after him?

Had he been phoning to warn her?

Why didn't I check my messages yesterday?

Standing up, her head swimming, she said, 'I'll be back in a minute, darling. Eat your lunch.'

She went out, stood in the porch, with the wind driving the rain on to her, and listened to it a third time. Just as the message finished, the phone rang. Startled, she pressed the answer button. 'Hallo?'

'Faith?'

It was Oliver.

For an instant, she thought this must be another message. Then she heard his voice again. 'Faith, can you talk?'

Trembling, she said, 'Oliver?'

'Harvey's been murdered. My brother. Jesus, Faith, it's just so terrible, I – I can't believe what's happened.'

'You're alive?' It was all she could say.

'I'm alive.'

'On the television news it – it said—'

'Harvey,' he said. He was crying. 'Oh, God, Faith, some bastard's killed my brother.'

'They said it was you.'

'I'm just so glad I got through. I needed to speak to you, I just needed to hear your voice, Faith. I have to go – the police – oh, Jesus. Can I call you later?'

'Yes.'

He said something she couldn't hear and hung up.

She stood where she was, leaning against the misted-up glass, watching her son busy with his food. She knew she shouldn't be feeling the way she did, because a man was dead – two men were dead – the brother of the man she loved was dead. A nice man, and she could recall him vividly. She knew she should not be feeling elated.

But she couldn't help it.

69

Outside, two floors below, a goods train was clanking past, heading towards the docks. It made a noise louder than scaffolding collapsing.

Spider, in a crumpled white T-shirt and underpants, on his hard bed in his cramped, bare-walled flat, had not slept. Grey light filtered through the grimy, curtainless windows. The television at the end of the bed was still on as it had been all night, sound muted. The smell of stale fat came from the plate on the floor beside his bed. A Coke can sat next to it, with the butt of a Marlboro Light crushed out on it.

It was Monday morning. He felt like shit. Sevroula was refusing to speak to him. None of his excuses for standing her up on Saturday night had washed. And Spider had seen an Identikit of himself on television. Half a dozen times already this morning. On ITV, on BBC 1, on Sky, on every fucking news programme.

An incredibly accurate likeness.

And he reckoned, gloomily, that along with his hopes of marrying Sevroula his green Subaru Impreza was down the toilet. He just hoped the bastard would give him back his deposit.

Now his phone was ringing. He picked up the receiver, hoping it was Sevroula.

A man's voice said, 'You asshole. What a fucking dickhead. You looked at the morning's papers?'

'No.' Spider's voice sounded lame and squeaky.

'They tell me you made the front page on three of them.'

'This isn't smart, calling me at home, Uncle.'

'You don't have to worry about that. If you had more than half a brain inside you and some small fragment of it was in working order, you wouldn't be at home, you'd be hiding in a cave on another fucking planet. Why didn't you leave your business card in their hands after you shot 'em? Make it even easier for the law?'

'It's not that good a likeness,' he said defensively.

'No? It's a perfect likeness of an arsehole. Not going to take the police long to work through the list of arseholes on their computer. Not when there's a fifty-thousand-pound reward out for you. What's that fucking noise?'

On the edge of his bed now, the train still clanking by, Spider said, 'It's a train.' Then, urgently, he said, 'Reward? I ain't seen nothing about a reward.'

'You don't have my fucking sources. The brother of one of your two fuck-ups, Dr Cabot, agreed it with the police yesterday – they've already been circulating it quietly in a few places where gun-dealers hang out.'

'Why's it been kept quiet, then?'

'Guess they didn't want to worry you, Spider. They probably thought you was worried enough already.'

Spider trembled. Fifty thousand pounds was big money. Big enough to tempt the weasel who'd sold him his piece?

Too big for him to fucking turn down.

And, oh, shit, he still had the Heckler and Koch in the flat. He hadn't wanted to dump it during his panic run through London on Saturday night. He'd just wanted to get as far away from Ladbroke Avenue as he could. On the far side of the park he had stolen a bike, and had cycled like the wind, for miles. He hadn't dared go back for his car, parked just a mile from Cabot's house, not knowing what kind of a cordon the police might have put around the area. Instead he'd gone home and hadn't left again until eleven last night when hunger had driven him to grab a takeaway.

'You didn't tell me he had a brother,' Spider said.

'I didn't tell you he had a mother either, or a father.'

Thinking of the Subaru, Spider said, 'I can still do the job – just give me a couple—'

'In your dreams. Take my advice and get the hell out of there – vanish.'

The phone went dead.

The train had passed now, and in the sudden silence the walls closed in, shrinking the room around him until it no longer felt like his home but a prison cell.

No time to wash or shave. He got dressed quickly, tripping over his clothes, trying to think clearly about what he needed to take, and where he could go.

Sevroula's place?

And if she said no?

He rammed the Heckler and Koch deep into his trouser pocket. Fucking Turkish drama queen was about to discover that, with Spider, *no* was not an option.

70

In the middle of a consultation, Ross's intercom buzzed. He picked up the phone.

Nodding a curt apology at his woman patient he said, 'Yes?'

'Mr Caven's in reception.'

'Tell him to make an appointment like everyone else.'

'He says it's urgent.'

'So are all my appointments.'

'He seems agitated.'

There was something in her tone that got through to him. 'I'll see him for two minutes after I've finished with Mrs Levine.'

When his patient left, the private detective came in, holding his laptop bag in one hand and a brown envelope in the other. He was looking pale, as if he hadn't slept, and reeked of cigarette smoke. Ross closed the door and did not offer him a seat. 'This had better be good,' he said. 'I have one hell of a morning.'

Caven handed him the brown envelope, looking at him with grave, accusatory eyes. There was a box-shaped object inside, which rattled. In his soft Irish accent he said, 'When you hired me, Mr Ransome, you told me you were wanting photographs. I think you should take a look at this.'

Ross removed the box from the envelope. There was a videotape inside it. 'What is it?' he said, but he already knew.

'Do you have a machine to play it on?'

Ross glanced at his watch, opened the cabinet containing the television and video-recorder, and put in the tape. Still standing, both men watched in silence.

It was black-and-white footage and the picture quality wasn't great, but it was good enough. It showed a wide-angle bird's-eye view of a large loft apartment. The place seemed to be in darkness. Then suddenly light flared as the lens adjusted, and Ross could see more clearly. A man who looked like Dr Oliver Cabot was coming in at the front door.

As he walked across the floor a figure appeared out of a doorway behind him, a small man or a woman in a smog mask and biking crash helmet, with a rucksack on his back, holding a pistol with a silencer in one hand and a black object in the other.

As if hearing his name called, the man who looked like Oliver Cabot turned round. The other figure lurched forward and rammed the black object against Cabot's arm. Cabot staggered a few paces then fell over backwards.

Ross and Caven watched in silence while the figure dragged the unconscious man a short distance across the floor, propped him up against a sofa, and shot him through the forehead. Immediately the figure disappeared through the doorway he had come from and emerged holding a torch. He hurried to the front door and went out.

Ross turned to Caven, white-faced.

Caven said, 'You can turn it off. It's just a small section I've copied for your benefit.'

Shakily Ross walked over to his desk, picked up his phone and buzzed through to his secretary. 'I'm going to be a few minutes, Lucinda. Hold the fort.' Then he sat down behind his desk, feeling drained, suddenly.

Caven ejected the tape, put it back into the box and replaced the box in the brown envelope.

It took Ross all his self-control to prevent himself blurting out, '*I warned Ronnie-fucking-Milward the place was under closed-circuit surveillance. Jesus, I warned him!*'

Instead he stared ahead of him in silence, looking everywhere in the room but at the detective, not wanting to catch his eye, not wanting to give the arrogant little Irishman any chance to pick up on any body language.

Hugh Caven sat down on the sofa and laid the envelope on the cushion beside him. After some moments he said, 'Mr Ransome, would you be familiar with Occam's Razor?'

'I've never heard of it. Should I have done, as a surgeon?'

'William of Occam was a philosopher in the four-teenth century. He based scientific knowledge on experience and self-evident truths. He believed in the Aristotelian principle that one should not seek to complicate issues beyond what is absolutely necessary. His principle became known as Occam's Razor. This was that any problem should be stated in its basic and simplest term. In science the simplest theory that fits the facts of a problem is the one that should be selected.'

'Please put that to me in some form I can understand.'

'Certainly, Mr Ransome. The simplest explanation is usually the one that is right.'

'And what exactly is the relevance of this to what we've just seen?'

Caven linked his hands, glanced around the room as if checking for bugs, and said, 'If someone is murdered, there is a reason. Ninety per cent of murders are within families. Of the other ten per cent, burglary is sometimes a motive, but we've just seen that that is not the case here. If the killer was just committing burglary, he didn't need to execute his victim – he'd already knocked him out with a stun gun.'

Caven cleared his throat. 'So, you suspect that Dr Cabot is committing adultery with your wife and you hire a private detective to establish this. Dr Cabot's brother, who could be his twin, is murdered in cold blood by what appears to be a professional assassin. Harvey Cabot is a good man, an eminent scientist, happily married, no obvious enemies. But Oliver Cabot has one very obvious enemy.'

Ross shook his head with a smile that was utterly devoid of any humour. 'Mr Caven, if I'm hearing what I think I'm hearing, that you're about to try to blackmail me, I just hope for your sake you've got a good solicitor. You've already committed two serious offences by installing those cameras – criminal damage and breaking and entering – and I'm sure you've contravened other laws with your bugging of Dr Cabot. I wouldn't advise you to compound them with an absurd attempt at blackmail. I want you to get yourself out of my office and out of my life.'

Caven did not move. Instead, very quietly, he said, 'Mr Ransome, a second man was killed on Saturday night – the man who was shot in the hall. He was one of my men, one of the best guys I ever worked with. He saw what was happening and tried to do something about it. You may be angry, but don't underestimate how angry I am. You didn't even know Dr Cabot. Barry Gatt was best man at my wedding.'

'Out,' Ross said, walking to the door. 'Send me your bill. I don't ever want to hear from you again or see you again.'

'You should calm down, Mr Ransome, we need to talk about—'

Ross tore open the door and shoved the detective through it, shouting, *'Get the fuck out of my life!'*

Then he slammed the door so hard a sliver of plaster fell from the wall.

71

Spider's thought processes had taken him to the point of believing he had allowed himself to be panicked by Uncle Ronnie. Standing at the washbasin, jaw covered in foam, cigarette burning in the soap-dish, some manic food programme on the television now – he hated food programmes – he went through the calculations again in his head. If there was a reward, the earliest the police could have known would have been yesterday, Sunday. Then they would have to have put the word out and about via a handful of informers, around the pubs and bars and clubs, and on a Sunday word would have travelled slowly. Very few people knew his address. He was in danger, yes, but immediate danger? He couldn't see it.

The fucking Identikit must have come from that screaming bloke who'd locked himself in his flat, and Spider was bitterly regretting letting him off the hook.

He pulled the razor down, drawing a clean stripe of flesh through the left side of the Charles Bronson moustache, which hid the botched hare-lip. The moustache that was now reproduced in perfect detail in the Identikit.

Sevroula told him she never got up before eleven. If he got there while she was still in bed he would have the element of surprise. Maybe she wouldn't like him so much without the moustache. Her problem.

The Identikit wasn't everything – you couldn't get convicted on an Identikit. That nude bloke couldn't have seen him for more than a few seconds – in a dark hall at midnight. How much weight would his evidence carry? At least he knew he'd left no fingerprints. But forensics were sharp now: they could get you from a single carpet fibre on your shoe. And DNA was a bigger problem still – a bead of sweat or a hair follicle. But the gun was the biggest problem.

Have to get rid of the gun.

That was an absolute priority. It was lying on the bed now, he could see it in the mirror, making an indent on the sheet, shiny, still smelling of cordite. Five bullets gone from the magazine.

The Channel was the best option. Overboard from a ferry in the darkness. Gone for ever. But the ferries would be watched now. It had to be put somewhere it could never be found, and the barrel never matched to the bullets found in the building on Ladbroke Avenue.

The little weasel he'd bought it from could run to the police in search of his fifty-thousand-quid reward, but unless they could find the Heckler and Koch and establish that this was the gun that had fired the bullets, what evidence did they have?

And then a really bad thought wormed through his brain.

Would Uncle Ronnie shop him for fifty gorillas?

A crazy notion – he did too many jobs for Ronnie, he was worth a lot more to him than a paltry fifty grand. No way would he—

Except Uncle Ronnie's temper was legendary. He'd had to leave England after an argument in a pub that had ended in him shooting a man in front of thirty witnesses. EXECUTED IN COLD BLOOD, one headline had said. And he remembered that bust in the hall of Ronnie's grand house at Chigwell, of some Greek geezer, Atrium or Arius or some name like that. Uncle Ronnie used to pat the bronze head and tell Spider that when this man fell out with his brother he killed his brother's children and served them to him roasted at a banquet.

Uncle Ronnie thought that was fucking heroic.

And for a long time during his childhood, Spider had been nervous of displeasing his uncle Ronnie. Scared that if he upset him, he, too, might find himself roasted and garnished, being served for lunch. And, as an adult, he knew that Ronnie Milward was capable of anything when he lost his rag.

And something else was just occurring to Spider. The fuck-up of killing the wrong man, then shooting the second man downstairs, went far beyond himself: it meant that Ronnie Milward had lost face with his client. That was the real issue here.

He'd made his uncle look a fool.

72

Faith paid the taxi and climbed out, pressing a pound coin into the hand of the doorman. Then she entered the lobby of the Marble Arch Hotel, negotiated her way through what seemed like the population of a small Japanese city, followed by an Olympic obstacle course of suitcases, and travelled up in a packed lift crushed between two huge American women in baggy shorts with even baggier flesh.

At the ninth floor she stepped out, checked the direction of the room numbers, turned right and found number 927 a short way down. She knocked softly, and waited. Somewhere a phone was ringing.

Oliver opened the door. He was barefoot, in a crumpled navy sweatshirt and jeans. His whole body seemed hunched and crumpled, his unshaven face gaunt, the colour of slate, with black rims around his eyes and deep pouches beneath, his hair matted and awry. For some moments he just stood and stared blankly at her, as if his eyes and brain were no longer linked to each other.

Faith was shocked. She had never seen grief like this.

'Faith, it's good of you to come.'

She threw her arms around him, wanting to protect him, to comfort him, needing to reassure herself that this wasn't a ghost. 'You poor darling,' she said, hugging him hard. 'Oh, God, you poor darling.'

For a long while they stood there in silence, her face pressed against his chest, his hands massaging her back, his breath riffling a few loose strands of hair across her forehead. 'Faith,' he murmured, 'tell me it isn't real, tell me it hasn't happened.' Then there was anger in his voice. 'How could anyone do this? This is London – it's meant to be safe. Harvey was a wonderful guy. Everyone loved him. Who would want to kill him?'

Her head was full of questions she wanted to ask him, but not now. Now was just a time for them both to try to calm down a little. Behind her, she could hear the rattle of crockery and cutlery: a room-service cart being wheeled past. In its wake came the aroma of bacon.

Still holding each other, they moved into the room and Faith pushed the door shut behind her with her foot. She looked up into his sad grey eyes, and felt as if they were staring into her soul. She felt a sudden quickening sensation, as if an electrical current had been switched on inside her. They stood together and she could feel the same current inside him, could feel the dull thud of her heartbeat, then his.

Excitement ran deep inside her, their eyes locked and they were moving across the floor, lips caressing. His felt so soft, gentle, moist. She was pressing harder against them now, pressing her body against his, the colour of eau-de-nil spinning round them, on the walls, the drapes, the chairs, tables. Images in the same colour slipped past, the window, grey light, another building a dirty brown colour beyond, then eau-de-nil again.

Her hands were inside his sweat-shirt on the firm flesh of his back, as he tugged at her blouse, pulling it free of her belt.

Then she felt a shower of sparks so deep inside her she gasped, as his hands went round her stomach, his fingers pressing inside her waist band. She could feel them now further down still in her soft flesh, pressing into the tendrils of her hairs, and in response she pulled open the buckle of his jeans, tore the pop stud and pulled down the metal zipper.

Slowly, sinking to her knees, taking his jeans and boxers down with her, breathing in the heady smell of his warm flesh, she buried her face into the thick, luxuriant tangle of his pubic hairs, holding him in her hands, holding his beautiful, incredible, rock-hard sex in her fingers. She stroked him in long, slow, gentle movements, feeling his whole body taut as wire, listening to the breaths exploding from his throat, then pressed her lips to the moist tip of this thing, this incredible, exquisite thing, Oliver's thing, the first time she had seen another man's, touched another man's, smelled another man's since – oh my God since – so long, so long before Ross. And this was different. Oliver was so much more beautiful than Ross, than anything, anything imaginable.

She pulled up his sweatshirt, kissing his stomach, then his nipples, teasing them with her tongue, and he pulled down her panties. Then they were on the floor, clothes part on, part off and she was guiding him into her, whispering his name, and he was silent, cupping her face in his hands, kissing her forehead, her cheeks, her eyes, and the world was a swirl of tangled grey hair and eau-de-nil and his warm minty breath.

She wanted to freeze the moment, to stay here for ever with Oliver Cabot, so deep inside her that she felt as if she was part of him. She called his name, as she felt herself being locked with him, gripped by him, filled totally and utterly by him. She closed her eyes, then opened them again, unable to believe this was real, that they were here, the two of them alone with each other. Scarcely able to contain the bursts of pleasure exploding inside her, bursts that were deepening every second, she closed her eyes again, praying for this to be real, praying for that look of happiness on Oliver's face to last, praying that this moment could go on and never end.

Oliver was close now, she could feel him growing

larger inside her, as she tried to hold back, to make the moment last. She felt the floor on her back, Oliver's stubble against her face, his hands holding her tight, pulling her up against him, and could sense a kind of crazed desperation bursting through the pleasure in his face as if this was the moment, the one unit of time, that they had both lived their lives for, that this was the one place where their destinies had intertwined.

She called his name again, shuddering, and he was shuddering too, his breath roaring in her ear.

Afterwards they lay cradled in each other's arms, in a kind of peace she had forgotten could be found in life.

73

Ross, in the spongy vinyl armchair, was sitting too low for comfort. He felt as if he was peering up at the psychiatrist from the bottom of a cliff.

From his attire, Dr David DeWitt looked more like an architect – or an arts critic, perhaps – than a doctor. A gangling, balding man in his early forties, he was wearing a crumpled brown corduroy suit, dark shirt, a tie inspired by Jackson Pollock, and grubby trainers. With his inane perma-grin, he was listening to Ross with the expectancy of a man awaiting the punchline of a joke.

This entire room felt like a joke to Ross – one of those private jokes you had to be in the know to understand. The exterior of the substantial terraced Regency house in Little Venice was all faded grandeur: peeling paint, crumbling steps, rusting ornamental lions. Inside it had been tastefully modernised by DeWitt's elegant wife – all except this room, which seemed to have been decorated by a colour-blind orang-utan with a spray gun.

The walls were painted to simulate leopardskin, the ceiling was a livid purple blotched with even more livid pink, the carpet was orange, and a Dayglo green spider hung from a metal filing cabinet. Almost every surface was stacked with precarious piles of files, receipts, books and papers. Anyone who had not been here before might have assumed that DeWitt was in the process of moving in, but Ross had come here some five years previously and it had looked exactly the same then.

That was when DeWitt had consulted him about his youngest son, Nick. The then five-year-old had a congenital facial disfiguration, with a hooded, elephantine nose. He had been so badly teased at school that he'd refused to leave the house. In a series of operations, Ross had corrected it, and Nick was now, according to his father, well adjusted.

The shrink was high-profile, constantly in the media and well connected. It was partly for these reasons that Ross had cultivated him. The other reason was DeWitt's speciality in body dysmorphic disorder. DeWitt's patients were normal-looking people who either imagined they were ugly or wanted some impossible ideal. He sometimes referred them to Ross, who would reassure them that nothing further could be done.

'Great seeing you on Saturday,' DeWitt said. 'A very good dinner. I particularly enjoyed meeting Michael Tennent – never met him before. And I liked your chief constable friend too.' He paused, then said, 'I'm sorry about Faith.'

'Yes.'

'Lendt's disease, you said?'

Ross nodded.

'But there is a glimmer of hope? This new drug?'

'It's the only hope.'

'But it's not working?'

Choking back well-rehearsed emotion, Ross muttered, 'No.' He dug out his handkerchief and dabbed his eyes.

'I'm sorry. She's such a lovely person. If there's anything I can do,' DeWitt said, 'Vickie and I are hugely indebted to you for all you did for Nick.'

'Thank you.' Ross pretended to pull himself together. 'Actually, there is, David, it's why I'm here. And I'm grateful to you for seeing me so quickly.'

'I had a lucky cancellation.'

David DeWitt, looking at Ross Ransome, saw an expensively clad man of similar age to himself who had a lot of flashy style. But Ross could earn more before breakfast than he could in an entire day. It was not a problem – but DeWitt felt there should be some compensation: surgeons ought to have a higher crack-up rate than shrinks, or lousier lives, or worse hours, but they didn't. They just made trainloads of money, dressed like successful bankers and acted as it they had graduated from charm school. But he *was* grateful to Ross for what he had done for little Nick. Two other plastic surgeons had told him that what he wanted could not be achieved. And Ross, who had performed three long operations on Nico, had refused to charge a penny. Now he was clearly distraught and desperate.

Something caught DeWitt's eye on his desk. A note from his wife, Vickie. She was going to be home late and this was a reminder to put food in the oven for their children's supper. He'd forgotten. It was five o'clock, they would already be home and, of course, since her job as a management consultant at Price Waterhouse Coopers was more important – in her view – than his as a psychiatrist, he was expected to break out of a consultation with a patient and put food in a microwave, the controls of which were beyond him.

'Do you have a microwave, Ross?'

'Oven?' Ross said, startled by the *non sequitur*.

DeWitt nodded.

'Yes. Why?'

'Wondered if you'd help me – I have to put the kids' supper in and it doesn't ever do what I tell it.'

Ross followed him downstairs into the basement kitchen, thinking that what everyone said about shrinks was true: they were barking mad.

A television was on, and he trod carefully around several toys lying randomly on the floor. The psychiatrist pointed to the oven and Ross peered at it closely. Reading from his wife's notes, DeWitt said, 'Six minutes at number two. If you can work out those controls, you can fly the space shuttle. So, tell me, how can I help you?'

Ross waited until they were back upstairs in his office, with the door shut and no one within earshot. Choosing his words carefully, he said, 'You've kicked up quite a controversy with your views on reforming the Mental Health Act. I heard you on the *Today* programme on Monday. Saw your piece in *The Times* yesterday.'

'Well, I believe the power to decide who is mentally ill and who should be detained in a secure institution should be in the hands of the medical profession and not determined by politicians. All *they* do is look at the bottom line of how much it costs to keep someone in a psychiatric hospital. They don't look at the bigger cost to society of releasing these people.'

'So you believe that the medical profession should take a more aggressive attitude to the psychiatrically ill?'

That perma-grin. 'Aggressive?'

'OK, that's a bit severe. Let's say proactive.'

'What exactly is your interest in all this, Ross?'

'I'm just coming to that.' Ross allowed his composure

to deteriorate once again. 'David, you see, Faith—' He allowed his voice to quaver. 'This disease is now affecting her mind – you've seen her yourself, for God's sake.' He fought back a sob. 'I'm sorry. I love her so much.'

'I can see.'

'Watching someone's mind go is a terrible thing. No one can imagine what it's like until they've been through it themselves. And although she's on the Moliou-Orelan drug it isn't working because she won't take the pills.'

'Why on earth not?'

'She thinks I'm trying to poison her. Instead she's going to some fucking alternative doctor.'

'What kind?'

'He's into everything. Homeopathy, acupuncture, psychotherapy, chicken entrails, you name it.'

DeWitt asked, 'How do you feel I can help you, Ross?'

'I need your co-operation. This is a big favour, David. You probably won't like it, but it's the only chance we have of saving her life. Sometimes you have to be cruel to be kind.'

74

On the bed, with Oliver's arm wrapped around her, the fingers of his other hand stroking her back, Faith lay serenely still, breathing in his scent, listening to the scrape of her eyelashes on the pillow each time she blinked, wondering what he was thinking.

Muted sounds of the London morning filtered through the double-glazed windows: the faint roar of traffic, a car alarm, the whine of a power tool, and the occasional shout. She didn't know what the time was and she didn't care: Alec was being picked up from school by a friend's mother and would stay with her until Faith collected him.

She couldn't remember feeling like this before, so calm. It should feel strange, she thought, to be lying in bed with another man, but it seemed the most natural, beautiful and comfortable thing in the world.

'I'm your doctor,' Oliver said quietly. 'I'm meant to be curing you, not sleeping with you.'

'I think you've just cured me,' she murmured. 'I'm better. I've never felt so good before.'

He kissed her eyes, the musky, intoxicating smell of sex rising from deep within the bed. She breathed it in deeply.

'You've just blown eight years of celibacy for me,' he said.

'That should be a criminal offence.'

'Breaking celibacy?'

'No. A lover like you being celibate.'

A thought flashed through her mind: *We didn't take any precautions*. But instead of being concerned she was glad.

She kissed him again, and he smiled, but then his expression darkened. He was still gazing at her but he wasn't seeing her now: he was watching some movie inside his head, or he had travelled to some parallel world where Harvey Cabot was still alive, in Switzerland, perhaps, giving his talk on particle physics, instead of lying in a mortuary refrigerator, disembowelled by a Home Office pathologist, with a name tag tied to his big toe.

And she searched her mind, trying to find a parallel world or universe, or some small kink in time she could slip through to see another version of herself, another Faith Ransome who had just made love to Oliver Cabot, a Faith Ransome who was fit and well and not dying of Lendt's disease. A Faith Ransome who wasn't having her neural pathways chomped away by a savage pack of kidney-bean shaped amoebae. A world where she could live to see her son Alec grow up, get married, have grandchildren. A world where she could make a life with this man in whose arms she lay and from whom she never wanted to be parted.

'I love you,' she said.

His hand squeezed hers in silent acknowledgement.

She squeezed back, and said, 'Is it hard for you to go home?'

'Home?' His voice sounded so distant.

'Your flat? Ladbroke Avenue?'

'Crime scene.'

For a moment she didn't understand. Then, 'You're not allowed back?'

'The whole building's sealed off. They let me in with a police officer to get a few things – said it would be about a week before I can go back. I don't even know if I'll want to go back there ever.'

'Do you – they – have any idea who killed Harvey?'

'If they do, they're not saying anything to me.'

'Who was the other man?'

'A private detective. Had a couple of convictions for assault some years back. He'd been a night-club bouncer, or something. Some kind of low-life. It's hard to see he had any connection with Harvey.' He released her hand and sat up a little. 'The police say it could have been mistaken identity. It had the hallmarks of a professional killing. They asked if I had any enemies.'

His eyes searched hers and a shadow slid across her soul. Yes, it had occurred to her moments after she had seen the news yesterday.

'Ross is a bully,' she said, 'but I don't think he—'

'I didn't mean—' Oliver said, but she interrupted him.

'Ross bought a shotgun several years ago because we

were getting overrun by rabbits – they were eating everything in the grounds, and digging up the lawns. But he only uses it occasionally, on rabbits.'

'No, look, Faith, no way did I mean to imply—'

'It was my first thought too. But I know him. He can make my life hell, and hit me, but I don't think he'd kill anyone. He's a doctor and that's in his soul. He lost a patient a couple of months ago and came home crying about it. He's a baby at heart, a baby who never had enough love.'

'Most psychopaths are people who never had enough love as children.'

'Not Ross,' she said. 'He's a lot of things but I don't think—'

They fell into a silence that was less easy than it had been minutes before. *Why am I defending Ross?* she wondered, and thought of him bugging the house, striking her and Alec. Ross had always been fanatically jealous, but with Oliver he had been over the top. Although she really didn't think he could kill anyone.

But did she believe that because it was true?

Or because it was easier?

75

Ross stood in the phone booth in Marylebone High Street, surrounded by hookers' business cards and stickers.

ORIENTAL DELIGHT – SENSUAL MASSAGE BY SUKI.

MISS STRIKKKKTTTT. DISCIPLINE.

NINETEEN-YEAR-OLD DANISH BLONDE. NEW IN LONDON.

The name on the last card was Kerstin, and in her photograph she didn't look nineteen, she looked north of thirty, and her breasts didn't bear the handiwork of God or DNA. To Ross's eye they carried the signature of a surgeon he knew but didn't care for, who had carved himself a lucrative niche doing cheap breast enlargements for the sex fantasy market.

The phone was ringing, and after some moments a male voice answered in Spanish.

'I want to speak to Señor Milward,' Ross said. 'Tell him I'm calling from England, and I'm not happy. He'll know who it is.'

'A moment. You hold, please.'

The faint crackle of static. Ross shoved in a pound coin, then Ronnie Milward's distinctive voice came on the line. 'Yeah – who is this?'

'It's me.'

'Ah. Thought it might be.' At least the hoodlum was smart enough not to say his name. 'The boy fucked up, he's being dealt with. What can I say?'

Ross was thinking about the twenty-five thousand pounds he had transferred to Milward's bank account in Zurich. And he was thinking about Dr Oliver Cabot, free to go on screwing his wife and poisoning her mind. 'What are you intending to do about it?' he asked.

'Might have helped if you'd mentioned the brother,' Milward said reproachfully. 'Caused a lot of grief, that.'

'You're saying it's my fault?'

'I think we should call it shared blame.'

'Meaning?'

'I'm happy to finish the job properly – but I wouldn't feel comfortable about a refund. I've had a lot of expenses.'

'Obviously not in your research department. And I'm not sure it's too smart to finish the job now.'

'Leave it a few weeks? See how the wind blows?'

'I think we'll do that. But if we call it off I'm looking for a full refund.'

'I don't operate that way.'

'Nor do I.'

'We'll leave it a few weeks. You know where to find me.'

'You'd better still be there.'

'Think I'm going to do a runner on you for twenty-five grand? I don't even get out of bed for that.'

Ross realised the line had gone dead. For a moment he thought Ronnie Milward had hung up on him.

Then he saw, from the flashing display in front of him, that he'd forgotten to put in any more money.

76

Spider's top-floor bedsit was accessed by a narrow staircase, leading up from a front door sandwiched between a betting shop and a Chinese takeaway. The door led out on to a high street that was busy and transient, populated by an uneasy ethnic mix of Indians, Pakistanis, Afro-Caribbeans, Chinese and, more recently, an influx of Serbs.

Dope was dealt on every corner by small tight-knit teams, with lookouts stationed further away, giving hand signals like bookies' runners. This was the kind of neighbourhood where every shop lowered grilles over the windows at night, where no one knew anyone else's business, and people walked fast, staring straight ahead, because eye-contact with a stranger could land you a knife wound. Low rent, high turnover, plenty to keep the law busy. Plenty of bigger fish to interest them than himself.

Except today.

Spider, in his tracksuit, holding his rucksack in one

hand, keys in the other, saw it just as he was pulling the front door shut behind him.

The blue baseball cap. The blue overalls.

The giveaway.

For an instant he froze.

Like fucking chameleons, the Firearms Squad could blend into any crowd but those caps and those overalls would always make them instantly recognisable to each other.

A band tightened around his gullet like a ligature.

Baseball caps bobbing out of the crowd, towards him. *Jesus fucking Christ.* A whole fucking swarm of them. They had been waiting.

Shit, shit, shit.

A voice erupted from a megaphone that sounded only yards away. 'DROP THE RUCKSACK, PUT THE RUCKSACK DOWN ON THE GROUND. DROP THE RUCKSACK!'

A shadow loomed towards him, a dark face beneath a dark peak.

The voice even louder now, deafening. 'DROP THE RUCKSACK!'

He stepped back, slammed the door, heard a tremendous crash and saw daylight squeeze in around the jamb as a copper threw his weight against it. The lock moved visibly away from the wall, the brass stretching like elastic.

Spider turned, vaulted up the stairs, made the first-floor landing before he heard the door splinter open below him.

The voice seemed to be coming out of the walls at him. 'ARMED POLICE. WE HAVE THE BUILDING SURROUNDED. COME OUT WITH YOUR HANDS UP.'

Footsteps clumping up the treads yards behind him. Brain racing, trying to think clearly. Fire-escape? No fucking good, would take him straight down. No other option. He sprinted on up to his room, somehow got the key into the lock, twisted it, pushed open the door, slammed it shut, rammed the bed against it, hurled the small chest of drawers on top, then in desperation the television and the fridge.

Hammering on the door now.

'Police. Open up!'

He pulled the Heckler and Koch from the rucksack, snapped off the safety catch. The door was giving, splintering, the bed was moving. He threw his weight against it, moved it forward, gaining a few precious inches. Then he backed away to the window, stared out and down.

Blue caps. *Shit.* Three of them, one behind a signal box with a rifle, another with a rifle behind a concrete stanchion, the third in the open, behind a chain-link fence, spreadeagled, handgun pointing straight up at the window. The door was moving and the legs of the bed scraped across the ancient linoleum.

Spider jammed the gun down inside his T-shirt, then lifted up the sash window. Two rifles with telescopic sights were trained on him, with two of the best fucking marksmen in the world squinting through them.

But they wouldn't open fire unless he fired first, he knew that. They wouldn't dare, not out in the open like this.

You have time, Spider, just think fucking straight, man.

The legs of the bed scraped again. *'Armed police! Open up!'*

He swung himself out through the window, then stood to his full height on the rotten sill. The pointing was crap in the brickwork above him, plenty of finger-holds. Below, another fucking megaphone bellowed, 'ARMED POLICE. YOU ARE SURROUNDED. CLIMB DOWN!'

He levered out a sliver of cement that was in the way, dug in his fingers, hauled himself up, finding a foothold on the top of the window. Had to get height, fast. Up again, hands on the guttering. Straining, taking all his weight on his hands, he pulled himself up. A voice shouted out of the window now, his bedsit window. 'FREEZE!'

He scrambled up the steeply pitched roof, sending tiles slithering down. It was wet from the rain, slippery as hell, his left foot momentarily lost purchase, and he lurched forward, crashing painfully down on his knee, then he was up again, almost at the top, gripping a strip of raised lead flashing, then a satellite dish. A pigeon sitting only yards away continued to clean itself, then suddenly jerked up its head in alarm and took off.

Spider looked up, too. *Fuck*. He heard the clattering seconds before he saw it, looming over the roof of the grey concrete council low-rise at the end of the terrace, then dropping out of the sky straight on to him. The down-draught from the rotor was whipping his clothes, shot-blasting clay dust off the tiles into his eyes.

Hovering right over him now.

He looked up. Straight into the muzzle of a rifle. Caught the glint of light on the front lens of the sight. And now, from above him, another megaphone.

'YOU ARE COMPLETELY SURROUNDED BY ARMED POLICE. CLIMB SLOWLY DOWN. YOU WILL NOT BE HARMED IF YOU CLIMB DOWN. REPEAT, YOU ARE SURROUNDED BY ARMED POLICE MARKSMEN. YOU WILL NOT BE HARMED IF YOU CLIMB DOWN.'

You won't dare fucking harm me anyway and you know it.

Below, sirens wailed. Spider ran along the roof ridge, buffeted in the down-draught, the roar of the rotor-blade deafening him. Glancing down to his right he could see the high street, strangely silent, a huge empty arc in the centre of it, people standing well clear, anxious to get a good view but not anxious enough to die for it. Two Alsatians were being released from the back of a police van.

Gardens to the left, then the chain-link fence, and the railway line. Open ground. The dogs would get him on foot unless he could scale that fence. But even then he'd be down on their level – here he had the advantage of height on them. Ahead of him the terrace ran into the wall of the council low-rise. A vague plan took him up the wall, in through a window, into an office, where he could take a hostage. Below the building there was a car-park he knew well – he'd taken a couple of vehicles from it.

If he could just get there. Into that building. Down into that car-park. Get to Sevroula.

The megaphone boomed above him. 'CLIMB DOWN!'

He glanced up and, in that fraction of a second, didn't spot the cracked ridge tile, which split in half when he put his weight on it, taking his left foot sharply downwards. As he stumbled, he felt the Heckler and Koch eject from his T-shirt.

No.

Lunging desperately after it with both hands, trying to correct his foothold, another tile gave way, beneath his right foot, and he was falling face first, surfing down the steep wet roof, helpless, tiles ripping past his face, tearing skin from his hands.

His jaw hit the guttering, which sheared from the wall, but somehow he seized it with one hand, and hung, suspended. For a moment he really thought he was going to be OK, that it would take his weight, that he could pull himself back up. Then the fixings came away from the crumbling brickwork and, with a shriek, he plunged down, head first into a greenhouse.

He struck a roof pane with his face, then crashed down on his back into a bed of tomatoes. For an instant, through his pain, he was aware of their sharp, humid smell, then caught a flash of what looked like a huge, translucent bird as a massive, jagged pane of glass dropped from the roof. Before the scream had even left his mouth, the pane landed widthways across his neck, instantly severing his jugular vein and his carotid artery.

His mouth filled with the taste of copper. His lips released a faint, frothy gurgle. A series of deep barks came in response, and now standing over him, snarling, was the last thing he would ever see: an Alsatian's face.

The dog didn't understand that he was bleeding to death. It just didn't like him.

77

'Sea room', sailors called it. Having plenty of deepwater ocean around you. Enough to drift in any direction without having to worry about rocks or sandbars or land. Hugh Caven called it 'thinking room'. It was where he always went when he had a problem to solve.

The prow of the *Sandy Lady* rose and fell with the swell, and behind him now, a long way west of his stern, was the Thames Barrier. The oil storage depots and refineries along the shoreline, the cranes, bunkering stations, warehouses, marinas and power stations faded into a charcoal smudge. In clear waterproof Cellophane in a locker beneath his feet were the admiralty charts for these waters. He knew the names on them by heart: Canvey Island, Foulness, Sheerness, Isle of Grain, the Swale, Isle of Sheppey, Maplin Sands, and dozens more. You could explore these waters all your life and only cover a fraction of the names and places on the charts.

He kept a copy of Ernest Hemingway's *The Old Man and the Sea* at home and thought it the most moving book he had ever read. Sometimes, sitting out here, he liked to imagine himself as Santiago, that determined, courageous, stubborn old man, desperately fighting the sharks to save his prize marlin, and salvaging a kind of triumph. Maybe that was all you could ever achieve in life, never a total triumph, always just a kind of triumph.

He was sad that Hemingway, with all his wisdom, had taken his own life: if a man with a mind as fine as his couldn't hack it, could anyone?

He needed to be out here this afternoon, in the Thames estuary in his sturdy little clinker-built boat, putting as much water as he could between himself and the world. 'I'm going to pay a visit to the thinking room,' he had told Sandy.

She understood.

And now, with the taste of salt on his lips, the comforting smells of petrol exhaust, seaweed, tarpaulin and rope in the air, the drone of the Yamaha outboard behind him, mixed with the dull, clattering resonance of its loose metal casing and the steady crunch of water, he was unwinding, his anger with Ross Ransome subsiding.

He sat back in the stern, a light wind on his face, hand steady on the tiller of the outboard, eyes flicking from the compass on the binnacle to the quiet sea beyond the prow, the blue cool-box with his cans of Caffrey's and sandwiches wedged between his ankles and, further up in the boat, his rod, bait-box, landing-net, gaff-hook.

There was something else inside the cool-box, too: the master copy of the videotape of the man in the track-suit shooting Dr Oliver Cabot's brother. The only other copy was the one he had left in Ross Ransome's office, and he was pretty certain that if the surgeon hadn't destroyed it by now, it would have been put in a place where no one was going to find it.

Spray fell away from the bow like crushed ice, and he

watched it for some moments. It looked so cool, fresh, hypnotic. Occasionally he turned his head to check on the stern: the wake churned by the propeller into a grubby brown rubble. Tankers and container ships might loom up behind you, without you realising it, and scare the hell out of you. But now there was nothing but a few gulls bobbing around in the water and a half-submerged spar that was fast becoming part of the horizon.

He looked ahead again, keeping an eye on a conical channel buoy about a nautical mile ahead, and on a large ship about five miles off, heading up-river towards him, and a police launch that was going round slowly, in a wide arc, about two miles to starboard. Nothing else to worry about. At least, not out here.

No need to worry about depth, either, but all the same he glanced at the Eagle echo-sounder fixed to the binnacle beneath the compass. Thirty-five fathoms. A continuous map of the seabed slid across the small green VDU screen, and every few moments a virtual fish would appear, in one of three different sizes, swimming from left to right. He'd bought this piece of kit as a birthday present to himself, to show him where the shoals were, and it was still a novelty to him.

He'd been thinking only last week, that, with an extravagant client like Ross Ransome, he might be able to upgrade his boat. Now he was going to have a hard time getting a penny out of the bastard beyond the deposit. But that wasn't what he needed to think through now.

His employee Barry Gatt was dead. Barry had left a widow, Steph, with triplets – the result of treatment for infertility. Her hormone system had gone wonky since giving birth and she was suffering from depression. She was able to mother them and just about run a home, but not much beyond that. She was going to need money.

And Barry needed justice.

But . . .

A big but. It had been a criminal offence to put those cameras in Dr Cabot's flat.

He could get a tidy sum of money from selling that video footage to a television company or a tabloid newspaper. Hot pictures. He could give the money to Steph Gatt, and although it wouldn't bring back Barry, it might make a difference to her life. Except the pictures would open a can of worms. The police would be on to whoever bought them in seconds, demanding their source.

He was caught between a rock and a hard place, and the more he thought, the less clear the solution became.

The water darkened ahead of him, and a spot of rain struck his cheek. He glanced up at the asphalt sky. Some day he would buy a boat with a wheelhouse. He zipped up his fleecy Henry Lloyd buoyancy jacket, pulled on his green fishing-cap, tugging the peak down low, and peered over the bow, mindful of the buoy, altering his course by a few degrees to give it a wide berth. The container ship was looming larger, but was not a problem, it would pass a good half-mile to his star-board. He held the needle of the compass on his new course, 92 degrees. Steady. The anchor rattled in the sudden chop.

He should take the video to the police. Withholding evidence was an even bigger crime than either breaking and entering or illegal surveillance. Under the circum-stances, the police might well let him off with a caution, if that. But he was a jailbird. A convicted criminal with a record.

The police might just love this.

What if they tried implicating him? He'd fallen foul of

them during his work on a number of occasions, and if they chose, they could make it very difficult for him. They would insist on him giving them Ross Ransome's name, and someone would make sure that that it hit the papers. And when that happened he could kiss goodbye to the rest of his fee for certain.

But if he did nothing?

The crime-scene boys might find the surveillance cameras but he doubted that: they'd be looking on the ground and the walls and at the furniture. Would they look up? Did they have any reason to? And even if they did, would they find those tiny cameras?

There had been a message on his voice-mail this morning from a Detective Anson, giving an incident-room number and two other numbers, and he hadn't yet returned the call. He couldn't until he'd decided what to say. Another good reason to be out here now.

It had been stupid going to Ross Ransome's office and showing him the tape. What the hell had he hoped to achieve by it? A confession? Certainly the surgeon might be guilty. Caven liked to believe he was. The guy was unstable: he had evidence that his wife was considering being unfaithful and it wouldn't be beyond a man like him to have someone killed.

He was safely beyond the buoy now. The squall had died and the air was calm as the rain fell. His watch told him it was three o'clock. Slack water for the next hour. He cut the motor, closed the air-cap on the petrol can, tore open a beer and drank the creamy froth that rose up through the spout to pool in the lid.

Then he lit a cigarette and drew the sweet smoke deep into his lungs. The boat rocked gently and water slapped softly against the hull. Overhead, a gull cried. He watched the rain spiking the water all around him.

Walk away from this one, Hugh, a voice said inside his head. *You can make amends to Steph without landing yourself in a shitload of trouble. Ross Ransome's a smart bastard. You'll be the one who gets screwed, not him.*

When he finished the cigarette, he made his decision. Reaching into the cool box, he took out the videotape.

Then he hesitated. The Dylan song came back to him, those words again about the roads. How many? How many roads would he have to walk? And he thought, sweet Jesus, I don't know the answer.

78

The *Daily Mail* lay on the kitchen table. The front-page headline said, 'DOUBLE-KILLING SUSPECT DEAD IN FALL'.

On the television screen, Bart Simpson was standing on a stage beneath a proscenium arch in the beam of a spotlight, singing. Alec, in a red sweatshirt, elbows on the kitchen table, spoon and fork in the air, spaghetti sliding on to his hand, chortled.

'Alec,' Faith chided, 'darling, elbows off, and put your fork and spoon down.' Her eyes returned to the story in the *Daily Mail*. She couldn't keep away from it.

Alec ignored her.

She glanced up again. 'Alec!'

He still ignored her.

She switched off the television.

The story was in all the other papers and had been a lead item on the news. Paramedics had been unable to save the man, who had bled to death. Now fresher news was replacing it.

'Mummy!'

'Bed!'

'But, Mummy, you always let me watch *The Simpsons*.'

She stood up, grabbed his arm, tugged him sharply

from the table. 'You're going to grow up with good manners. People with good manners don't watch television at the dinner table.'

'But you were late tonight. Otherwise I could have had my supper and then watched them.'

'Well, I'm not letting you put your elbows on the table and then ignore me.'

'You were late yesterday, too. I couldn't watch—'

'I was late today because I had an important committee meeting. We're trying to stop some of our beautiful countryside being taken away. It's something Mummy has to do.'

He was crying now. 'I didn't hear you telling me about my elbows.'

'Yes, you bloody well did.'

'No, I bloody well didn't.'

'Don't swear.'

'*You* did.'

On the landing she gripped him by the shoulders, struggling to contain the rage inside her. *Taking out my anger on my child*, she thought. *Taking out my resentment at having to leave Oliver yesterday afternoon to come home. And at not being able to see him all day today.*

Taking it out on my child. God. Calm down. Pull yourself together.

She was seeing Oliver in the morning. But that was too long to wait. She wanted to get Alec into bed and asleep, then she could ring him as she had promised.

She had felt better today. No nausea, none of that freaky dissociation from her body, her brain had been sharp and focused in the committee meeting, even though it had run on hours late.

Yesterday, after they had made love, Oliver had insisted on doing a little work on her, some hypnosis and visualisation. Afterwards she had felt rested and energised, but whether that was from their lovemaking, the hypnosis, simply being with him, or the herbal capsules he had given her, which she had to take every three hours, she didn't know – or care. All she knew was that for twenty-four hours she had felt good for the first time in weeks. Normal.

I'm going to beat this, she thought. I'm going to crush every last bastard kidney bean shaped amoeba to pulp.

'You swore, Mummy. You did. I want to see *The Simpsons*.'

Downstairs, Rasputin ran into the hall, barking excitedly.

Alec was sobbing, stamping his foot now. 'I want to see *The Simpsons*.'

'Next time Mummy tells you to take your elbows off the table, you take them off the table, understand?'

'Not my fault you were late.'

The front door was opening. Ross's voice. Oh, God.

'Hey, boy! Hey, hey, hey! Yes, good boy!'

Her heart sank. What the hell was he doing at home?

Go away. Go to London. Leave me alone. Ross was never at home on a Tuesday night. All this attention he had started paying her. Ironic. All the years when she had wanted him home he hadn't been around; he'd always been in London, or abroad, working or talking at conferences. And now, suddenly, he had become new Ross, caring Ross. And inside, silently, she screamed, *Get out of my hair.*

'Faith? Darling?'

He stood at the foot of the stairs, holding about as big a bouquet as it was possible for a man to carry.

Alec trotted down the stairs, forlornly. 'Daddy, Mummy won't let me watch *The Simpsons*. Bart was doing an audition and now I don't know if they're going to choose him.'

From the upstairs landing, Faith watched Ross put down the flowers, pick Alec up and kiss him. 'And why won't she let the big guy watch *The Simpsons*?' Turning his face up towards her, he smiled.

'Cos . . .' Alec wiped his eyes with his sweatshirt sleeve. 'Cos . . . I didn't hear her—'

Ross lowered him so his feet were back on the floor.

'Alec,' Faith said, 'kiss Daddy goodnight and come up and run your bath.'

Ignoring her, Alec said, 'I really didn't hear her, Daddy, honestly.'

'Go up and run your bath,' Ross said. 'Then I'll come up and read to you. Deal?'

Faith watched the lips pout, then the hesitation. Debating the toss. Sometimes his father had a strangely calming influence on him, and could get him to do things she couldn't. Alec nodded, solemnly. Then, infuriatingly slowly, as if this was the one way he could get back at her, he began to climb the stairs, gripping every upright in turn, doing a little swing around it, then taking his time to ponder each tread before he placed his trainer on it.

When he was half-way up, she called down to him, 'Alec, have you fed Spike today?'

His jaw dropped, guiltily, and he scampered up the rest of the steps and along to his room to feed his hamster. She stood where she was, staring down at her husband.

He picked up the flowers and held them towards her. 'I brought you these.'

'Thanks,' she said flatly, and reluctantly walked down the stairs. The paper and the Cellophane rustled in his arms. She leaned forward and smelt the scent. She recognised some as orchids but there were other exotic ones she didn't think she'd seen before. 'What are these, the long ones?'

'I can't remember their name, but they cost a fucking fortune.'

'I'll put them in water right away.'

'Amount they cost you'd better put them in champagne.'

He followed her into the kitchen. 'Pleased to see me home?'

'It's a surprise.'

'Nice surprise?'

She pushed the plug into the sink, ran the cold tap, then cast her eyes around for a suitable vase. Ross came up behind her, slipped his arms around her waist, nuzzled her neck. 'How about some champagne? Some of the vintage Pol Roger? Winston Churchill's favourite. To celebrate.'

'Celebrate what?'

'That we're going to beat this thing you have.'

She saw him glance at the headline of the newspaper. He would have seen in *The Times* that the suspect in the killing of Dr Harvey Cabot was dead. He would have heard it on the car radio. But he made no mention of it.

'What news of your patient who's so ill? Lady Reynes-Whatshername.'

'Not good. Her husband's been threatening to sue me and everyone else.'

'And they think she's picked up this meningoencephalitis in the Harley-Devonshire?'

'Seems probable. A case of septicaemia with the same strain of bacterium was diagnosed three days ago. With some of these bacteria, no one can be sure how they're carried. Could be in the air-conditioning, the water, anything.'

'Is it going to affect the clinic?' She didn't know why she was asking the questions, she didn't care, she was already viewing her life with Ross as history. It was something to distract him from nuzzling her neck.

'No.'

'Unless, of course, there are more cases?'

'I don't think it's likely,' he said emphatically.

She found a vase, ran some water into it, up-ended it and tipped out a dead spider. Then she filled it again. 'Why's that? If you've had two cases and don't know how they've caught it, how do you know there won't be more?'

'I'll get a bottle of Pol Roger up from the cellar.' He let go of her and turned away.

'What do you feel like eating?' she asked. 'I was only going to make myself a tuna salad. Are you OK with something from the freezer? Lamb chops? Pizza?'

'We'll go out, save you cooking.'

There was something – *something*, she couldn't put a finger on it – strange about his tone. Almost as if it wasn't Ross himself who was at home, but a lookalike who was acting him a little too perfectly.

'What about Alec?'

He looked at his watch. 'Bit late to start trying to get a babysitter.' He hovered by the cellar door, and shot a second, rather surreptitious glance at his watch. 'Suppose we'd better eat in. Let's not worry about it for a while. We'll have a nice drink, a good talk. I'll go down to the cellar – still got one bottle of the eighty-three and it should be stunning.'

Faith glanced at her watch: 6.55. Then she glanced at the kitchen clock. The same. Ross was fanatical about all clocks in the house keeping accurate time. She'd promised Oliver she would call him at seven. He was distressed by the death of the suspect. They'd spoken briefly at lunchtime: the police had given him information that had not been released to the media. The dead man had had traces of cordite on his clothes, showing he had recently fired a gun. He had been carrying a gun of the same calibre as the bullet that had killed Harvey Cabot. He was on police files and had done two spells in jail, once as a juvenile for a violent mugging, once for car theft, and he was known to have underworld connections.

The police, Oliver had said, were convinced that this was their man, but they had not yet found any connection between Harvey and the other dead man, Barry Gatt. They were lacking a motive, but still felt strongly that Harvey's death had been a professional hit.

Oliver was upset that the suspect was dead. He needed answers, explanations and, one day, justice. He was scared that, with this man dead, the police might not dig as hard as they should.

She called down to the cellar. 'I'll just whiz out – won't take me ten minutes – see what they have at the fish counter at Tesco. They might have some scallops,' she said brightly.

Ross came barrelling up the steps. 'No, I don't need scallops. I'll have a tuna salad, that's fine, I need to lose weight. Let's relax, for God's sake. You said a while back that we never get the chance to sit down together and have a drink in the evening. Let's go into the library, have a glass of champagne and relax. Yes?'

'I'll get the nice glasses out,' she said, trying to mask the reluctance in her voice. 'And I think there's a tin of those anchovy olives. Would you like some?'

'Why not? I'll go and take my tie off.'

In the bedroom, Ross checked his watch again. Seven. Opening the bathroom cabinet and taking out the box of Calvin Klein Obsession For Men, he did a swift mental calculation. Timing was everything now.

And quantity. That was crucial, too.

79

It was just over two weeks to the longest day. Normally Faith loved these early weeks in June when spring suddenly became summer, when the garden was lush, the colours vivid, everything coming into bloom, her tomatoes starting to ripen in the greenhouse, her Jersey Royals ready for digging, her courgettes hoisting their flowers like flags. At this time of year there seemed to be such promise in the air. Such confidence. And, on such days, in the face of such intense celebrations of life, it was almost impossible to think dark thoughts.

Today, though, the thought of winter disturbed Faith as it never had before. She was frightened that when this summer had gone, she might never see another.

'Cheers,' Ross said.

Through the bay window behind him, Faith watched a grey squirrel run up a grand old beech tree on the lawn. Tree rats, some people called them. The little bastard had stripped bare great patches of the beech's bark, and now it was at risk of infections that might kill it. A whole family of squirrels was doing all kinds of damage to the trees. Perhaps Ross should shoot them – but how did you decide what to kill and what to let live? Was the beech tree more beautiful than the squirrel? That was subjective. Was it more important to the planet? The squirrel didn't know it was doing harm, any more than the amoebae munching away at her central nervous system did.

Everything was trying to survive. Life. The eternal food chain. Here was an irony she did not enjoy: a sentient human being, a creature at the top of the food chain, was nothing more than a damned canteen to a billion brainless amoebae.

'Hallo,' Ross said. 'Darling, hallo! Cheers! Anyone home?'

She came out of her reverie and raised her glass with a bleak smile.

'You'll never taste a finer champagne, I promise you,' he said.

She took her first sip, and he was right, it was magnificent, honeyed, rich, incredibly moreish. And, what the hell? she thought, drinking another, larger sip. Maybe this would lift her mood. Oliver had told her of the importance of thinking positively, being determined throughout every waking minute to beat those bastard amoebae.

'It is good,' she said. It was after seven, she was thinking. She wanted to speak to Oliver. Tomorrow she would see him again. Tomorrow, she hoped, they would make love again. She wanted to lie with him in bed, wanted to touch his skin and to feel him inside her. She felt closer to him than she had ever felt to Ross. As if she knew him better than she could ever know Ross. She *must* speak to him tonight. With luck, Ross would go into his study to work while she made supper. She would do it then.

Ross beamed at her. 'You look beautiful. I haven't seen you looking this good for weeks. See the benefit from the pills already?'

She said nothing.

He passed her the olives. She took one and ate it, enjoying the briny tang of the anchovy, and she took another sip. Against her salty palate the champagne tasted even denser and richer, and she could feel it fizzing in her veins, lifting her mood.

Oh, no.

Just the faintest motion. As if the room was a railway carriage, travelling fast around a bend. The tilting sensation. So slight she thought she had probably imagined it. She drained the rest of her glass, needing suddenly to get that alcohol inside her, needing to feel it working her system, getting her going, cheering her.

'That's it, down the hatch!'

'You look worried,' she said.

'Me?'

His voice sounded stranger than ever. *Are you really Ross?*

'Why don't you smoke a cigar?' she said. 'It seems strange seeing you drink without a cigar.'

'The champagne's too delicate. The cigar will kill it.'

'Bullshit!' she said.

He grinned and she realised she was grinning too, like a Cheshire cat, and laughing. *God, I'm pissed! On one glass!* 'You're not Ross,' she said. 'I think you're an alien who looks like him and you've been sent here to get me pissed.'

Then, suddenly, he began to melt, turning to liquid, pooling into his chair. And there was a strange sensation inside her head, as if someone was trying, very slowly but firmly, to rotate her brain within her skull. They were succeeding: all she could see now was the inside of her skull, like a cave, uneven ridges on the walls, the curved bowl, then the weird pink helter-skelter shape of her ear, daylight filtering weakly down the corkscrew tunnel.

Now she could see out through her eye-sockets again. This was great! It was as if her brain was resting on a turntable: a lazy Susan, didn't they call it? She could just spin it round at random. Spin it until her eyes were at the back of her head. Giggling, she told him she had eyes at the back of her head.

Ross was solid again now. Solid but indistinct around the edges. There seemed to be intense orange light where the contours of his body met the air. He was looking out of the window. 'Are you waiting for a bus?' she asked. 'Or a train?'

Then she shivered as panic filled her. She was outside her body again. Not up on the ceiling this time, just not in sync with her organs. Disembodied. She heard a voice that might have been her own but she wasn't certain. The voice said, 'Ross, I'm feeling very strange.'

He was still looking out of the window.

I'm dead. That's why he isn't turning round. I'm dead and he can't hear me.

She tested herself, mouthing each word in turn, listening to see if her voice corresponded. She wasn't sure how she could move her mouth, but by thinking about it, it seemed to happen. 'Ross, please help me,' she said. 'It's happening again, this thing, please—'

A car was coming down the drive. A taxi. It seemed to be gliding. Rasputin was barking but she couldn't see him. She called his name, wanting him to come into the library so she could see him, see that he was real, and that she wasn't dead and imagining him.

'Am I dead, Ross?'

He didn't turn his head. He walked out of the room as if he hadn't even heard her.

Voices. It sounded like the chatter of a cocktail party. The dog barked. She wanted to go and join them but she was scared to leave her body behind in case she couldn't find her way back to it. Or in case someone took it, thinking she was dead before she could explain that she wasn't, not totally.

'Ross,' she heard a voice say. It sounded like her own.

'Rasputin?' That sounded like her, too, but Rasputin didn't come. Instead, a car was gliding down the drive, a similar car to the one her mother drove, a small blue Toyota.

A voice she recognised said, 'Hallo, Faith.'

A tall, gangly man with glasses was standing in the

doorway, looking at her. It was David DeWitt, the psychiatrist who had been invited here last Saturday night, for dinner with his wife. Why was he back? Had he forgotten something?

Then he came into the room, and standing in the doorway behind him was Michael Tennent, another psychiatrist, who had also been here for dinner on Saturday night. Had he forgotten something too?

Or was her brain getting time all confused?

'I think,' she heard her voice say, 'that things in the kitchen are going astray. You'll have to remind me whether we've eaten or not – it's really hard to tell at the moment, with these long summer nights.'

'How are you, Faith?' David DeWitt said.

A voice that might have been hers replied, 'How would you feel if you were part of the food chain? Do you have any idea how much damage bindweed can do to an asparagus bed?'

DeWitt and Tennent were looking at each other, some signal passing between their eyes. Behind them, Rasputin was still barking and she wished he would be quiet.

Suddenly, her mother was in the room, too.

'Mummy?'

Margaret was wearing something inappropriate for a dinner party: a lightweight nylon anorak. Maybe she was just going to babysit. She saw her mother's mouth move, but her voice seemed to come from somewhere different.

'Hallo, darling.'

'You might not be able to hear me,' Faith heard herself say, 'because I'm dead. Could you explain this to Ross, Mummy, please. He keeps ignoring me. Please explain to him that I'm dead and I need somehow to be back in my flesh again.'

Jules Ritterman was in the room now, staring at her.

He said something to Ross but she couldn't hear the words. Then he came towards her, followed by Tennent, DeWitt and her mother.

Now Ritterman was speaking to her in a gentle, scolding way as if it was her talking to Alec. 'Faith,' he said, 'Ross tells me that you aren't being a good girl, that you won't take the medication that's been prescribed for you. Is that right?'

She heard her voice say, 'I'm dead, you see. It doesn't help taking anything when you're dead.'

They were all asking her questions now. She heard Tennent say, 'Do you hear voices, Faith?'

DeWitt asked, 'Have you been experiencing visions?'

Then Tennent said, 'Tell me, Faith, have you had any unusual experiences?'

Another voice said quietly, 'She seems confused. Has she shown evidence of being suicidal at any time in the past?'

She answered some questions, but most of them drifted around in balloons inside her head. After a while everyone went out of the room but she could hear them talking in the hall, debating, her mother among them answering questions about her.

She heard Ritterman say, 'It's normal practice to bring a social worker into a decision of this nature.'

Ross said, 'We can get round that, Jules. It can be a close relative instead of a social worker.'

Faith drifted in and out of consciousness. Suddenly they were all in the room again, staring silently at her. Jules Ritterman was holding something in his hands, but they were hidden behind his back. She felt a prick of fear.

Ross went down on his knees in front of her. 'I love you, Faith, I love you so much, I just want to make you better. We all want to make you better. Please understand that.'

Now she could see what Jules Ritterman was holding. It was a hypodermic syringe and a small vial.

A scream filled the room.

It was her scream.

She tried to get out of the chair, but hands were holding her arms, pinioning her. Ross was holding her, and DeWitt.

'No, please, leave me, leave me!' she heard herself scream.

Her mother was standing in front of her now. 'We love you, darling. We're doing this for you.'

Someone was rolling back her sleeve. Her arm was being held in a grip of iron.

She felt a sharp prick. Something forcing its way into her arm muscle, some dense fluid. She saw Ross's eyes. Jules Ritterman's eyes. Her mother's eyes. Michael Tennent's eyes. David DeWitt's eyes.

Her mother said, 'We all love you so much, darling.'

The light in the room was fading.

In the silence, she heard a bird trilling outside. A sound of summer.

It was singing for her.

Then it stopped.

80

'Seven fifty p.m., Tuesday June the eighth. Tape nine. Detective Sergeant Anson interviewing Dr Oliver Cabot.'

The detective checked that both tapes were rolling, sat back in his chair, arms folded, his face greasy with perspiration, and popped a sunflower seed into his mouth. He was a tall man, even by Oliver Cabot's standards, dressed in a brown suit, white shirt and a club tie with shields all over it. He had huge shoulders, bulging eyes that hinted at a thyroid problem and a ridiculous haircut, the kind of pudding-basin style a mother gives a small boy to save going to the barber, shorn at the back and sides and brushed forward into a limp fringe on top.

Detective Sergeant Anson wanted to go home. They both did.

His way of policing was the kind shown in those television detective dramas everyone in England was so keen on, Oliver decided. Courteous, plodding, one step at a time, laborious notes on paper despite the tape-recorder that was always running. God, he wrote so many goddamn notes. And all the time, Oliver knew, the man was trying to trip him up.

Oliver was almost beyond caring, numb from the loss of his brother and from a whole day spent in this windowless interview room at the Notting Hill police station. For the first time in his life he was beginning to understand how confessions could be forced out of people. You could easily get to a point where you'd say anything just to be released from a room like this.

Outside it was a warm summer evening, but it could have been winter, could have been any damned time of the year, it didn't matter. Harvey was dead. Before Oliver had even got out of bed this morning, he had been exhausted, up most of the night on the phone, talking across the Atlantic to Harvey's widow, Leah, in Charlottesville, Virginia.

It had taken a day and a half for the news to sink in with her, and now she was probing, wanting to talk through everything that had happened from when Harvey had stepped off the plane in London, and then beyond that, every detail of his life, back into their childhood together. She wanted to talk about religion, philosophy, anything other than listen to the silence of her house or her kids sleeping.

You could be dignified in dying, Oliver thought. It was possible, too, that you could be dignified in death. It was harder to be dignified in grief, which stripped everything from you. It took away the floor beneath you, the chair you were sitting on, the walls.

Leah was a good woman, attractive, intelligent, caring. She didn't deserve to be a widow at forty-three. John-John, Tom and Linda, fourteen, twelve and ten, didn't deserve to lose their father. And this world didn't deserve to lose Harvey Cabot. He had too much to give, too much to teach.

And, Oliver thought, he did not deserve to lose his brother. Losing Jake had been already too much to bear. Aristotle said that the gods had no greater torment than for a mother to outlive her child. He could equally have said it of a father. And a brother to outlive his brother.

During a break for lunch when they went outside for air, DS Anson told him that his hobby was archery. That was how he relaxed: huge bows that took one hundred and thirty five pounds of pressure to draw them, with high-tech arrows that cost twenty pounds each. On Saturday night Oliver's brother had been shot dead, and one consequence was an impromptu lesson on archery: how to hold a bow, how to pull back the arrow, sight the bow, how to fire it. In the battles against the French, those English archers were tough guys, the detective had told him proudly. At Agincourt, English archers killed eight thousand Frenchmen in seven minutes.

The detective's big, archer hands were now in the air, rotating against each other, symbolising two gears not quite meshing. 'You and your brother, Dr Cabot. Would you say you got along well as boys? Any sibling rivalry?' He proffered the crumpled bag of sunflower seeds. Oliver declined. Anson popped one in his mouth and chewed. He had been pleased to discover that Oliver approved of them.

Faith occupied Oliver's mind right now. For the past hour he'd sensed that something was wrong, that she was distressed, needed him. He might be imagining it, he knew, and that was why he needed to hear her voice.

'It is quite normal for there to be an element of sibling rivalry,' Detective Sergeant Anson persisted. 'Perhaps you could cast your mind back to your childhood.'

Faith Ransome. She was the only beacon of light in this darkness, the only thing that made him want to go on living. And he was so scared for her. Scared that if he didn't make her better . . . Scared of what her bastard husband might do to her if Harvey's death had been his botched handiwork.

'What are you doing? Some kind of Freud thing on me?' he said, angrily. 'What the hell are these jerk-off questions you keep slipping in? I loved my brother, I did not shoot him and I did not hire a hit-man to shoot him.'

'Dr Cabot, I can understand how you feel—'

'Can you?' Oliver interrupted. 'Did you ever lose a brother?'

Ignoring the question, the detective said, 'Eighty per cent of murders in this country are domestic, within families. I need to be able to eliminate that possibility.'

'You already have the guy who killed my brother.'

'A suspect,' Anson corrected.

'Bullshit. You know he did it.'

'What we don't know is *why*. Was he acting alone, or did someone pay him to do it, and if so, who?'

'I told you that you should question Faith Ransome's husband.'

'I have his name noted. He will be interviewed as part of our enquiries.'

'But you haven't done it yet! For God's sake, this man

should be a prime suspect. Just because he's a doctor and has some veneer of respectability, you don't seem to be taking what I say about him seriously.'

'With respect, Dr Cabot, you are a doctor yourself.' He smiled.

Strangely Oliver found himself smiling back. The guy might be weird with his sunflower seeds and his passion for primitive weaponry but at least he had a sense of humour. Maybe they both needed to try to lighten up.

'I have ten experienced detectives working on this case. Your relationship with Mrs Ransome is noted. It is also noted that you claim it is not adulterous, but you believe her husband thinks differently.'

'He beats her up,' Oliver said.

The detective wrote this down.

At nine o'clock the detective said to him, 'Dr Cabot, I don't feel the need to formalise this, but I would appreciate an undertaking from you not to leave the country until our enquiries are completed.'

'You mean I can't go to my brother's funeral?'

'I'm sure you'll be able to. I don't imagine his body will be released by the coroner for a few days yet.'

'I'm intending to accompany the coffin back to the United States.'

'I understand.'

'You'll need wild horses to stop me.'

Ten minutes later, Oliver was in his Jeep. The detective had warned him to be vigilant. If it was he who had been the intended target, not his brother, then he was still at risk.

Oliver had assured him he would take care, but he didn't think about it as he left the police station. All he could think of was Faith and the troubled feeling he was getting about her. In the car he checked his mobile's answering service and the hotel voice-mail. There were several messages from work on both numbers.

Nothing from Faith.

81

Hugh Caven sat at his desk, shoehorned between two filing cabinets, an ink-jet printer and a colour photocopier, in the global headquarters of Caven Investigation Services, which occupied the confined space of the rear spare room of his home. Home was a small, detached modern box, strewn with toys, in a quiet close in Ickenham, in south-west London. He had a view from his desk down on to the strip of lawn. Sandy was pegging out washing. Sean, his three-year-old son, was playing with a boat in the tiny inflatable paddling-pool.

Lying on top of the piles of papers covering his desk was a copy of today's *Daily Mail*. Beneath it were several other newspapers, all of which carried the story that an unnamed man whom police had wanted to interview in connection with the double killing in Notting Hill Gate on Saturday night had died in a fall yesterday.

Hugh Caven had one friend in the police and this man had just called him back with the information he needed. The police were satisfied that the dead man was the killer of Barry Gatt and Harvey Cabot, and from the evidence he had just heard he could understand why they believed this. But the police had yet to find a motive and were now looking into the dead man's background. They were suspicious that it was a contract killing, but they'd been unable to find any connection so far between Barry Gatt and Cabot. They wouldn't, not from Barry's widow, anyway.

Barry was a pro. He'd never have told Steph where he was working or whom he was watching. He was also a private man, with a profound sense of decency, and Hugh Caven reckoned he knew exactly why his employee and friend was dead. Barry, watching the television images in Dr Oliver Cabot's flat, had seen Harvey Cabot being shot and had gone to his rescue. Occam's Razor. *The simplest explanation . . .* Simple as that.

Out in the garden Caven saw his son trip on the edge of the pool and fall flat on his face on the lawn. Through the open window he could hear him bawling. He watched his wife put down her laundry, run across to him, scoop him up and comfort him. She was a good mother, a good woman. He was lucky. Five years ago he had been in jail and had had nothing. Now he had a wife he loved, a kid he was proud of and a flourishing business.

And a close friend dead.

He could give the police the link they needed. He *must* do that. All his instincts told him that Ross Ransome was behind this. And in all his life he couldn't recall disliking someone so much as that arrogant man.

And yet . . .

The retainer he'd had from the plastic surgeon had been peanuts. He'd racked up several thousand pounds' worth of expenses in the past two weeks, paying round-the-clock money to his surveillance men, including wages he owed to Barry, plus the equipment he had put into Dr Cabot's flat that he would not now be able to recover.

He watched Sandy rocking Sean in her arms. She looked so beautiful and he was a lovely kid. *You two deserve the best I can give you – but what the hell is that? A father who sacrifices his principles for money? Or a father who risks going back to jail for his principles?*

Hugh Caven had hated every second of his time in jail. There had been a novelty factor during the first few days, but beyond that he'd loathed everything about it: the smell of the place, the corruption of the warders who wanted to sell you drugs and made life extra hard for you if you didn't want to buy them, the loss of privacy. Above all, he had disliked the other inmates. You didn't meet life's winners in jail, you met the losers, spent all your days surrounded by them. Losers like himself, who'd screwed up and were probably destined to go on screwing up.

Now he was faced with a golden opportunity to screw up again. If he went to the police, Ross Ransome was going to find out and he wouldn't get another penny out of him – which left him about six grand out of pocket. Six grand he could not afford to lose. On the other hand, once Ross Ransome had calmed down and thought things through, maybe he would pay a lot more than six grand for him not to go to the police.

82

Somewhere beyond the walls of her room, the screaming had been going on all morning. For a while there was a series of low, terrible moans that sounded to Faith as if a man was lying impaled on park railings. Then there were sharp, hysterical screams. It was bugging her.

But the Big Question was bugging her more.

It had been bugging her for quite a while, now – she couldn't tell exactly how long because her watch had gone. It had been replaced with a plastic tag, which had her name typed on it: Faith Ransome (Mrs).

She assumed someone had done this to help her. More useful at this moment to know her name than to tell the time. Everything they did here was helpful – wherever *here* was.

One minor problem was that the tag was narrower than her watch-strap. The white mark on her wrist untouched by the burning sun in Thailand showed either side of the tag. She had asked both the Nurse Who Brought Pills and the Nurse Who Removed The Bedpan whether she might have a tag that covered the white, but neither had thought that was going to be possible.

This wasn't the Big Question that bugged her, though, this was only a small preoccupation, a welcome distraction from the cries of the man impaled on the park railings.

It was the thing on the back of her hand. She'd seen these dozens of times, in every hospital drama she'd ever watched on television, but she'd never had one herself before.

Umbilical, she thought. Like being a baby again. Attached to Mother. A tall, silent, metal mother, just a metal rod with a metal arm, and a plastic bag suspended from a hook in the arm, out of which came the umbilical cord, which ran down into a connector that was attached by sticking plaster to the back of her hand.

What the hell was the word?

She was having big retrieval problems with her memory. One moment it worried her and the next she was relaxed about it. Cool. 'Actually, I'm really cool about this whole thing,' she said aloud. She found it good to talk in here, helpful to practise her talking: you had to use skills like these. 'Use them or lose them,' she said to no one.

The man on the railings moaned and for once, she

realised, he was agreeing with her.

She looked around, although there wasn't much to see, nothing that she hadn't already seen several times. Bare walls painted white – a nice white, the kind of white you could go on looking at, on to which you could project your thoughts, a real cinema-screen white. She'd already watched her thoughts up there several times. Now it was the intermission.

There were no pictures in this room and the only window was a kind of frosted skylight in the high ceiling above her through which diffused white daylight came. It might be a grey day or a fine day, impossible to tell through that glass. It did not matter.

There was no curtain either.

She noticed that more as an observation than a concern. Nothing concerned her right now: she felt as she had felt years ago when she was larking around with girlfriends, a little drunk, and that was fine. Hard to focus on anything for more than a few moments, but, hey, who needed to?

There was a lot all boxed up inside her head that she needed to deal with, different boxes, an Alec box, a Lendt's disease box, an Oliver Cabot box, but there just wasn't time. The day seemed to be divided not into hours or minutes but into visits. The Pill Nurse visits. The Food Nurse visits. The Nurse Who Came With The Resident Doctor visits. The Others Who Asked Her Questions visits. The Dr David DeWitt visits. The Ross visits. A lot of Ross visits.

They were all so friendly to her, probably because Ross was a medic, she assumed. The medical profession looking after its own.

The Pill Nurse was coming into the room now. Dark hair and breezy voice. 'And how are we?'

'Fantastic!'

The nurse frowned and Faith wondered why. Then

she was holding the tiny paper cup of water to Faith's lips. She sipped. It was too much of an effort to hold the cup herself and, besides, her body was so heavy, it felt as though lead was running in her veins, not blood. It was so easy just to lie motionless, like a tree, everything done for her. Two capsules shaken out of a tiny container and popped into her mouth, one at a time.

'There! Not so bad, are they?'

Faith swallowed. Talking was a big effort, but she needed to talk, needed the answer to the question that had been bugging her. The answer to the Big Question.

'This thing,' she said, her voice slurred. 'What'd they call th's thing?'

'The cannula? On your arm? The cannula that the drip line goes in?'

'Drip line!' Faith said, so pleased she repeated it. 'Drip line!'

'Intravenous drip,' the nurse added, helpfully. 'It's just a saline solution, salt and water. Your husband was worried that you'd become very dehydrated.'

Ross was coming into the room now.

'She's just had her lunchtime pills,' the nurse said to him.

'Good. How is she?'

'She's fine, stable, seems quite settled.'

Hey, I'm a person, I'm not furniture, you can talk to me! Faith nearly said, but she didn't want to sound rude. Anyhow, it didn't matter.

'I'll leave you alone with your husband,' the Pill Nurse said.

Ross kissed Faith's forehead. 'How are you, my darling?' he asked, so gently.

'I'm really having nice time,' she said.

She saw his eyes glance up.

'Drip line,' she said. 'Umbilical.'

Ross peered hard at her eyes, then went to the door, which was open.

'Don' – go – go – yet,' she said.

He closed the door, then walked back across the room, behind the bed, out of her line of sight. A shadow moved across her face and she looked up. The drip bag was moving. He was doing something to it. Disconnecting it.

A tiny swell of concern washed through her. 'What doing?'

'Checking,' he said. 'I want to make sure my darling has exactly the right amount – I don't want them being stingy with your supply.'

Now he was sitting in the chair beside the bed. Something wrong with his jacket, she thought. There was a bulge in one pocket. Had he taken the . . . ?

She looked up. The drip bag was there, the solution filling the tube, the line, the umbilical. He was just looking after her. Being a good husband.

Now he was standing at the sink. She heard running water. He was putting something in his pocket.

'I'm due in theatre in half an hour. I'll come by this evening,' he said, and kissed her. 'I love you, Faith.'

'I love you too,' she said.

The door clicked.

She looked up again at the drip bag. It was so good lying here, feeling so happy, so loved. She glanced away, but instantly her eyes were drawn back to the bag. *Umbilical*, she thought.

Mother.

A connection, a poor connection, a few crackly sparks, that was all. There was some kind of a link. The drip bag. Her mother.

Being here.

But now she was too tired to try to work it out. Her eyes closed then opened again. Christ, it was happening.

The walls of the room seemed to inch in towards her, then move away. Panicking she could feel perspiration running down her face, down her neck.

'Help me,' she said. 'Please help me, it's happening—'

Dying again. They had come for her soul. She was outside her body now, looking down at it lying in the bed, eyes wide open, lips moving, crying out, 'Help me, please help me.'

Oh, Christ, she really was dying this time. Dying, leaving Alec behind, and Oliver Cabot. Where was Oliver? Why hadn't he—

Now the door was opening. A nurse was coming in with a man in a white coat, and she had seen the man before, a doctor. He leaned over, looked at her face, shone a torch into her eyes, checked her pulse.

She heard him say, 'She's had these before?'

'Twice,' the nurse said. 'It's a symptom of the disease.'

'Yes,' he said, with the calm authority of an expert.

'Please get me back into my body,' Faith said. 'I must see my son before I die completely – before I go and don't come back.'

The man's voice replied, 'What you're having is just like a little panic attack, Faith. You're going to be fine. You've been a bit of a naughty girl not taking your pills, haven't you? That's why you're having these attacks. I'm sure within a few months we'll have you much better.'

83

In his office at the Cabot Centre, Oliver punched up the 141 code to mask the identity of his phone, then dialled Faith's home number. Four rings then the sound of Ross Ransome's voice telling him no one was at home.

He dropped the phone back on the cradle.

What have you done with her, you sick punk? Have you killed her? You screwed up killing me and now you've killed her instead?

His next patient was downstairs in the waiting room, and he was already twenty minutes late for her appointment. It had been a mistake coming to work today. He'd thought it might distract him, take him away from the hotel room where he'd been incarcerated all day yesterday, waiting for the call from Faith that never came.

Was it because they had slept together? Had she gone home and found it too heavy a trip? Decided to bail out and go back to her marriage? After all she had said to him?

Oliver didn't think so, yet he knew from experience that it was hard to read people and even harder to predict their actions.

But not Faith, he thought, she wouldn't do that, it wasn't in her nature. She had a fundamental decency. If she had gone home and changed her mind, or changed it after they'd spoken in that brief call on Tuesday, she would have told him.

But what other explanation could there be? Her mobile phones rang and his calls got straight through to the voice-mail. No one answered at her home. They had agreed to talk at seven on Tuesday. A definite arrangement, not an *if* or a *maybe*. Faith had said she would call him but she had not.

Now it was one o'clock on Thursday. More than forty-eight hours since they had spoken. What the hell could stop her calling him for so long? An accident? She might have had a car smash on the way to Legoland or on the way back. But he'd looked up the route she would have taken and had rung every hospital between her home and Legoland, and no one of her name had been admitted. In case she had been killed he had

339

checked with the police. Nothing.

So what were the options? Either she was deliberately not calling him, or her husband was preventing her. He ruled out that she was deliberately not calling him.

Which left her husband. Her bully of a husband, who controlled her life, who was obsessed by her, who hit her. Either he had done something to her, had perhaps imprisoned her somewhere, or—

He didn't even want to contemplate that option.

He sipped water from the glass on his desk. Downstairs, a beautiful young woman who'd had an innocent-looking white mark on the tip of her thumb two years ago, and now had no right arm, was waiting to see if he could help her defeat the cancer that had defeated all the doctors she had seen. He needed to be strong for her. He needed to be strong for all of his patients – and for Leah, especially when he returned to America with Harvey's body. Perhaps the strongest he had ever been.

I need you, Faith, I really need you badly right now.

And I don't like this silence from you. It's too loud. Way too loud.

84

At three seventeen in the afternoon, Dr Jonathan Mumford, the duty ITU doctor at the Harley-Devonshire Hospital, stood by Lady Geraldine Reynes-Raleigh's bed, filling in a death certificate. Under cause of death he wrote, 'Meningoencephalitis due to septicaemia.'

Thirty minutes later, after he had wheeled her body down to the basement cold-store that acted as a holding mortuary, a twenty-one-year-old general assistant named Jason Rillets slipped out of the rear entrance of the hospital into a mews off Devonshire Place, walked a few hundred yards and stopped in a doorway, safely out of sight of the hospital. There he made a call from his mobile phone, which he had bought for just such a situation.

The call was to a journalist called Will Arnoldson, who had approached him a couple of years back. He was a rather raffish character, with swarthy, middle-European good looks, attired in a smart business suit. He looked more like a James Bond villain than a newspaperman.

Arnoldson freelanced. He was socially well connected and made part of his living flogging gossipy pieces to the newspaper diary columns. He paid Rillets thirty pounds for any stories about the Harley-Devonshire's upmarket clientele that he could get printed. The last titbit Jason Rillets had fed him had been printed in the news section of *Hello!* a fortnight ago.

'Lady Reynes-Raleigh? Mean anything to you?' Rillets said, glancing around him.

'Yes, she's good value,' Arnoldson said. '*Very* good value. What's the story on her?'

Rillets told him.

As usual Arnoldson got more out of him than Rillets had intended to tell him. The journalist thought he could make it into a good story – embellish it a little. He might even get two different pieces out of this, work up two different angles, if Jason didn't have a problem with that. It might mean a double payment for him.

Jason had no problem with that at all.

85

'It's the second time he's called,' Lucinda said, on the hands-free in his office. 'I think you ought to speak to him.'

On Ross's desk was a Moliou-Orelan container. There were ninety-seven capsules in the container, and three lying on his desk. Holding one of these firmly on the blotter with tweezers, he slid the needle of the syringe into the join between the two halves and injected the same tiny measure of ketamine that he had laboriously injected into all the rest.

'What time am I operating tomorrow?' Ross asked, removing the syringe and holding up the capsule to inspect it in the light, before dropping it into the container.

'Eleven. You told me not to make it earlier. I've had to do some juggling around.'

'Do you think I ought to go to Lady Reynes-Raleigh's funeral?'

There was a pause, then a sharp, 'Why?'

'I – as her surgeon.' Then he added, lamely, 'Networking?'

'I don't think it's very good advertising to turn up at the funeral of a patient who died after you operated on her.'

'You're right,' he said. And he thought, What the hell am I thinking of? Am I cracking up? My bloody judgement's all to hell and back. 'Do you think we should send flowers?'

'Absolutely not. You have to dissociate yourself from her. Keep your name well out of it.' His secretary paused, then added, 'Anyhow, you didn't like the woman. Why would you want to send her flowers?'

'Courtesy.' He checked the barrel of the syringe, then picked up the next capsule with the tweezers.

'Are you going to take this call? Detective Sergeant Anson? He's still holding.'

Ross took it.

The doorbell rang and Rasputin raced into the hall,

barking. Alec followed him, shouting, 'Mummy's home! Mummy's home!'

'I don't think so, sweetie, I'm afraid.'

'It might be!'

His grandmother crossed the floor and had a quick look out of the library window to see who it was. She was always wary of opening the door to strangers.

There was a large blue off-roader that she didn't recognise on the drive, and a tall man in a suit, whom she had never seen before, standing in the porch.

She went across to the front door and, as a precaution, put on the safety chain. Alec peered up excitedly as she opened the door a few inches. The man looked well dressed and well groomed, she thought, but what did that count for in today's violent world?

'Can I help you?' she said, through the gap between the door and the jamb.

'I have an appointment at five o'clock to see Mrs Ransome.' His voice was pleasant, and he spoke with an American accent.

'Appointment?'

'Yes, we made it on Monday.'

'Who are you, please?'

He proffered a business card through the gap, which she took and read: 'Don Rosslyn, Director. Research and Development. Moliou-Orelan Pharmaceuticals plc, a subsidiary of Moliou-Orelan Corporation Inc.'

There were two addresses, one in London and one in Berkshire. She returned the card to him. 'I'm afraid Mrs Ransome isn't here,' she said.

'She's not?'

The man looked disappointed. She decided he didn't look like a rapist or a burglar, closed the door, released the chain, then opened it wider, keeping hold of Rasputin.

The man knelt down immediately and began to make a fuss of the dog.

Alec said, 'My mummy's not well, she's in hospital but my daddy said she'll be able to come home soon.'

Still stroking the dog the man said, with surprise in his voice, 'She's in hospital?'

'I'm afraid my daughter is not well.'

The man stood up. 'I'm sorry. Actually, that's the reason I'm here. She's on a clinical drugs trial with my company. We have a new drug she's taking, which we're hoping will help her.'

Faith's mother said, 'I know all about it.'

'We're, like, running a monitoring programme. I spoke to Mrs Ransome on Monday to make the appointment. We're learning about the efficacy of our drug as we go along, and by spending a little time with each of our patients we think we can get them to maximise the benefits. Is her hospitalisation related to Lendt's disease?'

Glancing at her grandson, not sure how much he should hear, she said, 'Yes.'

'Mummy is going to get better, isn't she, Grandma?'

'Of course she is, and this nice gentleman's going to help her. You go and watch television while I talk to him, all right?'

Reluctantly, Alec headed for the kitchen.

'She's having severe symptoms at the moment,' she told the man. 'We're hoping the problem is because she's not been taking the drug until now. She's very independently minded.'

'But she is taking it now?'

'Oh, yes.'

'All the more reason I should see her. If someone isn't taking the medication it gives us false data readings. What we want to do is ensure absolute accuracy. That's the only way we can help sufferers beat this horrible disease long-term. Can you give me the name of the hospital and the address?'

'I have it on a pad in the kitchen,' she said. 'I'll go and fetch it for you.'

Five minutes later, Oliver Cabot drove his blue Jeep Cherokee out of the front gates of Little Scaynes Manor. It was strange being here, strange talking to Faith's mother: he felt a closeness to Faith and a distance at the same time. The woman must have been attractive when she was younger; she had Faith's slim build and her small, straight nose, but she didn't look or sound anything like her daughter.

A few hundred yards along the lane he pulled into a lay-by and consulted his road atlas.

Hospital? Faith, my darling, has this damned disease worsened overnight?

Her mother had been cagey about exactly what kind of hospital. Its name meant nothing to him, but there were numerous hospitals in Britain he didn't know. How badly had Faith deteriorated?

He called Directory Enquiries and asked for the number of the Grove Hospital, then dialled it.

'I'd like to speak to Faith Ransome,' he said, when the switchboard answered.

'One moment.' There was a brief pause, then the woman came back, polite but cold. 'I'm sorry, she is not permitted telephone calls. I can put you through to the nursing station in her ward.'

'Sorry if this is a dumb question, but exactly what kind of hospital are you?'

'What *kind*?'

'Yes.'

'We're a secure private hospital,' she said, irritably.

'Secure?'

'Yes, for psychiatric patients.'

345

Oliver hung up.

Psychiatric hospital?

Faith had been concerned about her bouts of dissociation. Had she had a really severe attack? Severe enough for her husband or her GP to decide she should be admitted?

He closed the atlas and put the car in gear. It would take him about an hour and a half, he estimated. He rang his secretary and asked her to make enquiries about the exact nature of the Grove Hospital, and any information she could find on the reasons Faith Ransome had been admitted there.

She rang him back forty minutes later. 'She's been sectioned under the Mental Health Act to be detained in a private psychiatric hospital, Dr Cabot. She's on a twenty-eight-day order.'

86

It was ten past five. In the rush-hour traffic it might take half an hour to get to the hospital. Then he needed to allow a further half-hour with Faith once he was there – he had to make sure he had enough time alone in the room to make one final switch. Tonight, he calculated, her existing supply of Moliou-Orelan capsules would be exhausted, and tomorrow they would start giving her these fresh ones. Then life would be easier.

How the hell had he allowed himself to be bullied by Detective Sergeant Anson into meeting him at his flat at seven this evening?

Walking down the steps of the underground car park in Cavendish Square, Ross was thinking about the policeman's voice. It was pedantic – slow, precise and polite, yielding no hint of emotion. Just duty. A voice in search of the truth.

Ross hadn't much liked his voice, didn't like the fact that he couldn't read it, and wondered just how much the policeman actually knew or suspected.

No doubt Caven had gone squealing to the police after he'd thrown him out of his office on Tuesday. Fine. Caven knew nothing of his arrangement with Ronnie Milward. It was no offence to hire a private investigator to follow your wife – if Caven had broken any laws in the course of his work, that was his problem.

Perhaps, Ross realised, he shouldn't have lost his temper with Milward. Caven was a grotty little scumbag, but no more. Ronnie Milward was altogether different. He might tell Ross over the phone that he wouldn't get out of bed for twenty-five thousand, but if he saw an opportunity to get out of repaying it by making a phone call or two and having Ross Ransome stuffed, would he take it?

Was the Pope Catholic?

And yet Milward was smart. He would know that Ross had before and after pictures of his makeover. He would not be stupid enough to risk his freedom for that paltry amount of money.

He pushed open the door marked Level 2 and strode in the shadowy lighting past rows of parked cars, the familiar smells of warm engine oil, petrol, rubber and dust in his nostrils. The Aston Martin was parked in his regular numbered bay between a sports Jaguar and a small Mercedes saloon. As he reached it, he dug in his pocket for his keys.

Nearby in the silence, a warm engine ticked and pinged. He pressed the button on the fob, and as the Aston Martin's indicators flashed streaks of amber across the floor and walls, and the central locking clunked open, a figure stepped out of the shadows right beside him.

Ross jumped. *Ronnie Milward?*

Then he calmed as he recognised the man's voice even before he saw his face.

'Good afternoon, Mr Ransome. Off to visit your wife? Your third visit today, I'd be thinking.'

The soft Irish accent. The shorn hair, the small frame, the pallid little aged-rock-star face.

'Are you following me?'

The private investigator shrugged.

'What do you want, Caven?'

'You must love her an awful lot.'

'I don't have anything to say to you, so out of my way, you're obstructing me.'

'We need to talk, Mr Ransome, you and I.'

'You might need to, I don't. And I've just heard from the police. They want to interview me. I wonder why?' Ross glared at the man. 'What did you tell them?'

'I haven't told them a thing. That's why I'm here.'

'Oh, yes? Are they psychic then?'

Ross pushed past him, and opened the door of his car. The interior light came on, and the opulent smell of leather rose through the stale air.

'Mr Ransome, you *have* to believe me. I have not said a word to the police.'

Struggling to contain himself, Ross put his hands on the investigator's shoulders and gripped them hard. 'You're pond life, Caven. You're a little bottom-feeder.'

'We need to be sensible about this thing, Mr Ransome. I can understand you might—'

Ross did something he had not done since his schooldays. It was something he hadn't even thought about in twenty years. He head-butted the man.

Caven reeled backwards, struck the wing mirror of the Mercedes, snapping it off, and jerkily, like a crumpling rag doll, sat down on the floor, a dazed look in his eyes, blood running from his nose.

Ross climbed into the Aston Martin, slammed his door and locked it. Then he rammed the key into the ignition, twisted it, keeping an eye on the investigator in his mirror, pulled out of the bay and accelerated. As he turned right, heading for the exit ramp, he saw the man emerge from the bay and lurch into a run after him.

He drove up the ramp, turned sharp right, following the exit arrows, tyres squealing, and accelerated hard down between the parked vehicles. The tail of a car was nudging out and he blasted the horn hard. As he started the turn to the final ramp up to the pay desk, he saw Caven come out of a door. He did not want a further tangle with this man to delay him.

The barrier was down and the bloody attendant in the booth was talking on the phone. Ross hooted twice. Caven was only yards behind now. The attendant waved in greeting, and the barrier began to rise. Ross's car phone rang. Ignoring it, watching Caven in his mirror, he drove on up the ramp into daylight. The bastard was still running after him. He accelerated harder, eyes on the mirror.

Oh, Christ, no, no, no.

The great red wall in front of him.

He stamped on the brake pedal.

Shit, shit, shit, shit.

He heard the tremendous, deep metallic bang then, almost simultaneously, both his eardrums popped, there was a burst of white light in front of his eyes, a jarring pain in his shoulder and the car rocked to a halt.

An instant of numbed silence. His ears felt as if he'd dropped twenty thousand feet in an unpressurised aircraft. He pinched his nose with his fingers, blew, and his ears cleared a little.

The bonnet had flown up and a jet of steam rose from the engine compartment. Airbags hung like spent condoms from the steering-wheel and passenger dash-board. Beyond the bonnet he could see the crumpled side panels of a bus. A startled woman in big spectacles was peering down at him through one of its windows. The driver was climbing down from the cab.

Ross unclipped his seat-belt and tried to open the door. It would not budge. Hot, sweaty and furious, he barged it with his shoulder. It still wouldn't move. There was a musical tinkling sound.

His bloody car phone was still ringing.

He barged the door a third time. People were standing around the car now and he was feeling foolish. He reached over to the passenger door then realised why his own door wouldn't open: the central locking was still engaged.

He unlocked it, opened the door and climbed out, staring shakily at the growing swell of faces closing around him.

'Not big enough?' An angry man's voice. 'Not bloody big enough? Not big enough for you to see? If you can't bloody drive it, you shouldn't bloody have it.'

Ross looked around anxiously, trying to spot Caven. But he had melted away. No doubt standing smirking somewhere nearby, he thought, staring in desperation at the crumpled front of the Aston.

Someone was going to have to sort this mess out and he did not have time. He was a member of one of the emergency road services, the number was on a card inside his wallet. He could get a taxi and phone them, tell them to come and collect the car, sort it out.

'Excuse me,' he said, and tried to push out through the crowd. An arm held him back. It was the bus driver.

'Where do you think you're going?'

'My wife's very ill,' Ross said.

'You're not going anywhere until the police have been.'

'Fuck you,' Ross said, pulling the man's arm away. 'I'm a surgeon and it's an emergency.'

The man grabbed him more tightly. A large, beer-bellied man with a walrus moustache.

'Let fucking go of me.'

'You're staying here.'

Ross heard a siren. He balled his fist to hit the man, then glanced around at the onlookers and restrained himself. Great bloody headline: 'Plastic Surgeon in Road Rage Attack on Bus Driver.'

'You can let go, I'm staying.'

With threatening eyes, the driver released his grip. Then Ross stared back at his car. The bloody phone was ringing again.

By the time he had ducked in to answer it, the ringing had stopped. He climbed out feeling even more foolish, and angry, carrying the phone with him. Not wanting to meet anyone's eyes, he pressed the message retrieval button.

There was one new message. It was a customer-services representative from Vodaphone. They wanted to know if Ross was happy with their service.

87

To the Victorians, size counted. A man demonstrated the width of his wallet and the depth of his purse by the girth of his waist and the grandeur of his house.

Gothic revival became the must-have of the late Victorians. The more turrets, leaded lights, crenellations and gargoyles they could cement, carve and etch on their ugly country piles and their even uglier London homes the better. Balconies of wrought iron as fine as filigree, columns and pilasters borrowed from Ancient

Greece, spider's web fanlights ripped off from the brothers Adam.

The Grove Hospital had originally been such a private residence – more of a statement than a home, it was a red-brick edifice that had been built by a Victorian aggregates-and-munitions robber baron – and eventual lord mayor – on what had then been the outskirts of London. It was now in a mishmash street of houses and offices, sandwiched behind the racetrack of Wellington Road and a marginally quieter reach of Maida Vale. It was the kind of London architecture Oliver Cabot had never particularly cared for. He liked Georgian, Queen Anne and Regency light and elegance, not Victorian darkness and clutter.

He checked his mirror to make sure he wasn't being tailed, still aware he might be a target, then parked on a single yellow line just beyond the entrance. The Jeep's clock told him it was 6.10 – twenty minutes before it was legal. Chancing it, he climbed out of the car, then hauled his jacket off the rear seat and wriggled into it, his shirt clammy with perspiration despite the Jeep's air-conditioning. A sudden shadow caught his eye and he looked up to see a quarrel of starlings break formation above his head, bursting like a firework, splaying out in a hundred directions, then miraculously together again and dipping over the rooftops, heading north towards Regents Park.

It was a warm evening, the cloying London air listless and muggy. He wiped the shine of perspiration from his face with his handkerchief, adjusted his tie, clipped his cellphone to his belt and locked the car. Then, grimacing at the building, he walked up the steps to the panelled front door beneath a scrolled porch, turned the brass handle and pushed. It was locked. To the left there was a speakerphone with a surveillance camera lens visible above it; he pushed the button.

A crackly voice: 'Yes, who is it, please?'

'Dr Cabot – my secretary told you to expect me.'

A few moments of silence then the lock clicked. He pushed the door and this time it yielded. In stark contrast to the exterior, the inside was drab and featureless. He entered a narrow, characterless hall, dominated by a high mahogany reception counter behind which was perched an elderly receptionist with prim hair and a fretful face.

The lighting was poor and the general ambience stark, institutional: bare cream walls hung only with licences, certificates, a list of First Aid procedures and exit-indicator arrows. There was crimson carpeting on the floor and a strong smell of paint, as if the place had recently been redecorated. Through an open door to his left, he could see a waiting room. A large wooden table in the centre was covered in magazines and there was an assortment of chairs. A frail, Middle Eastern-looking man in a business suit sat on one, cradling a walking stick. Beside him on a sofa were two women in traditional clothes, with yashmaks. They were all staring ahead in a funereal silence.

'Dr Cabot?' the woman said, as if double-checking.

'Yes, I've come to see my patient, Mrs Faith Ransome.'

She handed him a clipboard with a visitor's log, asked him to sign in, then reached for her phone with more assertiveness than her increasingly worried demeanour belied, and said, 'Sheila, I have Dr Cabot in reception.'

Oliver scanned the log. The first visitor of the day had been Ross Ransome, in at 7.15, out at 7.35. Then further down he saw his name again. In at 12.32. Out at 1.05. He scrawled his own name, making it deliberately illegible and put down the time: 6.15 p.m. Then he glanced at a floor plan of the hospital taped to the top of the counter. It indicated that the building stretched further back than was evident from the exterior, into an annexe.

The woman replaced the phone and said, 'Take the lift to the third floor, turn right when you come out, walk down the corridor, through the fire doors. You'll see Neurology directly in front of you, and a sign to the left to Park Ward. Follow the signs and you'll find the nursing station.'

The lift was deep and wide enough for a stretcher, and painfully slow. Oliver stepped out into a windowless corridor and followed the directions. As he went through a fire door and approached the nursing station, he heard a man screaming in the distance, a series of deranged howls. A pretty ginger-haired nurse in a chequered blue uniform was talking to a serious-looking man in a white medic's coat, poring over a file. As Oliver approached, the howls worsened. The nurse looked up at Oliver and raised her eyebrows with the trace of a smile, as if acknowledging a problem beyond their control. On her lapel was a tag identifying her as Ward Sister Sheila Durrant.

'Good evening, I'm Dr Cabot,' he said.

The man continued studying the file without glancing up.

'Yes,' she said. 'Hallo. We're a little confused. We have down on the forms that Mrs Ransome's GP is Dr Ritterman.'

'I believe Dr Ritterman has been the family doctor for some while, but Mrs Ransome recently registered with me.'

She held up a fax. 'Well, your secretary sent this through to us. It's just that we have instructions that no one other than the staff doctors and psychiatrists here – and, of course, her husband – is to see her. We have been trying to contact Mr Ransome but we haven't managed to reach him yet.'

The man put down the file and said, 'I'll be back in an hour or so. If Mr Oberg doesn't calm down in the next fifteen minutes or so, give him another intravenous fifteen milligrams.' Then, affording Oliver only a cursory glance, he left.

'You have a Mental Health Act section order?' Oliver asked.

'Yes.'

'Can I have a look at it?'

She produced a file from under the desk and handed him a bunch of documents clipped together. Oliver read through them. Faith was being held for assessment under a Section 2 order for twenty-eight days. The applicant for the order was Ross Ransome, as the nearest relative. The separate supporting forms were signed by Faith's mother, Mrs Margaret Phillips, Dr Jules Ritterman, as Faith's GP, and by a psychiatrist, Dr David DeWitt.

He glanced through the notes of the consultant psychiatrist for the hospital, Dr David Freemantle. They confirmed symptoms in accordance with the advanced stages of Lendt's disease. Her current medication consisted of intravenous glucose solution, three milligrams of risperidone twice a day – a fairly heavy dosage – and Moliou-Orelan N646329 Entexamin capsules, two, three times daily with food.

'How is she?'

'She's under our consultant psychiatrist Dr Freemantle. It would probably be helpful for you to talk to him, but he won't be here until nine tomorrow. So far she's not responding well to sedation – she's very delusional and confused.'

'I really would like to see her.'

She glanced down and he could see the hesitation. 'Yes, well, I think you have every right to see her.' Then looking up at him again, she said, 'You seem familiar –

your face. I'm trying to think where I recognise you from?'

'I've been in the news this week.'

'Ah, right, that's what—'

He could see, suddenly, that the penny had dropped. 'Oh, God, it was your brother?'

He nodded, with a lump in his throat.

'I'm sorry.'

Falteringly, Oliver said, 'Life has to go on.'

'I'll take you to her room.'

Oliver followed the nurse down a long corridor of closed doors, calculating from his memory of the plans that they were now in the annexe. A series of long, low moans from Mr Oberg, whoever he was, accompanied them.

At the end of the corridor they turned right, along a further corridor of closed doors, passing on their left, he noticed, a fire escape external door. A male orderly wheeled a dinner trolley from one, bringing out with him the smell of boiled fish and stewed cabbage. Oliver noticed lurid green jellies on the trays. Kiddie food. Plastic spoons only and styrofoam beakers. A flash of anger burned inside him. Faith was being treated as a child. This beautiful creature reduced to eating kiddie food off cutlery she couldn't harm herself with.

Sectioned under the Mental Health Act.

His secretary had phoned him back and read out the relevant parts of the Act to him. It required two doctors and a social worker or a close relative to carry this out. Any order would be granted for an initial period and was then to be reviewed. Patients had the right to ask for a review, which could either be reassessment by hospital managers or a Mental Health Act commission in a tribunal comprising a psychiatrist, a lay person and a chair. Oliver knew from his training in the States that, if similar criteria applied, it was far harder to get such an order reversed than granted.

'Here we are.'

Her name was printed on a card in the slot on the door. The nurse opened it and went in first, quietly in case Faith was asleep. When she could see she was awake she said, 'You have a visitor, Mrs Ransome.'

Faith was sitting up, propped on pillows, her food tray untouched on the swing table over the bed. She was staring straight ahead and did not acknowledge the nurse, who walked across and checked the almost empty drip bag.

'I'll just replace this. You may be coming off it tomorrow. Dr Freemantle says your electrolytes are almost back to normal levels now. They were badly depleted by the nausea your husband says you were suffering – I don't think you were eating or drinking enough, were you?'

In a slurred voice, Faith said, 'My husband changes it for me. He'll be here soon. He changes it.'

'Your husband?' Sister Durrant said, amused. 'I don't think that's your husband's job.'

'He changes it,' she said.

There was an insistence in her voice that the nurse brushed aside. 'Well, he's not doing a good job because it needs changing right away and he's not here. We'll have to give him the sack, won't we?'

Oliver stared at her from the doorway, deeply perturbed. The room felt like a cell: stark white paint, the skylight admitting one miserly pane of evening light, and a bare lightbulb fixed to the ceiling providing the only proper light. The bed was in the centre of the room, making her look some kind of exhibit. The only other furniture was a table next to the bed on which was a paper cup and a plastic water beaker, a remote

357

control attached to a coiled wire, presumably to prevent it being flung or dropped, a drip stand with a line running down to her wrist, a wash-basin, and a television set built into the wall behind toughened glass.

But it wasn't the room that perturbed him, it was what Faith was saying.

She looked beautiful, even in the flimsy white hospital gown, her hair greasy and matted, and no makeup. A tad pale from lack of fresh air and any exercise, perhaps, but otherwise OK. He had to restrain himself from walking straight over to her, putting his arms around her and kissing her. Instead, from the doorway he said, 'Hallo, Faith.'

There was no reaction. He exchanged a glance with Sister Durrant. Her eyes told him that this was normal.

Walking slowly over to the bed, he said, 'How are you feeling?'

It seemed to him there was fear in her eyes. Fear and confusion. Just the faintest flicker of recognition, that was all.

'I'll pop back and change the drip bag, then I'll leave you,' Sister Durrant said, and went out, leaving the door ajar.

He waited, listening to her footsteps recede, before he spoke to Faith again.

'Do you recognise me, Faith?' Leaning close he could see that her pupils were dilated. From the medication she was on, this surprised him. 'It's Oliver.'

She spoke, suddenly, in an almost robotic monotone, staring dead ahead. Impossible to tell whether she was pleased to see him or not.

'It's true what I said. Ross comes in and changes the drip bag. First the nurse changes it, then Ross changes it again. They don't believe me. They don't realise I can watch him sometimes from the ceiling.'

88

In his head Oliver carried a detailed summary of all the published material on Lendt's disease he had been able to find. The symptoms and time-frame for the development of the disease seemed consistent throughout the three thousand cases so far identified. The first symptom was prolonged nausea, the patient usually feeling this for two to three months, then increasing disorientation and paranoia-related irrational behaviour, including night terrors, and psychotic hallucinations during consciousness. A gradual loss of motor-control functions followed.

Faith had returned from Thailand in late April. Today was 9 June. If she had contracted the disease out there, she should still be in the prolonged-nausea phase – the symptom she had been manifesting frequently when he had seen her. She should not be in the psychotic state in which she appeared to be now.

She should not have dilated pupils.

It's true what I said. Ross comes in and changes the drip bag. First the nurse changes it, then Ross changes it again. They don't believe me. They don't realise I can watch him sometimes from the ceiling.

Was it possible?

Harvey had been murdered. Over the years the two of them had often been mistaken for one another. Ross Ransome was a bastard and, whatever Faith said, Oliver had put him at the top of the list of his personal suspects and he had made that clear to the police.

He strode over to the door, looked up and down the corridor, then dashed back to the bed, disconnected the drip line from Faith's wrist, put the tube to his mouth, and tested the solution tentatively with the tip of his tongue. It tasted innocuous enough. Then he gripped the tube in his lips, took a couple of hard sucks, swallowed and replaced the line. He saw that the electronic controller clamped to the line was set for six hours.

Moments later the nurse came back into the room, carrying a fresh bag, which she exchanged for the almost spent one.

'Are you expecting Mr Ransome?' Oliver asked her.

'He said he would be here at about six o'clock.' She glanced at her watch. 'Twenty-five past.' Then, sensing something from his expression, she said, 'Shall I let you know when he arrives?'

'I'd be grateful.' Then he added, 'Tell me something – the drip, she's on a six-hour replenishment?'

'In the daytime. Dr Freemantle has it on twelve hours at night.'

Oliver thanked her. She left and closed the door.

It shimmered as she closed it. Oliver stared at it, puzzled. It was as if he could see every single atom in the door vibrating. And as he turned back to Faith, the door seemed to elongate and travel with him. Unsteady on his feet, he touched the side of the bed to balance himself, and felt Faith's wrist. His head was hot, suddenly, and he felt giddy. The floor seemed to be swaying beneath him.

A voice that he wasn't immediately sure was his own said, 'What do you mean, Faith, that you watch Ross changing the drip bag from the ceiling?'

It was himself speaking, and yet he felt as if he wasn't in his body.

That same monotone. 'He comes and he changes it. He thinks I don't notice.'

She seemed a long way away from him now, as if he were on the far side of the room. But he was standing right beside her. He stared up at the skylight and it looked now like a tiny orb of golden light, miles above his head. Something crawled down his back. It felt like a spider. As he reached behind him, he felt more creatures, down his chest, down his legs, down his neck.

Squirming, it took all his concentration to put the words together and get himself to speak them, as if his mind had to fire impulses to his vocal cords one at a time. 'Tell me what happened, Faith. Why are you here?' Ants were crawling down his arms. He took off his jacket, rolled up his shirtsleeves, but he could see nothing.

There was a long silence. 'They came for me.'

'Do you know where you are?'

She shook her head.

The ants were crawling over every inch of his body now. 'You're in a psychiatric hospital. Called the Grove.'

'Psych—'

The door opened. He saw the nurse, Ward Sister Sheila Durrant. Her lips were moving but her words seemed to take for ever to reach him. He could feel the pulses in the air that each one made. 'Would. You. Like. A. Drink. Dr. Cabot?'

He tried as hard as he could to remain focused on her. She was giving him an odd look. Could she tell he was in some strange space?

'Thank you, I'm OK, we're doing fine.'

She closed the door. This time the sound distorted, the click of the lock was like the volley of a gun echoing around a valley.

In his teens he had dropped acid a few times. The first trip had been beautiful, but subsequent ones had made him feel uncomfortable. He didn't like to be out of control and the sensations of being dissociated from his body had panicked him. He'd never taken another recreational drug.

Now he recognised what was happening to him.

Something in that drip he had sucked was doing this to him. He was tripping, but not enough to cloud his thoughts completely.

Faith must be tripping, too.

Ross was putting something in the drips he was substituting, but why? Was he trying to drive Faith mad? Was this his way of getting back at her?

He was startled, suddenly, at the clarity of his thoughts. Then he caught sight of his watch: 7.17.

Impossible. He'd arrived here before a quarter past six. No way could he have been here an hour, no—

The nurse had looked at her watch just before she had gone out. It had been 6.25. There was absolutely no way three-quarters of an hour could have passed. He picked up the remote control, switched on the television and then pressed the clock button: 7.18.

'This is nice,' Faith said suddenly. 'Having you here.'

Three-quarters of an hour had gone from his mind. He peered at her eyes and saw that the pupils were less dilated. 'How are you?' he said, to test his voice. It sounded better now, near normal. He was returning to the base line from wherever he had been.

And now he was certain. Ross Ransome was putting a very low dosage of some dissociative drug in the drip.

The walls of the room were glowing with an intensity of light. The drug was still working on him, and he knew that with all the dissociatives, both the serotonergic psychedelics, such as LSD, psilocybin, peyote, DMT, and the anaesthetic ones, such as ketamine and tiletamine, their effects could go on returning for many hours after the initial effects had seemingly worn off.

He tried to think of any other explanation, but nothing else made sense. If there had been a sedative in the drip, its effects would have been quite different on him. The bastard was deliberately keeping her in a psychotic state – and doing it on a prolonged basis like this carried a severe risk of brain damage. Was this man crazy?

The question barely needed answering. For anyone to treat a jewel like Faith badly they had to be crazy. Dangerously mad. Prolonged doses of dissociative drugs had been proven to burn tiny holes in the posterior cingulate and retrosplenal cortex as well as the hippocampus, olfactory areas and the limbic system. Memory and learning skills would be affected, as would social behaviour, motor-control and bodily functions, with epilepsy as an additional factor.

The most likely drug, he guessed, would be ketamine. It was frequently used for burns-trauma cases, and part of Ross Ransome's reputation was based on his work with burns cases. He would have easy access to the drug.

Ross Ransome, you are a sick man.

And where was he? Sister Durrant had been expecting him at six. No doubt he would show up shortly.

He could wait: he didn't have anything else to do or go back to, just a hotel room, and yet another long phone conversation with Harvey's widow, and some goddamn cheerful room-service waiter bringing yet another meal he had no appetite to eat.

'I don't want to be here,' Faith said.

Oliver looked down at her, and squeezed her hand. 'I don't want you to be here, believe me.'

There was a knock and the door opened. Oliver stiffened, ready for a confrontation. But it was just a cheery woman orderly come to take the tray away.

When the door was shut again, Faith said, 'Take me away from here, please.'

She had been here for two days. If she had been on the drug continually, there would be a considerable build-up in her system, and it would keep repeating strongly for many hours, but she seemed to him very lucid now.

'It's not as easy as that,' he said.

'I want to see Alec.'

'He's fine, I saw him a few hours back.'

'What do you mean? Where?'

Oliver told her, and then he told her also about the Mental Health Act section order.

'It's not me who should be in here,' Faith said. 'It's Ross. They can't do this to me, they don't have any right.'

'I'll be back in two minutes,' Oliver said.

'Don't leave me, please.'

He kissed her forehead. 'I'm not leaving you.'

He opened the door and hurried back to the nursing station. Sister Durrant was on the phone and it sounded like a personal call. Impatiently he waited at a polite distance until she had finished. Then he said, 'The drip bag you just removed from Mrs Ransome's room – where is it?'

She looked at him curiously. 'The drip bag?'

'Yes, the empty one.'

'I've thrown it away.'

'I need it – where've you thrown it?'

'Into the incinerator chute.'

'Can we get to it?'

'It'll be burnt by now.'

Thinking fast he said, 'Will you do me a favour? Will you take a blood sample from Mrs Ransome for me?'

'We have blood for our routine tests.'

'No, this is different. Could you please do that for me? Just a small amount?'

'Yes, yes, of course.'

'And put the date and time on it, please. How do I get to the basement?'

'The lift – just press B.'

He was already on his way. He took the emergency stairs, running down the concrete well, past the ground-floor sign and into the heat of the basement. A long low corridor, poorly lit, with massive duct pipes running just above head height stretched out in both directions. There was a whine of electric motors, and a mixture of smells – food, laundry, heating oil. He saw the woman who had removed Faith's tray emerge from the kitchens and asked her where he could find the incinerator. She pointed out the door at the far end of the corridor.

As he walked along he passed an open door into the laundry and ducked in. The air here was hotter and damper than it was in the corridor and the howls of the giant washing-machines sounded like the turbines of jet aircraft. Through another doorway he could see two Asian women and a man busily hauling sheets out of a dryer.

He went in and none of them even glanced at him. Suddenly, he was floating, not walking. *That's why they're not looking at me, they can't see me, I'm dead, I'm a ghost.* He panicked. *I'm dead. How can I—?*

The drug, he realised, the ketamine, or whatever, was repeating on him. That was all. He just had to go with it, try to ignore it.

He took a step forward and nearly stumbled as the floor plunged away beneath him, as if he had trodden on a huge pedal. *Just an illusion*, he told himself and took another step, then another, holding out his arms to stay upright.

He saw several bins. One contained a stack of white coats, and in another was a stack of chequered blue nursing tunics. Without any clear plan in his mind, he grabbed a coat and a tunic, rolled them tightly and crammed them as far as they would go into each of his trouser pockets, then went back out and down the corridor to the incinerator door.

It was marked, DANGER, KEEP OUT and there were ventilation slats along the top and the bottom.

He opened it. A blast of heat accompanied by the drumming roar of a burner greeted him, and he found himself staring at a wall of blue steel, dials and gauges. A voice behind him shouted, 'Yes, hallo! What you doin', man?'

He turned to see a bemused, grimy-looking black man in blue overalls.

'I need something that was dropped by accident down the chute from Park Ward,' he said.

The man gave a warm, gap-toothed grin and scratched his grizzled head. 'Dropped down the medical-disposables chute?'

'Yes.'

'Well, you got a problem with that one. You bring an asbestos suit with you?' the man said, jerking a thumb at the shaking metal casing of the thundering furnace. 'Because whatever you lookin' fo's going to be in there – and I'm afraid mine's at the cleaner's.'

89

'Look, Detective Sergeant, my wife is extremely ill in hospital. I was involved in an accident on my way there this afternoon.'

'Yes, you have already told me this,' Anson said.

Ross stood up and went over to the window of his flat. Five minutes' walk to the hospital from here. He looked at his watch: 7.30. By his calculations the drip would have been changed an hour and a half ago. Faith might be returning to normal – although she had been on the ketamine for forty-eight hours. He was anxious to get to her. 'Could we continue tomorrow?'

The policeman's voice and demeanour were respect-ful, the courtesy of one professional to another. Yet there was a firmness that brooked little leeway. 'I'd really prefer to wrap this up tonight, Mr Ransome. It won't take much longer.'

Ross knew it would have been polite to have offered the man something to drink on this sticky evening, but he didn't intend to. He studied Anson's huge frame, which was dwarfing the two-seater chesterfield, his bulging eyes – definitely a thyroid problem – his perspiring face, and his ridiculous combed-forward haircut. The man's white shirt was clinging to his skin and the collar was crumpled. *You're hot and thirsty and if I give you anything to drink it will encourage you to stay longer. You're not getting anything from* me.

'Were you aware, Mr Ransome, that your wife was seeing Dr Oliver Cabot, the deceased's brother?'

Ross was aware that he needed to be careful. Obstructing the police by lying was a serious offence, and he didn't want to say anything that might bounce back in his face. He had no idea what Cabot had said to Anson, nor the weasel Caven.

'Yes, I was.'

'And how did you feel about that?'

'Are you married, Detective Sergeant?'

A slight frown. 'I am, yes.'

'Let's say your wife arrived home from a shopping trip this afternoon and found, God forbid, your house had been burgled. How would you feel if instead of calling the police she looked in the *Yellow Pages* and phoned the number of some back-street private detec-tive?'

'I don't quite see the—'

'Tell me how you'd feel, that's all I'm asking.'

Anson ferreted around in his pocket and extracted a

wooden toothpick, which he examined. 'I'd feel she was being a bit daft. I'd be annoyed, I suppose.'

'Because the police are the professionals? And you feel something that important should be handled by professionals?'

'Indeed.'

'Perhaps you can understand how I feel. Our doctors are among the best-trained in the world and I want the best for my wife. I was furious when I discovered she was rejecting everything I had done for her and going to a charlatan.'

'How did you make your views known?'

'I told my wife.'

'Did you tell Dr Cabot?'

Thinking carefully, Ross said, 'I had no desire to get into a slanging match with the man.'

Anson smiled understandingly. 'Very restrained of you, sir. I'm not sure I would have had such self-control.'

Ross sensed that the two of them might just be on the same wavelength. Changing his mind about the drink, he said, 'Can I get you something? Something cold, perhaps?'

'I'd appreciate a glass of water.'

'Nothing stronger?'

'A glass of water would be fine,' the detective said.

Ross grinned. 'I've got some ice-cold Grolsch in the fridge.'

'Ah!' Anson looked at his watch. 'Well, officially I'm not supposed to drink on duty – but it's late and I'd like that very much, thank you.'

Ross fetched two lagers, then offered the police officer a cigar, which he declined.

Swallowing a long draught of the beer appreciatively, Anson asked, 'Forgive the personal nature of this question, Mr Ransome, but have you ever had any reason to doubt your wife's fidelity at any time in your married life?'

'Absolutely not,' Ross said, levelly.

'And – again, forgive me – did you have any reason to believe that your wife was visiting Dr Cabot for any other purposes than purely a professional patient-doctor relationship?'

Ross narrowed his eyes deliberately, holding his hands still on his glass, aware that the detective would be studying his body language intently. He was determined to give nothing away. 'What exactly do you mean by that?'

It was the detective who allowed body language to give himself away. He held up his hands defensively. 'Nothing, sir, nothing at all. I just needed to clarify that.'

And Ross thought, *This is incredible! This is very good news! Caven has said nothing to him. He doesn't know about Caven!*

Then he cursed himself for the way he had reacted to the private investigator down in the car-park earlier. That had been dumb. He had to get hold of Caven, and maybe do some kind of deal, buy the little shit's silence.

Tipping back his glass and almost draining it, Anson said, 'My father suffers from Parkinson's disease. A mate of his recommended an alternative doctor, who put him on some cranky herbal diet.'

Ross did not like this sudden shift. 'Yes?'

'Didn't make a blind bit of difference. Cost my dad over two hundred quid by the time he'd bought all the stuff. Swallowed the first lot and threw up for twelve hours. Licensed con-man, I'd say.'

Ross said, 'All these alternative medics are con-men.'

Anson nodded in agreement.

Better, Ross thought. *This is much better.*

90

Oliver took the stairs back up from the basement, getting to grips with the geography of the place, logging the fire-exit routes, his thoughts on just two things: first, to ensure that Ross Ransome did not spend another moment alone with Faith in that room, and second, to get her out of the confines of the section order.

He kept his hands jammed in his trouser pockets, trying to hide the bulges as he walked back past Sister Durrant at the nursing station, but she was engaged in conversation and barely acknowledged him. She just pointed to an envelope on the counter and mouthed, 'Blood sample', at him.

He thanked her and pocketed it. Faith was asleep when he went into her room. He perched on the edge of the bed and watched her face. He looked at the fall of blonde tresses across her forehead, the tiny wrinkles in the skin, her mouth slightly open and her lips in a beautiful pout, as if she had fallen asleep waiting for a kiss.

Her neck looked so slender, the skin firm but pale, like a Rossetti painting, he thought, and he would have loved to lean across and kiss her lips and her neck right now, while she slept. She looked so gentle and so beautiful. And so terribly vulnerable.

And it was wrong to be feeling this, but he couldn't help it: he felt deeply aroused just being here, so close to her. Yet he was aware that this was an assessment room, where new arrivals would be kept under observation for a few days. It was possible there was a hidden spyhole, maybe up in the light fixing or behind the protective glass of the television – or any damn place.

His thoughts were interrupted by the sound of the door opening, and he turned in alarm. It was sister Durrant. 'Dr Cabot,' she said, 'Mr Ransome has just arrived downstairs.'

The second Grolsch had been a mistake. Under its influence, Ross had let slip something to Detective Sergeant Anson about Faith and Dr Oliver Cabot. It was one of those off-the-cuff remarks that would have passed unnoticed if Anson had been a less observant man, but Ross could see instantly that the policeman had registered it.

They had been talking about medicine men in primitive tribes, and how shaman healers whipped people into a frenzied trance state through the use of drums, and Ross had interjected that Dr Oliver Cabot probably achieved the same effect with his dick.

He hadn't said enough to make it an outright accusation, but he had said more than enough for the inference to be clear.

Not smart.

Now in the reception of the Grove Hospital, perspiring after his walk here, he signed the register and scanned the rest of the day's visitors. He saw Dr Freemantle's name, and the name of a psychiatrist he had met a few times and rated, Roy Shuttleworth, and further down another psychiatrist he knew, Dr David Veale, but apart from them, the names meant nothing to him.

'The ward sister asked if you wouldn't mind waiting just a couple of minutes while they change Mrs Ransome's bed-pan.' Ross grunted his irritation at the doddery receptionist, and stood looking through the waiting-room door at the elderly Middle Eastern man cradling a silver-headed stick in his hands, and the silent women beside him. Good customers, the Arabs.

Preferred them to whingeing English boots like Lady Reynes-Raleigh any day of the week. He pulled out his handkerchief and wiped his face, feeling a little muzzy from the effects of the alcohol and the heat. The drip bag was weighing heavily in his jacket pocket. He checked for the pills, which rattled, reassuringly.

The phone beeped and the receptionist picked up the receiver. 'Right,' she said, 'Thank you.' Then, raising her voice a fraction, she said, 'You may go up now, Mr Ransome.'

'I'll go up whenever I fucking feel like it,' he said, and walked down to the lift, checking that his mobile phone was switched on, waiting anxiously for the private investigator, Hugh Caven, to return his call.

Head-butting him had been stupid, he now realised, ruefully.

The lift doors slid open jerkily, then took an eternity to close. It was stiflingly hot in here. His mind went back to Detective Sergeant Anson. He'd been going off duty, he told Ross. Going home to kiss his girls goodnight, have a meal with his wife, take his two retired greyhounds out for a walk. He would be back at his desk at seven in the morning. If Caven was sufficiently angry he could give the information to anyone in the incident room. But would he?

He tried to think back to what the private investigator had said to him in the underground car-park earlier.

I haven't told them a thing – that's why I'm here—

Mr Ransome, you have to believe me. I have not said a word to the police.

We need to be sensible about this thing, Mr Ransome. I can understand you might—

Sensible, Ross thought. *Need to be sensible . . .* The little runt wasn't sure of his ground. He was nervous, caught up in something bigger than he had expected, plying his grotty little trade, and finding it biting back at him.

The lift jerked to a halt. He waited for the doors to open, ready to step out, when he saw on the panel that this was only the second floor. A member of staff who looked vaguely familiar stepped in. A doctor, he guessed from the man's white coat, then changed his mind. The man's curly grey hair was cut longer than most doctors'. He was more likely a psychiatrist.

The man stood holding the door open with one arm, as if he was expecting someone, and extended the other to Ross, beaming at him in recognition. Now Ross was searching his brain, trying hard to work out where they had met before, just who the hell he was. Here? Had they met here?

His memory told him it was some other place.

'Good evening, Ross. Nice to see you.'

The voice, a rather mannered, pukka Oxford accent – like someone practising after an elocution lesson – rang no bells. Ross held out his hand and the man gripped it in a firm shake, and kept on holding it as he spoke. 'You look as if you've been working hard, Ross.'

'Yes – I – you know – as usual.' *Who the hell are you?*

'Damned hot! Having to wear these ruddy coats makes it even hotter, doesn't it?'

Ross found himself agreeing. There was a welcome breeze from the open door. He was scanning the man's coat for an identity badge but couldn't see one. 'Yes,' he said. 'Too damned hot.'

The man was smiling at him now, as if they were sharing some private joke. Clear grey eyes staring insistently at him, as if saying, '*Come on! You recognise me, for heaven's sake, man, surely you recognise me?*'

'Are you sure you're feeling all right, Ross?' The man leaned over, his eyes getting closer and larger, fixed on his own, filled with concern. 'Suffering from the heat?'

The man's face was so close, Ross could not focus. All he could see now was the blur of the man's eyes. 'I – I—' He stalled, the man was confusing him.

'It's so hot, so hot, Ross, it's so hot, Ross, hot, hot, aren't you so hot, Ross, so hot, so hot, hot, Ross?'

Ross nodded. He was hot, the man was right. So hot. Hot, hot.

'You're feeling a little sleepy now, Ross. In fact, Ross, you're feeling hot and sleepy, aren't you?'

'Yrrss.'

The lift doors were closing now.

'You find it strange that I'm holding on to your hand. But you're finding it hard to let go of my hand, aren't you?'

Ross tried to let go, but found he couldn't. It was his hand that was gripping the man's now, his hand that was doing the shaking. He was aware that the car was moving up. Then the stranger moved and it seemed as if the car had stopped between two floors.

The man smiled. 'We'll take it slowly in this heat, Ross. We don't want to rise up too fast, bad for the blood pressure, isn't it, changing altitude too fast?'

Ross, feeling giddily disoriented said, 'Yrrss.'

'What I want you to do now, Ross, is rest and relax, relax, I want you to relax, relax, and listen to my voice.'

Compliantly staring into those grey eyes, Ross nodded.

'OK, Ross, from now on, all you will hear is my voice and my voice alone, nothing else is important to you. You are feeling hot and tired . . . but what is it you have in your pocket, Ross, the thing that's causing the bulge?'

Ross stared back at him, his head spinning.

'It's OK, Ross, you can answer me. Tell me what it is, it's safe to answer me, I can help you.'

'Drip bag.'

'And who is the drip for, Ross?'

'My wife.'

'And what is in the drip, Ross?'

'Ketamine.'

'I see. OK, Ross, that's fine, just listen to my voice, you're feeling so hot and thirsty. Take the drip bag out.'

Ross pulled the bag out of his pocket.

'Now, Ross, look down into your left hand. What do you see there? You see a canteen of cool water. Aren't you lucky to have such a cool canteen of water in your hand on such a hot evening?'

Ross looked down, blinking, and saw an oval, military canteen.

'Shake it, Ross. Listen to the cool water inside.'

Ross shook it and heard the water slopping around. It sounded so cool, so wonderfully cool. He licked his lips, feeling a desperate thirst.

'You are thirsty, too, Ross, so thirsty, Ross, so hot, Ross, so hot, thirsty, Ross, so hot. Imagine what it would be like to drink, Ross, imagine, Ross, so hot, Ross, imagine what it would be like to drink, Ross.'

Ross thought about the ice-cold water inside. His mouth was parched.

'OK, Ross, just enjoy yourself now. Unscrew the lid and take a nice cool drink of water.'

Ross stared at the canteen. It turned into a polythene bag filled with fluid then back into a canteen again. Then back into a bag with two rubber bungs at the base. Then back into a canteen with a screw cap. He gripped the cap, twisted, pulled, and suddenly water, beautiful, ice cold water, dribbled down his chin. He held the teat in his mouth and sucked greedily.

'That's perfect, Ross, drink it, drink it all, you are so dehydrated, you must drink it all.'

Ross swallowed the entire contents.

'Good. Now you've enjoyed your drink, Ross, put the

canteen back in your pocket, forget you ever saw me and go and enjoy the rest of your evening.'

Ross, dimly aware that the lift car was moving again, rolled up the bag and put it into his pocket. Then the car stopped. The doors were opening.

'You have another floor to go, Ross. I'll let go of your hand and you will get on with your evening.'

The man was gone. The lift doors closed. The car was moving upwards. Ross lurched. The walls seemed to be closing in around him, trapping him like a rabbit in a hutch. He punched at them, trying to push them out, but they came in even tighter.

He screamed, kicking out. The doors opened, just a tiny gap. He lurched in panic through the gap, then stumbled sideways and fell, sprawling on his face on the grey-carpeted floor.

He tried to stand up but the floor was rising up sheer in front of him, like a cliff-face. His fingers slipped on the pile, which was short as stubble. He was sliding, sliding away, going to fall off this face.

'Help me!' he screamed.

Slipping.

'Help, help me!'

He clawed desperately at the stubby fibres, trying to get a purchase with his nails.

'Help!' he screamed again.

A blur. Something white falling towards him. Then it stopped in front of his eyes. Legs. Flat black shoes. Lurching with all his strength he just managed to grab the ankles.

'Please help me,' he said. 'Please don't let me fall.'

Sister Durrant stared down in horror at the spectacle of Ross Ransome, sprawled on the floor, seemingly blind drunk, babbling like a child and gripping her ankles in his hands as if his life depended on it.

Then she heard a shrill warble. His mobile phone, somewhere in one of his pockets, was ringing.

91

'Is there a problem?'

Sister Durrant turned her head. Oliver could see Ross Ransome propped in a chair at the nursing station, his head lolling and another nurse standing beside him, keeping a steadying hand on his shoulder. Two men, who looked like doctors, and a hospital orderly were standing there as well.

'Thssss walls,' Ross was rambling. 'All fall down.'

'I heard a commotion,' Oliver said. 'Wondered if you needed any assistance.' Then, feigning surprise, he looked at Ross, then back at the nurse.

'Mr Ransome? What's happened?'

Sister Durrant glanced around then raised her hand surreptitiously to her mouth and mimed tilting a glass.

'*Drunk?*' Oliver whispered.

She nodded, then shrugged.

'Climbing all over the walls, bigger than Mount Kilimanjaro,' Ross rambled on. 'What we really need here is a gimballed gyro.'

Quietly Oliver said, 'Pressure, you think? His wife being in here?'

'Must be,' the nurse replied. 'He loves her so much, he's so dedicated to her – it's breaking his heart to see her like that.'

One of the doctors leaned forward and smelt Ross's breath, then said, 'I think we'd better find him a bed for the night in here. He's too pissed to send home in a taxi.' Turning to Sister Durrant he said, 'Have you a room free on this ward? The sooner we get him out of sight, the better for his sake.'

'Nothing on this floor. I'll go down and check with Avenue Ward on floor three.'

As she turned to walk away, Oliver touched her arm and accompanied her for a few steps, away from the rest of them, then he said, very quietly, 'Nurse, when you come back up, check out his right jacket pocket.'

'Why?' she said.

But Oliver was already walking away, hurrying past the nursing station.

Faith was still asleep when he went into the room. He pulled the drip line out of her wrist and switched off the flow valve, then propped her upright.

She opened her eyes. 'Wh – what – wha—?'

'We're out of here.'

He helped her into the chequered nursing tunic he had brought up from the basement. Faith, in a state of confusion, was of little help. The build-up of ketamine in her system was repeating on her now. He sat her on the edge of the bed, and said, 'Wait there, OK?'

She nodded in vague comprehension.

He ran back down the corridor, and stopped a safe distance from the nursing station. Chaos. Three of them were trying to help Ross Ransome, who was all flailing arms, tripping legs and incoherent ramblings, along the corridor, the rest trying to get out of the way.

Oliver ran back to the room, rolled the bedclothes into the rough shape of a sleeping form, grabbed Faith's hand and half led her, half dragged her in her nursing tunic and disposable hospital slippers out into the corridor. He stopped and looked in both directions. A shadow fell to his right, and he jerked Faith sharply back into the room, pushed the door until it was almost closed and peered through the gap. A nurse he hadn't seen before walked past. He watched until she had turned the next corner, down towards the nursing station, switched off the light, led Faith out into the corridor and closed the door behind them.

Holding his breath, he checked both directions, then took Faith to the fire-escape door, pushed it open and helped her through.

They were standing on a metal platform, with the fire-escape descending below them into what looked like a loading area. Despite the hour it was still brilliant daylight, and he felt exposed. This was not smart. He didn't know whether he was breaking a law, but helping a patient detained under a Mental Health Act order to escape from an institution could land him in serious trouble, and he didn't have a prepared story if he was caught.

But right now his only concern was to get Faith out of here, out of the clutches of her husband. He would have to sort out the consequences later.

He led her down as fast as he could, taking care on each metal tread, and they finally made it to the bottom. Her co-ordination was so bad that walking was difficult for her. He was either going to have to carry her to the car or bring it round here.

Carrying her would draw attention, he realised. He would have to pass the front door of the hospital.

'Faith,' he said, 'I'm going to fetch my car. I want you to wait here. Don't move.'

He saw a gap between two large wheelie-bins. Not brilliant, but she'd be hidden from the street and from anyone looking out of a window. He pushed her in gently.

Faith wrinkled her nose at the stench of garbage, staring along the grey slab sides of the bins that rose up either side of her, and at the sliver of daylight from the loading bay. A fly buzzed in her face and she flapped it away.

She was lucid again now. Lucid and scared. Scared of

being in this horrible alley. Scared of what Oliver had told her, that there was a section order, that she was legally insane, that she was not allowed to leave the ward she was in, let alone the hospital.

Scared of what Ross would do to her and Oliver when he found out.

Sectioned.

They could come and get her. Take her away, lock her up, stop her from seeing Alec.

Great mother you have, Alec, she's locked up in an institute for the insane.

A sudden sweet smell: cigarette smoke. For an instant she thought it was her mother. She caught another whiff, stronger. Footsteps. The scrunch of something beneath a shoe. A dark shape crossed the gap in front of her. A security guard, she saw with alarm, hat under his arm, sneaking a quick cigarette break.

Go away.

She heard him cough, a hacking, throaty smoker's rattle.

Please go away.

Her face felt hot. Oliver would be back at any moment. The walls of the bins were moving, coming in towards her. Someone was pushing them together, someone who didn't realise she was in here.

She tried to push back, but both sides kept coming.

Going to be crushed to death.

Closer, she could only stand sideways now. They were pressing against her face, her back. 'Please,' she whispered, 'please I'm in here, please stop—'

They kept coming. She was panicking, taking deep, gulping breaths, as she sidled like a crab, whimpering, stumbling sideways, '*Please, I'm in here, please stop, please stop—*'

The sliver of daylight, which had been only a couple

of feet away now seemed a hundred yards distant, and was getting smaller as she looked at it.

She stumbled faster, pushing her way out with her hands, and suddenly she was free, standing in the loading bay. The security guard was walking away, a cloud of blue smoke billowing around his head.

The roar of an engine. Big blue car, Jeep, familiar, halting.

Oliver! He was getting out.

The guard turned his head, stared at her, frowning. An elderly guy, he looked tired and hot. She realised afterwards that, in her nurse's uniform, she should have just raised a hand and waved, and he'd probably have waved back, thinking she was a staff member who had slipped out for a quiet smoke in the balmy air.

Instead she ran.

A shout behind her. 'Hey! Hey, you, hey, miss, lady!'

She fell into Oliver's arms, turned her head. The guard was breaking into a lumbering run.

Oliver flung her up on to the passenger seat and slammed the door. The guard was only yards away. The car lurched as Oliver climbed behind the wheel. He shut his door and she heard a sharp clunk just as the guard reached her door-handle.

The central locking.

'Hey! Stop! Who are you? What's going—'

With a squeal of tyres the Jeep lurched forward. She heard a loud shout, and saw the guard running alongside the car, still holding the handle.

'Oliver!' she screamed.

Then suddenly the guard was gone. Turning her head she saw him bounce on the pavement and roll a couple of times, then he was lost from sight.

Oliver drove in silence, his immediate priority to put distance between them and the guard.

He reached the end of the road and turned right, then left, accelerating hard. No sign of the man in his mirrors. He went down the road for a quarter of a mile, then took a left down to Wellington Road, then he turned right on to the busy thoroughfare.

He said nothing, wondering if the guard had got his number. He wanted the shortest route to the motorway, deciding it would be safer to get out of town rather than risk being stuck anywhere in London congestion. He kept a wary eye on his speed, not wanting to risk being stopped. Even if the guard hadn't got his number, he would raise the alarm. It wouldn't take long before Faith's absence was discovered. Minutes rather than hours.

'Faith, can you do up your seat-belt?'

Looking bewildered, she groped above her shoulder for it. He leaned across with one arm, helped her pull it over and click it home.

He was concentrating so hard on the seat-belt that he almost drove over a red light. He braked hard, and the vehicle screeched to a halt. Faith jerked forward against her belt. Then, to his horror, a police patrol car pulled up alongside him. The officer in the passenger seat was looking up at him, and Oliver kept his eyes dead ahead, a welcome stream of cold air from the air-conditioning blasting his face. Were they going to pull him over? He prepared himself. Keep calm. There was no way the alarm could already have been raised, and even if it had been, it was too soon for any information to have been circulated by the police.

The lights changed. The police car drove on ahead, losing interest in him. After a few hundred yards it turned off to the right.

Concentrating hard on his driving, Oliver followed the signs for the M40, and five minutes later was travelling at a steady fifty over the elevated section of the Westway, visor flipped down, squinting against the harsh glare of the low sun over the far rooftops.

Suddenly he felt as though he was outside his body again. He could see the car in front of him, the road beyond it, the red needles of the speedometer and the rev counter, but it was as if something else was driving and he was looking down, like a ghost, from above.

The drug again, he told himself. *I am here, I am driving, I am holding the steering-wheel, this is me, alive.*

I think therefore I am. I'm driving therefore I am. I just have to keep calm, it will fade, just give it time.

'Where's your passport, Faith?' he asked.

His voice was strange, as if he was listening to himself speaking.

There was a long silence. He thought she was asleep. Then she said, 'At home. Sussex.'

He thought about it as he drove. It would take at least an hour and a half to get down there, but she could get some clothes too. There were so many dangers, though. The moment the police were alerted, that was the first place they would look for her. And every harbour, airport and the Eurotunnel would soon have been alerted. It was too risky to try to get her out of the country at this point and, besides, he realised, she had to be here if she was to appeal to the tribunal to get the order reversed.

He reached forward and dialled his mobile phone. A sharp crackle, then he heard a male voice.

'Hallo?'

'Gerry?'

'Oliver! My friend, how are you? I'm thinking about you all the time.'

Oliver began to feel better. Of all the people he had met in England, Gerry Hammersley was the one he had warmed to most. At fifty-five, with two successful businesses, one a small chain of suburban London estate agencies, the other a niche-market wine shipping company, Gerry was still trying to find the woman of his dreams. A short, energetic man, he reminded Oliver of Groucho Marx.

Gerry had come to see him six years back, after Oliver had been interviewed on a radio show about the treatment of acute anxiety through hypnosis. Gerry had been dumped by his fiancée and his self-esteem was then at an all-time low. Oliver had changed his life, Gerry told him.

'Gerry, your offer that I could use your place in the country if I ever needed some peace and quiet on my own – is it still open?'

'Of course. You can stay there as long as you like – have the place to yourself. I'm not even sure when I'll be down next, but it won't be this weekend.'

'I just need it for a day or two.'

'Fine. When do you want to go there?'

'Tonight, if that's possible.'

'Well, of course, yes. I'd have liked to have the cleaning lady air a bed for you but—'

'Not important.'

'There's bread in the freezer. Long-life milk. Tons of wine and beer in the cellar. Use it all, OK? Eat anything you can find.'

'I'll get some stuff.'

'You don't have to. You remember where the spare key's kept?'

'Sure.'

'And the code for the alarm?'

'Uh-huh. Look, I need one other very big favour from you, Gerry.'

'What's that?'

'That you don't tell anyone where I am. Not a soul.'

'Absolutely. You've had the most appalling tragedy, and you must be sick of the media. My lips are sealed. One of my ancestors survived six months of torture by the Inquisition in the sixteenth century. They crushed every one of his fingers and toes with a thumbscrew because he wouldn't reveal the names of any heretics. They stretched him on the rack, they hammered him into a spiked chair, they inserted a stretching tool up inside him, and split his rectum open so badly he was never able to sit on a chair for the rest of his life. We Hammersleys know how to keep quiet, Oliver. It's in our genes.'

As Oliver hung up, Faith said quietly, 'We have to collect Alec.'

'Alec?'

'Ross will use him against me if we don't.'

Incredulously Oliver said, 'You want to go to your house and get him?'

'We have to.'

'Do you understand what's happened to you and what we're doing?'

'I – I think so.'

Oliver talked her through it. Every few moments he tested her to ensure that she was lucid enough to take it in. She seemed to be. But when he had finished, she was still adamant they had to collect Alec.

Oliver looked at his watch: 8.35.

Faith touched his arm and turned towards him with fear in her eyes. 'Please, Oliver, I don't know what Ross is capable of any more. If something happened to Alec – if he did something to him to get back at me – I don't think I could ever—'

Oliver didn't like it but he understood. 'We'll get him,' he said. 'We'll go get him now.'

385

92

The safety chain was on the front door. Rasputin was in a frenzy. In the porch of Little Scaynes Manor Faith yelled, over his barking, 'Mummy, open this door!'

'I'm phoning the police. It's for your own good!' her mother replied.

Faith screamed, hammering on the door with her fists, 'Open this door!' Turning wildly to Oliver she said, 'Your mobile – phone the number here, quickly! Phone it and block it so she can't call out!'

'Give me the number.'

She told him. Repeating it to himself, Oliver ran to the Jeep and dialled it.

'Let me in or I'll break a window!' Faith shrieked, trying to think clearly. The key also worked for the kitchen door at the back, but there would be a safety chain on it, too, no doubt. Her mother was nervous of the isolation here.

'Mummy!' she screamed, even louder. 'Mummy! Damn you, let me in!'

Through the bay window of Ross's study she could see her mother, standing at the desk, picking up the phone. She was about to run across and pound on the window, smash it if necessary, when on the other side of the door she heard a little voice.

'Mummy! Mummy's home!'

'Alec! Darling! Undo the chain!'

The door opened and Rasputin leaped out, almost knocking her flat. Alec jumped up, locking his arms around her neck and hugging her.

Oliver stood behind her, mobile phone to his ear. Faith ran through the hall into Ross's study, grabbed the receiver out of her mother's hand and ripped the phone base away from the desk, tearing out the wires.

'He's poisoning me!' she yelled at her mother. 'You stupid woman, my husband is poisoning me and you're letting him!'

'Faith, listen, Faith – listen to me, darling, you're—'

'You listen to me,' Oliver said. 'Mrs Phillips, I—'

'I know you, you were here earlier. Who are you? What are you doing with my daughter?'

'I'm your daughter's doctor.'

'My daughter is under Dr Ritterman.'

Oliver signalled to Faith with his eyes. 'Passports,' he said to her. 'Clothes.'

Faith made for the door. Oliver went over to her and whispered in her ear, 'Tear every phone in the house out of its socket. Does she have a mobile?'

Faith shook her head.

'Two minutes and we're out of here.' He turned back to her mother. 'Mrs Phillips, do you know the drug ketamine?'

Standing barefoot in a baggy T-shirt and jeans, Margaret Phillips folded her meaty arms. 'What of it?'

'It's an anaesthetic that can cause hallucinations and seemingly psychotic behaviour. Your son-in-law has been giving this to your daughter.'

'My daughter is extremely sick.'

'No, she is not extremely sick, not yet. She has a disease I think we can cure. Your son-in-law is giving her a drug that is nothing whatever to do with this disease. He's giving to it her because he is insane.'

'You don't know what you're saying. Ross worships my daughter. He's the most wonderful husband to her and the most devoted father, and one of the most brilliant and dedicated surgeons in this country. Don't you start coming here telling me—'

'Mrs Phillips, please listen to me—'

'You listen to me,' she said. 'I had a phone call less than ten minutes ago from the Grove Hospital, telling

387

me that my daughter was visited by a Dr Oliver Cabot – presumably you – earlier this evening and that she had vanished. They asked me to let them know if she turned up here, and that is exactly what I propose to do.'

'Don't you love Faith?' Oliver said. He tried to engage her eyes but she was too angry, too fired up.

'She's my daughter, Dr Cabot. I love her deeply.'

'Then help us. If you send her back to the Grove Hospital, her husband is going to kill her.'

'Oh, yes?' she said, sarcastically. 'And I suppose you're going to give her some miracle cure.'

'A cure,' Oliver said. 'Not a miracle, just a cure.'

There was an instant of hesitation in the woman's face. 'My daughter is under a Mental Health Act section order. If you are really her doctor, I expect you to act according to the law and return her to the hospital where she was being held.'

'Mr Ransome drugged Faith to get that order. I have the evidence.' Oliver pulled the envelope from Sister Durrant out of his pocket, ripped it open and held out the vial. 'Your daughter's blood is in there. When I take that to the Path Lab tomorrow it's going to show ketamine. Someone's going to have a problem explaining what a trauma anaesthetic's doing in her system.'

'Whatever he may have done, he will have done it for the best of reasons. I would trust him with my life. Do I make myself clear?'

'I'm taking Faith and she wants her son to come with us. I will take them wherever she wants to go, and if you truly love your daughter, you'll let her go and you won't inform anyone about this.'

'I'm phoning the hospital the moment you leave here with her. If you really are her doctor, I would suggest you leave Alec here and take her straight back. If you don't, I think you're going to find yourself in a great deal of trouble.'

'Mrs Phillips,' he said, trying one last time, 'please believe me, please trust me. Tell me what I have to do to convince you.'

Her arms still folded, Faith's mother said, 'Ross has told me everything about you, Dr Cabot. You're a charlatan and you have some kind of hold over my daughter. I think you are a dangerous and evil man. You can't convince me, Dr Cabot. Hell will freeze over before you do.'

93

On the far side of an opaque glass wall a phone was ringing, the volume increasing with each ring. *Got to get to it, got to answer it, got to got to got to—*

He butted the glass wall with his head. Then again, harder. The glass was soft, it was polythene, it dented, and he threw his full weight against it, feeling it yielding, ripping, only now it was suddenly solid again, a wall of glass that was exploding into a million shards. Air blasted his face. All around him shards of glass were falling away and then, suddenly, they began like feathers in a squall to rise up and disperse.

Cold black waves the size of houses rolled at him. He ducked with a scream. Opened his eyes. Strange, translucent light. One light source, a doorway on to a corridor, bright light out there, darkness in here. The phone ringing. In bed. He reached across to the table but the table had gone.

Where the fuck am I?

Ringing louder still. Phone on his right. He slept on the left. Everything on his left. Water, book, handkerchief, alarm, phone.

The phone was on his right.

Memories were coming at him now. He reached out, found the mobile phone, dropped it, picked it up again, felt for one of the keys, pushed it, brought the phone to his ear.

An Irish accent. Familiar. 'Mr Ransome?'

Who the fuck was this? 'Yrr.'

Head spinning like a gyroscope through the void of darkness. Partly remembered thoughts glimpsed for an instant then lost.

'You phoned me earlier, you were trying to get hold of me. Is there something that you wanted?' The tone was insolent.

He knew the name, saw it stuck firmly to a patch of darkness, but had to wait to come full circle before he arrived back at it. Now he could see it again. 'Caven?'

'Maybe we should talk in the morning?'

'Morning?'

'We'll talk in the morning, I've woken you. Call me in the morning.'

Something screaming inside his head. Some urgency, emergency, some need not to let this – 'No! Now! I – I have – have to talk – we have to talk – now—'

'Have you been drinking?'

Black soup slopped around inside his skull. Had he been drinking?

Where the fuck am I?

'No – I'm – I've just woken – Caven – you and I – we have talks to have – there are things we need to talk—'

I'm in the clinic. I'm in the fucking clinic, I'm in a bed in the clinic! The Grove. Hospital. I came because—

Grolsch? Two Grolschs? The heat?

Something in a lift. Something had happened in a lift but there was a locked and bolted door at the entrance to that memory path. Caven. Why did he need to speak to him?

Then he remembered. The police! That was it! Had to

stop Caven talking to the police.

'We need to talk now, Caven. Wasstime?'

'Five past ten.'

'Night?'

'Yes, five past ten at night. You have been drinking, call me in the morning when you're sober.'

'No – no, hold. Hallo? Caven?'

'I'm still here.'

It was starting to come back now. The underground car park this afternoon. 'We – we didn't have a good meeting earlier – not at all good. Shwee – weesh –' Christ, his brain was all a mess, the words weren't coming out right. 'We – you, I, *we* – need to talk – somewhere now?'

'It's five past ten at night,' the private investigator said.

'Half an hour. Just need to get my head together.'

'In the morning.'

There were three sharp beeps. Caven had disconnected.

'Fuck you.' Ross stared, blinking, at the bright light of the corridor. His eyes were tuning in to the room now. He was in one of the private rooms, lying on a bed. Why?

It's five past ten at night.

What the hell time had he come here? Anson. Detective Sergeant Anson. They'd drunk a couple of beers and then he'd walked over here – eight – about eight – and then?

He hit the locked door in his brain.

Swung his feet off the bed, on to the carpeted floor. His shoes were off. The floor tipped sharply away from him. He stumbled forwards, then sideways, clung to something, anything, a side-table, falling with it now, crashing to the floor. The sound of breaking glass.

Then the room flooded with light.

He looked up. A nurse in a chequered tunic was looking down at him. He knew her face but the name was gone. She was looking at him as if he was a child. Then she bent down and helped him to his feet.

'Are you all right, Mr Ransome?'

'Sh-shokay.'

'You've cut your cheek – I'll put a little plaster on it. Lie down again. Let's get you back on that bed.'

He shook her away, panic seizing him, memory returning, the drip, should have changed the drip at half past six—

Staggering to his feet he said, 'Faith, my wife, I – have to go to my wife.' Then he realised his jacket had been removed.

The drip bag had been in the pocket.

'Where's my jacket?'

She pointed to the back of the door. He went over to it, unhitched it from the hook and could feel immediately from the weight that the drip bag wasn't there. Had she taken it? She was looking at him damned strangely.

'I'll go and fetch a plaster for your cheek,' she said, and left the room.

He dug his hands into the pockets. The right-hand pocket. Something damp and crumpled. Pulled it out. An empty drip bag.

His panic subsided. Relief. *I must have changed the bag!*

The nurse came back in holding a sticking plaster, a wad of cotton wool and a bottle of what looked like antiseptic. He sat on the bed while she dressed the cut.

'Howsh – how – howsh my wife?' He read the badge on her lapel. Ward Sister Sheila Durrant.

'Your wife has left, Mr Ransome.'

It took a moment to register. 'I – don't understand. Left what?'

'Here. She's gone. Disappeared.'

'Whaaaat?'

'I'm sorry.'

He stood up, backed away, fury erupting inside him. 'Whaaat? Left? Left?'

'Her doctor came to see her. Dr Cabot. They've both gone.'

'You're not serious?'

'I'm afraid I am.'

His fists balled at his side. 'How can she have left? This is a secure hospital for Chrissake – how? How? *How?*'

'No one knows.'

'She's sectioned – she can't fucking leave.' The inside of his head was revolving again. 'Where is she?'

'We don't know.'

'Have the police been told?'

'Yes.'

He slumped against a wall and it began to revolve like a fairground centrifuge. 'This creep Cabot, this charlatan, he's her lover. They're sleeping together. He's screwing my wife. You let her lover come in and take her away?'

'I'm sorry, Mr Ransome. You arrived here rather the worse for wear, to put it mildly, and it took everyone we had to get you on to a bed for your own sake – to avoid embarrassment for you.'

'Very fucking kind of you.'

'If you're going to stand there swearing at me, I'm going to leave you and I'll talk to you again when you've sobered up a little more. All right?'

'Not fucking all right at—'

She walked out of the door and slammed it behind her.

Ross sat down on the bed. The room was jigging up and down and there was a strange buzzing sensation inside his skull, as if some insect, a moth or a large bee, was thwacking around. He saw a mobile phone lying on the floor, realised it was his own.

He picked it up, ran through the programme selector until he reached the last call-received indicator, displayed it then pressed the button to dial the number.

Hugh Caven answered on the second ring. 'Yes, hallo?'

'Meet me tonight, Caven, and I'll bring you the money I owe you, plus more.'

'How much more?'

'Another thousand.'

'Where do you suggest?' Caven said.

'I – ah—'

'Where are you?'

'Grove Hospital – close – Wellington Road. Maida Vale?'

'There's a Hilton near you, opposite Lords cricket ground. Do you know it?'

'Fy – I – I – find.'

'There's a coffee shop and a bar just off the lobby. I'll meet you there in half an hour, but don't keep me waiting. They're showing the film of *Woodstock* on Sky television at midnight. That's a rare treat and I don't intend missing it. Are you hearing me loud and clear, Mr Ransome?'

'*Woodstock*, midnight. Crap hippie film. Loud and clear,' Ross replied. 'I'm on my way now. You've got to be sad to want to watch a film like that, Caven.'

94

Oliver drove in silence for twenty-five minutes, one eye almost permanently watching in the mirrors for police. It was just coming up to half past eleven. If the security

394

guard at the Grove Hospital hadn't reported his number, Faith's mother would either have got one of the phones working or gone round to a neighbour and called the police by now.

Just five miles to go.

Less than five minutes.

He cautiously pushed their speed from seventy-five up to eighty. Alec behind him was absorbed with his GameBoy. Faith, he thought, was asleep.

There was another sign ahead, pointing to the left, with the drawing of an aeroplane next to it. Gatwick Airport.

His nerves tightened. Just a minute or so more, that's all. Something in his mirror now, something with a light on the roof, *shit*, then he breathed out in relief. Just a taxi.

Entering the airport complex, the smell of kerosene seeping into the car, he followed the signs towards the long-term car-park, and halted at a booth. They could be just a couple and their kid parking their car and catching a late flight, like a thousand other families. He pulled a ticket out of the machine and, as the barrier rose, drove forward a few yards. Two car-parks to select from.

Choosing the NCP at random, he followed the signs along the perimeter fencing, then in through a gate into a vast lot, then through into another. There were acres of parked cars all around him.

Perfect.

He drove along one aisle, all the vehicles clearly visible in the sodium lighting. He passed a Jeep Cherokee, similar to his own, but the wrong year and colour. Tempting, but hopefully he could do better. He drove along another aisle, then another. Two more Jeeps, one also the wrong year and colour, the other too near to a bus stop where a man was waiting with a suitcase.

Then, at the far end, in a relatively dark area against the perimeter fencing, he saw a navy Cherokee, identical to his own. He drove round and cruised slowly past it. The licence plate showed it was the same year as his. And there was a space three cars along from it.

No sign of anyone around.

'Are we going in an aeroplane?' Alec piped up, his voice full of excitement.

'Not tonight,' Oliver said. 'We'll go in one soon.'

'Where?'

'Where would you like to go?'

'Ummm,' he fell silent, 'I think I'd like to go – I don't know.'

Oliver opened the door. Faith stirred as he climbed down. 'Won't be long,' he said.

He hitched his jacket from the rear seat, took out his wallet and removed his Mastercard. Then he scanned the car-park carefully. No sign of anyone walking around or sitting at the nearby courtesy-bus pick-up point. And all the parked vehicles looked like they were empty. An aircraft on its landing path thundered by only yards above his head in a blaze of lights.

He walked down to the parked Jeep, and put his hand on the bonnet. It was warm. Good, that meant it had only arrived recently. No one would park here in the long-term unless they intended to be gone at least twenty-four hours, and probably longer than that.

He knelt down in front of the Jeep and, working around the edge of the car's licence plate, found a weak spot, and pushed the card in a good half-inch. During a heat–wave the previous summer, Oliver's front number plate had fallen off. He had learned from the mechanic who repaired it that most Jeep plates were held on with double-sided sticky-tape.

He levered the card until the gap was wide enough for his fingers. Then he pulled steadily, but not too hard, nervous of breaking the plate, until he felt the adhesion giving way. Suddenly the plate was free in his hand, leaving the tape in place on the back. He laid the plate down carefully, sticky side up, and repeated the process with the rear plate, then did the same with both the front and rear plates of his own car.

Five minutes later, relieved to have plates on the car that wouldn't – he hoped – be flagged on any police computer, he was driving away from the airport, heading north to the M25, from where he would head west. He set the cruise control to 80 m.p.h., turned Classic FM on the radio up so that he could hear it without waking Faith, and settled down with his thoughts for a long drive.

Behind him, hunched over his tiny games screen, Alec saved them all by trapping a Venusaur in a Poke Ball.

95

'You're late, I was about to leave. I told you I don't want to miss the film.'

'I went to the Hilton in Park Lane,' Ross said. 'I didn't realise it was *this* fucking Hilton. Anyhow, don't you have a video? You could have recorded it.'

'I told you very clearly, the Hilton at *Lords*,' Hugh Caven said. 'I've been here forty minutes.'

The private investigator was lounging on a sofa in a white T-shirt and jeans, leather jacket slung on the cushions beside him, a bunch of keys nestled in the lining. Ross stood unsteadily above him, squinting through a haze of cigarette smoke around the huge, busy lounge bar, finding it hard to focus.

'I also said I didn't want to see you until you'd sobered up.'

'Not drunk.' Ross sat down heavily in an armchair opposite him. There was an empty coffee cup and a bowl of nuts on the table between them. Ross hungrily grabbed a fistful of nuts and shovelled them into his mouth, then tried to focus on Caven.

The man's nose looked crimson and one of his eyes was half closed, with a dark blue ring around it.

'Did you bring your cheque-book?'

'How mush d'you say?'

'Five thousand. And I'm wanting another thousand on account. You mentioned—'

'Wasshappen – your noshe?' Ross pointed at Caven's face. 'You had ackisdent?'

'Accident?'

Ross nodded. His mouth didn't seem to want to work properly and he was having the same problem finding words he'd had earlier.

'You mean my broken nose? You head-butted me, remember?'

'Ah.' The memory was returning.

Caven's expression was black fury.

Ross tried to be humorous. 'I'm a plashtic surgeon – I – could do you a nishe new noshe.'

'I wouldn't let you operate on my son's gerbil,' Caven said. 'And I think an apology might be appropriate.'

'Sh-shorry.' Ross pulled out his cheque-book, then fumbled for a pen. A waiter came over. Ross ordered a glass of water then nodded at Caven. 'Can I get you – a shdrink?'

'No, thanks. Two minutes and I'm gone.'

The waiter walked away. Ross was trying to think. Caven's face blurred. He had wanted to meet this man badly, things to ask him, *silence*, that was it, he wanted to buy the man's silence, that was one thing. And find Faith. And Cabot. That was the other.

'Lishen, sorry – the car-park – I – wash in bad mood, we need to talk, you and I.'

'We *are* talking,' Caven said. 'We're talking for exactly ninety more seconds, then I'm going home to watch *Woodstock* on my digital television.' He pointedly looked at his watch.

'You – you want six thousand pounds. Give you ten shoushand—' He stopped, the whole lounge was rocking around. 'Ten shoushand. We stay friends. Shilence. We understand each other?'

'I don't think that you and I are ever going to be friends, Mr Ransome.'

'No – wash I mean is, the polishe – Dr Cabot – the brother – someone shot – the brother. I would prefer – sh'reputation ash a shurgeon – my clientele – better if you didn't shay to the polishe about working for me.'

Caven's demeanour changed in an instant. 'Is that what you brought me out here to talk about?'

Ross did not care for the man's expression. Alarm bells were clanging. Said the wrong thing, he realised. Should have kept quiet. 'No – sh'not important. I – I neesh to talk to you because shish man, Cabot, my wife, Cabot, shish man's taken her away, I need you to find her – she – hash to have her medication. Have to find her for her sake.'

'She's left you?'

'He'sh taken her.'

'Dr Oliver Cabot has taken your wife? She's left you for him?'

Ross nodded, and opened his hands, helplessly.

'You don't know where they are?'

'No, sh'right, fuck knowsh where they're – they're—' He looked down at his cheque-book. A waiter brought over a glass and a bottle of mineral water and set them down on the table.

As the man walked away, Caven leaned forward, animatedly. 'In his car? Has he taken her in his car? In his Jeep Cherokee?'

'How fuck do I know? Pushed her away on a four-wheeled crocodile f'rall I know. 'S your fucking job.'

Caven tapped his watch. 'Time's up.' He stood.

'Shwait – plish – pleash—'

'You going to talk sensibly to me? You're right at the end of your overdraft limit with my patience, do you understand?'

Ross signalled for him to sit down. 'Sensible. Don't know what car.'

Caven sat back down. 'Your wife has gone somewhere with Dr Cabot? Out of town?'

Ross shrugged. 'Anywhere, could be.'

'I fitted a global positioning transponder to Dr Cabot's Jeep,' Caven said. 'It was one of the first things I did. I can plot his position on the computer in my office.'

Ross felt a boost of excitement. 'How accurate?'

'Call me in the morning and I'll look. If they've gone in Dr Cabot's Jeep, I can find them for you. I'll be able to tell you where the Jeep is, anywhere on this planet, to within fifty feet. Is that accurate enough for you?'

96

A wave of tiredness hit Oliver and he yawned, then opened the window, allowing a blast of night air to storm in and buffet his face. It was twenty past twelve. The traffic was thin, and the air was fresher now. On the radio the weather forecaster had announced earlier that a low was moving in from the Atlantic. Changeable weather tomorrow.

Junction 13. Swindon. Oliver turned off the M4, along the dual carriageway he knew well. He passed signs for Cricklade, then Cirencester. Just fifteen minutes and they'd be there. Fifteen more minutes to elude the police and they'd be safe.

In his mirror a pair of headlights materialised out of the night, coming up fast behind him, then slowing and keeping pace with him. Nervously he looked at his speedometer. Seventy-five. Oliver slowed to sixty-five. The car behind slowed, still pacing him.

Shit.

Anxiety rippled through him. If there was an alert out for him, the switch of the licence plates would cover him against being spotted by a vigilant patrol officer, but if he was stopped in a routine check, he would be in trouble, because he had no idea of the name and address of the owner of the Jeep from which he had taken the plates.

He continued at sixty-five. The car continued tailing him. Wild thoughts went through his mind. Did he know the back roads around here well enough to give the police the slip? He only needed to lose them for a few minutes and that would enable him to make it—

To his relief the car overtook him, exhaust blattering, deep bass thumping from the sound system, and raced on ahead into the night.

Just a bunch of dickheads.

Faith stirred from the noise.

'Where are we?'

'Five miles to go,' he said.

She turned to check on Alec, who was sleeping soundly. Faith closed her eyes again.

A Puccini opera, *Manon Lescaut*, was playing on the

radio. Manon was staggering in the American wilderness, singing a sad lament, a woman who had chosen passion over money, but had then wavered, with fatal consequences; a woman who had allowed indecision to corrode and ultimately destroy her life.

There were some things in life to which you had to give your all, where there was no room for doubt. Doubt killed you. *He who hesitates is lost.* That applied to medicine as much as to fighting or anything else. Utter conviction. He could heal Faith, get rid of the Lendt's disease. She was receptive enough, responsive enough, and she had the strength of mind and character. Within three months, if he was given free rein to work with her, he knew they would beat the disease. He knew this just as certainly as he knew that Moliou-Orelan wasn't interested in developing a drug that would beat Lendt's, or any other disease. There was much more money in keeping people dependent on medication for years and years than in curing them. If Faith was one of the lucky few she would be on that Moliou-Orelan drug for the rest of her life. And having to put up with whatever side-effects went with it.

He passed the signs to Cirencester industrial estate and Stroud, and turned off to head for the Cotswolds. There was a turning coming up in a couple of miles that was easy to overshoot. He passed the familiar landmark of the Hare and Hounds pub, and he slowed his speed further. Road signs ahead pointed to Bourton, Stow-on-the-Wold, Moreton-In-Marsh. Then to the left he saw the familiar sign, marked Chedworth, Withington and Farm Trail.

He braked hard and turned left into a wide lane. A couple of miles along he came to a familiar left-hand bend. A prominent for-sale sign was fixed to a large barn conversion that had been under construction for as many years as he had been coming down here. He turned right in front of it, into a narrow lane barely wider than the car, which after half a mile dipped steeply downhill into a village of grey Cotswold stone houses and dry stone walls.

It was easy to miss the entrance to the drive, and he kept his speed down as he left the village, going into a sharp right-hand bend, past a fine gatehouse and along the boundary of a walled estate, followed by a left-hander. Then just as the road straightened out, he saw the driveway ahead to his right. Breathing a low sigh of relief, he swung the Jeep in through the five-barred gate that was always open.

The tyres rumbled on the cattle grid. In the headlights a panicking rabbit darted to the right then to the left, then right again. Oliver slowed for it, and it darted into the hedge.

Alec's voice startled him. 'Are we nearly there yet?'

'Just going up the track now. Couple of minutes.'

'I can't see anything,' Alec said.

There was a shadowy cluster of farm buildings ahead. The headlights shone on an open-sided barn containing a stack of bales and a decrepit-looking tractor. Oliver smelt a sharp tang of rotting straw and muck, then the much stronger stench of pigs. A dog began barking.

He drove through another gate, and the track climbed at a sharp gradient for several hundred yards towards a copse of firs. Beyond them it levelled out, running between two stock fences over open pastureland. At the end he made a right turn through another five-barred gate and over another cattle grid. The track continued upwards, more gently for a few hundred yards, the tyres rumbled over a third cattle grid and then they were mashing gravel. He brought the car to a halt and pulled on the handbrake.

Faith touched his arm lightly. 'Well driven,' she said.

Oliver smiled, stifling a yawn, feeling a deep sense of

relief to be here. He opened the door and climbed out, breathing in the sweet night air, the silence broken only by the distant bleating of sheep, the ticking of the hot engine, and the crunch of his feet on the fine white pebbles.

He unclipped Alec's belt, then helped the sleepy boy to the ground. Faith hugged Alec to her and looked around. 'It's beautiful,' she said. 'So peaceful.'

The dark countryside was bathed in a faint sheen from the waxing quarter moon and the shimmering white specks of the stars. A long way in the distance was a weak orange glow from the street-lighting of Cirencester.

'I'm hungry,' Alec said. 'Where are we?'

'We're having a little holiday,' Faith replied.

'Is Daddy coming?'

Oliver watched her leaning forward, hugging her child hard. 'No, just you and me,' she said. 'And this nice man who has arranged the house for us.'

When Gerry Hammersley had bought the place twenty years back, it had been empty for over fifty years. Originally a tenanted smallholding, with a farmhouse, barn, and stables, a fire had razed the house to the ground shortly after the end of the Second World War. The estate that had owned it hadn't considered it worth rebuilding.

Gerry had converted the barn and granary into a beautiful L-shaped house, the stable block into a garage, and had put a swimming-pool at the back in a walled garden where the house had once been.

Oliver hefted Faith's suitcase from the tailgate, retrieved the key from its usual hiding-place beneath a flower-pot and unlocked the front door. Then he stepped inside, switched off the burglar alarm and turned on the hall lights.

'Wow!' Faith said, stepping into the tiled hall. 'It's beautiful.'

'It is,' he said. He had spent many peaceful weekends at Ampney Nairey Farm with Gerry, and Gerry's latest conquest, walking, mountain biking, playing tennis, lazing around the pool, barbecuing. If he had a favourite place in the whole world, this was it, because you could spend a whole week at this house and not see another soul, other than the cleaning lady and the gardener, who both came on Tuesdays, and the pool-man who came when it suited him, and the occasional farm vehicle out working the land. Not even the postman disturbed the tranquillity of Ampney Nairey Farm, but by arrangement left the mail in a box at the village post office for Gerry to collect. And there was only this one track up to the place. Access across the fields at the back was only possible by tractor.

You are safe here, Faith Ransome, you and Alec. Right now you're in the safest place in the world.

97

Hugh Caven's son, Sean, had taken recently to copying his dad. When his dad switched from cornflakes to Shredded Wheat for breakfast, Sean switched too. His dad had two pieces, and so did Sean. His dad sprinkled sugar on top, then poured the milk, and Sean did the same. Then, as his dad read the paper, Sean read his Beano, sipping his orange juice in the same grown-up way his dad sipped his, plastic mobile phone at his side on the table, just like his dad's real one.

The private investigator liked to read the diary page. He tried to tell himself that it was purely a business thing: he needed to keep up to speed on the famous because he never knew who might call on his services, nor on whom he might be requested to spy. But in truth he was as much attracted to the lives of the rich and famous as he was repelled by them.

This was why, every morning, the page of the *Daily Mail* he read first was Nigel Dempster's.

As he turned to it now, tired but elated from *Woodstock*, Jimi Hendrix's 'Purple Haze' still booming in his head, he read the lead story, about a Greek shipping tycoon offering to loan a yacht to the Prince of Wales for a summer holiday. Then, an item half-way down the page caught his eye.

GERALDINE'S QUEST FOR ETERNAL BEAUTY ENDS IN TRAGEDY

I was much saddened to hear of the death, at 47, of my old friend Lady Geraldine Reynes-Raleigh yesterday. Geraldine – best friend and close confidante of my cousin Lady Shasta de Bertin – was a feisty chum and an entertaining dining companion for all of us lucky enough to be in her circle.

Friends – myself included – were anxious when Geraldine decided to have plastic surgery on her nose, which, it now seems, may have led inadvertently to her death. Geraldine's grieving brother Mark, 50, said yesterday: 'We all felt the operation was unnecessary since she had a delightful nose, but she seemed determined. Of course none us ever dreamt that it would have such dreadful consequences.'

A spokesman at London's exclusive Harley-Devonshire Hospital would only confirm that Geraldine had died 'following complications' after rhinoplasty. The surgeon, society figure Ross Ransome, 42 – known to many of his clients as 'Golden Hands' – was unavailable for comment at his home in Regent's Park, London. Tragically, this is the second patient he has lost in recent months: Maddy Williams, 31, a British Airways computer programmer died last month during a similar operation.

There is no suggestion, of course, of any medical impropriety by Mr Ransome. But his long and glittering career as plastic surgeon to the stars has been something of a chequered one. Over the years, my enquiries show that as many as 12 other patients have died during or following surgery. In every case, the post-mortem has established that Mr Ransome was not to blame. Nonetheless, it seems the quest for beauty has a high price.

In the kitchen the toaster popped. Sandy, apron over her dressing-gown, called, 'Sean, hurry up, your egg is ready.'

Sean called back, 'Is Daddy having an egg today?'

'Yes, he is.'

Caven's mobile phone rang. He put down the paper and his spoon, pressed the answer button and lifted the phone to his ear. Across the table, Sean Caven brought his toy telephone to his ear and adopted a deeply serious expression.

'Caven,' the private investigator said.

'Good morning.' It was Ross Ransome, sounding as if he was suffering the effects of a serious hangover.

'And what can I do for you on this fine summer morning?'

'I don't know where the fuck you are, it's raining in London.'

Caven said nothing. It was raining here, too, and it wasn't worth the bother of explaining he had been joking. God had omitted to put in Ross Ransome's humour chip. He stared at the newspaper page in front of him, wondering if the surgeon had seen this.

'You said to call you in the morning for the compass co-ordinates.'

'I have them in my office, you'll have to hold for a minute.'

As Caven went upstairs, Sean told his client to hold, too.

They were written down on a jotter beside his computer. 'Are you still there, Mr Ransome?'

'Yes.'

'Fifty-one degrees, forty-eight minutes, fifty seconds, north, one degree, fifty-six minutes, eighty-one seconds west.'

'Where the fuck is that?'

'Somewhere in Gloucestershire, in the vicinity of Cirencester.'

'Is that the closest you get it?'

'Like I told you, it'll be accurate to within fifty feet. You need to avail yourself of an Ordnance Survey map.'

'I thought I paid you last night to tell me where she is.'

'You did and I've just told you. Now I'm going to finish my breakfast with my son. Good morning, Mr Ransome.'

Hugh Caven hung up and went back downstairs. Sean was talking into his phone.

'No calls at the table,' his father said, then grinned. This kid was so special – he was so proud of him it hurt sometimes.

Will you be proud of me when you're a grown-up? Will you still imitate everything I do? In case you do, please let me set you good examples now.

He picked up the *Daily Mail* again and reread the piece on Ross Ransome. Then he read it again.

He continued to stare at the page throughout the rest of the meal, eyes flicking occasionally to Sean. Upstairs in his wallet was the cheque from his client for six thousand pounds that he badly needed. Where was the borderline between decency and betrayal?

You're a killer, Ross Ransome. You killed Barry Gatt just as surely as you killed this Lady Reynes-Raleigh and the others before her. Don't ask me how I know, but I do.

When they had finished breakfast, Hugh Caven went back to his office, closed the door, phoned Directory Enquiries, and asked for the number of the coroner's office for the City of Westminster.

98

At some time around seven Alec had found a television. Faith had been aware of him slipping out of bed, then she had heard distant shouts, laughter.

She slept on and when she woke again it was half past nine. She smelt bacon. Oliver was standing in the room, in jeans, trainers and a pink polo shirt. He looked tired.

'Morning,' he said, and kissed her tenderly. 'Open the curtains?'

'Please.'

'It's a real English summer's day out there.' It was blustery outside with spots of rain on the glass. He closed the window then turned towards her. They held each other's eyes. 'Thank you,' she said, 'for all you did last night.'

He looked awkward. 'We got away with it.' He raised his arms apologetically. 'Had to borrow some of Gerry's clothes – just came down in the suit I was wearing and that was it.' He grinned. 'So, how are you feeling?'

'Rested,' she said. 'But tired still. Did you sleep?'

'A little. I always sleep here – this is where I come

when I need to sleep. But I guess my brain was a little busy.'

'Mine feels clearer this morning. We're fugitives, right?' she said.

'You've broken a Mental Health Act order and I've helped you. It would not be too smart to get caught.'

'And what happens now?'

'Breakfast. Alec was hungry, I made him a fry-up. I hope that was OK?'

'I think I'd like a fry-up too.'

'You're hungry?'

'Starving.'

'Good.' He looked pleased. 'You need to eat.'

She sat up in the large, soft, sleigh bed, exposed wooden beams above her head, antique French oak furniture in the room. 'What happens after breakfast?'

'I have to go to London, see a lawyer friend. We need to move fast.' He dug a small vial out of his pocket and held it up to her. It contained what looked like blood and had a handwritten label on it. 'This is a blood sample the ward sister at the Grove Hospital took from you last night and dated. I'm hoping it's going to show that you were pumped full of ketamine. I'm also hoping the ward sister did what I asked her to do and checked your husband's coat pocket, where she'd have found an empty drip bag with traces of ketamine in it.'

Alarmed, Faith said, 'Do you have to go? Couldn't you do it over the phone from here?'

'I need to get this blood sample to a lab.'

'We're in Gloucestershire?'

'Yup.'

'There must be labs here – in Cheltenham.'

He sat down on the bed, took her hand. 'It's Friday. Gerry's gardener and the cleaning lady come on Tuesdays. No one else comes here, except maybe the pool-man. You're over a mile from the nearest road and two miles from the nearest village. No one knows you're here. You just have to sit tight. Don't use the phone because that can be traced back. Trust me, OK?'

'Yes, I do. It's just—'

'You understand what your husband was doing to you, don't you?'

'Yes. You explained it to me.'

'Do you want me to talk you through it again?'

'No, I understand. It's just – What happens if you get caught?'

'I have the blood sample – the proof. And I don't know where you are. So what are they going to do? Torture me?'

She smiled. 'And if you don't come back?'

'I'll be back. In a few hours. If I need to speak to you I'll call you. I'll ring twice, hang up, then call again. OK?'

She nodded, with deep reluctance.

'You have your mobile? You picked it up last night when we collected your things from your home?'

She climbed out of bed, and walked, unsteadily at first, to her suitcase. She retrieved her phone from the jumble of clothes.

'Switch it on, but don't use it – I'll call in an emergency if for any reason I can't get through to the main number here, with the same two-ring code. But don't use it – any call you make or receive can be traced to the nearest cell. OK?'

'Keep it on but don't use it,' she said. 'You'll ring twice, hang up, then ring again.'

'Good girl. Now, one egg or two?'

'Two, please.'

'Sunny side up or over easy?'

'Over easy.'

They were good eggs, cooked well, and after Oliver left she continued to sit in front of the warm blue Aga, at the refectory table, listening to the squawking voices of the Cartoon Network on Sky on the huge wide-screen television in the next-door room, watching the rain falling outside, and the blue Cherokee driving away through it. She felt scared. She was trembling. Too agitated to eat, she got up from the table, walked to the front door and made sure it was shut and locked.

Then she explored the rest of the house. There were more doors everywhere, doors out from the conservatory into a walled garden where there was a swimming-pool with a blue cover drawn across it, out to a yard where the oil tank and the dustbins were housed. She checked them all to ensure they were locked.

Then she went back to the kitchen, forced a couple of mouthfuls of the food down her and scraped the rest into the bin.

Through the window she had a clear view of the driveway, which dipped down into an endless landscape of green and beige fields, clumps of trees and bushes, and a distant line of pylons strung out beneath a grey sky. A couple of morose-looking Friesians cropped grass on the far side of a barbed-wire fence.

There had been a power-cut recently. The clock on the electric oven next to the Aga flashed oo.oo. So did the clock on the microwave. And the one on the radio on the work-surface. Three sets of double-zeros flashing at her as if time had stopped. She looked at her wrist and realised her own watch had been removed at the hospital. What damage had they thought she could do to herself with a wristwatch? She dialled the speaking clock. Nine forty-six and twenty seconds.

In a drawer she found a pile of instruction booklets and manuals, and busied herself working out how to reset the clocks on the appliances. She managed the microwave and the radio, but the electric oven defeated her.

Alec walked into the kitchen. 'Can we go home soon?' he asked.

She stared out of the window. The sky was darkening and a sudden volley of rain spattered against the panes, rattling like lead shot. She felt the draught on her face, and thought, with a shiver of both cold and fear, I don't know where home is any more.

99

Bloody woman.

Margaret had left a message on his voice-mail, saying that the phones at home were out of order and she needed to speak to him urgently. How was he supposed to speak to her? He had called his mother-in-law three times at Little Scaynes Manor; each time the phone rang four times and voice-mail kicked in.

Ross hung up again and dropped the mobile phone back on to the passenger seat of the rented silver grey Vauxhall. Then he called Lucinda to see if she had any messages. He'd already spoken to her earlier and cancelled his day's work.

Sounding slightly shocked she asked, 'Have you seen today's *Daily Mail*?'

'What's in it?'

She sounded hesitant. 'A piece about Lady Reynes-Raleigh.'

'Good riddance to that bitch-queen from hell.'

'I've had a couple of calls – the *News of the World* and someone from the *Guardian*.'

'What are they saying?'

'They want to talk to you about the surgery you did on her.'

'I don't have time to deal with this crap right now, Lucinda. Tell them it's patient confidentiality and to take a hike.'

'I already have. I can't get through to the garage yet about your car.'

'Car?'

'Your Aston Martin.'

'OK, fine.' His mind was wandering, he didn't have time to deal with crap like this right now. 'Talk to you later,' he said abruptly, and hung up.

Rain was sheeting down and London's traffic was all snarled up. The traffic was always worst on Fridays. The wipers clunked away, the rubbers squeaking, the de-mister whistling out air on to the windscreen. Grosvenor Square was clogged up because of a reversing lorry. He jabbed the horn in frustration, then jabbed it again. Someone else a few cars behind him honked too.

The runt, Caven, had told him to look up the co-ordinates himself on an Ordnance Survey map. Great. Six thousand pounds and he had to buy his own fucking map. He'd been to three places in London so far: two had nothing; one had Ordnance Survey maps for every fucking square inch of England except the Cirencester area.

The traffic was inching forward. He finally reached the far side of the square, passed the American embassy, then turned left into South Audley Street, parked on a yellow line as close as he could to Purdey's, the gunsmith's, and ran into the shop.

It was a relief to be out of the traffic and in the dignified quiet of the handsome interior, with its rich smells of leather and gun oil. A well-spoken male assistant behind the counter recognised him immediately. 'Mr Ransome, good morning, what can I do for you?'

'I brought in one of my guns ages ago to have a scratch removed from the stock. I should have collected it in May.'

'I'll go and find it.'

Ross waited, drumming his fingers on the polished wooden counter. There was one other customer, a tall woman with a poodle on a lead, draping a silk scarf around her shoulders in a mirror. The dog growled at him, and Ross glared at it. Suddenly his face felt burning hot; the room seemed to shrink like a concertina, then stretch out again. He gripped the counter to steady himself as the floor pushed up beneath his feet, then sharply dropped away again. He saw a hand, long white fingers, neatly manicured nails, tufts of hair behind each knuckle.

It was his hand, he realised, with shock. His own disembodied hand.

'Here we are!' The assistant was holding Ross's leather gun case, with a tag tied to it. Ross was unsure whether the man was looking at him or at the woman behind him with the scarf and the dog.

'I'll show you what we've done in the workroom, Mr Ransome.'

The assistant was talking to him. His voice sounded strange, distant. The man was taking out his twelve-bore and presenting the stock to him for inspection.

Ross barely looked at it. He wasn't interested in the mark, he just wanted to take the gun and go. The atmosphere had turned oppressive. Through the window he saw a police car, and unease squirmed through him.

Got to get out.

'I think we've managed to polish it out pretty well,' the assistant said.

'Looks fine.'

'If you see, this is where—'

'I told you,' Ross snapped at him, 'it looks fine.'

'Very good.' The assistant's demeanour stiffened, but his courtesy was unaltered. He replaced the gun in the bag. 'Will that be all for this morning, Mr Ransome?'

'I need a box of cartridges. Number Six shot.'

Ross handed him a credit card, signed the slip, then went outside, relieved to have the gusting air and rain on his face, relieved that the police car had gone. A traffic warden was writing a ticket, but she was several cars away from the Vauxhall. He opened the boot, a little revived, his face icily cold in contrast to the burning sensation of a few minutes back.

The next shop he wanted was only a few doors away. He'd passed it many times, often stopping to look in the windows, but had never entered it before. Its window displays announced that it sold spying equipment, everything from night-vision goggles to briefcases with in-built recorders, tiny microphones and video-cameras. He went in and asked if they sold global positioning systems.

They had a wide range, just about any option he could think of. He bought a receiver, which looked much like a mobile phone, and an attachment into which the assistant inserted a CD of Ordnance Survey maps covering Gloucestershire and much of the rest of the west of England. The assistant helped him programme in the two sets of co-ordinates Hugh Caven had given him this morning, and showed him how to get the computer to read them.

When he returned to his car, he was lugging three bags. In addition to the GPS he had bought a pair of military specification Zeiss binoculars, and a slim pencil torch, which he had already clipped inside his breast pocket. There was a ticket taped to the windscreen and the warden had vanished. Ross tore it off, dropped it into the gutter, then climbed back into the car. It was twenty past eleven.

He removed the receiver and the computer from one bag and laid them out on his lap, then looked at the screen closely, adjusting the brightness, making it sharper. He saw a village named Lower Chedworth. Roughly a mile to the west of the village he saw a long track, finishing at a building marked Ampney Nairey Farm, which was right at the epicentre of the co-ordinates. It had to be this place. There was no other building around.

He dialled home to Little Scaynes once more. Again he got the voice-mail, but this time it was accompanied by a sharp beep from his mobile. The low-battery warning indicator was flashing. He cursed, and switched it off to conserve what power remained.

Then he started the car and threaded his way towards Park Lane, from where he would make for the Cromwell Road and then the M4. The hatred burning inside him was intensifying with every minute that passed. He could see images in his mind of Faith and Dr Oliver Cabot kissing each other, naked in bed together, their surprised faces as they grabbed the sheets, trying to cover themselves as he stood over them in the bedroom with the light snapped on and his shotgun in his hands. Faith's expression, followed by the music of her screams as he blasted Dr Oliver Cabot, first with one barrel, then the second. The sheets ripped open, turning crimson with his blood then drenched in darker, uglier colours from his shredded viscera. Her eyes staring at him as he reloaded.

A small flashing display on his new GPS told him he was 116.075 miles from the target destination. As he inched forward in the traffic, the distance displayed on the instrument decreased.

Twenty minutes later, as he approached the Hammersmith flyover, Ross saw a garage on his left and pulled on to the forecourt. He bought a five-litre petrol can from the shop and filled it to the brim. He also bought a cheap plastic lighter.

100

It went like that some days. Quiet. Just a sad wino found dead beneath a pile of newspapers and cardboard, or an elderly woman who'd dropped dead straining on the lavatory. Other days it was crazily busy, like today. A despatch rider who'd gone under a bus. A suicide who'd jumped from an office block. A middle-aged woman who'd died of complications after surgery.

A dozen cadavers had been brought in overnight. The ones where murder was suspected, like the floater who'd been brought in from Westminster Bridge and the stabbing victim found in an alley off Oxford Street, would be examined by a Home Office pathologist. The rest were down to Harry Barrow, a retired pathologist of sixty-seven, who was doing a locum in Westminster while the consultant was away in Capri on holiday.

'All right for some, isn't it?' he said. 'Lying on their backs while the whole of ruddy London drops dead on us.'

Harry was a short, blunt, irrepressibly cheerful northerner, who habitually wore a bow-tie. He sported a nicotine-stained moustache that was too big for his face, and wire-framed glasses that were too small for it. He liked to moan that he kept getting dragged back, kicking and screaming, from retirement to do locum jobs. But the truth was that he was bored stiff with retirement, and seized any opportunity to escape from his nagging wife, Doreen, who loathed his pipe smoke, criticised his drinking and was only interested in bridge, which she played all day, every day, save for her hour in church on Sundays. He liked to jest that he found the dead more fun to be with than his wife.

Dressed in his green scrubs, white boots and rubber gloves, Harry Barrow stood over the naked corpse of Lady Geraldine Reynes-Raleigh, talking into his dictating machine.

In the glare of the fluorescent light, her flesh was the colour of tallow. She had been cut open down her front from her neck to her pelvis, the skin was folded back exposing her internal organs, and her yellowy intestines coiled out of her midriff. Her breasts, skilfully enlarged and lifted by Ross Ransome, now hung, still erect from the implants, on each side of the stainless-steel table-top. Her scalp had been peeled back and lay like a membrane across her face, the skull cap had been sawn off and put to one side, and her brain lay nearby on a metal trolley. A buff identity label hung from her right big toe.

'. . . and the suturing and bruising on her face is consistent with her recent sessions of cosmetic surgery.' He switched off the dictating machine, walked across the room and put it down, selected a knife then returned to Lady Reynes-Raleigh and picked up her brain. Placing it on the white plastic cutting board behind her head, he made a careful slice through it. Then he looked at the assistant pathologist, Annie Halls, who was standing beside him and pointed. 'You can see the damage from the meningoencephalitis here and—'

He was interrupted by another assistant, a handsome, good-natured Indian woman in her mid-forties, called Zeenat Hosain, who came into the room.

'Dr Barrow, Sarah from the coroner's office is on the

phone. She says it is most very important to speak to you right away.' She nodded at the cadaver. 'It is concerning this lady.'

The pathologist removed his gloves, and went over to the phone on the wall. 'Sarah? Good morning.'

'Morning, Harry. We know you're busy, but we've had a strange phone call about Lady Reynes-Raleigh. It might be nothing, but the coroner would like you to take an extra close look at her.'

'What was the gist of the call?' he asked.

'It's someone who wouldn't give his name but claims to know Mr Ransome, the surgeon who operated on her. He thinks her death might have been intentional. We're not taking the call seriously enough to turn it into a murder inquiry at this stage, but please be extra thorough.'

Harry Barrow returned to the cadaver deep in thought. There was little doubt in his mind that the cause of death was meningoencephalitis – that was clear from looking at the state of the brain. The first area he decided to take a closer look at was inside the skull, to see if he could find anything there, any abnormality that might be linked to the meningoencephalitis, although frankly he doubted it.

Touching the loose flap of the scalp, through which there was a faint indentation from the woman's nose and chin, the pathologist said, 'You know, think I could set myself up as a cosmetic surgeon. Do one of these scalp flaps a lot cheaper than that bugger Ransome.'

Annie Halls sniggered. Black humour was the universal currency of mortuaries.

Serious again, he studied the interior of the skull. An infection causing meningoencephalitis could enter the body in a host of ways. He knew from pathology lab tests done while the woman was alive that it was a strain of septicaemia, and probably cross-contamination in the hospital, but it could have been transmitted in the air, the water, or through a wound.

Suddenly something caught his eye in the cribriform plate, on the ethmoid bone, which separated the nose cavity from the cranium: a tiny fracture in a straight line. Unnatural. And he saw as well that there was a small amount of haemorrhaging in the tissue around it.

He walked across to his tools, selected a pair of forceps and pulled the edge of dura, the thick white membrane lining the inside of the skull, away from the bone. Beneath, he could see the damage to the cribriform plate more clearly. It was possible that the surgeon's chisel had gone too far during the rhinoplasty operation. Clumsy – particularly for a man of Ransome's reputation.

But it would have taken force to do this.

He carefully cut out a section of bone. He would fix and decalcify the plate in the laboratory, then examine the damaged section microscopically to look for any evidence of pus or inflammation. It would take a few days for the acid solution to remove the calcium, but he would then be able to see the damage more clearly.

The more he thought about it, the more the damage bothered him. The cribriform plate was relatively remote from the operative field in a rhinoplasty where the chisel would pass up between the skin and the outer aspect of the nasal bones. What was a surgical implement doing within the nasal cavity at its weakest point?

He dictated his concerns into his machine. And he decided that when he had finished with the woman, he would speak to the coroner's officer and tell her his concerns. It was probably nothing, but he had learned in a long career that you were never safe taking anything for granted. Your instincts were your best guide. And right now Harry Barrow's instincts told him something wasn't right.

101

Oliver decided he was right to ignore Faith's plea to find a local laboratory. She would be safe at the house while he was away, and the evidence in that blood sample was crucial; he needed a lab he could trust not to ruin or lose it, as well as one with an established reputation for forensic work, whose evidence would stand up in any tribunal or court hearing.

There was a regular fast train service from Swindon to London – he had used it a couple of times in the past. In the car on the way to the station, he tried to phone his solicitor, Julian Blake-Whitney, a partner in the law firm Ormgasson, Horus and Sudeley. Blake-Whitney had acted well and efficiently for the Cabot Centre and Oliver trusted his judgement. In turn, Blake-Whitney trusted Oliver: he and his wife had brought their twelve-year-old son, William, who was suffering from chronic asthma, to the Cabot Centre, and within a year the boy's symptoms had gone.

Blake-Whitney was in court all morning, but his secretary got a message to him and, within minutes, he rang Oliver from his mobile. He would cancel a lunch appointment and meet Oliver at one o'clock.

Oliver left the Jeep tucked safely among a mass of cars in the station car park, and caught a train that would get him into King's Cross shortly after eleven-thirty. If he travelled by underground he would have just enough time to get to the lab then on to his meeting with his solicitor.

He sat alone in a first-class compartment and made a

call on his mobile to the house, using the code he had agreed.

'It's me,' he said, when Faith answered. 'How are things?'

She sounded tense. 'OK. How soon will you be back?'

'I'm on my way to London. I have to use a lab that's accredited with the police and I've fixed a meeting with my lawyer – his firm are the top medical specialists in the country. I want to get this section order lifted on you today somehow. How's Alec?'

'He's sitting in front of a wide-screen digital television watching Sky, and eating caramel-crunch ice-cream I found in the freezer. That's about as good as it gets for a small boy on a wet Friday morning.'

Oliver laughed. 'And you?'

'I'm just – thinking, I suppose, just finding everything a little hard to take on board.'

'I'll be back mid-afternoon.'

A train thundered past and for a few moments he couldn't hear what Faith was saying. Just as he picked up her voice again, they went into a tunnel and he was disconnected. When they emerged on the far side, he redialled.

'Sorry,' he said. 'How are you feeling?'

'OK – apart from eating too much breakfast.'

He grinned. 'No relapses from the drug?'

'Some weird flashes – and occasionally the floor moves around. But nothing else.'

He was pleased by how normal she sounded. She was strong, she was a coper. 'Is there anything you need?'

'No,' she said. 'Just you. I love you, Oliver.'

'I love you too.'

'I really love you,' she said. 'So much.' She was breaking up. For a moment he wondered if it was the connection, then he realised she was sobbing. 'Everything's going to be all right, Faith. I promise.'

At ten past one, Oliver and Julian Blake-Whitney were seated in a cramped booth at the back of a packed wine-bar just off Chancery Lane. It was a couple of years since they'd last met and in that time the solicitor had put on weight, lost some hair, and sprouted a mosaic of broken veins on his cheeks. He was squeezed into a grey chalk-stripe suit, a Jermyn Street shirt with a cut-away collar and a sombre silk tie, and had a learned air about him, enhanced both by his half-moon glasses and his confident, authoritative voice.

Oliver, in his polo shirt, felt under-dressed.

'I'm sorry to hear about your brother,' Blake-Whitney said.

'Yup. Tough call.' Oliver swallowed. He found it hard when people spoke of Harvey's death.

'Have the police got any ideas about who did it?'

'I talk to the detective in charge every day. They don't have any solid ideas at all yet.'

'And the other man – was there some connection between them?'

'Low life. Some kind of private dick or something. Used to be a night-club bouncer, but now his widow won't tell the police what kind of work he'd been doing.'

'Sounds like drugs.' The solicitor gave a sympathetic grimace. 'Anyhow, you're looking well, Oliver, you haven't changed a jot.' He patted his belly. 'But I could do with losing a few pounds off this.' He grabbed a menu, summoned a waitress and got the ordering out of the way: garlic bread and lasagne for himself, a salade Niçoise for Oliver, and a bottle of the house claret. Then he looked at his watch. 'Got to be back in court at two sharp, so tell me the problem.'

Oliver talked him through the events of the past few

weeks, and in particular of last night. Their food arrived as he was finishing.

'OK,' Blake-Whitney said. 'It's good that you had the nurse sign the vial. You've had this blood sample analysed?'

Oliver shook his head. 'The lab won't be able to get a result until Monday afternoon at the earliest – and that's pulling out all the stops.'

The solicitor tore off a chunk of garlic bread then offered the rest to Oliver, who raised his hand in a polite refusal.

Munching hungrily, Blake-Whitney said, 'Well, as it's Friday afternoon, we're not going to get anything in motion until Monday at the earliest. Mrs Ransome will have to be examined in advance by at least one independent doctor. I think we're looking more likely at Tuesday or even Wednesday to get all our ducks in a row, and we're looking at a minimum of a week after that if we apply to the hospital managers, and two weeks if we go for a Mental Health Act commission.'

'There's nothing you can do faster?'

'Unfortunately it's a damned sight easier to get someone sectioned than to get it reversed. That part of the Mental Health Act is there to protect the public.'

'The public should be protected against her goddamned husband,' Oliver said.

'Well, he's going to be in big trouble if you find what you're hoping to find in that blood sample.'

'So what happens between now and next week?'

'As your lawyer, I have to advise you to return Mrs Ransome to the Grove Hospital.'

'No way, Julian. I'd only return her to the hospital if you got an injunction preventing her husband coming within a mile of her until the hearing.'

Glancing anxiously at his watch, the solicitor nodded. 'I gave you that advice as your lawyer,' he said.

'So now give me some advice as my friend.'

'You're sure no one knows where this lady is – other than this chum of yours who lent you the place?'

'Absolutely.'

'Then go back to Gloucestershire, make yourself scarce, give me a phone number and we'll talk on Monday.'

'I could hug you.'

'Go and hug Faith. I'm not into all this male-bonding crap. Just get me the result of the blood tests. Hugs embarrass me.' He gulped some more wine and smiled. 'Nothing personal.'

102

'There was a grey car, Oliver.'

Faith was stammering and he could hear the fear in her voice. There were two other men in the compartment with him, so he got up and went into the corridor. Rain was sheeting down outside across the lush green Berkshire landscape.

'I'll be at Swindon in an hour. I'll be back with you by half past four.'

'It came up the drive.'

'What kind of a car?'

'A saloon – I'm not sure – a Vauxhall maybe.'

'Did you see who was in it?'

'No.'

'How close did it come to the house?'

There was a burst of static on the line and he missed what she said next. When the line was clear he said, 'I didn't hear you.'

'I don't know – a few hundred yards, then it turned round. I saw it driving away.'

'How long ago?'

'About two hours.'

Trying to calm her, but concerned now, Oliver said, 'It was probably someone trying to find the farm who had gotten lost – that happens sometimes.' It had actually happened once.

'It might have been Ross,' she said.

'What car does he drive?'

'A blue Aston Martin.'

'So it wasn't Ross, right? Anyhow, Ross has no idea you're there.'

'Please come back quickly, Oliver, I'm really scared.'

'Are the doors and windows locked?'

'All of them.'

'Listen, Faith, don't worry. If you see the car again call me. I'll be there as quickly as I can.'

'Please hurry.'

'I'll go bribe the engine driver.'

103

In his office overlooking the back garden of his home, Hugh Caven was staring at the spikes of rain in the paddling-pool. He had just come off the phone after a traumatic conversation with Barry Gatt's widow.

The coroner was releasing Barry's body, and Steph had arranged the funeral for next Tuesday. He knew how hard up she was, and had finally persuaded her to allow him to pay for Barry's funeral. He told her that Barry had died while in his employ and he really wanted to do that.

Then she'd broken down and told him of the debts Barry had left and she didn't know how she would cope. Caven told her he would help. He lied that there was life insurance covering his employees and that he might be able to get something for Barry's death from the policy. In truth he planned to give her what he could himself. It wouldn't be much – he had enough debts of his own – but it would salve his conscience.

And his conscience was troubling him badly right now, as it had been all day. Ross Ransome was a dangerous bastard. He was regretting having given him the compass co-ordinates this morning of where Dr Oliver Cabot's car was located. If Ransome had been behind the killer of Cabot's brother – and Barry Gatt – who was to say he wasn't intending to finish the job off?

Why the hell else would he want the co-ordinates?

To get his wife back?

Sure.

He dialled New Scotland Yard and asked to be put through to the incident room for the Cabot and Gatt murders.

After two rings a voice-mail told him that all the lines were busy. He left a message that he had information relevant to the death of Barry Gatt, and asked for someone to call him back.

He said it was urgent.

104

It was *you, bitch!* Ross could see her clearly now, through the binoculars. *It was you looking out of the window when I drove up earlier. You were there, and then you were gone. I was too far away to be sure.*

She was staring out of the window straight at him, only she couldn't see him, of course, and there was no sunlight to reflect off his lenses and give him away. He'd learned that deerstalking in Scotland. There was a time when he went regularly, a group of young doctors together, their annual boys' hunting trip. A gamekeeper in Braemore had also taught him how to move silently through undergrowth. And how to remain invisible.

Deerstalking had taught him patience too.

He was lying, shielded by a clump of ferns, in a ditch on the edge of a copse of firs, close to the track and with a clear view of the house. A long green Barbour jacket, waterproof trousers, wellington boots and a rain-hat, which he'd bought in an outdoor shop in Cirencester an hour ago, along with the canopy of branches above him were keeping out most of the weather, except for one persistent trickle of water down the back of his neck.

A beetle was crawling past in front of him, up and down every undulation of the soil, laboriously navigating through the fronds of dripping greenery. A solitary bird was tweeting somewhere above him. The smells of moist earth and pine cones brought back those deerhunting days vividly to him. Good times. Those early years with Faith when they had been so happy together. Before Dr Oliver Cabot had come on the scene to steal her from him.

Where are you Dr Oliver Cabot? Is your car hidden away in the garage or have you gone out to buy more condoms to screw my wife with?

She was in what looked like a kitchen, wearing some kind of blue top, and her hair could have been tidier.

You look like a slut, today, Faith. Is that what Dr Oliver Cabot does to you? Makes you into a slut? Do you do slut things to him?

Faith needed him. She might not realise it, but she did, she really did. She was looking like a piece of trash.

You've rejected me, and now look at you.

His mind went back twenty-eight years. To his mother lying on the bed in her small, grim flat, with her legs scissored around her lover's waist.

I thought at least you would have left me for a

paradise, and that all I could have done would have been to stand in awe if I ever saw you.

I really would like it if you could explain how you could do this to me, Faith.

A sharp clatter some way behind him startled him. The sound of wheels on a cattle grid, he realised.

A second clatter, louder, and now the sound of an engine. A vehicle travelling quickly. Tyres on the rough surface, splashing through puddles.

He could see the front now. A blue off-roader. A Jeep Cherokee, passing by just yards from him. The silhouette of a tall man driving, with long grey curly hair.

Through the binoculars he watched the Jeep pull up outside the house. The stupid bastard stopped right in front of the door, blocking his view of it. Ross strained to see through the windows of the Jeep but all he could see was blurred shapes moving, then the door closing.

Faith, his beloved Faith, was there, opening the door to Dr Oliver Cabot, welcoming him back to their love-nest. She was probably pulling down his zipper now, taking him in her mouth, the way she had once long ago when he'd arrived home on a hot summer evening after she'd had a long, boozy lunch with a friend.

You are going to be sorry, both of you, so—

He swung the binoculars. She was in that kitchen window again now. Dr Oliver Cabot was standing next to her. Faith was pointing in this direction, they were talking, discussing something.

For an instant he panicked that they could see him. Impossible.

The car was safely hidden away, parked out of sight at the back of a pub half a mile along the main road. Dr Oliver Cabot wouldn't have seen it. Ross was aware that they would be looking out for strange vehicles, that Faith would have told him about the silver car she had seen come up the drive, so he had trudged up here in his country clothes, and could have passed for any local out for a walk. He hadn't seen a soul and he didn't think anyone had seen him. It was now ten to five. It would take him about twenty minutes to get back to the car. How long were they going to remain here? They had stayed last night, which meant they thought they were safe. He had a feeling they'd be here tonight as well, and that they intended staying longer than that.

With luck if the weather held like this it would be a dark night. The wind and the rain were a real bonus: they would mask any sounds he made when he returned.

105

'Mummy, can I show you something? Please!' Alec stood at the bottom of the stairs, looking breathless with excitement. 'Can I? Can I?'

In the huge living room, Oliver was kneeling down, trying to light the wood-burning stove. Faith, relaxing on a sofa, was staring through the huge picture window at the lush flower beds and lawn of the walled garden, and at the rain pooling on the cover of the swimming pool. The *Evening Standard* Oliver had brought down from London was open on her lap, and she was sipping a glass of Australian Chardonnay which tasted like nectar.

It was the first newspaper she had read in days, and the first alcohol she had drunk in almost a week, and the wine was going to her head. It was a good feeling. She felt safe now Oliver was back, and the room was filling with the crackling sounds and the cosy smell of burning kindling. She drank some more.

There was nothing in the paper about Oliver's

brother's death. Old news already. She smiled. 'What is it you want to show me, darling?'

'You have to come up and see it.'

Alec had been good all day, busying himself playing with his Star Wars Lego, in between watching either Cartoon Network or the Trouble channel, and exploring the house.

'OK,' she said. 'Let's go – it had better be good!'

Standing up, she realised how tired she felt. Drained, zapped, utterly exhausted.

Maybe even a little sloshed?

Alec scampered up the oak staircase and she followed him slowly, each tread an effort, up on to the galleried landing. The room Oliver had slept in was to the left, and the one she had shared with Alec was straight ahead. Alec ran down to the right and in through a door.

She followed him, and found herself in another bedroom, attractively decorated with antique pine furniture, and a white lace bedspread over a king-size bed. Alec was looking at her mischievously.

'Mummy's very tired, darling. What am I meant to be looking at?'

He ducked into a wardrobe and came out with a long pole with a hook on the end, then stared upwards. Faith followed his gaze and saw a loft door.

'Alec, I don't think this is a good—'

But he was already hooking the pole into the metal eye on the door as deftly as if he had been doing it all his life. He gave a sharp tug and the hatch door lowered. A compacted metal ladder was attached to it. With another flick of the pole he had the ladder telescoping open to the floor.

He began to climb up it.

'Alec, darling, I—'

But he was already disappearing through the hatch.

Moments later a light came on. Never comfortable with heights, Faith gripped the ladder and climbed, very slowly.

When she reached the top she stared round in amazement. It was a kid's paradise up here. A huge insulated loft with a wooden floor, a bed with a Batman cover, and toys strewn everywhere over the floor, bulging out of an open trunk. At the far end, side by side, were a huge electric train set and Scalextric track.

'The man said I could sleep up here tonight, Mummy. Can I, please?'

'Oliver said you could sleep up here?'

Alec nodded. He knelt and pulled on a Hallowe'en mask with an eyeball hanging loose.

'That's a big improvement, darling.'

Through the mask, he boomed, 'Can I? Please can I?'

'You'll be lonely up here.'

'I won't.'

She went over to the bed and pulled back the counterpane. It was all made up and the sheets were bone dry. 'This isn't our house, I don't think we should use this bed.'

'The man said I could.' Still wearing his mask he went over to the Scalextric and pressed a switch on the wall. Then he picked up one of the controls and squeezed the button. With a sharp whir a sports car hurtled along the track and somersaulted off on a bend. 'Have a race with me.'

'Later. I'm going to get your supper now.'

As Faith went downstairs, she was greeted with a thick pall of smoke, and an ear-splitting whine. Alarmed she hurried into the living room. Great black clouds were billowing from the fireplace, and the whining sound was even louder – a smoke detector, she realised.

Oliver was coughing. 'I'm going to have to let this go

out – goddamned chimney must be blocked by a bird's nest or something.'

Faith busied herself opening windows. It was several minutes before the smoke cleared and the alarm stopped.

'Not such a smart idea,' he said.

She smiled, picked up her glass, and drained the rest of her wine. 'Can't win them all.'

He came over to her, his hands black and his face smeared with soot, and kissed her lips. 'Where's Alec?'

'Up in a loft that's full of toys. He said you'd told him he could sleep up there – did you?'

'If he wants to, sure. Gerry keeps the place for any kids who come down – he has a raft of nephews, nieces and godchildren who visit.'

She caught the look in his eye, and grinned. 'So if he sleeps up there, we might get to spend a little time together?'

'Had crossed my mind.'

She put her arms around him, held him tightly, then stood on tiptoe and kissed his eyes, then the tip of his nose and his lips. 'I think that's a very good idea,' she murmured. 'It's much the best idea you've had all day.'

106

Horse brasses. Horse brasses irritated him tonight. Everything was irritating him. There were horse brasses nailed to the beams and to the nicotine-stained walls wherever he looked. A bridle with brass studs, a brass buckle and brass medallions engraved with brass fucking horses was hanging from the wall right by his head. A pall of cigarette, cigar and pipe smoke eddied around him. His table wobbled every time he put anything down on it.

The pub was heaving. Ross hated crowded pubs. Steam was rising off sodden clothes. The chatter of all the people in here infuriated him, their sudden cackles of laughter, and the braying voice of a posh-looking know-all in a baggy yellow jumper and yachting loafers.

His hands opened and closed on the tumbler: just a drop of Macallan's remained at the bottom. The stub of the cheap cigar he had bought in here smouldered in the cracked Martini ashtray, next to his unfinished ham sandwich.

It was dark outside the window now. Twenty-seven minutes past eight. Ross drained the whisky, then cradled the glass in front of him. It was the third double he'd drunk since coming in here just before six. Or maybe the fourth.

Suddenly his chair was moving, sinking steadily down through the floor. Nobody noticed. The floor was caving in, and he was disappearing down through it. He was staring up at all the faces in here, watching them receding, blurring, vanishing into the smoke and the ceiling.

A loud crack, like a gunshot, startled him.

It was his glass, he realised. It had slipped from his fingers and fallen on to the table without breaking. His knees were banging together so hard they were hurting.

Get a grip, man. Drunk too much. Shouldn't have had that last one.

The cold air would clear his head. It was dark enough now. Time.

What things were the bitch and Dr Oliver Cabot doing to each other now?

Ross crushed out the cigar stub, slipped the box of matches he had bought into the same pocket as his lighter, pulled on his jacket and his wet hat, and trudged outside. The rain was coming down harder and the wind had whipped up into a frenzy.

This was good. This was the night coming right for him.

It was not quite as dark out here as it had seemed from the inside, but it was dark enough now. He climbed into the Vauxhall, fumbled to get the key into the ignition, then to find the light switch. The instrument panel lights came on, glaring at him, like creatures of the deep, poking their luminous heads out of their holes in the dashboard.

Closing his eyes, giddily, Ross could feel the whisky burning deep in his gullet. *Drank too much. Shouldn't have had that last one. What are you doing to my slut wife, Dr Oliver Cabot?*

Opening his eyes again, the creatures turned into instruments, then back into creatures again.

Go fuck yourselves.

Two tasks, he remembered. The interior light was one. He opened his door and moved the switch so that it stayed off permanently. Then he climbed out, opened the boot and removed the bulb from the light in there. No tell-tales to give him away.

He started the car, and drove back along the road for half a mile, then turned left, through the gate and over the cattle grid, his face pressed hard against the windscreen, trying to see through the rain and the mist and the dark.

After another half-mile he saw the shadows of the farm buildings again. The headlights, on low beam, picked out the open-sided barn and the ancient tractor.

He wasn't sure how far away the headlights would be visible in this weather. Although the track couldn't be seen below the copse of firs from the bitch's love-nest, there was a danger that if they were looking from a dark window they might see the glare of the headlights. He stopped the car on the far side of the barn and switched off the lights. The sea creatures darted back into their caves in the dashboard.

Plenty of time. All the time in the world. Just take it slowly, stick to the plan, don't try to jump the gun.

He switched on the radio, but that was no good, because too much light emitted from it. He needed total darkness.

Are you in bed yet? Are you lying naked, with your hair untidy, and dirty dishes in the kitchen, bitch? Are you lying naked with your legs around Dr Oliver Cabot's waist, bitch?

The car rocked in the wind.

Hatred rocked his mind.

Dr Oliver Cabot in his blue Jeep Cherokee driving past up the farm track earlier. Driving past to Faith, *to his wife*, who was waiting, waiting with her untidy hair at the door of their love-nest. They might be lying on a sofa together now, arms around each other, watching slut trash on the television.

You're trying to ruin my life, Dr Oliver Cabot. You are screwing my wife and you are polluting her mind. You are killing her, you selfish bastard. Killing her with your fucking charlatan witch-doctor mumbo-jumbo.

After a while, his eyes had adjusted to the darkness just enough to see the track. He started the engine and, without turning the lights on, drove slowly forward.

He went through the second gate, and up the steep gradient. As he approached the copse, he could see a flickering pinprick of light through the trees.

He turned the car off the track and drove over bumpy ruts into the thick of the copse, out of sight from every direction. He had tested earlier to make sure the ground was firm enough to take the vehicle.

Taking his binoculars from the boot, he walked to the edge of the copse and, leaning against a tree for support, raised the glasses to his eyes.

There was light coming from three windows in the house: the kitchen window where he had seen the bitch looking out, a window beside the front door, and a Velux window up in the roof.

No sign of the bitch or of Dr Oliver Cabot.

The luminous hands of his watch said ten to nine. He stayed where he was, leaning against the tree, raising his glasses, training them on the house, lowering them. *Come on, bitch, you have to come into the kitchen sometime, you need fuel for your lovemaking, you need to feed your lover.* Sheep were bleating in a field, and a bat was flitting around overhead, but otherwise there was only the sound of the wind, the creaking branches of trees and the pouring rain.

At twenty past ten Faith came into the kitchen, and pressed her face up against the glass, staring straight out at him, looking worried.

You stay worried, bitch, you've got plenty to be worried about right now.

Then Dr Oliver Cabot came and stood right behind her. Ross could see them, framed, as if he was watching them on television. Cabot slipped his arms around the bitch's waist and nuzzled her ear. She smiled, turned towards him, cupped his face in her hands.

Ross churned with anger. The bitch slut was kissing the charlatan on the mouth. Kissing him like she had some hunger inside her, some frantic desperation. They were pawing at each other, caressing each other's faces. Dr Oliver Cabot was gripping the slut's hair now, pulling her head back and working his mouth around her bare neck.

'Get your hands off her!' Ross shouted into the wind. 'Get your hands off her you fucking bastard. That's *My wife, fuck you, Cabot*!'

He lowered the binoculars, seized them by the strap

438

and in fury swung them hard against a tree until the lenses shattered.

His chest was pounding and the whole night was a blur in his eyes as he marched back to the boot of the car, opened it, and with the light of his pencil torch, removed his shotgun from its carrying case, loaded it, and shovelled extra cartridges into each pocket. Then he took out the can of petrol, and slammed the boot lid.

He clipped the torch back in his pocket. Then, with the can in one hand and the gun in the other, he began to walk towards the house. After a few moments, the kitchen light went off. He walked at a steady pace, eyes fixed on the house.

The house.

He stumbled in a pothole and nearly fell, just catching his balance in time.

The house.

Getting nearer, step by step by step. He reached the cattle grid and stopped. Light spilled out on to the gravel ahead from the window by the front door. Too risky to walk on gravel, too much noise. Around the perimeter barbed wire fenced off pastureland. Boots squelching on the boggy grass, he went round the side of the house to the back.

There he set down the petrol can, leaned the gun against the fence and climbed over, cursing as he snagged his trousers then tore his jacket on the barbs. He was in an orchard. A high brick wall ran along between him and the house. There was a light on in an upstairs room behind drawn curtains, and weaker light showed through another Velux window in the roof.

Half-way along the wall he saw a wooden gate. Leaving the gun and the can where they were, he opened the gate a fraction. It was stiff and scraped loudly. He stopped, then pushed it further, wincing at the sound, until there was a gap wide enough to get through.

It led into a formal garden, with a lawn, shrubs and a swimming-pool. He could see a patio with a swing chair and some other garden chairs, a table, a kettle barbecue.

Cosy love-nest you have here, bitch.

He went back out, collected the gun and the can, and walked on, along the outside of the wall, and arrived at another gate. This one opened on to a paddock, at the far end of which he could see a tennis court. He stopped. There were several windows on this side of the house. Flickering light came through one. Keeping close to the house, he walked along, pausing to test a door, which was locked, then detoured around a massive rhododendron and approached the window where the light was coming from.

It was a sizeable snug, with two huge sofas, oak beams and a large television with a cartoon playing, the source of the flickering light.

He moved on. The next window was dark. He shone the torch into it and saw a small study, with a desk, computer, photographs on the walls. The door was shut.

This was good.

The wind was howling even louder, shaking his jacket, tugging at his hat. The windows were all shut, but the panes were large. He picked up the gun by the barrel, and waited. There was a lull in the wind. When the next gust struck, the wind howling even louder, he rammed the butt of the gun against the glass.

With a horrifyingly loud bang, it bounced off.

Shit.

He stood there, listening, staring up at the house, frozen in panic. Just the howl of the wind. Nothing else.

He removed his hat, put it over the butt, then swung it at the pane again, using all his strength. It went through with a crash of shattering glass that sounded as loud to him as an entire greenhouse collapsing.

'Jesus Christ, Jesus goddamned Christ.' He moved away from the window, pressed himself flat against the wall and waited, trying to hear voices, movement, anything above the wind and the roar of blood in his ears.

He didn't know how long he stood there. Five minutes, maybe ten. Then he did a half-circuit of the outside of the house, stopping at the gravel. Still the same lights on, no sign that anyone had heard him.

He went back to the study window and shone the beam in again. There was a low sill, with a cloisonné vase on a low plinth, which he moved to one side. He also tugged away a few jagged shards of glass and dropped them on the lawn. Then, holding the torch in his mouth, he climbed in as quietly as he could, lowering his feet on to the floor, and reached out for his gun and the petrol. He laid them both on the carpeted floor and removed his wellington boots.

He went to the door, lifted the rustic latch, and peered out. He saw a long passageway, walls lined with hunting prints, and a closed door at the far end. No sign of anyone.

He carried the gun and the can into the passage, then closed the door behind him. In the silence as he walked he could hear the petrol sloshing and gurgling in the can. And there was another sound he could hear too, right above him. A creaking sound. Steady, rhythmic.

He looked up, his mouth dry with hatred. Then he quickened his pace. Light spilled beneath the door at the end of the passageway. In his rough calculations of the geography of the place, he decided this must be the light from the entrance hall.

He was right. The door opened on to a wide hall, with a beamed ceiling, terracotta floor tiles, several fine

Italian marble statuettes on plinths, and large framed oil paintings of rural scenes. A wooden staircase led up to the next floor.

Above him, he heard a moan as gentle as the sigh of a summer breeze.

The creaking sound was louder now, and faster.

Then it stopped, abruptly. He looked up, confused. He was in the kitchen of a small flat: dirty plates piled in the sink, an open tin of spaghetti rings sitting on the draining board.

Then, suddenly, he was in the hall in darkness again. This wasn't the hall of his mother's flat but he could hear his mother's voice, muffled, but unmistakably her voice, crying out, 'Oh, yes, don't stop, oh, God, oh, God, keep doing that!'

He climbed the stairs swiftly, stealthily, then stood at the top listening to her voice coming through the door.

'Yes, oh, yes, do that! Do that, do that! I love you so much.'

Ross unscrewed the cap on the petrol can, and walked the length of the landing, pouring the petrol steadily out. Then he stood at the top of the stairs, listening to the screams of pleasure, and watched petrol flow down each of the wooden treads.

Scream, bitch. You'll be screaming differently in a minute.

'Oh, God, yes! Oh, yes, don't stop, oh, God, oh, God, keep doing that!'

He opened the bedroom door, and let the last of the petrol gurgle out, watched it spread across the bare oak boards towards the white rug that surrounded the bed. It was a huge, ornate wooden bed, with a carved spike rising from each corner, like four phalluses.

Whore's bed.

There was just a cosy glow in the room from one bedside lamp. In its light he could see two figures asleep.

His bitch wife and *Dr* Oliver Cabot. Now, suddenly, they weren't asleep any more. He was in his mother's bedroom, watching the white bony buttocks of a naked man pumping away between her thighs. Saw her bare legs around his waist, her back arched, her hair scattered around her face and the pillow, her cheeks red with exertion.

He let the can fall with a clank to the floor, and that was when she woke up and saw him.

'*Oliver!*'

The scream of terror was the sweetest music to his ears.

'*Oliver, oh God.*'

Dr Oliver Cabot was awake now, too, blinking in confusion. They were both naked, sitting up in the bed, mouths open, goggling at him in fear, holding the sheet right up to their necks, trying pathetically to keep themselves covered.

He held the gun tightly, pointing it straight towards them.

'*Ross. No, Ross. No, please, Ross. Please no, please no, Ross, no no no.*'

Ross smiled. For the first time in a very long time he felt calm. 'Breathe deeply,' he said. 'Breathe deeply, both of you.'

The charlatan smelt it first. Ross saw his eyes widen even more. Then the bitch smelt it.

Her voice dropped several octaves into the bellow of a wounded animal. 'Oh, no, no, Ross, don't do this, no, Ross, no, no, no.'

'Get out of the bed, Faith, and put your clothes on.'

'Please, Ross, no.'

'I said, get out of bed and put your clothes on, slut.'

Without taking her eyes from his face, she slipped out and hobbled over the floor. Ross's gaze went from her to the quack charlatan and back to her. Her nakedness disgusted him, the wobble of her breasts disgusted him, her bare knees disgusted him, her bony feet disgusted him.

She stooped, picked up her knickers, whimpering, lost her balance trying to put them on and had to clutch a bed post. He looked back at the charlatan and a flicker of recognition sparked inside his brain. Somewhere. Recently. They had been together.

Photographs from Caven?

No, they had met. Somewhere.

'Mr Ransome,' the charlatan said, his voice quavering, 'don't harm your wife. I'm the guilty one. Let's talk about this.'

'Shut up,' Ross screamed, aiming the gun even more closely. 'One word and I shoot. Just one fucking word.' He turned back to Faith. 'Come on, bitch, hurry! You got them off fast enough.'

'Mr Ransome—' Oliver Cabot said.

Ross pulled the disposable lighter he had bought at the petrol station from his pocket and brandished it, thumb on the top. 'I said shut up, quack.'

Oliver stared at him in silence, eyes darting from him to Faith, nostrils twitching.

Faith had on her jeans and was pulling on her blue knitted top, then pushed her feet into her shoes. 'Please let's talk, Ross.'

'Tie him up,' Ross said.

Trembling she said, 'How – how do you mean?'

'Just tie him up, you slut. Bondage. You used to like it.'

Ross saw a dressing-gown at the end of the bed. He pocketed his lighter, reached forward, stripped the belt out of the loops and threw it at her. 'Around his wrist, then around one of those posts.'

Swinging the gun from Faith to Dr Oliver Cabot, Ross marched across the room to a wardrobe with sliding doors. He pulled one open and saw a rack of ties. He yanked a bunch down and flung them at her. 'Tie him with those.'

'Mr Ransome – Ross—' Oliver said.

Ross pistol-whipped the barrels of the gun into his jaw, splitting open his lips and sending a fragment of tooth flying on to the floor. 'I said silence, quack. Aren't you used to silence with all the transcendental-meditation shit or whatever other shit it is you do?'

'Ross,' Faith begged. 'Ross, please—'

She tied Oliver, spreadeagled on his back as Ross directed, an arm to each post and a leg to each post. Then Ross pulled back the sheet, leaving him naked.

'No erection, quack? How sad.'

Blood dribbled from Oliver's mouth. Faith looked at her husband. 'Please talk to me, Ross. This isn't any way forward for anyone – this is crazy.'

'Get out of the room, bitch.'

Faith looked at Oliver with desperation in her eyes, then back at Ross. 'I'm not leaving him, Ross. If you're going to kill him, you're going to have to kill me too. I'm dying anyway – a few more months, what the hell does it matter?'

'Get outside.'

'No.'

Ross pulled out the lighter and held it up again, his hand shaking. Faith looked at Ross's face, at the gun, then at the lighter. There was a flicker of something in her eyes, something he couldn't read, something he didn't like. And before he had any chance to work it out she launched herself at him, sinking her teeth into his hand.

With a howl of pain he released the lighter, which fell to the floor, and squeezed the trigger.

Nothing happened.

And he knew, in that split second, what the bitch

queen from hell had seen. He'd taken her shooting clays in the past, and she knew this gun. She'd seen that the fucking safety catch was on.

Faith jabbed her thumb into his eye, and punched him with her free hand, then again, so hard her fist hurt, but she barely noticed. She scratched him, tore at his hair, still gouging the eye with her thumb.

He staggered and went over backwards. Clinging to him she fell over with him. Out of the corner of her eye she saw the gun.

Pushing herself away from him, she grabbed it, and threw herself at the door. Out on the landing, she crashed against the top of the banisters. Turned. Ross was lurching towards her. She lifted the barrels of the gun towards him, then realised. The petrol. Mustn't fire, God, *must not fire*.

She hurled herself down the stairs, and ran over to the front door. *Noooooo*. Oliver had put on the safety chain.

Ross was half-way down the stairs now. She yanked at the chain, pressed the release button, grabbed the latch and the door opened.

A hand grabbed her by the throat.

Screaming, struggling for breath she was propelled forward, her legs were kicked away, and she fell face first on to the gravel. She heard the gun clatter down somewhere beside her, but before she could do anything, Ross jerked her head up by the hair then smashed her face down into the gravel. She felt blinding, giddying pain, and when she looked up, Ross was stumbling to his feet with the gun in his hands.

'Get out of the fucking way, slut.'

She stood, blocking the door, gagging. 'No, Ross, don't do this.'

He raised the barrels at her. 'Move out of the way.'

Suddenly, finding strength from deep inside her she

said, furiously, 'Ross, you are bloody well going to listen to me.'

For an instant he looked startled by her sudden change of tone.

Softening her tone she said, 'Ross, if all these things you've ever said to me about how much you love me are true, then you've got to turn round and walk away from here.'

He blinked. There was fleeting hesitation in his face. Then he said, 'Get away from the door.'

'I mean it, Ross. I'm dying, you know that and I know that. Maybe these pills will work, but I don't believe so and I don't think in your heart you believe so either. If you really love me, Ross, then you have to let me go, so I can live whatever I have left of my life the way I want to.'

'Get away from the door.'

His tone had changed a fraction. The hesitation was growing.

'If you kill Oliver, Ross, you are killing me.'

'Move.'

'Do you think it takes guts to stand there pointing a shotgun at me? I thought you were a man with guts, Ross. The kid who came from nowhere and made it to the top of the toughest field of medicine. A man everyone admires. Are people going to admire you if you gun down your wife?'

'Move out of the way, Faith.'

'If you want to show guts, Ross, then leave us. That's what would take real guts.'

Ross stared at Faith, then at the tiny red sight at the end of the barrels, then back at the slut. He heard the pity in her voice, then saw her lying on her back with her ankles around the naked waist of Dr Oliver Cabot, heard her moans of pleasure . . . And then another sound, ringing through the night, the wind and the rain.

He turned his head and over his shoulder saw a spangle of blue light shoot across the darkness. Then another.

A wailing that was getting louder.

A siren.

'You called the police!' He hardened his grip on the gun, took up the slack on the trigger.

'I didn't – for God's sake, how could I?'

He raised the barrels so the red sight was dead centre between the breasts he had sculpted so beautifully. Then, suddenly, he was sinking into the ground the way he had sunk into the floor at the pub. He saw two Faiths. Then four. He swung the gun wildly at each of them.

The siren was getting closer.

And now Faith was pin sharp again. Then something hurled her sideways. A tornado was coming out of the door at him. The charlatan, naked, hurtling headlong at him.

Ross squeezed the trigger. The fucking safety catch! He jabbed it with his thumb, pulled again. The deafening boom of the gun sounded right in his ear as he crashed forward over the body of the naked man. And searing heat singed his hair, sucked the air from his lungs.

The interior of the house erupted in flames.

And he heard a howl way above the shriek of the approaching siren.

It was coming from Faith.

'*Alec! Ross, our son is in there.*'

Ross hauled himself to his knees and saw in her face what he already knew from her voice. She was telling the truth.

'You idiot! You bloody fool! He's in there, for God's sake, he's asleep in the loft.' Frantic, she ran towards the raging flames.

Ross stumbled after her, hauled her back, feeling the heat on his face. 'Where?'

'In the loft, you bloody moron.' She turned on him, raining punches on his face and biting him. 'Lemme go! lemme go! My son, he's in there!'

Trying to hold her at bay, to calm her, he said, 'How do you get to the loft, Faith? Answer me, woman! *how do you get to the loft?*'

She tore free, ran again to the inferno in the doorway. Ross grabbed her and jerked her back. She turned, jabbering, hysterical, trying to break free to run into those flames. Ross punched her in the face, knocking her out cold.

'You goddamn fucking madman, your kid's in there.'

He turned. Dr Oliver Cabot was standing, dazed, blood pouring from his mouth and nose, and from the top of his head where a swathe of his hair had gone as if he'd been scalped.

'Jesus, oh, Jesus,' Ross gibbered, near hysterical himself now. 'Alec. Oh, Jesus.' He looked up at the Velux with the light on.

Pushing the charlatan away, Ross ran to the right, then the left, frantically staring up at the house, looking for his son and a way in that was free of flames. The window he had broken. At the back. 'Alec!' he called. '*Alec, it's Daddy!*'

He sprinted round the side of the house, vaulted the barbed-wire fence, raced along the back wall, calling frantically, 'Alec! Alec! Alec!' No flames on the ground floor yet. Round into the paddock, along the side of the house, and he climbed back in through the broken study window. Then he crossed to the door he had shut earlier and opened it.

He'd operated in the past on scores of burns victims who'd done exactly the same thing: they'd opened a door from a room with an open window, giving a fire the fuel it needed. Creating a tunnel of oxygen.

The solid wall of fire avalanched down the passageway towards him, sucked the air from Ross's lungs, and pulled him, screaming in shock and agony, right into the searing, blinding vortex of the flames.

Oliver, climbing up a drainpipe, heard an explosion of glass below him, and looked down. A screeching adult human form, alight from head to foot, was running in a crazed zigzag across the grass. 'Alec!' the figure screeched. *'Alec! Alec! Alec!'*

He saw the figure fall, roll, steam rising all around him, roll again, frantically trying to beat out the flames. 'Help me, I can't see, I can't see. Where am I? Help me. Help me find Alec! *Help me find my son!'*

Oliver looked away. He had to keep going up.

Alec, I'm coming, just hold on, I'm coming.

Choking on the dense smoke rising all around him, he got one hand on the guttering, grateful that Gerry Hammersley had put up decent, solid, cast-iron guttering, not plastic crap. He scrabbled for a foothold, found a tiny ledge, levered himself higher, then somehow, he was up on the roof, climbing on all fours like a monkey up the slippery tiles. At last he reached the Velux where the light was coming from, in the loft roof where Alec was sleeping.

Christ.

Through the glass he could see Alec standing by his bed in his pyjamas, flames licking up through the hatch. If he broke the glass, he risked a fireball. He ripped a tile from the roof and rapped on the window with it. Alec looked up.

Oliver realised the child probably couldn't see him. He pressed his face close to the glass and yelled, 'Alec! It's me, Oliver! Can you close the loft hatch?'

Alec was staring, mouth open in terror, but couldn't hear him.

He would have to risk a small hole. He chipped at the glass until a small fracture appeared. Then he pushed his thumb through it and put his mouth over the hole. 'Alec, you are going to have to be brave. Get a pillow-slip, soak it in the wash-basin, put it over your head, then reach down and pull that hatch shut.'

Alec shook his head, stammering with fear. 'No, no, no.'

'Alec, come closer, put your face really close to mine.'

The boy didn't move.

'Alec, you can trust me, come closer.'

He backed away towards the hatch.

'*Stop!*' Oliver called in near panic. '*Alec! Stop!*'

One more step and he would fall through the opening into the flames. Oliver thought, desperately. He couldn't break the glass – the boy would be engulfed in a fireball.

Then he heard an explosion as something – a gas cylinder, perhaps – detonated, and a shower of burning wood and debris hurtled up through the hatch and fell all around Alec. Screaming and shaking burning embers off himself he ran towards the skylight and reached up on tiptoe towards Oliver, his face a mask of terror.

'Come closer still.'

Alec reached up further.

'Can you see me, Alec? Can you see who it is?'

The boy nodded.

Behind him, Oliver could see the flames starting to catch on the beams above the hatch entrance. 'OK, Alec, I want you to be calm, I want you to be calm, Alec, to be calm, Alec, you are going to calm down, Alec, down, down, down, listen to my voice, you are calm, listening to my voice, don't think about anything, just do what I tell you, think how calm you are. Are you calm now, Alec?'

The boy stared, as if unsure what to answer

Oliver cursed. It wasn't working. 'Alec,' he said, 'Alec, can you hear me OK?'

Alec mouthed a silent, 'Yes.'

'Look at my eyes, just keep watching my eyes, don't look at anything else, eyes, just my eyes.'

He was engaging him now. His eyes swung right then left, mirroring Oliver's. 'My eyes, just keep watching my eyes, just be calm, don't listen to anything but my voice, be calm, think about your eyes, just your eyes on my eyes, keep your eyes, your eyes, keep your eyes on my eyes keep calm keep your eyes on my eyes and do what I tell you. We're going to play a game. This is an important game, keep your eyes on my eyes, keep your thoughts on my thoughts.'

Staring at the boy, concentrating as hard as he could, squeezing out the flames, the flecks of scalding ash that touched his face and hands, Oliver continued for a full minute until he could see from the dilation of the boy's pupils that he was now under.

'We're going to play a game, Alec, we are going to play fire-fighters. You are going to take a pillow-slip, soak it in cold water, put it over your head, and go over to pull that hatch shut. I want you to do that now, then come back.'

Alec nodded and did exactly as he had been told. He walked without fear towards the hatch, put the pillow slip over his head, ducked down, pulled up the ladder, and moments later the hatch door slammed shut.

Then Oliver smashed the glass, grabbed the child, removed the pillow slip and took a quick glance at his badly burned hands. The boy was silent, still in a trance, still feeling no pain.

He scooped him into his arms and swung him up on to his back. He told Alec to hold on tight.

Then he climbed out on to the roof. There was a ferocious crackle in the air and a choking smell of burning paint. All around him sparks and smouldering embers floated in the air like spent fireworks. He inched his way down until his feet reached the guttering. Miraculously, the one part of the house that wasn't burning was directly beneath him.

A police car was parked just short of the cattle grid. He could see Faith slumped in the front passenger seat. No sign of Ross.

'Hey!' he yelled. 'Hey! Help! Help!'

Seconds later a beam was shining in his face. Then he saw two police officers below him.

Oliver yelled, 'There's a ladder, but we don't have time to get it. One of you hold the drainpipe, the other get on his shoulders and I'll pass the kid—'

His voice was drowned in a massive roar, as if he was standing on an erupting volcano. The roof was moving. The house was collapsing. Both officers looked up in horror and stepped back. One cupped his hands and yelled, 'Jump!'

In sheer panic, Oliver lobbed Alec, like some giant rugby ball, straight at them, then leaped as far out into the darkness as he could.

107

Sean was restless at breakfast. Hugh Caven couldn't work out whether his son was looking forward to starting playgroup again today or not. Every time he asked him, all he got was a silent shrug. It was the first day of the winter term, although ironically it seemed that summer had finally arrived in England: a real

Indian summer, the temperatures well up in the eighties, far higher than normal for the first week in September.

The private investigator was also restless. Among the envelopes in the morning post he'd scooped from the letterbox was one he didn't like the look of: a buff, letter-sized envelope with a police crest on the outside.

He didn't know what it contained, but there were several possibilities and none of them good. It might be notification of a traffic violation – maybe he'd gone through a speed camera, or had been photographed jumping a traffic light, or perhaps his tax disc was out of date.

More worryingly, a couple of weeks ago he'd been grilled by a policeman after being observed snooping round the back of a house, when he'd been trying to photograph a couple having an affair. Could be something to do with that. Or there was still a possibility it was to do with the bugging of Dr Oliver Cabot's flat.

He remembered back in June when he'd finally taken the plunge and phoned Detective Sergeant Anson, now promoted to Detective Inspector, quite how cool his reception had been. It had seemed to him then that the policeman was more interested in the fact that he had illegally entered Cabot's flat than in his information that Ross Ransome might be linked to the murders of Barry Gatt and Harvey Cabot. He had dutifully taken down the compass co-ordinates and the address in Gloucestershire where Caven told him he thought Ransome was going, and where he had warned Anson that there might be an ugly scene, but he had taken them down only under duress and had not sounded convinced.

As soon as Sandy had driven away with Sean, Caven took the post upstairs to his office, lit his first cigarette of the day and ripped open the buff envelope.

Police Headquarters, Notting Hill Police Station,
101 Ladbroke Grove, London, W11 3PL

Mr Hugh Caven
Caven Investigative Service
5 Claremont Close
Ickenham
IK12 7BD
5 September 1999

Dear Mr Caven,
Reference: 37 Ladbroke Avenue, London.
I am writing with respect to your activities in
unlawfully entering the premises of Dr Oliver
Cabot at 37 Ladbroke Avenue in June of this
year, and further, in placing illegal surveillance
devices in these premises.

  Having given careful consideration to all the
circumstances, I have decided to take no further
action on this matter. However, I must warn you
formally that any recurrence of offences of this
nature in the future will be viewed very seriously
by the police, particularly in light of your
previous record, and you may be liable for
prosecution.

      Yours sincerely,

Detective Inspector D. G. Anson
Senior Investigating Officer

Nine months later, Hugh Caven received a second letter
from the same police officer.

Notting Hill Police Station,
101 Ladbroke Grove, London, WII 3PL

Mr Hugh Caven
Caven Investigative Service
5 Claremont Close
Ickenham
IKI2 7BD
8 June 2000

Dear Mr Caven,

I have the pleasant duty of informing you that a reward was offered in June of last year for information leading to the arrest and successful prosecution of the killer or killers of Professor Harvey Cabot. The award was sponsored by the late Professor Cabot's brother, Dr Oliver Cabot.

Our investigations have led us to conclude to our satisfaction that the prime suspect, who was responsible also for the unlawful killing of Mr Barry Gatt, is now deceased. These same investigations, partly as a result of information supplied by yourself, have resulted in the issuing of a warrant for the arrest of Mr Ross Ransome, of Little Scaynes Manor, Little Scaynes, West Sussex, on a charge of conspiracy to murder.

As Mr Ransome's medical condition is such that it has as yet not been possible to serve any warrant, and nor does it seem likely he will ever be in a fit state of health to attend trial, I am instructed by Dr Oliver Cabot to inform you that he would like to make you an ex gratia payment of £10,000 (ten thousand pounds sterling) as a token of his gratitude for your contribution.

If you are willing to accept this award, kindly contact the undersigned at your convenience.

Yours sincerely,

Detective Inspector D. G. Anson
Senior Investigating Officer

The cheque arrived ten days later. Hugh Caven paid it in at his bank, without telling his wife about it. Times were still hard, and he knew exactly what she would say, with a five-year-old son and a seven-month-old daughter to feed. He wasn't intending to give her the chance.

He allowed five days for the cheque to clear, then went to the bank and drew out the entire amount in cash.

Late that same night, he drove to the street where Barry Gatt's widow lived with her triplets who were now two years old. He parked a safe distance away, so that he wouldn't be spotted if she looked out of a window. He was relieved to see that no lights were on in her little house.

He pushed the cash through the letterbox in a bag, then returned to his car.

As he headed home, he kept the radio switched off, preferring to listen to the music playing inside his head. It was an old Bob Dylan song, and as he drove, singing the words with the window open and the air blasting his face, a weight lifted from his heart and began blowing in the wind.

108

In the small room annexed to the low-dependency ward in the burns unit of East Grinstead hospital, Faith glanced at the nurse, then back at the figure in the bed. When she had first come in, she had found it hard to look at him.

From the skewed parting of the scaly purple mass of scar tissue between the remnants of his nose and his chin came a long, low moan. Then once more the sucking, watery sound of a breath in, followed by the long, slow rasping as he exhaled.

He lay on his back with his arms raised, fists clenched like a boxer. To a stranger it might appear that this was some bizarre act of defiance against his condition, but Faith had been told by the nurse at the plastic-surgery unit of this hospital, where he used to operate himself one day a week, that this was not so. It was a phenomenon in severe burns victims known as the pugilistic attitude, where the limbs remained permanently flexed due to the shortening of the flexor muscles caused by shrinkage of the skin and the muscle tissue from the heat.

The pugilistic attitude was more usually seen in dead bodies recovered from fires, and it was unusual in a victim still living. But Ross Ransome was a rare case, and the sheer strength of his will to live had amazed everyone. Few people, other than young children, survived sixty per cent burns. Yet two years on, Ross was still alive after suffering almost seventy per cent burns. If, as Faith thought, this could be called living.

Life-support had been switched off with her consent as next-of-kin, three months after that June day when he had been transferred here from Cheltenham, suffering second- and third-degree burns. The skin across almost all of his torso, arms, legs and head had fibrosed into scar tissue, and he had sustained severe damage to his internal passages, airways and organs, in particular the kidneys and, by far the most serious, his brain. His hair had gone, as had his vision, but EEG tests showed that he still retained some hearing.

Ironically, instead of weakening and gradually slipping away, as the medics had hoped, his pulse seemed, month by month, to be getting a little stronger. No one knew, with the condition of his brain, whether he was capable of feeling pain, but every few hours he released a moan, and for this reason he was kept on a constant morphine drip.

Patches of his body were covered in bandages. For the past two years he had undergone an endless series of grafts, as his former colleagues fought a constant battle against areas of his skin dying because of his damaged circulation.

Faith wasn't sure why she had come. The hospital said he had been calling her name as if he had something he urgently needed to say, but the thought of seeing him had scared her. He still wielded power over her, the power to come to her in her dreams and frighten her, to overshadow her waking thoughts.

And she had seen the evidence that had been amassed against him on some of his patients, although it didn't appear likely he would ever be brought to trial. She slept badly most nights, lying in bed, thinking, unravelling those years of her marriage to him, looking for the signs and clues pointing to the monster she had missed. The only thought that appeased her conscience was, as Oliver reminded her repeatedly of the words of Sören Kierkegaard, that life can only be understood backwards but it must be lived forwards.

Standing as far away from him as the small room allowed, she watched him warily, glad of the company of the nurse, scared that somehow, even in this state, he could reach out and harm her. It seemed to Faith that he was aware of her presence and desperate to speak.

One of the hardest things to bear had been Alec's persistent questions about his father, but they were becoming less frequent. She'd decided from the start to stick as close to the truth as she could. She told him his daddy had been badly injured and was in hospital a long way away, and did not want Alec to see him until he got better. Oliver was good with him and Alec was clearly fond of him, but there were still times when she could see sadness on his face as he drifted into some space of his own inside his head.

The words came out suddenly, sharp and clear. As clear as if the past two years had been sloughed off and they were back at Little Scaynes Manor together in the library, the drawing room or the kitchen, chatting.

'How's Alec?'

Then silence.

Faith stared at the nurse, wondering if she had imagined it, but she could see that the nurse had heard him too.

In a trembling voice, Faith said, 'He's fine.'

There was no response, just the ragged sounds of his breathing.

She waited a full minute, maybe longer and then, she couldn't help it, tears welled in her eyes. 'He's just had his eighth birthday party,' she said. 'We had a bouncy castle, a conjuror and a barbecue.'

She glanced at the nurse, who encouraged her with a nod to continue. 'He – he liked it best when we turned off the air pump for a few seconds, and the castle started to deflate. And he scored thirty runs in cricket at school last week. He's going to be a good sportsman, just like his dad. He's shooting up now too. He's going to be tall and strong, like you.'

She dug into her handbag, pulled out a handkerchief and wiped her eyes. 'And do you know what he said the other day? He told me he wants to be a doctor when he grows up. He said he's going to be a plastic surgeon, just like you. He wants to fix that bump on my nose – the one I got after you biffed me in the face to stop me running into the burning house to try to get him. You broke it – that's ironic after all the surgery you did on me, isn't it?'

Her voice was faltering. Then she gave a little laugh. 'I told him he'll be needing to do more than just rhinoplasty on me by the time he's qualified. I think all that great work you did on me will be in need of top-up maintenance in thirty years' time.'

The tears were flooding down her face now. She turned away, racked with emotion, walked out of the door and quickly down the corridor.

Epilogue

Three months later, on a fine autumnal morning, in the middle of breakfast, Faith received a phone call from the hospital, telling her that Ross had died during the night. The duty houseman said he hadn't thought there was any point in waking her at four in the morning.

She thanked him and hung up, unsure how she felt. Relief, certainly, but it was more complicated than that. She was still technically his wife, which meant, she remembered from her father's death, that she would have to register the death and organise the funeral.

She wished Oliver was here to put an arm around her and give her a hug. He would understand the jumble of emotions inside her; he seemed to understand so much about people, about life.

Heavy-hearted, she sat down at the kitchen table of the house Oliver had bought near Hampstead Heath, and watched Alec munching his cereal. Rasputin sat as usual by his feet, ever hopeful that a stray cluster of granola might fall his way. He was usually lucky: Alec was a messy eater.

Both she and Ross had been living on borrowed time. In a way, all of them were, Alec, her mother and Oliver included. All of life was borrowed time, really.

She remembered, a long time ago, walking through a graveyard in North London with Oliver, and she could recall vividly something he had said as he had looked at a gravestone.

'*You know what fascinates me? It's the dash. That little mark between the dates. I look down at someone's grave, and I think, That dash represents a human being's entire life. You and I are living out our dashes right now. It's not important when someone was born or when they died, what matters is what they did in between with their lives.'*

He had gone on to talk about a temple that existed in another dimension, a temple that humans could only enter after they had died. In this temple were stored the Akashic Records, which comprise the history of each soul.

She wondered if that was where Ross had gone now. If he was in that temple, thumbing through the pages, trying to find that point where everything in his life had changed, that one moment where maybe the paths had forked and that something – no one would ever know what – had got into his mind, and he'd gone from being a good man to a bad one.

Something positive to have come out of the horror was that her mother and she had bonded. Their relationship was far stronger and closer now than it had ever been. To her delight – and amazement – Margaret, who had developed osteoarthritis, had become a regular patient of the Cabot Centre, going there weekly for acupuncture, aromatherapy and Reiki, and, even more to Faith's surprise, had accepted a course of homeo-pathic remedies from Oliver for a cold.

It was two years and four months since her first diagnosis of Lendt's disease. The check-ups were down to every three months now. The last two had been clear. There were people who went into remission then had the disease return and wipe them out, but two years was pretty much the outer limit.

Medicine was an inexact science as all the pages of information on Lendt's disease on the Internet showed: arguments for and against the new Moliou-Orelan wonder-drug, Entexamin; arguments for and against all kinds of natural remedies. She had no way of telling whether the route she had chosen with Oliver Cabot was the right one to beat the disease, but every time she questioned it in her mind, she remembered a conversation she'd had right at the start of her treatment from him.

'At this clinic we're not against science, Faith, anything but. Science is just a method of getting at the truth, and we no more believe that the extract of the antennae of some Amazonian ant will cure arthritis than the regular medical profession does, until it is properly tested. But we also know that we're treating people not cars. And people get better because they want to get better. We know from a number of well-run studies that there is an intimate connection between the mind and body. If we make the mind feel good, with massage, good music, pure, natural foods and, of course, love, the body will have a much better chance of healing.'

'Is that what you want to do to me, Dr Cabot, cure me with love?' she had asked.

'Mummy, we're going to be late for school.'

Faith looked up and stared at her son through a mist of tears.

'Why are you crying?' he asked. 'Are you sad?'

She nodded. 'Mummy's sad this morning. She's very, very sad. But she's also happy.'

'You can't be happy and sad at the same time.'

'You can,' she said, dabbing her eyes with a napkin. 'It's a secret they don't teach you at school.'

She stood up. 'Come on, get your bag and your coat. You're right – you *are* going to be late.'

Rasputin started barking.

'What else don't they teach you at school, Mummy?'

She grabbed the keys off the hook on the dresser, gave the dog a biscuit to keep him quiet, got Alec's coat on him and his bag over his shoulder, then scooped her son out of the door.

In the car he repeated the question.

She didn't reply. The journey was too short and the answer too long.

If you have enjoyed this book you can email Peter James on scary@pavilion.co.uk or you can look up his other books on www.peterjames.com

available from

THE ORION PUBLISHING GROUP

☐ **Dreamer** £6.99
PETER JAMES
978-0-7528-7678-8

☐ **Twilight** £6.99
PETER JAMES
978-0-7528-7679-5

☐ **Alchemist** £6.99
PETER JAMES
978-0-7528-1729-3

☐ **Denial** £6.99
PETER JAMES
978-0-7528-2688-2

☐ **Host** £6.99
PETER JAMES
978-0-7528-3745-1

☐ **Prophecy** £6.99
PETER JAMES
978-0-7528-1737-8

☐ **Faith** £6.99
PETER JAMES
978-0-7528-3711-6

☐ **Possession** £6.99
PETER JAMES
978-0-7528-3746-8

☐ **Sweet Heart** £6.99
PETER JAMES
978-0-7528-7677-1

☐ **The Truth** £6.99
PETER JAMES
978-0-7528-1666-1

All Orion/Phoenix titles are available at your local bookshop or from the following address:

Mail Order Department
Littlehampton Book Services
FREEPOST BR535
Worthing, West Sussex, BN13 3BR
telephone 01903 828503, *facsimile* 01903 828802
e-mail MailOrders@lbsltd.co.uk
(Please ensure that you include full postal address details)

Payment can be made either by credit/debit card (Visa, Mastercard, Access and Switch accepted) or by sending a £ Sterling cheque or postal order made payable to *Littlehampton Book Services*.
DO NOT SEND CASH OR CURRENCY.

Please add the following to cover postage and packing

UK and BFPO:
£1.50 for the first book, and 50p for each additional book to a maximum of £3.50

Overseas and Eire:
£2.50 for the first book plus £1.00 for the second book and 50p for each additional book ordered

---

BLOCK CAPITALS PLEASE

name of cardholder ....

address of cardholder ....

....

....

postcode ....

delivery address
(if different from cardholder)

....

....

....

postcode ....

☐ I enclose my remittance for £................................

☐ please debit my Mastercard/Visa/Access/Switch (delete as appropriate)

card number | | | | | | | | | | | | | | | | | |

expiry date | | | | Switch issue no. | | |

signature ....

prices and availability are subject to change without notice